'*The Shadow Glass* is like the old children's movies it worships: sometimes dark, but never heartless; gritty yet soulbaring. It embraces its referents as a whole: their beauty with their ugliness, the healing power of nostalgia with its potential to poison the present. But it never goes cynical, never loses faith. It stands proud with a VHS copy of its favorite movie held aloft, daring you to say it's not the greatest film ever.' **Edgar Cantero, author of *Meddling Kids***

'Wonderful. A bold and heartfelt adventure from another world, another time—and our own.' **Max Gladstone, Hugo and Nebula Award-winning writer**

'The fantasy adventure my 80s-loving heart needed! Loaded with unforgettable characters, a thrilling quest, and the best 80s pop culture references, I loved every moment.' **Kat Ellis, author of *Harrow Lake***

'Henson Heads, rejoice! Of the myriad of pleasures Josh Winning conjures within his stunning novel *The Shadow Glass*, perhaps my personal darling is the rendering of a complete and hereunto unexplored cinematic fantasia that could easily stand alongside such practical FX classics as *The Dark Crystal*, *Labyrinth* and *The NeverEnding Story*. I was instantly transported back to the video store of my youth, sent down the fantasy aisle once again, where these pre-CGI pleasures of puppetry reside... and magic still exists.' **Clay McLeod Chapman, author of *The Remaking* and *Whisper Down the Lane***

'Bringing together an artful blend of nostalgic references, emotionally-wrenching characterisation, and stunning worldbuilding, *The Shadow Glass* is a delight of a debut.' **Tori Bovalino, author of *The Devil Makes Three* and *Not Good for Maidens***

'A blast of big-hearted fantasy fun, *The Shadow Glass* will have 1980s nostalgists digging back through their VHS collections with glee.'
Matt Glasby, author of *The Book of Horror*

'You don't have to be a child of the '80s to appreciate *The Shadow Glass*. There's enough magic within these pages to dress you in leg warmers and take you there. Nostalgic, heartfelt, and bristling with humor. An absolute corker!' **Rio Youers, author of *No Second Chances***

'Epic, edge-of-your-seat fantasy in its own right, with just enough horror to keep things interesting. The world-building is fantastic, but it's the beautifully drawn characters that I think will capture readers' hearts, as they force us to think about growing up, growing old, and the importance of hanging on to that sense of wonder that the best fantasy (like *The Shadow Glass* itself) can inspire.' **Elizabeth Corr and Katharine Corr, authors of The Witch's Kiss trilogy**

'Packed with heart and featuring a plot as fiendish as any Goblin King's labyrinth, *The Shadow Glass* is a masterpiece!
William Hussey, Award-winning author of *Hideous Beauty* and *The Outrage*

'A thrilling and deeply emotional coming-of-age-in-your-30s quest that perfectly conjures up the feeling of being a viewer fully immersed in the tantalisingly dark worlds of Jim Henson's 1980s fantasy films while also weaving a heartfelt tale about grief, denial, the complicated relationships between parents and children, and reconciling one's childhood with the adult you've become. Suspenseful, funny, imaginative, and often as creepy as a Skeksis banquet, *The Shadow Glass* is a must-read for any fan of Henson or '80s fantasy in general who ever dreamed of what it might be like if the Creature Shop actually came to life.' **Robert Berg, HensonBlog.com**

THE SHADOW GLASS

JOSH WINNING

TITAN BOOKS

The Shadow Glass
Print edition ISBN: 9781789098617
E-book edition ISBN: 9781789098631

Published by Titan Books
A division of Titan Publishing Group Ltd.
144 Southwark Street, London SE1 0UP
www.titanbooks.com

First Titan edition March 2022
10 9 8 7 6 5 4 3 2 1

A CIP catalogue record for this title is available from the British Library.

Printed and bound by LSC Communications

THE SHADOW GLASS

"Keep believing, keep pretending."
Jim Henson

"Well, c'mon feet."
Sarah, *Labyrinth* **(1986)**

Film, Inc. *magazine review of* The Shadow Glass
(December 2011 issue).

THE SHADOW GLASS (PG)
FILM ★★★★ EXTRAS ★★★★★

OUT NOW // DVD, BD **EXTRAS** // Featurettes,
Commentary, Storyboard track, Galleries

"Although it's now 25 years old, this film remains resolutely one of a kind," says Bob Co. creative producer Amelia Twine on this anniversary re-release of *The Shadow Glass*. "One thing that still stands out is the fact that it's a film children can enjoy that is uncompromising in its darkness. There's no sugar-coating the world of Iri. But that's a good thing. It's one of the things that makes *The Shadow Glass* so special."

She's not wrong. On top of the remarkably adult themes, mind-boggling ingenuity abounds at every level of director Bob Corman's 1986 feature debut, and the extras on this two-disc set fondly explore everything from the cleverly concealed puppeteers to the lovingly crafted nooks and crannies of the film's vast sets. "We used a special type of dirt to give the characters a lived-in, grubby feel," reveals Jenny Bobbin, creator of many of the film's remarkable puppets, confirming that *The Shadow Glass* is nothing like the clean-cut kids' entertainment of Corman's earlier puppet series *Fuzz TV* (1975–79).

Yep, this remains nightmare-inducing stuff, set in the world of Iri (pronounced "eerie"), which is home to a plethora of astonishing creatures including skalions, kettu, wugs and a terrifying, bug-eyed soothsayer. The plot sees fox-like pup Dune embarking on a quest to rescue his world from a tyrannical queen, encountering colourful characters along the way (the pom-pom-like "lub" is a shameless scene-stealer) and learning a hero's lesson in self-worth.

There's no mention of the controversy that surrounded the release of Corman's prequel comic series *Beyond the Shadow Glass*, which inspired a book-burning protest in the 1990s, but perhaps this isn't the place for that. The wealth of extras include storyboards, photo galleries, and commentary from the rarely-glimpsed Corman, and the love and passion that went into the film is clear for all to see. "This film is my life," Corman says at one point during his chat track. "People think I'm being disingenuous when I say that, but it truly is." Delivering everything a fantasy lover could ever dream of, *The Shadow Glass* is a dark and bewitching tale unlike anything ever seen again.

ROSIE FLETCHER

WHAT TO WATCH NEXT...
The NeverEnding Story (1984)

More puppets, this time of the doggy variety. Plus the terrifying Nothing. Pillows for hiding required, plus a hairbrush to sing the theme tune into.

Game of Thrones (2011–)

We've only had one season of this book adaptation but, so far, it's proved a huge thrill – a grown-up fantasy for grown-up *Shadow Glass* fans. We can't wait to see where this one goes.

The Fuzz TV Christmas Special (1979)

The skalions would eat Flick, Bucket and co. for breakfast, but we still love them, and the musical numbers in Corman's festive favourite are to die for.

1

Jack Corman swore as he seized the window shutter and forced it to stop flapping. It had been striking the frame when he arrived at his father's house, making a sound like gunshots that echoed across the street, and he was surprised the neighbours hadn't come out to complain. Then again, Kettu House wasn't just any house. People tended to approach it with caution.

Gritting his teeth, he wrestled the shutter back. Like everything to do with his father, it resisted, and Jack's knuckles ached with the cold as the wind bit into them. His suit jacket squeezed his torso, making it difficult for him to move, and the shutter bucked and jerked as if attempting to throw him off.

Jack gave it one last shove, then swore again and gave up.

Wiping perspiration from his top lip, he stepped back to appraise the building. It was craggier than he remembered, its face weathered and beaten by time. From outside, Kettu House looked like two red-brick Georgian semis with their front doors side by side. In reality, one of the doors was a fake. His dad had been a joker—before it all went wrong.

Over thirty years ago, Bob Corman knocked through both properties to create one scowling super-house, and it only got weirder inside.

The thought of the labyrinthine interior caused Jack's stomach to clench.

He'd grown up in there, spent most of his adolescence desperate to escape it, and it was only when he went off to university that he was finally free of it. That was over a decade ago and he dreaded to think what he'd find. In the intervening years, the place had grown larger and more confused in his mind, evolving into a house of mirrors. He fought the urge to get the hell out of there.

Instead, he swiped his unruly fringe from his eyes, suppressing the panic.

It's just a house, he told himself. *Just a house.*

His hand slipped into his breast pocket, his fingers brushing the envelope nestled there. Through the paper, he felt the modest brass key, and his mind calmed. It had turned up at his flat a week ago, his father's writing on the front. Bob must have sent it before he died and, even though Jack couldn't understand why Bob wanted him to go into the attic, he recalled what was stored up there and his plan took shape. He just had to find the courage to go through with it, then everything would be peachy keen.

Scene change. Fresh take. Action, cut, print: *Welcome to your new life.*

His gaze moved up to a window sticking out of the roof like an eyelid.

He frowned, certain he'd seen movement behind the pane.

No, it was just clouds being buffeted by the wind.

The shutter started banging again.

'Christ's sake,' Jack muttered, regarding it with a mixture of anguish and disdain. It could wait. If he didn't go into the house now, he never would. His hands shook as he took out his keys, preparing to mount the steps to the front doors.

'Um, *hi*! Hello?'

Jack stiffened as a voice called out behind him. A skinny teenager stood just inside the front garden, hovering by the oak tree. The kid's eyes were too large for his oval face, and his teeth flashed white against his brown skin, a nervous grin that made his age difficult to guess. Seventeen, Jack thought, maybe younger.

'Sorry, I didn't mean to scare you.' The kid winced. 'It's just, I mean, you're *him*, aren't you?'

'Who?'

'Jack Corman.'

Jack's eyes narrowed. 'Never heard of him.'

'You *are*! You're Jack Corman! *Man*, I can't believe it. I mean… Gurchin! You're really here! I heard you'd moved away or… I don't know… there are crazy theories, like you became a botanist. Even I had trouble believing that one.'

The kid's bony shoulders jerked with amusement and Jack squinted at him. Daylight had all but bled from the garden, ushering in a blustery autumn evening, but Jack saw that underneath the boy's blue raincoat he wore a T-shirt that read *I LUB YOU*. Jack groaned aloud.

'Look, mate, I don't have time for—'

'Toby.'

'What?'

The teenager stuck out his hand. 'Toby. It's an honour to meet you.'

This. Wasn't. Happening.

Usually *Shadow Glass* fanboys stuck to the internet. That's where they felt most at home, poring over the film, dissecting it frame by frame, exchanging first-viewing stories and creation myths and trying to figure out if you really could see a crew member in the final battle sequence.

Jack hadn't encountered one of them in years and that was just the way he liked it.

He ignored the hand, filled with the need to get away. 'Sorry, Toby, it's been a shitty day. You'll have to excuse me.'

He started up the steps, but Toby's voice followed over his shoulder. He was hot on Jack's heels.

'Sorry, it's just… You have no idea what *The Shadow Glass* means to me. I know it's for kids, but it's not just a kid's movie. It's real and scary and it's not *safe*. Like, it feels so *real*, even though it's over thirty years old. I always tell Huw—he's my boyfriend—I always tell him that's the sign of a true classic. It only gets better with age.'

'*Mhmm.*'

Jack had heard it all before. It was just his luck that the first time in years that he visited Kettu House, he was ambushed by an Iri nut.

'Sorry, Toby, I've got to go.' He jiggled the door lock, relieved when it clicked.

'But I—'

Jack hurried inside, shutting the door harder than he had intended. Silence settled around him.

He took a moment to catch his breath, squinting in the dim light of the hall.

Any relief he felt at escaping the teenager vanished as the musky air filled his nostrils. He sneezed, doubling over and sneezing again.

'This place,' he muttered as he straightened to survey his surroundings.

The hall was even more cluttered than he remembered.

Knick-knacks and keepsakes crowded the passage, giving the impression of a pokey antique shop. A grandfather clock stood surrounded by bone-dry potted plants, while Japanese *Shadow Glass* posters were mounted on the walls. A shelving unit groaned with VHS tapes, DVDs, a Walkman and a cassette tape library, and there were books everywhere. Feathered with age and heaped amid swirling dust motes.

Jack's neck creaked as he turned his head to take it all in.

The curios were familiar but also different to how he remembered them, as if he were viewing them through mottled glass. They looked decayed. Relics from another time. A life he had almost forgotten he'd lived. And this was just the hall. From where he stood, he glimpsed the rooms and passages beyond, wending in a disordered muddle, combining to form a house of riddles. A place in which to get lost.

He stilled, frowning at the distant point where the back hall turned into the kitchen. He was sure he'd seen movement there. He pictured his father still roaming Kettu House, tall and narrow as a telegraph pole, shuffling in slippers and a moth-eaten cardigan, fingers scratching his beard. He could still hear the whispers of a man who had long since relinquished his grip on reality.

'In a forgotten time, in a forgotten world, deep within a forgotten chamber few have ever seen, the Shadow Glass sees all.'

Jack gritted his teeth and shook off the image. That was years ago. Bob was dead and the house was empty—of anything living, at least. He couldn't get distracted.

Aiming for the rickety staircase, he went further inside, his fingers tapping one of the bottles in a drinks cabinet. He recalled being fourteen and smashing bottles in the street, furious at his father for his latest drunken tirade.

The memory stung, and even though Jack wasn't a drinker, his mouth felt parched. He uncapped the bottle, taking a defiant swig as he started up the stairs. The whisky seared the back of his throat.

'Jesu—' he coughed, then froze as a shadow crossed the wall.

He didn't move.

He'd only caught it out of the corner of his eye, but he was certain it had reared up from the skirting board and flashed across the wallpaper.

Stiffly, he listened, sensing eyes on him.

Ch-ch-ch-ch…

Jack's arm hair bristled and his gaze snapped to the ceiling. He had heard something above him. A skittering of claws on floorboards.

'Hello?' he called.

The house swallowed his voice. He wasn't sure he had even spoken.

Ch-ch-ch-ch…

Apprehension pinched Jack's chest. He'd definitely heard it that time. A scratching above his head.

Somebody was up there.

More fanboys, maybe, come to pick over the remains of his father's empire.

Maybe they were already in the attic, claiming the thing he'd pinned his entire future on.

Adrenaline flooded his veins and Jack battled his way down a landing cluttered with *Shadow Glass* props, framed movie cells and fake, otherworldly plants that tangled between his feet. He stumbled against a door, knocking it open to reveal his teenage bedroom. It hadn't been touched since he moved out. Band posters on the walls, single bed beneath the window, headphones plugged into a hi-fi system that he would crank up to eleven to drown out his life.

Above his head the scratching continued, and Jack left the bedroom, clambering up another, even narrower set of stairs that shrieked as he climbed.

He came to a stop outside the attic door.

Of course the sound was coming from there.

Above the rasp of his own wheezing, he heard it louder than before: a scraping like nails on the inside of a coffin. His throat thickened with fear.

For a second, he was fifteen again, crouched in the stairwell while his father told him to go back to bed. Jack had woken in the night and followed voices up to the attic. He'd listened through the door as they echoed in the dark, and he couldn't tell if Bob was in there watching a movie, or if Bob was making the voices himself. Maybe the newspapers and magazines had been right. 'Bonkers Bob' really had lost his mind.

Crouched outside the attic now, twenty years later, Jack felt darkness grasping at his neck.

Was his father still in there?

He should run. Get out of there before it was too late.

No. He shook off the memory. This wasn't some teenage fantasy. Somebody had broken in. They could be making off with the very thing he was there to claim for himself.

He took the envelope from his pocket, removed the key, and ground it into the lock. Throwing open the door, he charged inside and—

Tripped.

His toe caught something in the dark and he lost his footing. He crashed forwards, striking the floor painfully as he crumpled onto his front. Somehow, he managed to prevent his head cracking against the floorboards, and found himself staring at a pair of knobbly claws resting on the floor in front of him.

He clutched the miraculously intact whisky bottle and craned his neck up at the thing looming over him.

An amphibian creature with boil-pocked green skin leered in the gloom. It was squat and slimy-looking, its too-wide mouth hanging open to reveal glimmering rows of needle-sharp teeth. Its bulbous eyes were heavy-lidded, vacant and staring, and while it looked like something that had slithered out of a swamp, it wore mechanised armour, the kind of sci-fi tech that seemed purpose-built for deep space.

Jack's heart slammed the floorboards as he recognised the character. A skalion.

Just a puppet, he told himself as he eased into a kneeling position. *It's just a puppet.*

They'd given Jack nightmares as a kid. The skalions were villains by design, created for the sole purpose of terrorising the heroes of *The Shadow Glass*, and the sight of one now made his skin itch. Not just one. A whole battalion crowded together in a sneering pack, each around four feet tall and bigger than any puppet had a right to be.

Now that quiet had settled over the house, Jack felt stupid. He was letting his imagination get away from him. Nothing was moving in here. How could it?

They were just puppets.

He got to his feet and fumbled for the light switch. As a bare bulb blinked on, he felt the burn of a hundred eyes.

More puppets.

Too many to count were dotted all over the attic, their smiles fixed, their frowns unmoving. Not just skalions but wugs, too. Wizened little gnome-like creatures in woolly hats that snuggled together amid the spider-webbed furniture.

Jack surveyed it all with an uneasy familiarity. When he was a child, these characters meant everything to him. They were his friends. His family. His playmates. Now, though, they stirred only distaste and, somewhere beneath that, a distant sense of longing.

For a brief window before Bob retreated into himself, before the TV interviews and 'Crackers Corman!', before the delirium and the drinking and the blackouts, before Bob's inability to show up to a single important event in Jack's life… Jack had been happy.

He felt the weight of the bottle in his hand, and was about to take another swig when he spotted a glass cabinet in the corner. It towered over the surrounding furniture like a monument. The sight of it caused a shiver to travel through him.

'Dune,' he murmured.

There it was. In the dark of the cabinet's interior stood another puppet. The reason Jack had fought his way through this haunted funfair ride of a house.

The fox-like figure almost looked alive, as if it had been waiting for this very moment, and as he approached, Jack discerned the adoring detail that had been lavished upon Dune's creation. The eyes held galaxies of feeling and Dune's lips were parted as if preparing to speak, his fur-tipped ears alert.

He was crafted out of foam prosthetics threaded with dense black and rust-coloured fur, and he wore hardy kettu attire that protected him from desert storms. A mud-stained breast plate, brown leggings and a pair of lightweight leather boots. The very best a movie budget could buy.

As a kid, Jack had wished more than anything that Dune would talk. He would hold staring contests with him across the breakfast table, or he'd lie in bed at night and whisper in his ear, *'I know you can, I promise I won't tell.'*

But Dune was stubborn. Most kettu were. It was the quality that separated them from just about everything else in the world of Iri. The hero-making quality.

'Hi, Dune,' Jack said quietly.

He already felt like a traitor for what he had planned. Jack raised the bottle and took another hit of whisky. Before he could lose his nerve, he dug out his phone and dialled.

'Jack?' The man who answered sounded older than Jack remembered, his voice nasal and hard.

'Hello, Mr Smithee.'

'Alden. Please, call me Alden.'

'Sorry, Alden, hi.' He took a breath. 'I thought you might like to know who I'm looking at right now.'

'Oh?' An expectant breath came down the line.

'Dune is in the original cabinet. Hasn't been touched in years. He looks just the same as he did in the movie.'

A pause, then Alden Smithee sighed. 'Marvellous. You understand my apprehension, I'm sure. We aren't discussing a used car, here.'

'No, I understand. It's a lot of money.'

'Oh, don't worry about that. I'm more concerned about the puppet himself. He's an important cultural artefact and I want you to rest assured that I intend to give him a good home.'

Jack shook his head. Alden Smithee sounded just like the teenager who had jumped him outside. Just like the bloggers and YouTubers who praised Bob and all he had created. He swallowed his irritation, remembering that fifty thousand pounds was sitting on Alden's table.

Beggars really couldn't be choosers.

'Would this weekend be convenient to complete the sale?' Jack asked. 'Tomorrow? Around six?'

'Oh! Yes. Yes indeed.'

Jack turned away from Dune, ignoring the constellation of eyes seeking him out in the attic. His tongue felt swollen with booze.

'It's Kettu House on Knight Street, New Cross. Drop me a text when you're on your way. Goodbye, Mr Smithee.'

'Goodbye, Jac—'

He hung up.

His hand ached around the phone.

Tomorrow his bank account would be in the black for the first time in a year. He could pay off his debts and start again. The ship hadn't sunk yet. He could still turn it around.

Forget about the unfinished business degree and the dead-end jobs and interviews, the fact that he was on the wrong side of thirty and hadn't paid his rent in two months. Not to mention that he'd burned his way through five brief relationships and a dozen incendiary flings.

Jack's mouth pinched at the corners, a smile devoid of amusement.

Things were going to be all right.

He could do this.

He forced himself to look at Dune, and was unnerved by the sensation that he was in the presence of an old friend. He raised the bottle again, his eyelids heavy, and fought the onslaught of memories the puppet conjured, but they assaulted him in waves.

When he was seven, he would race home from school every Friday to watch *The Shadow Glass* with Dune and his dad. They would sit in his study and Bob would hum as he fed the VHS into the machine—

No.

Jack struggled free from the memory. There was no point going back there.

He looked down at the phone digging into his palm, and was about to pocket it when he noticed the call list on the screen. Every call he had received in the past few weeks. Towards the bottom, a name stood out in red. A missed call from a month ago. The day Bob died.

Dad.

'*What happens next, Dad?*'

It was the question Jack always asked when the credits rolled on *The Shadow Glass*. Because when he was seven, before he hated the film and everything it stood for, he couldn't bear the story to be over.

'*Well, there's no such thing as a happily-ever-after.*'

'*What does that mean?*'

'*It means there's always another story.*'

'*Does Dune go on another adventure?*' Jack would ask, even though he knew the answer.

'*Oh yes, many adventures, some even more dangerous than the fight to reclaim Iri from Kunin Yillda.*'

'*When can I see Dune's other adventures?*'

His father took a moment to reply. He brushed crumbs from his beard with a large hand. '*One day, my boy. One day.*'

Staring at the call log, Jack felt unsteady on his feet.

He found himself flicking through to voicemail and his thumb hovered over the most recent message. It was only fifteen seconds long and he had only listened to it once.

He hit play.

A whispering voice crackled through on speaker.

'Jack? Boy-o? Are you there?'

His father's voice was hoarse, short of breath, and there was no power to it. None of the resonance he had possessed as a younger man. He sounded lucid, though. Sober.

Jack glanced at Dune, searching the puppet's face for any sign he recognised the voice of his creator. Feeling stupid, he looked back down at his phone, but his vision blurred as his eyes grew wet, and all he saw was a rectangle of light from which his father's voice croaked.

'I need you, Jack. Will you come? Please?'

He hadn't.

[Shot of a panel table with the MCM Comic-Con backdrop]

RICH WENDIGO: Welcome everybody to the 'Fantasy Worlds' panel at MCM Comic-Con 2002! *[applause]* I'm Rich Wendigo, comic writer and movie journalist, and I'm honoured to be here as your host. Let's give a big round of applause to our panel: horror author Gina Powers, artist Todd Campbell and— Oh. It seems Bob Corman has ducked out for a minute. Somebody check the toilets for Bob Corman? *[audience laughter]*

BOB CORMAN: I'm here! I'm here!
[Bob Corman climbs onto the stage, struggles with a chair, and sits down]

RICH: Here he is! Everybody, please welcome filmmaker and puppet master Bob Corman! *[applause]*

BOB:	Sorry about that. I had an urgent Iri issue to deal with.
RICH:	Haha, that's great. Sorry, Bob, if you just move slightly back from the mic that'll fix the feedback issue.
BOB:	Like this? Hello hello this is ground control to Major Tom, can you hear me?
RICH:	Perfect. Ahem, right, Gina, let's dive in with you. Tell us, what do you think makes us fall so hard for fantastical worlds?
GINA:	Sure, great question. I personally love worlds that show us something unexpected. The ones that put a twist on familiar environments and explode them somehow. Make them spectacular.
RICH:	Absolutely. Bob, this sort of applies to your film *The Shadow Glass*—

AUDIENCE MEMBER: YEAH!

[Bob stands]

BOB: All right! Who here loves *The Shadow Glass*?

[smattering of applause]

BOB: No, really. Shout 'I LOVE IRI!' No, better, 'I LUB IRI!'

AUDIENCE MEMBER: I lub Iri!

RICH: Right. Uh, so Todd! You created Battleworld for your book series The Rage of—

BOB: Battleworld? Did he say Battleworld?

GINA: Yeah, Battleworld.

BOB: See, this is what I don't get about fantasy nowadays! It shouldn't be about the battles. I— Wait, is that a kettu in the audience?

RICH: I think that's somebody dressed as a fox.

[Bob climbs onto his chair]

BOB:	It's a kettu!
TODD:	Here, do you want some water?
BOB:	Don't patronise me.
RICH:	I think we should move on—
BOB:	Argh, everybody's so hung up on conforming these days! Nobody wants to stick out. Be different. Look at *The Shadow Glass*. The system was stacked against us! You know what I say to that? Fuck the system!
AUDIENCE MEMBER:	Yeah, fuck the system!
BOB:	That's the Iri spirit! See, there's none of this corporate bullshit there. Raise your hand if you believe in Iri! Come on! Say it with me! 'I BELIEVE IN IRI!' You'll see— *[Bob loses his balance, falls off the chair and crashes onto the table. He rolls over and lands on the warehouse floor]*

RICH:	Shit, Bob, are you okay? Is he okay? Can we get a medic in here?
	[crew members run in to surround Bob, who lies motionless on the floor]
BOB:	*[just audible]* Nobody gets it. Nobody.
10:28	*[Transcript ends]*

Comments

Troyville / seven years ago

Corman was a genius! publicity stunts like these make him LEGENDARY! Anybody believes this is a real drunken meltdown is an IDIOT, he was doin' it for the press

Baylaymania / seven years ago (edited)

What a mess. No wonder his film sank.

Lub1te / six years ago

BOB 4EVA YEAH!!!!!!

A distant hammering woke him.

Jack squeezed his eyes shut and lay listening, tangled in what he assumed were bedsheets, wondering why his head felt like it was being smashed between two rocks. His mouth tasted like a slug had crawled inside and died.

As the hammering persisted, he rolled onto his back and scraped open his eyes, staring up at a wall papered with peeling nineties movie posters. *Scream, The Guesthouse, Pulp Fiction,* and an array of Spielberg classics. There were bands, too. Jimmy Eat World and Foo Fighters, a whole bookcase of CDs and cassette tapes.

For a crazy moment, Jack thought he had woken up in the past, because this was his teenage bedroom. The one he had hidden in for most of his youth, turning up the music, losing himself in angry American rock. Jack had been particularly pleased with the Spielberg posters because they were like a middle finger to his father. Spielberg had the career Bob dreamed of.

With a sinking feeling, Jack realised he was still at Kettu House.

He raised a hand to his head and recognised the exquisite agony of a very adult hangover, and he remembered he had found his room sometime around midnight. He must have passed out, because now light was poking through the curtains, and the hammering that had roused him wasn't the window shutter flapping loose again, but somebody relentlessly assaulting the front door.

He waited for them to stop.

They didn't.

'Christ!'

Jack grabbed his suit trousers and shirt from the floor, dressing as he struggled onto the landing. If it was another fanboy eager to share his love of all things Bob, Jack would happily give them a piece of his hungover mind.

'What the f—' he began as he yanked open the front door, but the sight of the woman killed the remainder of the sentence.

'Jack!'

His cousin was a vision in purple. Her floaty trouser suit matched her nails and her brown hair was pinned up from a smiling, make-up-free face. Jack stood paralysed by her blue-eyed stare. He almost didn't recognise her.

'Amelia.' He coughed. His throat felt sore, as if he'd been gargling toilet cleaner. Maybe he had.

'You're here.' Amelia hesitated and then moved forward to hug him, but it was a professional embrace. Their torsos didn't touch. 'Gosh, it's so good to see you, J.'

'How'd you know I was here?' he asked, his eyes watering at the brightness of the day. Behind her, the morning was brittle and cold, the road wet from an overnight downpour. The oak tree dripped white pearls. He had no idea what time it was. It had to be early.

'Female intuition?' Amelia smirked. 'Okay, there's a chance I also spent an hour banging on your flat door before your neighbours complained. Charming people, by the way. Very loud voices. Anyway, I figured there was only one other place you'd be, although I have to say I'm surprised.'

They blinked at each other, the air thick like an invisible screen between them. Jack fought the surreal feeling that they were kids playing dress-up, pretending to be adults, the way they did when they were younger. But rather than the cousin he remembered, a stranger stood before him.

'You wouldn't leave a woman on the doorstep, would you, J?' Amelia's smile was tight against her teeth. Was she nervous? Begrudgingly, he stepped back to let her in.

'Wow, the old place hasn't changed,' Amelia said as she strolled into the lounge, bold as brass. The drapes were only part open, filtering in a shaft of light that gilded the fireplace. Amelia took in the sunken sofas and winged armchairs before turning to settle on Jack, who stood in the doorway.

'Remember those shows we used to put on in here?' she said.

How could he forget? When they were kids, he saw Amelia every day. They were the original *Shadow Glass* super-fans, and they'd watch the film and draw comics at every opportunity. Jack had been excited to have a friend who loved kettu as much as he did, even if she was his cousin and therefore a by-default playmate, not one you had to earn.

A week after Jack's eighth birthday, though, Uncle Grant and Aunt Gill had followed their restaurant-chain dream to America, and Jack and Amelia rarely spoke again.

Now Jack thought of it, he was sure that was when things went downhill with his father. Amelia wasn't there to confide in when Bob turned up at Jack's school for parents' evening wearing open-toe slippers and a dressing gown. She wasn't there when Jack broke a peacock-like *mesaku* figurine in Bob's study, and Bob refused to look at him for two weeks. She definitely wasn't there when Bob made his infamous television appearances, and Jack could barely walk through school without somebody dropping a 'Crackers Corman' joke.

Jack had been alone with his father's demons.

And the biggest joke of all was that Amelia now ran Bob's studio. She was the one Bob mentored when she returned to the UK looking to get into filmmaking, and now she looked every bit the knuckle-cracking movie executive. Jack still had no idea what made her different. How she was able to drag Bob out of his cocoon. Maybe Bob saw something in her that he couldn't in Jack.

Amelia gave him a hooded look. 'So? How've you been, J?'

'Good. I just got promoted.'

He'd said it before he knew the words were coming.

'Really? That's great!'

'Yeah, at a publisher.'

'That's… Wow, publishing!'

Jack's temple thudded. The publishing gig had only lasted a month because they said he kept turning up late, or not at all, and even though there were always reasons, he couldn't remember them now. Meanwhile, the interview yesterday had gone so badly he wasn't sure he'd ever get a job.

Jack shrugged. 'Better than messing around with puppets, anyway.'

The flash of irritation in her eyes was so familiar he couldn't resist a satisfied smile. He knew he was being juvenile, but he couldn't help it. Blame waking up in his old room. Blame the house or the hangover or the fact that just being there made him feel seventeen again in the worst possible way.

He rubbed his aching forehead, wishing he had water and paracetamol.

'What do you want, Amelia?'

'Right.' His cousin brandished a large folder he had been too addled to notice, setting it on the coffee table. 'I wanted to show you these, figured I'd bring Bob Co. to you. I won't even apologise for the ambush, it comes with the showbiz territory. Also, the funeral wasn't the right place to talk, and I wasn't sure you were getting my messages.'

'I got them.'

'So you were avoiding me.'

'Trying to.'

Amelia didn't seem offended. She flipped open the folder and stepped back. Irritated by his own curiosity, Jack moved forward.

Illustrations filled the portfolio. The first showed a glittering lake teeming with broken ruins, mystical symbols etched in stone. Another depicted bug-like creatures hauling themselves out of the ground. The style was familiar, ranging from full watercolours to charcoal sketches.

Breath hitched in Jack's throat.

'Are these Rick Agnor originals?' He recognised the style of the artist who helped Bob create the world of Iri. Whole books had been dedicated to his eye-popping concept art.

Amelia nodded in answer to his question.

'Rick's drawing Iri again?'

Amelia rolled her eyes. 'I forgot you were this slow. It's art for a new movie, J. A new *Shadow Glass*.'

Jack didn't move. He struggled to process what she was saying. Bob Co. were making a sequel? That didn't make sense. When *The Shadow Glass* flopped in 1986, Bob and his studio moved into special creature effects, providing puppets and monsters for films like *A-Maze*, *Riddlemaster* and *Man-Hero*. It sustained them for thirty-plus years.

But they didn't make movies. Not after *The Shadow Glass*.

A noise came from upstairs.

Amelia showed no sign she had heard it, so Jack pretended he hadn't, either.

'I thought the BBC thing fell through,' he said, remembering the sequel mini-series that almost got made five years ago, until Bob's vision was deemed too expensive and the deal collapsed.

'Right,' Amelia said. 'But eighteen months ago we ran market research on the original film. It's bigger than ever, thanks to the nostalgia renaissance. All those kids like us who grew up in the eighties are craving more of their childhood favourites. Plus, a lot of those kids are parents now. They're introducing *Shadow Glass* to a whole new generation.'

She cracked a smile. 'Either way, the numbers were clear. Audiences are desperate for more Iri and Dune.'

Jack stared at her, dumbstruck.

'Look,' Amelia said, 'with Uncle Bob gone we're sort of feeling our way in the dark here. We've gone through eight script treatments in eighteen months and none of them work. None of them are *him*. Which is why I want to bring you in.'

Jack snapped from his daze. 'Me?'

'You know this world better than anybody. Better even than

me. We need you, J.'

Jack's jaw had gone rigid. 'To write your script?'

'Please,' Amelia said. 'Say you'll try?'

'I'm done trying.'

Ch-ch-ch…

The sound needled under his skin. He scratched the back of his hand.

'And here's the thing,' Amelia said. 'The Shadow Glass prop is missing. Nobody's seen it since the eighties, but we need it. Big time.'

Her expression hovered between entreating and resolute. Jack could see how much she needed this.

'We're going for absolute authenticity here,' Amelia continued. 'The nostalgia crowd want the real thing. But it's not at Bob Co. and I've exhausted all my contacts trying to track it down. I figured if it was anywhere, it'd be here. Have you seen it?'

Jack laughed.

'You're unbelievable.'

Bob had been in the ground for two weeks and Amelia was here not as family, but on business. *Shadow Glass* business. He was sick of that film getting between him and everything.

'We're done here,' he said coolly, even though he felt anything but. He went to the front door, opening it and waiting. Outside, it had started to rain.

Amelia joined him, clutching the folder by its handle.

'Jack, will you—'

'Don't. You've said enough.'

Something banged so loudly they both jumped. At first, Jack thought it was the noise from upstairs, but then he saw Amelia had heard it, too.

He snorted with irritation as he realised the window shutter had come loose again.

Out in the rain, he took the steps down into the front garden, his body numb to the downpour. He felt back-to-front. Bob and *The Shadow Glass* had become inseparable in his mind and they were confusing everything. In his hungover state, Jack felt like he was coming unstuck. Reality was blurring at the edges.

Amelia wanted his help with *Shadow Glass 2?*

He had to be dreaming.

'It's because of me, isn't it?' Amelia demanded as Jack caught hold of the shutter. 'The reason you're acting like this? Because I'm running Bob Co.? Your dad—'

'Was a drunk!' Jack shouted, unable to bear it any longer. He faced her. 'He was a pilled-up, drunk ex-hippy who took too many psychedelics in the sixties.'

Amelia looked stunned. 'I can't believe you're saying that.'

Jack was trembling. 'You have no idea what it was like growing up with that man.'

'So tell me.'

He tried not to, didn't want to, but the words erupted from him nonetheless.

'Remember 2002? His big Comic-Con appearance? That was the day of my graduation. I was leaving school, going off to university. Dad knew it was the same day as the Con, and you know what he chose? The crowds. The fans. The strangers whose adoration he craved. Not me. Not his own son.'

He sneered at the memory of the press the next day.

BONKERS BOB STRIKES BACK!

Emotion clogged his throat. More words crowded in, but a lifetime of practice stuck them fast. He returned to the shutter.

'I'm sorry that happened,' Amelia said. 'I'm sorry, that sucks. And I'm not saying he was perfect. Bob made a lot of questionable decisions in his time. But you can't blame me. You turned your back on him a long time ago, Jack. I couldn't turn him down.'

'Why won't this thing *cooperate?*' Jack grunted, forcing the shutter back into place.

'Please, J.' Amelia drew herself up. 'If you don't want to help us with the film, fine. But if you just tell me where the Shadow Glass is, I'll leave you alone. Forever, if that's what you want.'

He stared at her, unable to believe what he was hearing.

'Bye, Amelia. Good luck with the movie.' He held her gaze without blinking, even though the rain was coming down hard now, ice-cold on his skin.

Amelia stood searching his face, as if looking for a sign that he would give in. Then she shook her head.

'I'm not saying Bob was perfect,' she said again. 'Not by a long shot. But when I came back from America and needed a friend? He was there for me.'

She stalked onto the street. Jack watched her get into a black Land Rover and speed off.

He remained motionless, soaking up the rain, flabbergasted by what had just happened. How couldn't she see that he was the one who had been wronged? She came to Kettu House demanding his help when she should have been apologising.

'*He was there for me.*'

Bob had never been there for Jack.

And for all he knew, knowing that work was happening on *Shadow Glass 2* could be the reason for Bob's stroke.

A thunder-boom shook the street and the wind screamed in his face, spitting leaves and grit as Jack hurried for the front steps.

He had to get Dune ready for Alden Smithee and figure out his next move.

As he started across the garden, though, somebody shouted behind him.

'Hi! Jack?'

Jack slipped on the mulching grass but remained upright, turning to find a figure standing by the oak tree. The trespasser wore black trainers, a rucksack and a blue raincoat with the hood fastened so snugly it squashed his face. Toby, the teenager from the day before. Why was everybody suddenly so interested in him?

'What are you doing here?' Jack asked, battling the wind to get to the steps.

'I wanted to apologise,' Toby shouted over the storm. 'I—'

Another clap of thunder swallowed his words.

'What?' Jack shouted.

'I said I think we got off on the wrong foot. I shouldn't have just showed up like that.'

'Forget about it.' Jack already had.

'It's just, I'm trying to put on an anniversary screening of *The Shadow Glass*, in Bob's honour. But I don't have a budget to cover the rights, so I was hoping you could sign it off.'

Jack squinted at him through the downpour. That was his reason for being here? 'You'll have to ask Bob Co. about that.'

'Nah, I already tried them. They hit me with a cease and desist. You're my last hope.'

A spark of annoyance spat in Jack's chest but he ignored it.

Not his problem.

'I'm sorry,' he said.

A flash of white glanced off the house, followed by a thunderclap that vibrated in Jack's bones. The storm was overhead.

Toby glanced up. 'What's with this storm?'

'Pathetic fallacy,' Jack muttered.

'What?'

Jack gritted his teeth, preparing to excuse himself, when Toby said, 'I'm so sorry about your dad. The stroke. I cried for a week when I heard. It's so awful. Like, he was amazing. His *mind*. And he wasn't even that old. He had so much more to give. It's just such a tragedy.'

Jack's upper back tensed, hardening into rock.

'It must've been tough,' Toby continued, 'dealing with it all. I guess that's why the puppets weren't there. At the funeral.'

Jack's gaze narrowed. 'What are you talking about?'

Rainwater dripped from Toby's nose, but he didn't seem to notice. 'In the December 2001 edition of *Film, Inc.*, Bob Corman—sorry, *your dad*—said that when he died, he wanted the *Shadow Glass* puppets at his funeral. I mean, he might have been joking, but you never know, right? Especially as he loved them so much. They were like his family.'

The noise of the storm dimmed as Jack stared at the teenager. The only way he could know about the funeral was through the papers. He shuddered at the memory of a press photographer snapping away with his camera from across the crematorium car park.

ONE-TIME CULT DIRECTOR DIES AGED 71.

It wasn't Toby's opinion on the funeral that burned. It was his implication that the puppets were more than just props to his father. Jack had no time for anybody who even remotely entertained Bob's fantasies.

'I think you should leave,' he said.

Toby's face fell. 'Sorry, I didn't mean to— Hey, watch out!'

At Toby's cry, Jack twisted in time to see the shutter spinning through the air. It had torn free from the house. His arms were too slow getting to his head and then Jack felt wood bludgeon his skull. It was as if a glass shard had cracked against bone.

'Fu—!' he began.

Then there was nothing.

Darkness pressed in around him.

A blank void.

And a stabbing pain somewhere near his eyes.

'Jack? JACK?'

Something shook him but Jack resisted. He couldn't take any more. He wanted to surrender to the darkness.

Let it claim him and his shitty life.

'JACK!'

Jack's eyes snapped open and he stared up into a panicked face. Toby's mouth moved but all Jack heard was howling wind. Above Toby, the sky swirled in a black-and-grey soup that seemed to be sucking the city into its depths. Jack realised he was lying on the wet ground, still in the front garden, and his skull felt like it was smashed all over the grass.

He put up a hand, surprised to find his head intact but wincing as his fingers brushed a welt near his hairline.

'Can you get up?' Toby yelled. His fingers dug into Jack's forearm and together they got him on his feet. Jack saw pink and white stars and gripped hold of Toby.

'Can you manage the steps?' the kid shouted in his ear.

Jack nodded, then wished he hadn't because it made his head hurt. Leaning on Toby, he laboured up the stone stairs. A gust of wind ushered him inside and, together, they slammed their backs against the door, panting as the storm became muted beyond the walls.

'*Wooooow.*'

Toby's hushed exclamation made Jack wince. The kid had taken a few steps down the hall and stood peering around like he'd been given the keys to nerd paradise. Jack sagged against the door, unsure if he could hold his own weight.

The house trembled under the storm, its timber frame creaking. Jack eased away from the door and limped to the living room. A damp patch stained the ceiling and water ran down the walls.

'Just perfect,' he said. If water was coming through the ceiling, that meant there was damage upstairs, too.

A crunching *smash* made him spin on the spot, and he saw thick, wet branches thrusting through the lounge window, tearing the drapes as they reached for him. The oak tree had wrestled its way inside.

'Holy shit!' Toby shouted.

Another flash and boom shook the house and sparks spat from the light fixtures.

'The whole place is going to explode!' Toby panted.

'No way,' Jack said, just when the loudest clap of thunder yet set the floor rocking.

It didn't stop. There was no lightning now, just a dissonant booming, over and over, like the beat of a primal drum. Sparks sprayed from the light fixtures and the water glittered, dripping in slow motion. His father's possessions shivered and jerked, the sofas creeping across the floor while, in the cabinets, grinning *Fuzz TV* puppets hopped where they sat. Jack avoided looking at them, their lifelike movement spreading anxious heat up his back.

'We should call—'

Toby fell silent as a new sound came to their ears. An almighty crunch like a rockface cracking open.

What if the oak in the back garden had collapsed, too? It would destroy half the house.

But Jack was sure the sound was upstairs, somewhere above their heads.

He thought of the skittering and scratching noises, but this was different. Louder.

Had somebody broken in? For real this time? The more he listened, the more it sounded like feet on floorboards.

He ran for the stairs, which swung from one side to the other until he blinked them back into focus. Not caring, only thinking about who was ransacking the house, if they'd made it to the attic and Dune, he took the stairs two at a time.

THUMP, THUMP, THUUUMP.

It was directly over his head. A primeval heartbeat. Bone striking bone. He didn't stop to guess what was going on up there. Clinging to the wall, he hurried up the narrow staircase to the attic. He threw open the door and charged inside, right into the middle of a waking nightmare.

Dark shapes thrashed around him in the gloom, some thin and agile, others squat and wide, all jerking and shuffling. He heard the ring of steel and caught sight of clashing blades, just one sound amid a chorus of snorts and screams. He couldn't make out what was going on and leapt back just in time as a sharp object swung past the tip of his nose.

A sword.

Something shot through the air and he ducked, narrowly dodging an arrow that twanged into an overhead beam. He stared at it in disbelief.

'What's going on?' Toby demanded at the door.

Even if Jack had tried to answer, he couldn't have spoken, for at that moment, in the shadows of the attic, a crouched figure turned towards Toby's voice.

Twin embers shone through the air, finding Jack. A pair of eyes. Their gaze intensified, and then the shape separated from the others, darting with terrifying speed towards him.

Jack yelped as something solid crashed into him and he was thrown onto his back. Whatever had landed on him wasn't heavy, but it was strong, pinning him with ease. His head ached, a fresh wave of nausea consuming him, and his vision swam.

Panting, he blinked until the thing pinning him came into focus. He stared up into bright yellow eyes, the darkness picking out the creases in a face that wasn't fleshy and human but downy with fine golden hair. For an insane moment he thought it was Dune, but the features were too delicate and a plait lay over her shoulder, which was clad in leather armour.

As he gawped up at her, the stranger leaned in to hiss with a voice as unyielding as the blade at Jack's throat.

'Quick! Tell me before I cleave the tongue from your mouth. Where is the Shadow Glass?'

Jack tried to swallow but he couldn't.

As chaos raged around him, he stared up at the woman. No, not a woman.

A kettu.

Excerpt from The Shadow Glass *screenplay, dated 1 Dec. 1984,* *written by Bob Corman.*

INT. HUT – NIGHT
CLOSE-UP: DUNE's eyes SNAP OPEN.

He SITS UP with a jolt and discovers he's in a BED,
covered in multicoloured blankets. His arm is
BANDAGED, his fox-like ears alert and swivelling.

He blinks, looks around, sees that he's in a SMALL,
TOASTY HUT. Pots BUBBLE on a STOVE and
HUNDREDS OF TREE ROOTS twist in curtains from
the ceiling.

> ### DUNE
> (to himself)
> Where am I?

> ### OLD VOICE
> (o.s.)
> Safe! Or as safe as anyone
> can be in Iri.

DUNE startles as the tree roots SHIFT and WRITHE.
Or, he thinks they are roots.

As they PART, they reveal an OLD MAN with BARK-
LIKE SKIN hanging upside down from the ceiling. He

drops to the floor and faces Dune. His hands resemble
GNARLED twigs, his EYES YELLOW-GREEN and
PIERCING.

                    RILL
          Welcome, welcome! I am Rill and
          this is my home.
                    (looks around)
          Hmm, such as it is.

                    DUNE
                    (in awe)
          The mystic. You're Rill the mystic!

A dozen startled eyes BLINK open around the room:
furry creatures with enormous ears dozing on shelves
and tables. Rill has a lot of LUBS.

                    RILL
                    (squinting)
          Heard of me, have you? Don't believe
          everything you hear out there. Most
          times, the truth is far, far worse.

Jack opened his mouth but only garbled syllables choked out.

'Speak!' the kettu ordered, and the blade thrust against his Adam's apple.

'I... I... Ca—'

Jack stared into her face, seeing a humanoid creature with eyes like planets and a nose almost as pointed as the fur-tipped ears atop her head. Breath snorted from her nostrils, which was impossible because he could see the uneven dye in her fur, the near-invisible seams along the backs of her arms where stitches were hidden. She was a puppet. But she was moving.

'ZAVANNA!' a male voice bellowed.

The kettu's head snapped to the side and then her weight lifted off him. Jack lay stunned as she plunged across the attic. His eyes adjusted to the midday gloom and he watched in a daze as the kettu clashed with the saw-toothed blade of—

A skalion.

Crackling fear forked through Jack's abdomen.

They were as familiar as the rest of his father's possessions, but wrong. They shouldn't be moving. They shouldn't be *alive*.

Jack's gaze swept over the figures, looking for the puppeteers. Maybe somebody had fastened them with strings to manipulate them from above. But the beams were empty. There were no puppeteers.

The skalion emitted a reptilian rasp.

'Kettu scum! Kettu die!'

It was a foot taller than the kettu, its razor teeth gnashing in its wide, lipless mouth, a purple tongue squirming as it parried in its mechanised armour.

Jack felt like he was watching a projection of *The Shadow Glass* but it was happening for real, in his father's attic. He could smell them, the earthy perfume of the kettu mingling with the slimy reek of the skalions, and fresh horror foamed in his stomach as he attempted to process what he was seeing.

Skalions.

Creatures of nightmare.

Merciless. Fearless. Mad.

And here. Right here in the attic.

'Wha—? How?' Jack watched in terror as the creatures fought. The kettu moved with the grace of a dancer, her blows landing with deadly force, but the skalion was immovable, solid as wet clay, fielding her attack while gurgling with laughter. A second kettu fought further back, surrounded by hissing skalion soldiers, and this couldn't be happening. It couldn't—

A throwing star smashed into the floorboards between Jack's legs and he jerked into motion, scuttling backwards across the floor like a crab until his back struck something solid. The door frame.

Sweat slid down the side of his face and panic clawed at his chest.

He had to get out of there. Or wake up. Whichever came first.

Before he could move, though, his limbs jammed tight as blue light winked at him.

It beamed from the centre of the attic, where a hunched shape squatted. It was smaller than the amphibians, its narrow face dominated by insectoid eyes that sparkled with ice-blue light. Over its skeletal frame hung a rag-like dress, and its skin was tough and midnight-black, like a shell. Its gnarled claws squeezed together as it beheld him and cold blistered through his bones.

'Nebfet,' Jack choked.

He felt his sanity fraying, coming unpicked one thread at a time.

The creature's mouth tugged into a gap-toothed smile and the attic faded to black around it. Jack saw only those segmented blue eyes, that emaciated skull-like face, and he felt a stabbing presence at his temple, something ravenous needling its way inside.

'Earthling, that is what you are, hmm?'

The voice grated in his ears, echoing around him and inside his own head. It was accompanied by a chittering sound like insects that caused his arm hair to bristle, although he couldn't tell where the sound originated.

He had seen this before, on-screen; Nebfet the seer working her dark magic in *The Shadow Glass*, sinking psychic hooks into the minds of wugs and shredding what she found. However painful it had appeared on-screen, the reality was a hundred times more agonising.

'Show me this world. Show me now, earthling.'

He felt the power of her mind. The unbending will, so strong it pulverised his own. He was a worm snared in her beak, powerless to do anything other than be devoured, and no matter how much he repeated in his mind that this wasn't happening, he couldn't stop it.

'*Show me.*'

Images flickered across his vision. London streets. Buses. The river.

'*Yesssss,*' the creature hissed, and he felt her brain tremble with pleasure.

A scream loosened her grip on his mind and Jack felt the alien presence snap away.

The attic returned in all its crashing, shrieking mayhem.

He saw the female kettu astride a skalion soldier, her blade buried in its chest. No blood oozed across the floorboards, though, only bits of stuffing and armour that surrounded the body, as if she had shredded a feather cushion.

'Go!' Nebfet screeched, raking a fleshless finger towards the window.

Jack watched as the toad-like soldiers hurled themselves forwards, smashing through the glass and vanishing outside. At least a dozen of them.

'Hmmm,' Nebfet said, and Jack flinched as her iridescent gaze lingered on him for a second more. Then she turned and scuttled to the window, leaping outside.

Silence settled over the attic, broken only by the drumming of rain on the roof.

Jack remained leaning against the door frame, his mind shredded, his forehead throbbing.

At the centre of the attic, the female kettu who had attacked him stood panting over the skalion corpse. She was actually panting. Jack watched her breast expand and contract, her ears twitching as she surveyed the damage.

At the window, a second kettu, the male one, peered into the street, his snout trembling. Lightning flickered in the distance, but the storm had faded to a far-off purr.

'Gone,' the male kettu said. 'For now.' He was darker than his companion, his build broader, the fine fur oak-brown with black markings like soot smudges. Jack tried to remember his name but failed. He wasn't one of the main *Shadow Glass* players. Perhaps a side character with limited screen time.

'That was amazing!' Toby cried.

All eyes snapped in his direction. He stood in the door, rainwater dripping from his coat. He pushed back his hood and unzipped his coat—on his T-shirt, a furry lub wore a sombrero and played the maracas. For a moment Jack feared the female would throw herself at them again. Toby didn't appear to share Jack's concern. He looked elated, as if he had stumbled into the best live theatre performance ever.

The female kettu took a confident step forward, her black-and-red tail stiff behind her.

'What are you? What is this world?' she demanded.

Something about her suspicious tone struck Jack as funny.

His laughter filled the attic and he winced, because laughing hurt his head, made it feel like a cracked egg. Then he laughed again and struggled to his feet.

'Brilliant, just brilliant,' he said.

'Jack?' Toby asked.

'I thought I had a few more years before I lost it, but fine, I'll take it. It was good while it lasted.'

The kettu blinked at him—he remembered *kettu* was both plural and singular—their ears flicking the air, paws still ready with weapons.

Jack couldn't stop. He shook with hysteria, his whole body vibrating at the sight of the puppets, and he didn't ever want to stop finding it funny, the most ridiculous thing he had ever seen, them glaring at him, because if he stopped finding it funny he didn't know what he'd do.

He bit his lip to control the sound.

'Let us begin again,' the female said, her voice tight, as if she were only just controlling her emotions. 'I am Zavanna and this is Brol. Are you friend or food?'

Transcript from an interview with Bob Corman broadcast on BBC Radio 1, 27 June 1986.

INTERVIEWER: It is a question all creatives get asked, but the world of *The Shadow Glass* is so rich, so alive, I have to ask. Just where did it all come from?

BOB CORMAN: *[laughs]* What if I told you I've seen it?

INTERVIEWER: Seen what?

BOB CORMAN: Iri.

INTERVIEWER: I suppose you mean metaphorically? Spiritually?

BOB CORMAN: Metaphorically, literally… Iri is real to me. I've seen the things that are now up on the screen. I suppose that's why it feels so real, because Iri is real. It truly is.

4

'I knew it!' Toby cried. 'Zavanna, you're Dune's sister! And Brol, you were in some of the battle scenes, right? Are you part of the Vex tribe, too?'

Zavanna's eyes became slits. 'How do you know this?'

'You were only bit-parts in the film but there's a comic about you, Zavanna. It's really difficult to find now. I got an old copy on eBay. I'm right, aren't I?'

'Ha!' Jack surrendered to the laughter. 'Dune's sister, yeah, right. Got it. Why the hell not?'

He'd always known this would happen. Bob's mental decline was genetic. It was only a matter of time before Jack succumbed to it, and now *Jack* was the one in the attic hearing voices. He'd even created a fanboy character to give his delusions a contemporary spin. Bob would be proud.

The kettu named Zavanna hunched as she faced them, as if prepared for another attack.

'Speak plainly,' she spat. 'Are you allies of the skalions?'

'Hell no.' Toby made a face.

'Explain how we came to be here.'

'I can't explain it. Jack?'

Jack couldn't speak.

The kettu bared her teeth. 'Who are you? What is this realm?'

'That's Jack, and I'm Toby,' Toby said. He raised his hands. 'We're pacifists. We're pro-peace, right Jack? And this is Earth, or at least a room in a house on Earth.' He gave an apologetic shrug. 'Sorry, but you're not in Iri anymore.'

Zavanna remained motionless, studying them. Jack shuddered under her gaze, wondering what she was thinking. *How* she was thinking. He had no idea how Toby was handling this so well. There was no fear in his dark eyes, only delight. It was as if Toby had been waiting his whole life to talk to a kettu and he wasn't going to waste a second of it.

'You are carnivores, predators,' Brol said. 'Beady eyes in front. What is your prey?'

'Beefburgers?' Toby said.

'The malodorous one is injured.' Zavanna nodded at Jack's forehead.

Instinctively, his hand went up. The skin felt hot and solid where the shutter had struck him, and the reality dawned on him in a fevered rush. 'Oh thank god. I'm concussed. Or I'm unconscious. That's what's going on.' He slapped his cheek. 'Somebody wake me up, will you?'

'Jack, you're not unconscious,' Toby said.

'Seriously, hit me.'

Toby shook his head. 'I've never hit anyone. Jack, stop hitting yourself!'

Zavanna gave Jack a final look and then dismissed him. 'The

manchild is an imbecile.' She paced on the spot, talking to the rafters. 'We had the Glass within our grasp! It was so close I could *touch* it. Iri could have been saved. But then all was confusion, screaming and thunder, and then we were here. This is madness!'

She scanned the attic. 'The Glass *must* be here, also.'

She fell upon a cardboard box, tearing it open to scour the contents. With a frustrated growl she shoved it aside and tore at another, her claws shredding the material like it was tissue paper.

'Hey,' Jack said. 'Stop.' He stepped forward and a fresh wave of nausea rolled through him.

'Stay back if you value your pelt! You will not keep us from the Glass!' Zavanna continued to demolish boxes, searching under furniture, turning the attic upside-down.

Jack was about to tell her stop again when a new thought occurred to him. Less than an hour ago, somebody else had come to the house looking for the Shadow Glass.

'Did Amelia put you up to this?' he demanded.

'What is a Melia?' Brol asked.

'That's it, isn't it?' Jack searched the rafters for hidden cameras or radio transmitters, anything that could control the puppets remotely. 'You're some kind of animatronic for the new movie.'

'New movie?' Toby asked.

'Do you have cameras in there?' Jack stepped closer to Zavanna, waving a hand in front of her face. 'Nice try, Amelia, but I'm onto you. You're getting nothing out of me.'

Zavanna snarled and suddenly Jack was on his back again, pinned to the floor by the kettu. This time he was sure he'd be sick.

'There is no *Melia*. I am Zavanna of the Vex tribe and I have been charged with locating the Shadow Glass before the skalions destroy our world. Now *tell me* where it is.' She forced her arm down, increasing the pressure against his Adam's apple.

'I don't know!' Jack twitched beneath her. 'I don't know where it is!'

She held fast for a second and Jack stared into her face, seeing her pupils dilate, his face reflected in them, and the scratches in the glass orbs that doubled as eyes. He couldn't breathe. It was too much. It didn't make any sense.

'Don't hurt him,' Toby said. 'He can help! You want to find the Glass, right? He's the son of Bob, the creator of the Shadow Glass.'

Zavanna's ears pricked and she considered Jack warily.

'You are the son of Bob?'

Slowly, Jack nodded.

The kettu took in his bruised face, his shabby suit, and Jack knew what she saw. The disdain in her expression was clear. He felt as insignificant as a midge.

'Lies,' Zavanna muttered, releasing him. 'He is no son of Bob. He is as wise as an inebriated wug. He is nothing.'

How does she know Bob?

As she moved away, Jack seized her arm. He felt the mechanical skeleton of the puppet beneath its foam muscles, and also the warmth of a living thing. Somewhere inside, the puppet may have veins expanding with blood, and it had breath, too. Was there a heart in there, fluttering with new life?

'How are you alive?' he rasped.

'Unhand me.' Her paw flashed and Jack winced as claws raked the back of his hand. He let go.

'You're really real,' he said, staring at the welts between his knuckles.

'Rithmar spare us.'

The thought was too big for his skull. He felt unsteady, the adrenaline bleeding from his body to leave him hollow.

Somewhere in his mind, a voice whispered, *He tried to tell you. He tried to tell everybody.*

No. Bob had been unhinged. A drug-fried hippy. An emotional wreck.

There was an explanation for this, Jack just hadn't found it yet.

'How wondrous! Zavanna, behold!' Brol held a Rubik's cube, which he must have found in the box on the floor by his foot. 'Is it a teller of fortunes? Might it guide us to the Glass?' He shook it by his ear.

Toby laughed. 'It's just a toy.'

'Christ,' Jack muttered. He got to his feet, then sank into an armchair, feeling broken and deflated.

'Time is wasting,' Zavanna said sharply, facing Brol. 'The boy is a liar and the manchild is a half-wit. We must keep moving, locate the Glass before Nebfet sinks her talons into it. We do not need the natives.'

She tugged her sword free from the dead skalion. The creature remained motionless, playing dead or maybe actually dead, never alive to begin with. Jack didn't know what to think. Zavanna went to the window, drawing a cloth from her armour to clean her sword.

'Wait, don't go,' Toby said. 'You said you saw the Glass, before you turned up here. What happened?'

Brol looked at Zavanna's back. When she gave no reaction, he cleared his throat, placed a foot on a wooden trunk and rested an arm on his thigh. Classic hero-explains-the-plot pose. Jack fought a fresh wave of delirium.

'We were protecting the wug village. Zavanna, myself and Dune. The Shadow Glass had been stolen from the kettu castle and the skalions believed the wugs were concealing it. They invaded with their full army. The Vex tribe went to their aid and we fought amid a storm unlike any we had ever experienced. We discovered Nebfet the seer in a chamber below ground, working some dark enchantment on the Glass, attempting to twist it to her own diabolical means.'

He hesitated, looked pained, then continued, 'In the confusion, Dune perished, slain by a skalion warlord. And then the Glass cracked, erupted with a blinding light, and we were here.'

Jack barely heard the last part of Brol's story because his chest had cramped. 'Dune's dead?'

He blinked and rubbed his face. No, this wasn't happening. Dune wasn't dead because he wasn't real. None of this was.

'Yes, I am afraid so,' Brol said.

'No, he can't be.' Toby looked crestfallen. 'I can't believe it.'

Brol straightened. 'He died the death of a hero.'

'Dune.' Jack's gaze moved to the corner of the attic where Dune stood in his glass cabinet. He looked exactly the same as he had the previous night, staring out with his mouth slightly ajar, his face immobile. A silent observer.

There came a clatter from the window and Jack saw that Zavanna had dropped her sword. She flew to the cabinet, pressing her palms to the glass.

'Brother?' Her breath steamed the pane. 'Dune?!'

She stared into his face, searching.

'What have the natives done to you?! They have bewitched you! Dune! Hear me!' She spun to glare at Jack, the whites of her eyes showing, and he thought of rabid dogs and werewolf movies. The marks on his hand stung.

'I didn't do anything,' he said, worried she'd do worse than floor him this time.

'It's, uh, a statue,' Toby said. 'In his honour.'

'Look, none of this is real!' Jack cried, leaping up from the armchair. 'The story, the characters, Iri—Dad made it up. It came out of his head. You're puppets, for god's sake!'

'*Puppets!*'

A high-pitched cry came from the other side of the attic. Jack's mouth fell open as a number of potato-shaped heads popped up around the room like a living version of Whack-a-Mole.

'Wugs!' Toby shouted.

A couple of the creatures had gathered in front of a cracked mirror. They were barely two feet tall, resembling old men with stubby limbs that poked out of knitted cardigans. Woolly hats were tugged over their misshapen heads, their skin cracked with age, leathery and smooth.

Their toothless mouths hung ajar as they stared at their reflections, then at their fabric bodies, and shrieked, button-black eyes pinned wide.

'*Puppets!*' one of them wailed, and the attic erupted in chaos as the wugs scattered, howling as they crashed into old furniture and collided with one another like bowling pins.

Amid the tumult, a new shape leapt out from behind the bookcase. A mewling black-and-white animal zipped across the floorboards and leapt into Toby's arms.

'What now?' Jack groaned.

Toby stared down in shock at the thing trembling into his raincoat. His face lit up. 'Oh my god, it's a lub!'

Jack eyed the creature nuzzling into the crook of his arm. Its furry, bat-like ears were too big for its head, and its eyes seemed to be all pupil. A small mouth was set in a fuzzy line and a long, black-and-white tail wound about Toby's forearm. The creature resembled a cat crossed with a raccoon, its tiny paws drawn in to its fluffy chest as it shook and trilled.

'Oh man, I always wanted a lub.' Toby soothed the spot between the creature's ears and its eyelids dropped. 'There, there, it's all right. You're safe now.'

'Those things are dangerous,' Jack murmured.

'Not even!' Toby said. 'Look at it!'

As the wugs continued to race about the attic, Jack massaged his own forehead. He kept waiting to wake up. Any second now, he'd blink and find himself in the front garden, the storm still raging, the shutter lying at his side. It was all a whisky-induced fever dream.

'Silence!'

Zavanna's voice brought the wugs to a standstill. They stood huffing, catching their breath, and in Toby's arms the lub watched them with interest. Zavanna cast a look at Brol and then herself, as if noticing for the first time that they, too, were made from latex and fake fur. She blinked and her expression hardened.

'Whatever is happening, it is happening for a reason,' she said to Brol, her voice barely above a whisper. 'I do not understand it but I will not surrender hope of finding the Shadow Glass. If its will spirited us here, then its will altered our state. We must trust in the Glass and we *must* find it.' She went to the window, retrieving her sword and staring out at the sky. 'The lunium is in one cylar. If we do not reclaim the Glass before then, Iri will be lost to the skalions.'

'*Cylar* means *day*,' Toby said.

'Yes, I know.' Jack didn't need a fanboy education in his father's lore.

Toby frowned. 'But what's the lunium? I've never heard of that.'

Brol cleared his throat again. 'It is the prophesied cosmic window of time when good and evil may fight to rule Iri for the next millennium.'

'Iri will not last another millennium,' Zavanna said to nobody in particular. 'Not if the skalions triumph.'

'Holy shit, like an Iri end of days?' Toby said. 'That's immense! How have I never heard of that before?' He balanced the lub on one arm and took out his phone. 'There's a full moon tomorrow night. Funny, I guess it's like our version of the lunium?' He paused, bobbing the lub. 'Wait, you said there was a storm, right? That must be how you came through to our world. There was a storm here, too. Maybe there was some kind of mystical convergence that allowed you to cross over. That's how it always happens.'

'Always?' Brol raised a bristled eyebrow.

'Uh-huh. *Stargate, Coraline, Narnia, Masters of the Universe, Time Bandits...* they all had portals. I mean, portals are sort of off-trend right now, but that doesn't mean one didn't bring you here.' His forehead crinkled. 'That's assuming Iri is a real place, which would be un-freaking-*believable*, even though I have no idea how that's possible.'

'The small one is excitable,' Brol said to Zavanna. She didn't appear to be listening, instead rooting through her satchel, pushing aside old scrolls and clinking trinkets.

'You said the Glass exploded in Iri,' Toby continued. 'What if it was destroyed? Maybe that's why it sent you here, in its final moment. The Shadow Glass still exists in this world.' He looked at Jack and added, 'As a movie prop, anyway. Maybe its power transferred to the Glass in our world, just like the kettu and the skalions.'

Jack massaged his aching temple.

'Jack, you know where Bob kept it, right?' Toby said.

Brol stepped forward. 'Manchild, if you truly are the son of Bob, then we beseech your help.'

'He is not Bob's son,' Zavanna said. 'He is an imposter.'

Jack felt the full force of the kettu's gaze and cringed. He didn't know what to say. Didn't want any part in this.

Toby went over to him. 'We have to help them,' he hissed. 'Don't you get it? Bob was telling the truth! All those interviews he gave about Iri and alternate realities, how he said he'd seen things... he wasn't making it up!'

More than ever, Jack felt like he was trapped in a nightmare. He had seen first-hand how erratic Bob was, how demented he could be. Jack had spent too many years trying to forget all of that for anything to change his mind.

'This isn't real,' he said, as if repeating those words would force the world to realise it had glitched. Reset.

Toby gestured at the kettu. 'They look pretty real to me.'

Jack watched Brol put his hand to Zavanna's elbow. They appeared deep in discussion and then Zavanna said something and broke away. Brol looked hurt. It made Jack uncomfortable. It was pure fantasy. The eighties alive and shrieking in his father's attic.

'Bob would want us to help them,' Toby said.

'I don't care what he'd want.'

Toby's forehead creased. 'You don't?'

He looked more confused by that than the fact that the puppets were alive.

'Jack, didn't you hear Brol's story? The Shadow Glass was stolen from the kettu castle, Nebfet was enchanting it when Zavanna found her... none of that happened in the movie. We're in new territory. We're in a real-life sequel to *The Shadow Glass*! I always wanted to find out what happened next, and now we're *living it*!'

Jack dabbed the sore spot at his hairline. It ached more than ever and he had a feeling this wouldn't go away unless he made it.

'Fine,' he said, squeezing the bridge of his nose. 'Let's just get this over with.' He faced the kettu. 'We'll help you.'

'We do not require—' Zavanna began, but Brol cut in.

'Peace, Zavanna. They are native to this world and appear quite harmless. The skalions have all but destroyed Iri and now that they are in this world, they will seek to claim it, too. The natives require our help as much as we do theirs.'

Jack eyed the smashed attic window. He was right. Skalions devoured everything they encountered and their appetite was limitless. If he wasn't losing his mind, if the skalions really were loose in London, there was no saying what havoc they might wreak.

'I feel certain Dune would trust them,' Brol said.

Zavanna looked like she wanted to tear out his throat. They stared at each other without blinking and Jack wondered if they were going to fight. Then Zavanna scowled and sheathed her sword between her shoulder blades while muttering, 'If you wish to make pets of them, so be it.'

Brol sniffed, then he bowed to Jack and Toby. 'We accept your gracious offer, most gangly and peculiar new friends.'

'All right!' Toby actually punched the air. The lub squeaked like a chew toy. Zavanna watched the sky, perhaps seeking a way to navigate without them, ignoring them all.

'If the Glass is anywhere,' Jack said, 'it'll be here in the attic. The quicker we start looking, the quicker we can get this over with.'

'Zavanna says the same of washday,' Brol said.

A growl sounded near the window.

★

They each took a corner of the attic. Jack sensed the tension in the air, the wariness that existed between them, and tried not to think about how easily Zavanna had subdued him. How sharp her claws were. Only Toby appeared impervious to the strained atmosphere. While they picked over boxes of Bob's possessions, he asked the kettu an excitable stream of questions, listening intently as Brol answered.

'How many pups are in a kettu litter?'

'Why do gripyorns lay eggs in the brains of blibs?'

'Have you ever heard of Sigourney Weaver?'

Jack focussed on sorting through vinyl records, time-crinkled notebooks and old board games. Nearby, the wugs helped. Sitting in a row, they examined each new object with wonder, 'oohing' and 'aahing' as they passed dead batteries, old lighters and painted egg cups between them.

A couple of times Jack caught Brol shooting him a curious look, but Zavanna seemed to have forgotten Jack existed. She opened drawers and scoured their contents with increasing impatience, throwing aside old clothes and moth-eaten cushions, her movements jerky with frustration.

In one of the notebooks, Jack found a black-and-white photograph of the Shadow Glass. Just the sight of it caused his pulse to quicken and he went to shove the picture away, but something stilled his hand. He peered closer.

The Glass was large and oval-shaped, its black wood frame expertly carved so that it danced with Iri beasts. The mirror itself was dark, almost black too, and mottled with age. It really did look like a relic from a forgotten time, a forgotten world, beautiful and sinister and ancient.

But it was just a photo. There was nothing to say where the Glass was now.

Jack blinked and returned it to the notebook.

After an hour, they had found nothing more than a couple of spiders' nests and a box of seventies horror paperbacks with titles like *The Wasting* and *She Goes into Houses*.

'It's no good,' Jack said, his head aching. 'It's not here.'

'It could be somewhere else in the house?' Toby suggested.

Jack shook his head. 'If it was anywhere, it'd be in the attic.'

'So what do we do?'

They fell silent, out of ideas.

Across the attic, Zavanna dumped an eyeless doll back into a picnic basket and began searching through her satchel.

'Zavanna?' Brol asked.

'I shall perform a sight voyage,' she said.

'Zavanna, it is too dangerous.'

Toby frowned. 'What's a sight voyage?'

'It is how certain mystics commune with the ether,' Brol explained. 'We possess herbs that are powerful enough to transport the consciousness out of the body and into the Other Place.' He gave Zavanna a troubled look. 'But they are a known poison. Zavanna, if you enter the Other Place, there is no guarantee you will ever return.'

'It is worth the risk.'

'I cannot lose you, too.'

Zavanna glared at him and Jack struggled to keep a lid on his apprehension. Not because the kettu were arguing, but because if the Shadow Glass wasn't here, he knew exactly where it was likely to be.

'Listen,' he said, attempting to form the words even though he didn't want to. 'If anybody knows where the Shadow Glass is, it's Jenny Bobbin.'

Excerpt from 80s Flicks: A Celebration, *by Matt Glasby (Rough Tirade Press).*

Medusa. The Witch King. Maleficent. More than any other movie genre, fantasy boasts an embarrassment of villainous riches. And if we're talking the 1980s? Fuhgeddabouddit. Between Bavmorda, the Nothing and Frank Langella's sublime Skeletor, the '80s were the golden age of Hollywood villainy. This was the era when so-called 'kids' films made it their mission to scare the living shit out of you. If you weren't having nightmares, they weren't doing it right.

Deserving of her own putrid corner of the genre is Kunin Yillda, the skalion queen who dominated cult puppet masterpiece *The Shadow Glass*. 'I imagined the most horrible thing I could and there was Kunin,' said director Bob Corman of his turgid creation, an amphibian-like swamp dweller whose acid-seared armour and tangles of string-like hair suggested her role model was the Iceni queen Boudicca.

Just why is Kunin Yillda so scary? Well, on top of being lethal in battle and possessing her own meddlesome psychic (the terrifying Nebfet), she's also representative of the very worst of '80s excess.

Created by legendary puppet designer Jenny Bobbin, she's an anti-Yoda, a fantasy version of Gordon Gekko who's hellbent on more, more, MORE, no matter the cost (although she'd make short work of Michael Douglas's *Wall Street* suit). If 'greed is good', Kunin Yillda makes great work of the eating.

'The best kind of movie villain,' theorised film critic Roger Eggers in 1988, 'is one who reflects back at us the things we fear about ourselves.' Kunin Yillda certainly achieves that. Her vulnerabilities about her rancid appearance are all-too relatable, as are her ravenous appetite and take-all attitude (the single-minded sadism maybe not so much). After all, what's scarier than something that just wants to consume?

Jack floored the accelerator, steering the Volkswagen down a street strewn with wet newspapers, egg cartons and mulched food. The storm had wreaked havoc on more than just Kettu House, and south London looked as frazzled as Jack felt. Even the noir-ish wash of midday light couldn't help it.

'Marvellous,' Brol sighed from the back of the van, his seat belt fastened. 'We are truly humbled by this majestic chariot.'

Beside Jack, Toby chuckled, the lub curled up in his lap.

'How hard and grey this world is,' Zavanna said. Her eyes barely reached the window.

Jack focussed on the road.

After patching up his forehead with some gauze, he'd found the green camper van in the garage, sitting beside an equally clapped-out orange Beetle. The Volkswagens had been Bob's pride and joy, purchased in the seventies with one of his earliest *Fuzz TV* cheques, but neither had seen the road in years. Jack only hoped the engine wouldn't catch fire as they drove.

He couldn't shake the sense that this was all his father's fault. Bob had sent the key in the mail. Bob had tempted Jack back to Kettu House. Would any of this have happened if Jack hadn't unlocked the attic? Did Bob know the puppets would start talking?

His grip tightened on the wheel.

It would be easier to ignore the kettu in the back if Brol would stop talking. While Zavanna sat in frosty silence, Brol explained that he was a kettu lieutenant, that the siege at Wugtown was his thirteenth, and that he had fallen in love with Zavanna when she rescued him from something called a 'tunnelling fizzverm' during the Battle at Jewelhaven.

'I knew right there, as I lay choking on the embers of battle, that I had found my mate.'

Jack remembered kettu partnered for life and wished that information wasn't in his brain.

He also wished Zavanna would stop staring at him. He kept catching her glare in the rear-view mirror, a mixture of contempt and suspicion in her eyes. He couldn't tell if he felt ill at ease because she was a puppet, or because she seemed perfectly capable of killing him in a breath and feasting on his corpse. He made a mental note not to do anything that would rub her fur the wrong way.

I really didn't need this today.

'What was he like?' Toby asked, and Jack realised he was talking to him.

'Who?'

'Bob.'

Just the mention of his name made Jack's palms clammy.

'I wish I'd had the chance to meet him,' Toby said. 'All I have to go by are the interviews and blog posts. You're the only person

I know who knew him for real, so I wondered… what was he really like?'

'You don't want to know,' Jack muttered.

He felt Toby looking at him for an uncomfortable moment, but he couldn't do it. If he told Toby the truth about Bob, the way his obsession with *The Shadow Glass* infected everything, the awful things he'd said in a stupor and forgotten about the next day, he'd crush his dream.

Toby stroked the lub in his lap, and Jack ignored it, too. He was sure that every time he looked at it, the puppet inflated, its eyes igniting with scorn. Lubs had always seemed sweet in *The Shadow Glass*, but Jack knew better.

Toby must have sensed his discomfort because he turned to look at the kettu.

'You said the Shadow Glass will save Iri from the skalions, but how?' he asked.

'The Glass possesses the very soul of Iri,' Brol said. 'The skalions have poisoned the land with their accursed teck-noll-gee, causing Iri's soul to wither. Once we have the Glass, it will choose a worthy subject, a champion who might pass into its mirror realm and replenish its soul, reset the balance. Iri will recover and the skalions shall be banished back to the swamps from which they crawled.'

'Mirror realm? That's not in the film.'

'Film?' Brol asked, his head cocked.

'It's like a story, but with pictures.'

Brol's voice became hushed. 'It is drawn on parchment? In the manner of the Kettu Sagas?' He gazed into the middle distance. 'I have always felt my victory at Crooked Rock would make for a glorious addition to the Sagas. Tell me, are you acquainted with these Scribes of Film?'

Toby laughed. 'I'll see what I can do. You were saying about the mirror realm?'

'Yes, of course. The mirror realm is said to lay bare the champion's soul. The very essence of their being. The champion must face their darkest truths to prove themselves worthy of the Glass. And once they have done so, they can ask one thing of the Glass. They can salvage Iri's soul simply by wishing it so. Save the world.'

Convenient, Jack thought. It sounded like typical fantasy film garbage. They all had some mystical solution to the plot's key problems. He remembered Bastian naming the Empress in *The NeverEnding Story*, the wannabe magician tricking the evil queen in *Willow*, and the teenage witch learning the value of her non-magical friends in *The Magical Adventures of Ellen Dritch*. He hadn't thought about those movies in years.

'At this very moment, Iri teeters on a blade's edge,' Brol said. 'The skalions' greed has wreaked hell on the landscape, gutting communities, wiping out species and habitats. The kettu deserts have been ravaged beyond recognition. If Iri is not restored by the lunium, there will be no going back. Iri will become a bleak, barren land, one unable to support life, one that will fester and decay until, eventually, it perishes, and us with it.'

'But how does the Glass know who to choose?' Toby asked. 'Who's worthy of it?'

Brol released a breath. 'That is the great mystery. Those who enter the Glass never return to share what they have learned.'

All this talk made Jack nervous. 'How about some music?' he said, jamming the buttons on the radio.

An eighties rock anthem blasted from the speakers, turned up so loud that it vibrated in his clothing. In the back seat, the kettu clamped their hands over their pointed ears.

'Is this used to torture information from captives?' Brol shouted. 'It would surely break them most swiftly!'

Toby shut it off.

'Sorry, you guys have crazy hearing, right?'

Zavanna shook out her ears, looking furious.

'A kettu is nothing without their hearing,' Brol said, adding thoughtfully, 'or their sense of smell.'

'Or their sword,' Zavanna said darkly, massaging the hilt of her blade in a way that made Jack nervous that she would sooner run him through than tolerate him for another second.

Thirty minutes later, they pulled up outside a bungalow on a quiet street in Putney. It looked like something out of a fairy tale. Grandma's house. The front door was varnished red and the windows were decorated with lace netting that obscured the interior.

Jack observed it nervously. If Jenny Bobbin had the Glass, they could end this. Quest complete. Collect your glowing trophy and return to reality.

Spurred on by the thought, he reached for the door handle and told the kettu, 'Stay in the van.'

Zavanna's gaze frosted over. 'Stay? You are not my commander. If the Glass is here—'

'If anybody sees you moving about like that, you're fucked,' Jack said.

'What is "fucked"?' Brol asked.

Toby cackled. 'The PG puppet just F-bombed you.' At Brol's questioning look, he added, 'Uh, it means things are really, really bad.'

Brol nodded slowly.

'What if you played dead?' Toby said to the kettu. 'Go limp.'

'Limp?' Zavanna's nose wrinkled.

'Yeah, like…' Toby let his head hang forward. 'Easy.'

'It's the only way you're going anywhere near that house,' Jack said.

★

A few minutes later, Jack stood outside the red front door, amazed that he'd reached it even though every sinew in his body had screamed at him to get back in the van. He clutched Brol, feeling the kettu's warmth and wondering if this felt weird for him, too. To his credit, the kettu was a natural, his head tipped forward and his limbs hanging loose against Jack's torso. Maybe this would work after all.

Toby's backpack wriggled and he hushed it over his shoulder as he held Zavanna. From inside the bag, the lub mewed and fell silent.

Jack knocked. His neck knotted painfully as he waited, then he heard the click of locks and the door opened.

Warmth and light spilled out, along with the chirpy melody of Annie Lennox's 'Walking on Broken Glass'. A woman peered out at him and Jack nearly choked as he tried to swallow.

'Yes?' The woman's voice was husky, mismatching her slim frame, and purple paint smeared her cheek. It was in her white hair, too, which was fastened in a clip, and her green boiler suit was covered in rainbow flecks and dashes. Her pale blue eyes were as intelligent as ever.

'Jenny?' Jack said.

'Jackie? Oh my gosh, is it really you?'

Her California accent was as strong as ever, breezy and somehow big, and the sound of it made Jack's heart ache. When he was a kid, he'd lived for that sing-song voice, so exotic and different. She had stuck it out with Bob for eight months before he ruined their relationship.

Jenny went to hug him but stopped herself, raising her paint-covered arms. 'You caught me mid-masterpiece. Won't you come in?'

Toby nudged Jack and he stepped into the hall. His gaze skipped over the collection of frames, china figurines and marionettes that filled Jenny's home. It was cluttered, but it was clutter with a philosophy. He breathed deep, checking around for any sign of the Shadow Glass, but he saw none.

'I'm Toby,' Toby said.

Jenny smiled. 'It's nice to meet you, Toby.' Her attention went to the puppet in his arms. 'Is that who I think it is?'

Toby seemed to have forgotten about the kettu. He lifted up Zavanna and Jenny moved closer. Jack tensed, but the kettu remained motionless. If only he could pull off the same trick, people might leave him alone.

'My, it's been years,' Jenny breathed. 'It's good to see you again, Zavanna.'

'You remember her,' Toby marvelled, 'even though she's only a secondary character.'

'Of course I remember her. I made her.'

Toby grinned.

'They, uh, need fixing up,' Jack said, bobbing Brol in front of him.

'Yes, I can see that. Come in, come in. This way.'

As Jack followed her down the hall, he couldn't help feeling Jenny had purposefully avoided looking at his patched-up forehead. She led them through the kitchen, passing the table where Jack's father had once sat with a guitar playing a number from *Fuzz TV*, and continued into the garage.

It wasn't a garage, though. It was even more packed than the hall, shelving units running along the walls, every available surface crammed with curios. A stack of canvasses rested against the garage door.

Jenny silenced a paint-covered CD player. 'Welcome to my studio.'

'Holy cow.' Toby cracked Zavanna's head against the door frame as he hurried inside. 'Sorry! Oh my god! Is that the thimble from *Ash Knight*? And that's the mermonster from *Waves of Fortune*!' He practically hyperventilated as he dashed from shelf to shelf. He halted by a miniature white peacock, its wings spread in flight. 'I didn't even know figurines of the mesaku existed!'

Jenny's laugh was rich and warm. 'You should see the ten-foot head we created for the movie. Pretty terrifying. Here.'

She took Zavanna from Toby and set her on a stool, then poked through drawers full of buttons, needles and thread. Jack placed Brol beside Zavanna, scanning Jenny's collection for the Shadow Glass, but there were no mirrors. Nothing tucked among the canvasses or bundled in bubble wrap.

'We're looking for—' Jack began, but Toby's shout interrupted him.

'Jack, look!'

Toby pointed at a cabinet in the corner. It was almost identical to the one in the attic, except instead of Dune, it contained a potbellied four-foot puppet. A memory of childhood fear spat somewhere inside Jack.

'Kunin Yillda,' Toby whispered.

The skalion queen was even uglier than Jack remembered. Like all skalions, she was scaly and sick-looking, her head as wide and irregular as a beat-up football, topped by a thorny crown that nestled in limp grey hair. Boils pocked her grey skin and her bulbous eyes were fixed on Jack in a death stare. He swore he could smell the swamp musk coming off her.

'Wait,' he said, 'don't get too close.'

Toby hung back a little.

'Ah, my most glorious creation,' Jenny said, pausing mid-thread, Zavanna's arm lifted. 'She was always my favourite. Your father let me keep her after shooting wrapped.'

Stiffly, Jack crossed to Kunin Yillda's cabinet and peered in. The puppet remained motionless, so he ran his hands along the wooden frame, checking for any sign it had been opened recently.

'You'd be surprised how valuable that thing is,' Jenny said. 'She's older than Toby here.'

Jack forced himself to peer into the creature's craggy face. Was she still a puppet? Or was she just good at pretending? He couldn't believe he even had to question it.

'Has she,' he began, struggling for what to say. 'Has she… moved recently?'

'She's been in that cabinet for over a decade,' Jenny said.

'Not has she *been* moved,' Jack said. 'Has she *moved*.'

Jenny frowned. 'Jack, she's a puppet.'

He found he couldn't stop looking at Kunin Yillda. He tried not to blink in case he missed a twitch. Jenny was saying something but her voice was distant, as if she were talking in another room rather than right behind him.

He shook the cabinet. Kunin Yillda didn't react.

'Move!' Jack shook the cabinet harder. '*Move!*'

Kunin Yillda rocked forwards, her forehead butting against the pane, but the puppet had only moved because he had shaken her loose.

He felt a hand press into his forearm and jumped, then released a scratchy breath.

'Jack, how about a cup of tea?' Jenny said softly.

He let go of the cabinet.

At the kitchen table, he dropped wearily into a chair and watched Jenny fill the kettle. Toby had remained in the garage to drool over the props and, as Jenny took down a couple of mugs, Jack felt nine years old again. It was almost as if no time had passed and he had come here after school.

When he thought about the eight months Jenny dated his father, he remembered a feeling of lightness. He had known Jenny his whole life, ever since she worked on *The Shadow Glass*, so he barely noticed when she started spending more time at the house. She would make dinner and open the curtains and sometimes she was there for breakfast, which was how he knew it would be a good day.

His father had seemed different, too. He spent less time in his study and Jenny had a gift for conjuring laughter from him, the way a magician pulls flowers from a hat.

That seemed like another life now. A distant, far-flung time, like an island that he had long since left behind. It hadn't lasted between Jenny and his father. How could it have? Everything his father touched in those years turned to ash.

'Are you still working at the paper?' Jenny asked, pouring boiling water into the mugs. 'I was surprised when your father told me how much you were enjoying the ads team. Work's work, don't get me wrong, but you were always such a creative kid.'

'You stayed in touch with him?' Jack asked.

'On and off over the years.' Jenny set a steaming cup in front of him. She sat in the chair opposite. 'Of course, he made it difficult, but I cared for the idiot. Never could stop. I visited him a couple of times now and then.' Her voice softened. 'Jack, how are you really?'

'I'm fine.'

'Yes, you seem it.'

He ignored her tone.

'Did you see him much before the stroke?' she asked. A thread of silver hair whispered against her cheek. 'He always talked about you. He'd be happy that—'

'You don't need to do this,' Jack interrupted.

'I'm just trying—'

'To make me feel better, like always.'

She didn't care, not really. If she cared, she would have stuck around when he needed her.

Jenny sighed, contemplating her tea. 'Your father was a complicated man, Jackie. It's what I loved about him, even when we stopped seeing each other. When he happened upon a new idea, it was like watching fireflies in the night. Of course, that kind of creativity often comes with a side order of less desirable qualities. It's part of the reason things didn't work out with us.'

'Let me guess, he tried to brainwash you with his metaphysical mumbo-jumbo, too.'

'There was that,' Jenny said. 'I guess I was too much of a realist, and boy did your father make it difficult to have a normal conversation. When things ended between us, I got job offers from all over the world, so I took them. I'm afraid my pride was somewhat bruised by the whole thing. I'm sorry I couldn't be there for you. I would hate for you to think it was because I didn't want to be. I loved you, kid.'

Jack realised he had never spoken to Jenny as an adult. Hearing her side of the story was surreal. In his nine-year-old mind, Jenny had been there, and then suddenly not. He hadn't ever considered her feelings, only what her departure had done to him.

'I saw him,' he said before he could stop himself. He took a breath. 'I saw Dad a year ago. He showed up at my flat saying he wanted to talk. We hadn't seen each other in years, not properly, so we went for dinner. It seemed okay at first.'

He paused, the memory prickling through him. 'He barely touched his food, but he asked about me, wanted to know what I was doing with my life. Then he started on about the BBC deal, the fact that the money people still didn't understand his vision, that Iri was in crisis…'

He tried to stop but he couldn't. 'He knocked his plate on the floor, made a mess trying to clean it up, and people were staring. It was The Bob Show all over again. I can't believe it took me almost an hour to realise he'd been sneaking booze in the toilet. I used to be an expert at spotting that stuff.'

'That's the last time you saw him?' Jenny asked.

Jack nodded.

He'd left out the part where he only agreed to go for dinner because he needed five thousand pounds to clear his debt. He didn't even get the chance to ask before Bob unravelled. Jack wished he could forget the way Bob had pleaded with him, his beard damp with tears.

'It's all falling apart, boy-o. It's crumbling around them. Iri needs you more than ever.'

He'd walked out without looking back.

'He came to see me, too,' Jenny said, her eyes glistening. 'Two months ago. He was ill. He had some kind of liver condition. Didn't know how much longer he had left.'

Jack frowned.

'You didn't know? Christ. Perhaps he was trying to protect you.'

It would be the first time Bob had protected Jack from anything.

'I wasn't blind to his flaws, Jack. I knew he turned to drink when things got tough, but back then I rationalised it to myself.

He drank so rarely, and never in front of you.' She exhaled. 'I was a fool. If I could go back to that time, I'd stay.'

Jack knew she was trying to make him feel better but he couldn't bear it. Bob may have hidden the drinking when Jack was nine, but by the time Jack was a teenager, Bob was practically pouring it on his breakfast cereal.

He met Jenny's gaze and something weakened within him. He wanted to open up to her. Tell her the words Bob said when Jack was fifteen, during one of his worst episodes. The ones that finally destroyed their relationship for good.

'He said…' Jack began, but his throat sealed shut.

'Jack? Boy-o?'

He heard again the rasp of his father's voicemail.

There was no air in the kitchen. He had to move.

Jack kicked back his chair as he stood. He hurried for the back door and burst out into the garden.

The air was icy on his cheeks and he sucked in great lungfuls of it, his eyes stinging. He wouldn't cry. He wouldn't break.

He blinked in the fading afternoon light, wishing the shuddering in his ribcage would stop.

'Jack, I'm sorry.'

He sensed Jenny behind him, but he couldn't turn to look at her. His hands balled into fists. This was all Bob's fault. Even from beyond the grave, he was messing everything up.

'I shouldn't have said anything,' Jenny murmured. 'I can only imagine how it's been since your father died.'

'We're looking for the Shadow Glass,' Jack said, because at least that was something he could say without feeling like his internal organs were in a blender.

'The Glass? That's what this is about?'

'Sort of. Do you have it?'

Jenny's voice sounded tight. 'I've not seen that thing in years.'

'Do you know who has it? Or where we can find it?'

She went quiet for a long moment, then she said, 'I don't know where it is, but I thought it got dismantled. At least, that's what I heard.'

He turned in surprise. 'Dismantled?'

'Broken into pieces. Easier to transport that way.'

Jack stared at her. A groaning sound wheezed from his throat. Of course. He had forgotten the most important part of his father's movie. Dune's quest revolved around him tracking down the four fragments of the Shadow Glass. They were scattered throughout Iri and it was only when Dune united them that order was restored.

Whatever cosmic force was behind this whole impossible adventure, it had a sick sense of humour. Because they weren't looking for one movie prop, they were looking for four.

Jack almost lay down in the garden.

'I didn't—' he began, but then a movement caught his eye. A flash of something in the shadows by the fence.

'Shhh,' he hissed, scanning the flower beds for anything that could have moved.

Ignoring Jenny's questioning look, Jack moved down the path, expecting a dark shape to hurtle from the bushes at any moment. As he reached the end of the path, he stepped on something and instinctively jumped back. He peered down at a viscous substance that pooled at his feet.

'What the—'

Steam rose from a wet pile just in front of him. Grimacing, Jack crouched down and a putrid smell curled into his nostrils. He pulled up his suit jacket to cover his mouth.

'What is it?' Jenny asked, standing over him.

Jack reached down to tease up the material, grimacing at the slimy texture. It was as thin as paper, a single piece of something like white fabric, soaked through with gelatinous fluid, long and curling at the edges. He fought the urge to vomit as he realised what it was.

Skin.

Something had shed its skin.

He turned it towards the light, recognising the scaly pattern etched into it.

'Skalions,' he whispered.

A crash resounded within the bungalow.

'Toby!'

Dropping the rancid material, Jack rushed past Jenny and went back into the kitchen just as a figure hurtled from the garage into the house, smashing into the kitchen table.

Brol didn't lie still for long. He bounded quickly to his feet, tail alert as he scooped up his sword and prepared to plunge back into the garage.

'Skalions?' Jack asked.

The kettu nodded. 'They are here, new friend Jack.'

Excerpt from the article Corman, blimey! *from the June 2001 issue of* Film, Inc. *magazine.*

WHATEVER YOU'VE HEARD ABOUT BOB CORMAN, YOU'RE WRONG.

On the fifteenth anniversary of the cinema release of *The Shadow Glass*, *Film, Inc.* was granted a rare audience with the director, whose career took a nose-dive after his puppet-animated fantasy adventure failed to draw audiences in 1986.

Serving tea at his New Cross home, the fifty-one-year-old founder of Bob Co. is far from the addled recluse you've read about. Wearing a colourful cardigan and brown leather shoes, he still has his iconic beard, which is as bushy as you've seen in archive pictures. Although quiet-spoken, he possesses a resonant voice, and remains pragmatic about the film's box-office shortcomings.

"You have to remember, *The Shadow Glass* came out amid a glut of sci-fi and horror sequels," he says. "Nobody knew what to do with Iri and its inhabitants. This was the '80s, the last era of optimism. People wanted sparkling adventure and cute aliens but that never interested me. I wanted to make a film that said something."

Not everybody was listening, though. In the years following the release of *The Shadow Glass*, Corman practically lived on the press trail, trying to drum up interest in his film. However, his appearances stirred only a bemused interest in Corman himself, and his TV chats often devolved into feverish monologues about transcendental meditation, wormhole theory and the healing powers of crystals. 'Bonkers Bob' was a hip new circus act and there wasn't a TV sofa in town that wouldn't have him.

Shortly after his most famous TV meltdown—a segment in which he attempted to get the interviewer to commune with the world of Iri via a live meditation session—an article ran in *Zeppelin* magazine in which a rock star claimed Corman took psychedelic drugs with him at college in the late '60s. The papers loved it.

Now, Corman dismisses that period in his life as merely "tricky". And the one thing he will not be drawn on is the ire of so-called fanboys who, ten years ago, held a demonstration after the publication of a prequel graphic novel series. Mass burnings of *Beyond the Shadow Glass*, written by Corman, led to a number of arrests as protests got out of hand. One fan, Wesley Cutter, remained unrepentant and branded Corman a "world-trashing hack".

Looking troubled at the mention of the incident, Corman won't directly address Cutter's actions and will only say, "People love the world of Iri. They feel protective of it. In the end, that is the greatest compliment I could ever receive."

Brol leapt back into the garage.

'Jack?' Jenny asked from the back door, her features pale. He wasn't sure if she had seen Brol but she looked more confused than disturbed.

'There's somebody in the house,' he said. 'Stay there. Please.'

'But—'

Before she could argue, he shut the door and turned the key, trapping her in the garden. As she stared open-mouthed at him through the glass, he flicked off the lights, plunging the bungalow into darkness.

'Jack! Open! This! Door! *Now!*'

He ignored her, seizing a carving knife from the counter and darting into the garage. It took him a moment to process what he found.

On the other side of Jenny's studio, a large hole had been torn from the garage door, the corrugated edge glowing ember-orange. Five skalions sparred with Zavanna and Brol, blades clashing as the reptilian soldiers drooled and cackled.

Jack realised they looked different. Their green skin shone with slime and their musculature was more defined. Their stench clogged the garage, a reek like rotting vegetables, and Jack breathed through his mouth. He thought of the skin he'd found in the garden and shuddered.

'Get back!' Toby yelled as a skalion charged towards him.

Brandishing the kitchen knife, Jack threw himself forwards, tackling the skalion from behind. He seized hold of the collar of its armour and jerked it off balance. The creature rolled to one side, easily bouncing back to its feet. Despite the cumbersome armour, they were surprisingly nimble.

The creature hissed at Jack, jerking its head forward to reveal a sheath of poisonous darts that protruded from its spine.

'Oh shi—'

Jack dropped just in time. The darts whistled over his head, embedding in one of the shelves.

The skalion released a hissing shriek and rushed him, its padded feet slapping the cement floor. Jack was too slow in rising and yelped as the creature bowled into him. He found himself on his back, the skalion clambering on top of him, its armour rattling as it raised a serrated blade and prepared to plunge it into Jack's heart. Before it had the chance, a furry blur knocked it sideways. The skalion crashed into the wall and Jack stared up at Zavanna, who remained crouched, ready to strike.

'You're strong,' Jack panted.

She flashed him an irritated look. 'Stay out of the way, manchild.'

She pirouetted on the spot, thrusting her sword into the skalion's belly. The creature screamed and black blood erupted from its torso.

Jack stared in shock.

Blood.

Not foam like before.

It gushed from its wounded belly, slopping to the floor as the soldier thrashed and twitched. Finally, it released a death rattle and collapsed, lying still.

'No! Get back!'

Toby's shout drew Jack's attention. A skalion was advancing towards him with a deadly glint in its eyes.

'Give usssss,' it rasped.

It seized Toby's legs, yanking them out from under him. As Toby flopped to the floor, a second skalion bounded over him, smashing open the cabinet and gripping the frame in webbed claws. It clambered inside to reach for Kunin Yillda.

As two more skalions went for Zavanna and Brol, Jack scrambled to help Toby, seizing the armour of one of the skalions and wrenching it away from the teenager. The creature gibbered and spat at Jack, and Toby jumped up to tackle the soldier already tugging Kunin Yillda out of the cabinet.

They had come for their queen, but why?

She was still just a puppet.

Whatever the reason, it couldn't be good.

As Toby heaved the skalion away from the cabinet, the creature squinted in irritation, released its queen, and flicked a switch on its armour. A transparent visor flipped over its head while green gas pumped from its back, enveloping Toby and mushroom-clouding into the garage.

The other skalions engaged their visors, cackling, their boiled-egg eyes agleam.

Jack coughed as his vision clouded and he inhaled a lungful of the reeking mist. It burned his lungs, stinking like something found festering in a watery grave, and he released the skalion he had been wrestling.

Through the fog, he spotted four bulky shapes surrounding the cabinet.

'Stop them!' he cried, retching as he inhaled more of the toxic air. He threw himself at the nearest skalion, knife raised, moving on instinct alone. He had no idea if he could actually plunge the blade into the creature. Vaguely, he wondered when he'd started thinking of them as creatures rather than puppets.

He didn't get to find out because the skalion heard his approach. It whipped around and pain spasmed through Jack's hand.

The creature's claw had flashed out quicker than he imagined possible. Its fingers gripped his, squeezing so tightly Jack felt his bones creak. He bit his lip to stop from crying out and he lost his grip on the knife. It shook free, clattering to the floor; unlike his hand, which the skalion held on to.

Its visor flipped back and its eyes seethed with white fury.

'Jaaaaaaack,' it rasped.

Then, with a shriek, it dragged Jack's hand into its mouth and bit down.

Jack screamed.

Agony like nothing he had ever experienced blazed in his hand. Jack bucked and wrenched, attempting to pry it free, but it was useless. The skalion's razor teeth gripped his flesh, scraping bone and shredding sinew as it grunted with pleasure.

Jack screamed again and finally tugged his hand free. He fell back, crashing against the wall, trying to think through the pumping pain in his hand. As he leaned into the bricks, he raised his right hand and felt light-headed at the sight of it.

His index finger was gone, replaced by an oozing red stump.

'My finger,' he whispered, unable to process what he was seeing. 'My finger...'

The skalion's bulbous eyes gleamed at him, Jack's blood dripping from its mouth as it chewed and swallowed.

'Tasty earthling,' it gibbered.

Jack clutched his injured hand to his chest, attempting to stem the flow of blood. In a daze, he watched the skalion swivel back to the cabinet, but Brol leapt before it, tackling all four skalions at once while Toby's voice echoed somewhere in the fog.

Jack's fingers were slippery and warm but a freezing chill crept through him. He couldn't think. The garage spun in circles around him, even though he was sure he wasn't moving. He tried to remain upright, but then his shoulder struck something solid, the wall maybe, and he collapsed against it, sliding to the floor.

'My fuh...' he whispered, trying to focus. The garage felt distant. He was looking the wrong way through a telescope and everything had shrunk and become distorted. The toxic gas seemed to cushion sound so that it reached his ears in a muffled confusion.

'Manchild,' Zavanna said, appearing at his side. Her voice snapped the garage back into focus. 'Bite this.'

He tried to resist as she wedged a piece of wood between his teeth, but she was determined. She tugged at his injured hand, attempting to pry it away from his chest, but he held tight, afraid she'd hurt him even more than the skalion had.

'Let me help you,' she spat, and he couldn't understand why she was even trying. So far, Zavanna had shown nothing but derision for him. He felt too weak to fight her, though, and relented. She took his injured hand and looped something around the stump. Too late he realised it was a makeshift tourniquet. He screamed and wood splintered between his teeth as she yanked the string tight.

'Get off me!' he cried, spitting wood chips.

'Cease your squawking,' Zavanna hissed, removing a strip of fabric from her satchel and fastening it around his finger. 'Anybody would think you'd lost something important, like an eye.'

He may as well have. He could barely see through the white haze of discomfort. His finger throbbed, his *missing* finger, and bright red pain burned where Zavanna pressed the bandage.

'Kunin,' he groaned.

As if on cue, Brol was kicked to the floor at Jack's feet and the shadowy outlines of the skalions surrounded the cabinet once more. Through the settling gas, Jack discerned the frontmost creature seizing Kunin Yillda from the case, yanking her free, and then leaping through the garage door, vanishing. The others followed, shrieking with triumph.

Whatever they wanted the puppet for, they had succeeded.

'Remain here,' Zavanna told Jack, darting outside after them, Brol right behind her.

Jack felt his consciousness slipping. He hugged his hand. The pain was unrelenting and it was all he could think about. But they were getting away with Kunin Yillda. And what about Jenny? Gritting his teeth, he struggled up from the floor using the wall for support. Cradling his hand, he staggered for the ruined garage door.

'Jack?' Toby said.

'The Glass is in pieces,' Jack murmured, clinging to his hand. As Toby's mouth fell open, Jack ducked through the hole in the door, almost tripping on his way outside. On the drive, he gulped down fresh autumn air and it helped clear his head.

Ahead, the kettu cast about in the middle of the road, but it was no good.

They were too late.

The skalions were gone.

'Jack?'

He saw Jenny struggling over the garden fence, one leg slung over and scraping for purchase. With a cry, she dropped down into the driveway, huffing and swiping her hair out of her face as she ran to join him.

'Christ on a bike! What happened?' she panted, staring at the smoking garage door.

'They took her,' Jack said, hearing his voice as an echo as his gaze swept the empty road. 'They took Kunin Yillda.'

★

Back at the van ten minutes later, Jack sagged into the driver's seat and let his skull sink into the headrest. He tried to think of anything other than his hand, but the makeshift bandage was soaked through and the wound itched, felt wrong, his hand both heavy and weightless.

'Of course the Glass is in pieces,' Toby trilled as he got into the passenger seat. 'That makes total sense! Why didn't we think of that?!' He looked through the windscreen. 'The kettu must have taken shelter somewhere nearby. We should circle the area to pick them up.'

Jack said nothing. He felt cold. Somehow, he had managed to convince Jenny not to call the police, urging her to give him a couple of days to get the puppet back. She didn't look happy about it, but at least she'd agreed. He suspected his injured hand had worked in his favour.

Toby unzipped his rucksack to stroke the lub. The creature crooned in relief, its batlike ears seesawing up and down. It must have heard the whole thing.

'Are you okay?' Toby asked.

'I'm fine,' Jack said.

'Oh, I meant the lub.' Toby stopped. 'What happened to your hand? Did you cut it?'

He hadn't seen. The skalion gas must have shielded Toby from the horror of Jack's ordeal. Jack was about to explain when a sombre voice spoke from the back seat.

'You are safe.'

Jack would have jumped if he had the energy. Instead, he rolled his head to look in the wing mirror. The kettu sat in the back of the van, grubby and weary-looking, skalion blood smearing their armour, seat belts fastened.

'How did you get in here?' he asked.

'We thought it best the artist woman did not see us,' Zavanna said. 'You appear to be a nervous people.'

Toby laugh-coughed. 'It's so good to see you guys.'

'Were you harmed?' Brol asked, his gaze flitting over them.

'Show me,' Zavanna said.

He felt a pull at his elbow and found her reaching for him between the front seats. He raised his hand, closing his eyes as she peeled away her bandage. She was surprisingly gentle.

'Oh my god, Jack,' Toby cried.

'It ate my finger,' Jack murmured. He felt like he was sinking into a car-seat marshmallow. Everything seemed hazy and distant.

'I think I'm going to be sick,' Toby said. 'Does it hurt?'

Jack didn't have the energy to answer.

Zavanna pressed something to his hand and ordered him to

hold it there while she retreated to the back. 'I shall fashion a balm,' she said, and he heard her going through her satchel, rustling what sounded like dry leaves and clinking something wooden.

While she worked, Toby filled the kettu in on what Jack had said about the Glass being dismantled.

'That is problematic,' Brol breathed. 'And now they have their queen. We failed to stop them.'

'But she wasn't their queen,' Toby said. 'She was still just a puppet. What use is that to them?'

'Maybe they've figured out how to bring her to life,' Jack murmured. 'Bring her here.'

Toby shuddered. 'I really hope not. Kunin Yillda's poison kills you dead in seconds. Although, I guess it's the only reason they'd want her. Kunin Yillda gives the skalions something to live for.'

'If they succeed,' Brol whispered softly, 'it is not just Iri that will suffer. Kunin Yillda desires everything she sees, including the Glass. She will not stop until this new world is under her rule, also.'

Jack massaged his aching head with his good hand. This wasn't going away. He had hoped that by humouring the kettu and Toby, he would nip whatever was happening in the bud before it got out of control. Instead, it was getting worse.

'What does Kunin even want with the Glass?' he asked.

'The skalion queen prizes shiny baubles,' Brol said.

'She uses them to distract from her hideous countenance,' Zavanna added.

'And the Glass is the shiniest bauble of all.' Brol shook his head. 'She means not to use the Glass, but to prevent others from claiming it. Merely by possessing it, she dooms Iri.'

'Nobody ever taught her to share,' Toby said. 'How did they even know she was there? At Jenny's? In fact, how are they even *surviving?* London's huge. The skalions should be freaking out, not organising military operations that leave us royally fucked.'

'Nebfet,' Jack croaked. He shivered as he recalled those blue eyes pulsing at him in the attic. The soothsayer had sucked information from his brain like a wheel bug.

'Of course,' Toby said. 'What if she figures out where the Glass pieces are?'

'Then we are truly fucked.' Brol's ears perked up. 'Is that the correct usage of the word?'

As Toby laughed, Jack sensed the life draining out of him. His limbs felt like ten-ton weights. His wounded finger pulsed angrily and he wanted to lie flat, slip into blissful unconsciousness, but then Zavanna was tugging on his arm again. Something cool covered the wound and he smelled herbs and soil.

'A soothing balm,' Zavanna said. 'Now I shall redress the wound.' She worked quickly and Jack realised the balm was already doing its job. The pain was replaced by a pleasant numbness. He could breathe a little easier. His eyelids were heavier than ever, though. When Zavanna was done, he found himself staring blearily into her face.

'You helped me,' he whispered, still trying to understand why.

'You fought with the elegance of a newborn barhogg,' Zavanna said, 'but you fought, nonetheless.'

Her tone was less sharp than it had been before.

But only in the way that a blade can be blunted by overuse.

Jack's eyes refused to stay open any longer.

'Jack, move over,' Toby said, attempting to push him across to the passenger seat. The lub beeped from the dashboard, and Jack was only vaguely aware of lifting his legs across to the other side of the car and then sinking into the passenger seat. As the van's engine kickstarted, he surrendered to the darkness.

Excerpt from the novelisation of The Shadow Glass *by S.M. Johnnie, based on the screenplay by Bob Corman.*

Dune peered up into his grandfather's face, noting the whiteness of his hair and the wisdom of his eyes. There was something comforting about sitting by his side in the firelight, knowing how old he was, the things he had seen. His grandfather was a reminder that not all kettu died in battle. Some survived to tell dead men's tales.

'But what happened to the Glass?' Dune asked.

His grandfather's whiskers trembled. 'It was broken apart during the Pack War.'

'Broken?! How?'

'The four packs failed to agree on who should command the power of the Shadow Glass, and so, in a rage, the Vex general hacked it to pieces and left the tribes to squabble over them.'

Dune pondered this new information. 'Did that fix it?'

'No. The general was killed and the Pack War raged for another arran.'

'Wooow. Where are the pieces now?'

His grandfather released a breath. 'That, my pup, not a soul in Iri knows.'

'We're here!'

Jack bolted upright as the car rocked to a standstill.

'We're where?' he asked. He went to rub his eyes but then he felt the weight of the bandage, the twinge in his finger, and reality flurried back in a suffocating rush. He blinked down at his hand, which Zavanna had neatly patched up, and a wave of nausea travelled through him. He couldn't bear to think about what had happened to his finger, so he peered out the window.

The sky had bled a sickly green, the clouds torn into ragged strips, and Jack didn't recognise the neighbourhood.

'You drove?' he asked.

Toby smiled sheepishly. 'Dad's been teaching me.'

'This is your friend's abode?' Brol breathed, staring out at a red-brick townhouse.

'Huw's parents are loaded but tighter than a badger's chuff.' Toby unclicked his seat belt. 'Jack, can you move?'

'I think so.' The pain had eased a little but his hand felt wrong, the wound tight and pulsing. His whole body ached. 'We're at your boyfriend's place?'

Toby nodded. 'I'm late for a Guild meeting and, well, Sumi's a student nurse. She could take a look at your finger.'

'The manchild's finger has been treated,' Zavanna said pointedly. 'We must focus on the Glass.'

'If anybody can help find the Glass, the Guild can. We meet every Saturday and, between us, we know everything about Iri and Bob Co. and *The Shadow Glass*.'

A growl rumbled from Zavanna's throat and she looked poised to kick open the car door and go on without them.

'Patience, Zavanna.' Brol placed a paw on her shoulder. 'There is yet time. We must trust in new friend Toby's gilded comrades.' He looked at Toby. 'Go. We shall keep watch.'

Zavanna shrugged him off and began rooting angrily through her satchel. Jack felt a twinge of sympathy; he knew what it was like to want something only for it to constantly elude you.

'We'll be quick,' he said, noting the time on the dashboard. Four p.m. He had to be home in two hours to meet Alden Smithee. Grimacing, he eased himself out onto the pavement.

'Here.' Toby attempted to pass Brol the lub, but it chirruped and tightened its tail around his wrist. 'Hey, it's okay. I'll be back soon.' He tickled it under what Jack assumed was its chin and the tail loosened. Brol took the creature, wincing as its claws sank into his arm.

'Those little pricks *smart*,' he told the lub. To Toby, he added, 'Be swift.'

'Swift we shall be!' Toby beckoned Jack down a driveway that ran alongside the house, and they skirted into a small back garden. He bounded down a set of cement steps and threw open a door below ground level.

'Children of Iri, fall at my feet!' he yelled.

Jack followed but hung back by the door, surveying the snug basement as three sets of eyes crinkled in his direction. A couple of girls sat on the sofa and the coffee table was laid with the *Shadow Glass* board game. A bookcase was crammed with colourful volumes and a snarling leviathan figurine, and posters were fixed to every available surface: *NeverEnding Story, Ellen Dritch, Flight of the Navigator, The Shadow Glass*. The latter was signed, his dad's signature swirling in gold.

'You're late.' A pale guy with glasses and messy brown hair got up from the sofa. He kissed Toby on the lips, so Jack assumed he was Huw.

'We almost had to do four-player,' said a blonde girl from the sofa.

'Which means tie-breaker,' said the Asian girl beside her.

'Right, sorry.' Toby shot his friends a timid look. 'I got caught up with something. But, guys, this is Jack.'

They all blinked in Jack's direction. Jack raised his good hand in a nervous wave, the other clutched to his chest.

'Holy shit,' said Huw.

'What the—' whispered the blonde girl.

'What's going on?' asked a woman as she came in from the house. She was older than the others, maybe forty, pear-shaped and wearing dungarees, her hair a kaleidoscope of pinks, blues and greens.

'This is Jack,' Toby repeated. 'Jack Corman.'

'Shut the front Dorr,' the woman said. The way she said it made Jack think she was punning on the kettu from the movie.

'*The* Jack Corman?' whispered Huw. 'Gurchin?'

Jack winced.

Gurchin.

On the rare occasions he thought about *The Shadow Glass*, a special bit of his soul died every time he remembered the creature known as Gurchin. His dad had called it a lightning strike of inspiration, casting his toddler son as the rubbish-dump-dwelling goblin who lived in the bowels of the city of Rapell, devouring its trash like a bin-bag connoisseur.

With his enormous ears and tusks, Gurchin featured on almost as much tie-in memorabilia as the lub. T-shirts, mugs and tea towels all bore his catchphrase, *'That's good eatin'!'*, a line Bob dubbed in post-production because Baby Jack could barely talk at that point.

Gurchin was the reason fanboys and girls always gawped at Jack like he was Yoda in the flesh. Everybody loves a scene-stealer.

By the basement door, Jack tensed as the guy in glasses hurried over to shake his hand. 'I'm Huw. Wow, you're Jack. *The* Jack. Gurchin's in my basement. I don't know what to say. I'm hot. Is anybody else hot? Wow, there's like a hundred things I imagined saying to you if I ever met you but I can't think of a single one.'

Huw was still clasping Jack's hand. Jack looked down at it.

'Right, sorry, personal space.' Huw released him and fiddled with his glasses. 'Shit. Hi. Welcome. Gurchin! Would you like to sit down? Can I get you a drink? We're playing *Shadow Glass?*'

'Huw?'

He looked at Toby.

'Breathe.'

'Right.' Huw released a breath. He cleared his throat and straightened, pressing a hand to his heart and half-covering a faded kettu emblem on his T-shirt. 'As president of the Shadow Glass Guild, it is my great honour to welcome you to our gathering.'

'Co-president,' said the Asian girl.

'*Co*-president,' Huw said.

'Funny how you always forget that part.' The girl waved a hand covered in rings. 'I'm Sumi.'

'Anya,' said the blonde.

'Nell,' said the older woman with multicoloured hair, setting the snacks on the coffee table. Jack assumed she was Huw's mum. He couldn't think of any other reason she'd be at a Guild meeting handing out nibbles.

'Is-it-true-there-was-a-musical-number-that-got-cut-from-the-final-film?' The words erupted from Huw's mouth as if he had been fighting them for the past minute. 'Sorry. I remembered one of the things I wanted to ask.'

They all stared at Jack and he resisted the urge to flee up the steps. The way Toby's friends looked at him made his injured finger pulsate. He'd been around fan-kids when he was little. They thought he was special. That just being near to him made a difference. That it brought them closer to Iri.

He realised they were all waiting for him to answer Huw's question.

'I don't know,' he said.

Huw looked disappointed. 'I heard it was shot but never released, and it's not on any of the DVDs, but I read an interview with one of the puppeteers who said they shot this great musical sequence in the ruined village that ended up on the cutting room floor.'

'Sorry,' Jack said.

'See.' Toby nudged Huw. 'It's just a myth. Like that story about how you can see a crew member in the castle fight.'

'That's true,' Nell said. 'If you pause it just right—'

'You see a reflection of the back of Dune's head,' Sumi interrupted. 'It's not a crew member, it's just a reflective surface showing the back of the puppet.'

'I heard it was Bob you could see,' Anya said, looking at Jack. 'That's what really happened, right? He got caught in one of the shots.'

'Guys!' Toby said. 'Can you keep the nerd-ons under wraps for like two seconds?'

They fell silent.

Jack's head spun. He thought he might need to sit down. All his energy was focussed on his injured hand. He didn't have any in reserve to cope with a fan club.

Huw frowned at Toby. 'Does this mean you got permission? For the memorial screening?'

Toby's eyes became hooded. 'Uh, not exactly.'

'So what's going on?' Huw asked. He looked at Jack. 'Are you coming to All T'Orc tomorrow?'

'It's a mini-convention,' Toby told Jack. 'You know, fans get dressed up and buy merchandise and hang out. It's awesome, especially All T'Orc, as it's hosted at Rick Agnor's art studio.'

Jack tried to think of a reply but his mouth had sealed up. He couldn't handle this. These kids loving everything about the thing he hated. It made his skin crawl.

'Jack needs our help,' Toby said, seeming to remember his injury. 'He got hurt. His finger, well, it's gone.'

Sumi frowned and got up from the sofa, approaching Jack. Gently, she took his bandaged hand and inspected it.

'You severed your finger?' she asked.

'It's gone,' he confirmed.

'Have you already been to the hospital?'

He shook his head. 'No. A friend patched me up.'

Friend was a bit of a stretch.

'Hospitals freak him out,' Toby said. 'Besides, I figured you'd be able to help.'

Sumi's gaze flicked between them and she looked confused, perhaps a little suspicious, but then she led Jack to the sofa and told him to sit while she checked his bandage. Jack's back felt clammy. He was hyper aware that everybody was looking at him, and their attention on his injury made it too real.

'Do you mind if I take a look?' Sumi asked.

He shook his head, even though the thought of exposing the wound made him shake. Sumi had a serenity about her, though, that relaxed him. She seemed to know what she was doing, her grip firm but gentle. Jack looked everywhere except at his hand.

'What happened?' Huw asked.

'It was a—' Toby began.

'Dog,' Jack blurted out, and Toby hesitated, then nodded.

'Right, a dog. Rabid. Really scary.' He looked uncomfortable. Jack got the impression he didn't lie much. 'Look, we're trying to solve a mystery.'

'Like how a musical number could ever get cut from the greatest film ever made?' Huw offered.

'Yes, exactly like that.' Toby rolled his eyes. 'We're trying to track down the Shadow Glass—the *real* Shadow Glass—and we only have until tomorrow to find it.'

'You mean the movie prop?' Nell asked, handing round the crisp bowl.

'Correct.'

'Forgive me,' Nell said to Jack, 'but aren't you the one who should know where it is?'

He nodded. 'I guess so. But I don't. I don't remember ever seeing it, to be honest.'

A jag of pain ran through Jack's finger and he sucked air through his teeth.

'Sorry.' Sumi had removed the bandage and he felt sick at the sight of the stump, caked in Zavanna's balm.

Huw was at the bookcase, removing chunky volumes and flipping through them. Jack noticed a postcard-sized framed picture of his father on one of the shelves. It showed him sitting in Kunin Yillda's black stone throne, his colourful socks peeking out beneath corduroy trousers.

'Didn't they reuse it for another film?' Anya said, lowering her phone. '*Man-Hero* or something? It shot at Bob Co., so it stands to reason they could use the same props on different films.'

'But the Shadow Glass is the Shadow Glass,' Toby said. 'It's the name of the film! They couldn't just recycle the main prop in something tacky like *Man-Hero*.'

'Excuse me, *Man-Hero* is a work of art,' Nell said.

'Says the Guild member who was alive when it was released,' said Anya.

'Hey! No ageism in the Guild! And I stand by *Man-Hero*, in all its bare-pec'd, *Conan*-pilfering beauty.'

'Hear, hear,' said Toby. 'Also, we love having an older member of the Guild. It gives us credibility.'

Jack coughed. They all looked at him. He didn't want to admit he had thought Nell was Huw's mum, and now that he knew she was part of the Guild, he felt even more on edge. Nell was around his age and clearly a big-time fan. She was exactly the kind of woman he had dated in the past, and it had never worked out. One of his girlfriends changed when she found out he was the son of the guy who made *The Shadow Glass*. She stopped looking at him as a boyfriend, and instead saw him as some kind of celebrity, even though Jack felt like anything but.

He wasn't arrogant enough to think Nell would be interested

in him, but her presence made Jack uneasy. He cleared his throat, trying to think of something to say.

'Uh, *Man-Hero*'s great,' he said.

'Thank you!' Nell high-fived the air.

Jack avoided her gaze.

'I suppose I could close the wound,' Sumi said, pushing her dark hair behind her ear as she considered Jack. 'But I really think you need a graft and a specialist who knows what they're doing. Plus without anaesthetic, it'll hurt. A lot.'

Jack rubbed the back of his neck, his knee juddering. He felt so tired, he wished he could forget about all of this. But as long as the kettu were around and the skalions were out there, maybe animating Kunin Yillda at this very second, his life would remain in limbo.

He had to get this over with.

'What do you need?' he asked.

Sumi ordered Huw to bring her the ingredients for a home-made saline solution, plus whatever painkillers he could find, and his sewing kit. While Anya heated a needle over a lighter, Sumi cleaned the kettu balm from Jack's wound and he took a couple of super-strength paracetamol, then lay back into the sofa, closing his eyes, pretending he was anywhere other than at a Shadow Glass Guild meeting.

There had been nothing like this when he was a kid. Aside from Amelia, he had been alone in his love for *The Shadow Glass*. He'd have killed to meet and dissect it with friends, keep the story alive the way the Guild were. A story only kept going if people remembered it, if they lived it over and over again. If it was forgotten, it evaporated. Ceased to exist.

Sumi began working on his finger and Jack tried to find his happy place, but happy thoughts had been in short supply for so long that all he could think about was the skalion's teeth, the death-reek filling the garage, Jenny's disappointed frown and Zavanna's disdain.

As gentle as Sumi was, her needle wasn't. It speared his torn flesh and his armpits grew damp with sweat. He resisted yanking his hand away, even as the needle bit his stump over and over, the sensation of tugging thread making him want to tear his whole hand off to escape it.

He swore that if he ever saw another skalion, he'd run fast in the opposite direction.

Huw and Toby went through the bookcase one volume at a time before admitting defeat.

'So what I'm hearing is *no*,' Toby said dejectedly. 'We have no idea where the Shadow Glass is.'

Huw hopped into the armchair and opened his laptop. 'Just give me like, thirty minutes. I bet I can track it down.'

'Want to bet a lub keyring on it?' Anya asked, smirking as she swiped at her blonde fringe.

'Arrrrgh! Sometimes I wish you didn't remember everything.'

Of course they had in-jokes. Jack squeezed his eyes shut at another sharp tug in his finger.

'There,' Sumi said, moving back, and Jack released a breath. He forced himself to look down, seeing that she had fixed a fresh bandage.

'How do you feel?' Sumi asked.

'Great.' He didn't.

'I just hope I haven't caused any permanent nerve damage.'

She looked genuinely worried and Jack realised he should be grateful. He *was* grateful. 'Thank you,' he said, meaning it.

'It's almost six,' Huw said from the armchair. 'I vote takeaway. I always research better with dough balls. Jack?'

Jack shook his head. There was no way he could eat. Then he processed what Huw had said and he lurched up from the sofa so quickly he almost toppled straight back over.

It was almost six p.m.

Alden Smithee would be at his father's house any minute to buy Dune.

'Shit, I have to go,' he said. What if he missed him? The thought sent a bolt of panic through his gut.

'Jack?' Toby stood.

'I have to be somewhere,' Jack told the Guild. 'But thanks.'

'But we haven't figured out where the Glass is,' Huw called.

Jack wasn't listening. He hurried for the door, ignoring Toby's shouts as he clambered up the basement steps with legs that barely felt like his own. He went through the garden and made for the street, anxiety flushing through him. He *had* to get back to the house.

'What's going on?' Toby panted, chasing after him.

'I have a meeting.'

'But it's Saturday night! What about the Glass?'

Jack's eyelids scratched as he fumbled with the keys to the VW, jerking open the door. 'It can wait.'

'We are departing?' Brol asked from the back of the van. Jack eyed the kettu nervously and got into the driver's seat.

'Stay here, be with your friends,' he told Toby.

'But the quest… Bob wants us to find the Glass—'

'Bob's not here!' Jack cried.

Toby startled, but Jack couldn't bear the idea that he'd miss Alden Smithee because they were fighting over something his father may or may not have wanted. He felt the atmosphere of Huw's basement in his skin. It had been like a shrine and Jack was exhausted of people blindly worshipping the very man who had made his life so miserable.

'It doesn't matter what he'd want,' he said, trying to keep calm. 'Even if he was here, it wouldn't matter, because trust me when I say he wasn't that great when he was alive.' He knew he should stop but he couldn't. 'Look, you think he was this all-knowing hippy-happy movie genius. You want the truth? Bob Corman was an egotistical, self-obsessed drunk who never thought about anybody except himself.'

Toby's face went rigid. He looked like he was about to cry. He shook his head. 'I don't understand—'

'There's just something I need to do,' Jack said, battling the guilt rising through him. Toby had to see it. He couldn't keep talking about Bob like he could walk on water. Nobody understood and they never had.

'This is no time for personal vendettas,' Zavanna said, while the lub made a wailing sound. 'The Glass—'

Jack hammered the wheel with his good hand.

'It can wait!' He tried to calm his breathing. Make them understand. This was going to turn his life around. If he didn't get back for the deal with Alden Smithee, he could kiss goodbye to fifty thousand pounds and he might as well evict himself from his flat. This was the plan. The *only* plan.

He started the engine.

To his surprise, Toby got into the passenger seat and shut the door, sitting stiffly.

Jack ignored him. If this was the way he had to do it, this was the way he had to do it. This was *reality*.

Grimacing, he bumped the VW over the kerb and sped off down the rain-soaked street.

There is ONLY The Shadow Glass.
We do not recognise the existence of extraneous
'franchise' material, including but not limited to novels,
graphic novels, and so-called 'tie-in merchandise'. Such
material is non-canonical and damaging to the integrity
of *The Shadow Glass*. When we refer to *The Shadow Glass*,
we refer solely to the movie as it was released (on film)
on 15 June 1986. We actively condemn any subsequent
versions, whether digitally 'cleaned up', re-edited,
re-released or otherwise.

It is our belief that *The Shadow Glass* was perfect upon
release and stands entirely on its own merit.

NO SEQUELS. NO SPIN-OFFS.

NO FRANCHISE.

Long live Iri.

They made it to Kettu House in thirty minutes. Jack's phone buzzed all the way there, but he couldn't answer it one-handed. He just hoped Alden would wait. When he reached Knight Street, he parked the van behind a black Mercedes that must belong to Alden, and he nearly cried out with relief when he spotted a man waiting at the top of the steps.

'You should go home,' he told Toby as he shut off the engine. 'Or stay here. Just let me deal with this.'

Toby frowned. 'What about the kettu?'

Jack was already hastening out of the van and dashing up the steps to the front door.

Alden Smithee resembled an undertaker, dressed in black, his chalky complexion devoid of colour. He might have been handsome once but his cheekbones were too sharp, his mouth too big, crammed with wonky teeth, and Jack had trouble guessing his age. He could be anywhere between forty and a hundred.

'Mr Smithee,' Jack said, running up to meet him. 'I'm so sorry, traffic was hell.'

The man gave him a wan smile. 'Please, don't apologise. I completely understand.'

Something about his calm made Jack's teeth hurt.

'Thank you,' he said. 'I appreciate it.'

'It looks like you've been through the wars.' Alden's gaze passed over his bandages.

'Oh, these? Just a scratch. Please come in.'

Jack's hands shook as he unlocked the front door, ignoring the pain in his newly sutured finger, and stuck his head through to check the hall. It was empty. There was no sign of the wugs or anything else that could have crept out of Iri. The house was eerily quiet.

'My, you've had some storm damage, too.' Alden wetted his lips as he looked around the hall. 'Is he ready?' His voice was little more than a whisper. Jack noticed his eyes were different colours. One green, one brown. The effect was hypnotic and he found his gaze flicking between them.

'Dune?' the man prompted.

'Right.' Jack pressed a palm to his forehead. It was moist with perspiration. His whole body felt swollen and he was having trouble breathing.

'If you wouldn't mind waiting here?'

Alden's mouth pinched into a smile. 'Of course. I've waited so long, another minute won't hurt.'

Jack left the man in the hall, hurrying up the stairs two at a time. By the time he reached the attic, he felt like he was having a heart attack. The air stuck in his throat and he was sweating through his clothes. But the attic was as quiet as the rest of the house, deserted of wugs, and Jack thanked his luck, stumbling to Dune's cabinet.

He wavered before it, unable to look into the puppet's face. Something stilled his hands for a moment and he stopped moving, his eyes inching up to peer into the kettu warrior's face.

'Dune?' he murmured.

The puppet didn't react. It remained motionless in the shadows of the box, its lips parted, its expression rigid.

No, Dune wasn't alive. He was just a puppet. Nothing special. Not to Jack.

Jack gritted his teeth and seized the cabinet, struggling with it as he carted it towards the stairs.

Back in the downstairs hall, he set it down on a table in front of Alden, wincing at his throbbing right hand.

The man's eyes shone as he looked at Dune and he hovered on the spot, his fingers anxiously knitting together. His lips looked painfully dry.

'There he is,' he whispered.

Jack stepped out of the way as Alden approached. 'You can take him out if you want.'

The man seemed to have been waiting for permission. Hastily, he unfastened the cabinet's clasp and opened the door. He reached in for the puppet but his hands shook and he paused, taking a sip of air. When they had settled, he removed Dune. He held him before him like a trophy, raising him to the light. His breath rasped.

'There you are,' he said. 'Well met, Dune of the Vex tribe.'

Jack wasn't paying attention. He was listening out for anybody else in the house. The last thing he needed was for a warbling wug to interrupt the sale. He wondered what had happened to them, if Toby had gone home, what the kettu were doing. His mind darted everywhere except to the present moment, the man clutching Dune in his bony hands.

'You know, I met your father once, a long time ago,' Alden said, still examining the puppet. 'I was so envious of him. He was a man with ideas. So many ideas. He was quite remarkable.'

'Thank you.'

'Were you close?'

Jack's heart became a fist pounding his ribs. He just wanted to get this over with.

'Not really,' he said.

'No?'

'I mean, everybody has issues with their parents, right?' He gave a tight laugh which quickly died. 'Dad could be difficult.'

Alden addressed the puppet. 'You are not a *Shadow Glass* fan?'

Jack snorted. 'No. I mean, maybe when I was a kid. But to be honest, I mean no offence, but it's a bit shit, isn't it? Sorry, I meant… Well, it's fine for what it is, but in the grand scheme of things it's no *Blade Runner*.'

He scratched the back of his neck, feeling his damp hair. There was no air in the hall.

'Interesting,' Alden said. He peered into Dune's face. 'You were always my favourite. Brave Dune, the saviour of Iri. His story is one of triumph and resilience. What is a hero but a normal person overcoming their own failings to defeat the demons of their soul?'

He shook his head. 'The so-called fans have never grasped that. How could they? All they see is an entertaining children's story with puppets. I see the true meaning of your father's tale. The poetry at its heart. It all comes down to this fellow and his quest.'

'Mhmm.'

'I must say, though, the tie-in material left something to be desired. Did you ever…?'

'Read it? The comics? No, I was never into all that franchise stuff, the stuff they built around the movie. I guess I outgrew it, or I guess I knew the way Dad was then. I don't know if he knew what he was doing.'

Alden appeared to grow younger as he stared at Dune. The seams around his eyes smoothed and a splash of colour bloomed in his cheeks.

'Are you satisfied?' Jack asked.

Alden nodded quickly. 'Oh yes. Very satisfied.' He guided Dune back into the cabinet, replacing the clasp.

'Just the small matter of payment,' Alden said, taking out his phone. He swiped the screen and then his phone pinged. He showed Jack the screen to confirm the amount had been released.

Fifty thousand pounds.

Jack felt sick.

'I suppose I should leave you to your evening.' Alden heaved the cabinet from the table, tottering back a pace as he attempted to retain his balance.

'Would you like a hand?' Jack asked, moving forward.

'No!' Alden drew a breath. 'No, I'd like to do this myself, thank you. Call me sentimental.'

'All right.'

Jack went to the front door and opened it. He tensed in surprise as he found two figures on the doorstep. Toby and his cousin Amelia.

'Ame—' He choked and tried to swallow. 'Amelia. What are you doing here?'

Her hands were buried in the pockets of a camel-coloured trench coat, the blue of her eyes even more vibrant than usual in the porch light.

'I thought we should talk—' she said, but she stopped at the sight of Alden. She closed her mouth and then opened it again.

'Jack, what's going on?'

'Nothing.' He gestured for her to move aside. 'Here, Mr Smithee, you should be able to fit through.'

'Thank you.' Alden cleared the door, struggling under the weight of the cabinet. He paused for a second to look at Amelia and Jack frowned at her frosty glare. Her whole face had tensed. There was no mistaking the contempt in her eyes.

'Mr Smithee, is it?' she asked sharply.

'Hello. I'm sorry, this cabinet is rather heavy,' he said, attempting to manoeuvre past her.

'Where's he taking Dune?' Toby asked, crushing the straps of his rucksack.

Alden adjusted his grip on the cabinet and raised his eyebrows at Jack. 'It was a pleasure doing business. And, please, if you discover any other curios, do let me know. I'm sure we could reach an agreement.'

'What's he talking about?' Amelia demanded. 'And what's happened to your hand?'

'If you don't mind…' Alden began, trying to step by.

'No.' Amelia remained where she was. 'Jack, what's wrong with you? You're selling? To *him*?'

'Excuse me, young man,' Alden said, and Toby begrudgingly stepped aside to let him pass, although his eyes burned with the same resentment as Amelia's.

'Don't go another step,' Amelia said.

'Amelia, stop it,' Jack hissed.

'Me stop it? Me?! Do you seriously have no idea who that is?'

Alden was already halfway through the front garden, quick-stepping away from the house.

Toby spoke up in a miserable voice. 'That's Wesley Cutter.'

GLENN LOCKE: Who started the fire?

WESLEY CUTTER: I don't remember.

GL: Did you go to the park intending
                 to burn the books?

WC: No comment.

FRANCINE RIPLEY: Mr Cutter, we know you organised
                 the protest. We know you printed
                 up flyers calling for people to
                 gather at Clapham Common
                 this afternoon.

WC: It was a peaceful protest.

GL: Where did you get the petrol?

WC: No comment.

FR: What is this book, anyway?
                 Beyond the Shadow Glass?

GL: It's a kids' book.

WC: It's not a kids' book.

FR: What do you have against it?

WC: It ruined everything.

'You're wrong.'

Jack stared after Alden Smithee as he loaded Dune into the boot of the Mercedes and then went to the driver's door. As the car sped away, Jack thought he glimpsed a second person in the back, a small shape sitting behind the driver's seat, but his eyes felt dry and he had probably imagined it.

'You've lost it,' Amelia said, glaring at him from the doorstep. 'You've actually lost it. How could you not recognise him?'

'That wasn't Wesley Cutter.' Jack's voice echoed in his ears, distant and feeble.

'Oh, I'm sorry.' Amelia threw up her arms. 'I must be thinking of another two-faced arsonist fanboy with a DVD bargain bin where his heart should be.'

The muscles in Jack's back spasmed and he wished she'd stop looking at him.

'Why'd he take Dune?' Toby asked.

'Tell me you didn't just sell Dune to Wesley Cutter.' Amelia's eyes danced with fear and fury.

He felt himself shrinking under her gaze, but he couldn't comprehend what she had said. He hadn't heard that name in years. How could the man he had just invited into Kettu House be Wesley Cutter? It didn't make any sense.

Jack recalled the newspaper pictures of a teenage Wesley Cutter, the jaw-thrusting young man who coolly stared down the barrel of the photographer's lens, defiant and unrepentant. In Jack's mind, that white-faced teenager grew more gaunt, ageing into the sallow-featured man who had just driven off with Dune.

Cutter and Smithee. Different but the same.

Jack's voice emerged in a disbelieving monotone.

'I just sold Dune to Wesley Cutter.'

He turned to stagger into the hall. The reality of what he had done squeezed in around him and his heart raced painfully. He'd sold Dune to the Bob Co. version of the Antichrist. But he hadn't known. How could he? It wasn't Cutter he'd done business with, it was Alden Smithee.

'Was this to get back at me?' Amelia asked, storming after him into the water-damaged lounge. 'I thought we could talk, maybe apologise. Boy, was I dreaming.'

'I didn't recognise him.' Jack held onto the fireplace mantel, certain his legs would give way if he let go.

'You didn't...' Amelia stared at him as if he was speaking a foreign language. 'Did you get a lobotomy after I moved away? How could you not recognise the monster who created the hate campaign against Uncle Bob?'

He hadn't forgotten, just sealed it away in the same box as everything else Bob-related. It had been easier that way. He could focus better, pretend to be somebody else. Now, though, the memory box had opened, its contents flapping in his face like spooked moths. Jack had been seven when, in 1990, Wesley Cutter gained notoriety for masterminding the protest against Bob's graphic novel, *Beyond the Shadow Glass*.

'He said Dad ruined *The Shadow Glass* with his comic,' Jack said.

'The one-shot starring Zavanna that revealed the origins of Iri,' Toby added.

Amelia looked lit up with rage. 'He held the burning ceremony in Clapham, where all those angry, hormonal nerdboys burned their *Shadow Glass* memorabilia.'

'He had a sick brother,' Toby said. 'Leukaemia, I think.'

'Right.' Amelia nodded. 'He only had a few months to live. Cutter wanted Uncle Bob to publicly condemn his own work so his brother could die without worrying that Iri was ruined. His brother was called—'

'Alden.'

Jack's stomach felt like a dirty rag being twisted and wrung out. The truth had been staring at him the whole time.

'That's when Dad stopped leaving the house. JESUS! He looked so different, I didn't recognise him.'

It was like he'd been asleep for years. How could he forget? He had spent so long trying to get away from his father, that reek of failure, he'd forgotten everything. He recalled the police coming to the house, talking to Bob, and then things changed.

Bob stopped coming out of his study.

Stopped showing Jack *The Shadow Glass*.

Stopped caring.

'Cutter can't do that,' Jack said, grasping for a lifeline. 'He can't use a fake name to do a business deal.'

'Alden Smithee isn't a fake name,' Amelia said. 'Cutter legally changed it after the court stuff in the nineties.'

'How do you know that?'

Amelia looked at Jack as if wondering whether or not to tell him something. Finally, she massaged her forehead and started pacing.

'A couple of years ago, the prop master at Bob Co. reported some items had gone missing. A couple of kettu cups and some paper fortune tellers we created for *The Guesthouse*. They were small pieces that could easily have been misplaced or mislabelled, nothing to warrant too much attention. A few weeks later, though, a *Fuzz TV* puppet disappeared.'

She grimaced. 'That's when we knew we had a problem. After an internal investigation, it became pretty clear that only one person could be responsible. The janitor. A guy called Trevor Kane.'

'Who's that?' Jack asked.

'He worked at Bob Co. for eight months until we fired him for stealing. It was only when we took him to court that we discovered he was a friend of Cutter's.'

'He said he was a collector,' Jack said. 'Cutter said he bought and sold movie curios.'

'That part's true, I guess. He made a success of himself, no doubt thanks to the items he got Kane to steal from us.' Amelia scowled. 'Cutter was running a business out of his mum's basement. Talk about a cliché. We could never prove Cutter was working with Kane, though, and we never found the missing props. Either he sold them on the sly or he hid them, but without proof, the case was thrown out.'

'He's such a fake,' Toby said. 'He's the kind of Snyder Cut fanboy who thinks women ruined *Star Wars*.'

Jack couldn't believe what he was hearing. How was it possible that some teen who organised a book-burning protest in the nineties still held a grudge against a long-past-it movie director? He should have got over it years ago. Grown up. Moved on. The way Amelia was talking, though, Cutter had only got worse, his obsession curdling into something monstrous. But why?

'So he hired Kane to get rich off the memorabilia?'

Amelia's gaze sharpened. 'Honestly? I think he has grander ambitions. He's been hassling our lawyers for years, reporting fan sites for breach of copyright. We have to be seen to enforce copyright law, so any website found using *Shadow Glass* imagery was sent legal letters. Naturally, Cutter got one too, but he contested it and won.'

'Cutter's the reason the sites have been closing?' Toby asked. 'The Guild had to close ours after Huw got a scary email.'

'Is that why you sent the cease and desist about the anniversary screening?' Jack asked, recalling that was the reason Toby had come to him in the first place. He wanted to screen *The Shadow Glass* in Bob's memory.

Amelia's forehead crinkled. 'Cease and desist?'

Jack nodded at Toby to speak.

'We wanted to put on a screening of the film,' Toby murmured, looking embarrassed. 'But you guys threatened legal action.'

Amelia appeared stunned. 'Wow. I'm so sorry. I had no idea.'

'If Cutter's not trying to get rich, why is he doing this?' Jack asked.

'He's decided he's the Iri conservationist,' Amelia said. 'Calls himself the Keeper of Iri.'

'Big surprise, *keeperofiri.com* is the only site that hasn't been shut down,' Toby added pointedly.

'He thinks Uncle Bob messed up by trying to franchise *The Shadow Glass*,' Amelia continued. 'He actively hates the Zavanna novel, and he's taken it upon himself to preserve the original movie, like it's some sort of religious text.'

'But that's—'

'Insane? Tell me about it. He's twisted everything. Ever since the book burning, he's amassed a vocal and dedicated following, fans who think just like him. It's grown over the years, thanks in part to the press attention he received after the burning. And, of course, he used the court battle with Kane to his benefit.'

Jack released a breath. His body had stopped shaking and a more familiar emotion had taken root. Anger. Cutter had purposefully misled him to get his hands on Dune. Perhaps owning Dune lent him fresh legitimacy in the eyes of his followers.

'So this is all about Iri?' he asked. 'Cutter wants to stop any more material being produced?'

'I think it's bigger than that,' Amelia said. 'After we fired Kane, one of our employees revealed they had caught him trying to get into Bob's old office.' Her jaw tensed. 'I think he was looking for a way to bury Bob Co. from the inside. I think that's been Cutter's intention all along.'

Jack's pulse ticked in his temple. Even though he wanted no part of Bob Co., could he really let Cutter destroy it? Could he watch from the sidelines as everything his father built was torn apart?

'What if he wants the Glass next?' he murmured.

'No,' Toby said in horror. 'He can't.'

'You said it yourself this morning,' Jack told Amelia. 'The Glass is the most important part of the movie. If Cutter finds it, he owns you. He might already have it.'

Amelia spoke through clenched teeth. 'If he does, we'll rain legal hellfire on him.'

'And he'll fight you to the last breath. How much are you willing to pay to beat him? How much can Bob Co. even afford these days?'

Amelia opened her mouth and then shut it. She knew he was right.

'The question is: what do we do now?' Jack said.

'What do you *want* to do?' Amelia asked, her tone steely. 'You've made it pretty clear you want no part of Uncle Bob's legacy.'

He couldn't deny that. It was true.

'What happened to your hand?' Amelia asked.

'A dog,' Jack and Toby said in unison.

Amelia's eyes narrowed. 'A dog?'

'Look, there has to be a way to fix this mess. All of it,' Jack said.

Amelia flashed her palm. 'Fine, don't tell me what happened to your hand, but you're right. Something will get us out of this mess, and I'm betting Uncle Bob's study contains that something.'

She went into the hall and started up the stairs. Jack chased after her, struggling to keep up as anxiety thrummed in his ribs.

'You can't go in there.'

'Watch me.'

She was already on the landing, striding towards Bob's office. The door was closed, just the way Jack liked it. He watched her fingers meet the handle, pushing, and Jack reached her just in time to seize it and slam the door closed again.

'Get away from there.'

Her eyes widened in surprise. He was panting, face screwed up, and he didn't know what he'd do if she tried to go in there again. She took a step back.

'Jack—' she began.

'No.' His teeth clenched painfully. 'You need to go.'

'Look—'

'He left the studio to you, isn't that enough? You got the studio, but this house and everything in it is mine.' He blocked the door. 'Get. Out.'

She seemed to be about to say something, but then she pressed her lips together and turned on her heel. She vanished down the stairs.

Jack collapsed against the door, waiting for the pounding in his hand to stop. His head hurt, too, the welt throbbing, and he felt so tired he wasn't sure he'd ever be able to move away from the door.

He had sold Dune.

'*Boy-o? Are you there?*'

He put his hands over his ears, trying to block out the voice in his head. That didn't stop the memories, though. He remembered standing outside this very door, bags packed for university. Eighteen and about to walk out of the house. His father's lined face had appeared, looking more shrivelled than ever, his beard an overgrown tangle.

But he'd only wanted to get back to his desk. The half-typed page on the computer screen. The honey-coloured liquid in the glass by the keyboard.

He barely seemed to notice Jack was leaving.

'Are you okay?'

Toby stood a few feet away, eyeing Jack as if he would snap at any moment.

Jack lowered his hands from his ears. 'Never better.'

You sold Dune.

The accusation shone in Toby's eyes, even if he didn't say it. For a brief moment, Jack envied him. Toby would never have sold the puppet. Toby was more put-together as a teenager than Jack had ever been, then or now. And what had Jack done? He had shouted at him, shattered his vision of Bob, all but called him a moron for loving *The Shadow Glass*. What kind of a man was he?

When he did speak, Toby said, 'I left Zavanna and Brol in the van. They're probably getting hungry by now. Lubs need to eat every few hours, too. I was thinking about going to the shop?'

Jack wiped sweat from his forehead. 'Sure, great.'

'Okay, uh, I guess I'll see you in a bit.' Toby hesitated, then he turned and went downstairs.

Jack was alone.

After a few seconds, he took the door handle and went into his father's study.

★

He knew instantly somebody had been there. The office was usually disorganised and groaning with his father's possessions. Now, though, fairy lights winked as they tangled through the handful of bookcases. Branches were propped against the walls and, everywhere Jack looked, little rectangles spun. Photos, he realised, on thread.

He felt a tug at his sleeve and looked down. A toddler-sized creature gawked up at him, its marble eyes watery and black, its woolly hat removed to reveal fine hairs on a soft scalp.

The wug wore a tentative expression. 'Come,' it said. 'Look.'

Jack had forgotten they were here. He almost laughed at its determined expression, and the anger he had felt in the hall cooled. He allowed himself to be led further into the study.

A handful more of the potato-shaped creatures tended to the grotto, humming in harmony while they pruned the branches. He recognised the leaves: the wugs had chopped down the parts of the oak that had crashed through the living-room window.

A wug polished a movie-poster-sized picture of his father that leaned against the bookcase. It was a larger version of the picture he'd seen at Huw's. Bob in his prime, sitting on Kunin Yillda's throne. The beard was trimmed around a crooked smile, his chin resting in his palm.

'What is this?' Jack breathed.

'For you,' the wug said. 'For Bob. Must remember. Bad to forget.'

Jack gazed around the grotto, the motor in his chest sputtering.

'Bob love us,' another wug said. 'Big heart.'

Another tugged Jack's trouser leg. 'And you. Come. Sit.'

Its eyes were so earnest he found himself sitting cross-legged before the TV, seeing himself reflected in it. The same old set they had watched *The Shadow Glass* on every Friday after school.

'*Dad, come on! Put it on!*'

'*A kettu must master patience above all else,*' Bob would say, feeding the VHS into the player.

The memory pricked the back of his throat and Jack saw himself aged seven, sitting in this exact spot, bobbing as he hugged Dune.

He remembered the screen crackling to life, thunder vibrating from the speakers, an aged male voice saying, '*In a forgotten time, in a forgotten world, deep within a forgotten chamber few have ever seen, the Shadow Glass sees all.*'

The words THE SHADOW GLASS were animated to resemble a darkly glittering mirror, and Jack would sigh, melting into the world of Iri, with its gilded mountain ranges and squelching bogs. A little thrill would tremble through him when Dune appeared, scuttling between villagers as the rumour of war spread, and Jack marvelled at his bravery when, under cover of nightfall, Dune spotted caped figures heading for the skalion lands, and followed. His quest had begun.

Now, Jack sat as the wugs gathered around him, a dozen of them, holding hands. They began to sing. He didn't know the words but he recognised the tune. It was their ritual for the dead. The melancholy sound stole through him, making his body heavy, stirring the bedrock of his mind.

He had almost forgotten what Bob was like before the burning.

It was easier to forget how good things were. The way Bob tucked him into bed as a kid, regaling him with stories about Iri.

As the wugs sang, Jack felt the fight leave him.

He'd been fighting to escape his father's fantasies for so long, but all that had done was bring them crashing into his life.

A warm hand touched Jack's and he looked at the wug that had led him into the study. Its face wrinkled like an old man's as it smiled. The singing had stopped.

Jack squeezed its hand. 'Thank you.'

The creature dipped its head and, one by one, the wugs filed out of the room.

Jack found himself alone. He peered around the study, the memories moving through him. All those years he had spent angry. Had he really been so blinded by his own hurt? He couldn't see that his father was suffering, too.

In that moment, Jack realised he couldn't let Bob Co. burn. He had to find a way to stop Cutter.

Stiffly, he got up from the floor and went to the desk. It was cluttered with books and rolls of paper, pots of pens and film cells. At the centre of it all rested an ancient computer. Somewhere here, there must be a clue that would lead them to the Shadow Glass.

Something about the familiar scent and clutter made him feel closer to Bob. For once he didn't mind.

'The boy is distressed.'

Jack spun around at Zavanna's voice. She stood by a bookcase, casually examining the rows of volumes and figurines.

'You shouldn't be in here,' Jack said, both annoyed and awed by the fact that she'd made it across the room without him hearing.

'It must be difficult, being so full of corrosive feeling.'

He almost laughed. 'Because you're a ray of sunshine.'

'A kettu warrior learns to channel her emotion. Yours erupts with the childish fury of a starving lub.'

'Says the kettu who nearly brained me twice.'

'Perhaps you deserved it.'

'Perhaps you're not as enlightened as you think you are. Only stubborn.'

Zavanna's paw went to the dagger at her hip. 'Do not presume to speak as if you know us. You do not care to know us. That much was clear from the moment we met.'

'Yeah? Well, you didn't want to know me either.'

Zavanna's feral glare caused a flame of fear to spark in his belly, but he refused to back down. He wanted to see how far she'd go. If she'd tackle him to the floor again.

After a second, the kettu's hackles settled and she looked away.

Jack's heart raced. He tried to reconnect with the calm he'd felt after the wugs' song, but Zavanna's presence made him nervy. How could it not? She was a creature from another world, supposedly, and he never knew what she was going to do or say. How could they ever hope to find common ground?

He remembered what she'd said.

The boy is distressed.

'I'll talk to Toby,' he said. 'If he comes back.'

'I would not blame him if he did not.' She still looked tense but her tone mellowed as she added, 'What you call stubbornness, I call tenacity.'

'Splitting hairs if you ask me.'

'I did not.'

Jack swallowed the urge to spit back at her. He was too tired. Tired of fighting. Tired of people making assumptions about him.

He raised his bandaged hand, recalling the relief he'd felt after Zavanna applied the balm. She'd helped him when he needed it. There must be something in her that wasn't cold and hard.

'Thanks for what you did with my hand, okay? It helped.'

'You are welcome.' At his steady look, she sniffed and added, 'You aided us when the skalions struck. For that you have my gratitude.'

Jack nodded.

It was the closest they'd come to civility since she showed up in the attic.

But the atmosphere felt even more awkward now. It was almost easier to fight. That way he didn't have to think about what he was really feeling.

As if sensing it herself, Zavanna tugged a large hardback from the shelf and opened it. Jack watched her gaze skip over the pages, wishing he could pretend he didn't find her the least bit interesting.

But she was a kettu, and kettu were never uninteresting.

'It is Iri,' Zavanna said. Her usual terse tone was threaded with melancholy. She ran her fingers across a watercolour illustration of the kettu plains. A white tree snaked out of blood-red sand, its limbs twisting into the air. One of Rick Agnor's masterpieces.

'Home,' Zavanna said. 'In these pages. How can that be?'

'I'm wondering that about all of this.'

'You talk of Iri as if it does not exist, but it is as real as me and Brol and Dune.' She looked at him. 'If you truly are the son of Bob, you must value what he created. The world he built for us.'

'I'm still trying to figure out how any of this is possible,' Jack said.

Zavanna considered him, then her gaze went to the dream-catchers at the window.

'I once conversed with Bob the Creator. In Iri, those in turmoil may find direction and guidance by embarking on a spirit quest. It is a dangerous journey through the unforgiving west. If you make it to the black mountain, and then its peak, you find a cave in which an oval glass is embedded in the rock. Through it, Bob the Creator offers guidance.'

Jack didn't understand.

'You met him?'

'I undertook the spirit quest at a time when I was directionless and angry. I met with Bob. He was kind and sad and humble. He showed me the way. He spoke of his son, too. He described him as creative and brave. I presume you have a brother.'

The dig didn't land because Jack's mind was spinning in circles, trying to fit together what Zavanna had said.

He had seen the notes, the script drafts, the paintings by Rick Agnor. Bob and Agnor had created Iri together. This very room was full to bursting with material that had never made it to the screen.

'How could Dad be in Iri?' Jack said.

'I do not know.' Zavanna shrugged. 'Sometimes it is better if there are no answers.'

An oval glass high in the mountains.

Jack thought of his father talking in the attic.

What if his father had been talking to Iri?

What if the Glass movie prop offered a window into the world Bob created?

It seemed ludicrous, but no more ludicrous than the past few hours.

'All I know,' Zavanna said, 'is that he spoke of Iri and said it was ours. Iri ceased to be his the moment the first Iridian was born.

He made the first stitch and then the fabric of Iri began to weave itself. It has a life beyond what he first imagined.'

For the first time, Jack wanted to know more.

'What's Iri like?' he asked.

A conflicted expression moved across the kettu's face.

'Before the skalions, it was wondrous,' she said, closing her eyes, still holding open the book. 'When the suns rise over the Lyylan Deserts, their light touches everything, invigorating the sands, burning life into the sky.'

Jack sensed her longing. He blinked at a picture on the wall behind her, certain it had shifted. The painting of a sandy plane brightened, the serpentine peaks rippling as if caressed by a dawn breeze.

'The suns call the burrowing cribbs from their hollows and ignite the rainbow colours of the flocking witterbirds,' Zavanna continued. 'In the forests, you can smell the dew in the air, feel the spirit of Iri moving through you, nourishing you, urging you to grow.'

One by one, images around the room shivered and stirred, as if awakened by her words. Jack stared in astonishment. All around them the canvasses whirled, leaves rustling as creatures dipped in and out of view while a hulking painted leviathan opened its fanged mouth to roar at a bleeding sky. Jack almost thought he heard it.

'It is wild,' Zavanna said. 'It is Iri. It is home.'

She opened her eyes and the room stilled.

The paintings became static once more.

Jack rubbed the back of his neck, unsure what he had witnessed.

It was as if Zavanna had conjured Iri. Offered him the briefest glimpse of her world.

And it wasn't enough. He wanted more.

'*It's all falling apart, boy-o.*'

He heard again the words his father had said a year ago, during their ill-fated dinner. Jack had dismissed them as part of The Bob Show. Now, though, Jack wondered if there was some truth in Bob's tirades.

Was it a coincidence that Zavanna's world had started to fall apart right around the time Bob died?

'*Iri needs you,*' Bob had said. '*More than ever.*'

A chill ran the length of Jack's spine. What if Bob was right?

Quietly, he said, 'I think I'm the reason you're here.'

Zavanna regarded him with a question on her brow.

'The storm this morning, the fight with Amelia, the shutter nearly killing me. It was too much. I remember lying there and wishing for something, *anything* that would make it better; anything that would save me from my joke of a life. A few minutes after that, you and Brol turned up.'

Zavanna's lip curled. 'I am not here to save *you*.' After a moment, though, she added, 'We were searching for a way to save Iri. We thought the Glass was the answer, but then the Glass exploded and we found ourselves standing before a manchild who claimed to be the son of Bob.' She shrugged. 'Sometimes, answers are not what you expected them to be.'

Jack couldn't tell if it was his imagination, but he was sure the kettu's face had become more expressive. The fleshy inner lining of her mouth had become pinker and her nostrils flared in a way he hadn't noticed before. He thought of the skalion's blood oozing across Jenny's studio floor, its razor-teeth around his finger, and swallowed.

The kettu's gaze shifted around the room. 'They can be difficult, fathers. Mine lost his life in the Battle of Torth. It was an honourable death, and his name is etched into the Yggram tree along with the other kettu warriors who dance in the afterlife. One day, I shall join them.'

She said it with a mixture of reverence and detachment. Jack wondered if that was what she really wanted.

'My father was a difficult kettu,' Zavanna continued. 'A hard kettu who never spoke of his emotion. I might have been invisible a lot of the time. Dune was always his focus. But, Jack Bobson, to deny one's feelings is its own kind of death.'

He saw pain in her face and it caused a lump to bristle in his throat. He knew that look. Grief.

Dune.

A pit opened in Jack's stomach.

If this *was* real, that meant Dune really was dead.

He almost couldn't bear the thought.

'I'm sorry about your brother,' he said.

Zavanna looked distant, her gaze fixed on her reflection in the TV set. For a long moment, she said nothing. Finally, her voice emerged, filled with a yearning that Jack felt in his heart.

'I can still feel him,' she said. 'It's as if Dune is on the other side of a pane of glass, just waiting. So close yet I cannot reach him.' She shook herself, her jaw setting. 'We must finish what he started. Save our grief for later. By saving Iri, we honour Dune's memory.'

She was so strong. So certain.

'Did you ever fix things with your father?' Jack asked.

Zavanna's ears twitched. 'He was stubborn.' A flicker of a sad smile. 'He died before either of us could speak our truth. It can be different for you, though, Bobson. Maybe by doing this, by finding the Shadow Glass and saving Iri, you can begin to repair the ill feeling that haunts you. Maybe we both can.'

He didn't know what to think, how to begin to process all those years of pain.

'Let's keep looking, then,' he said.

He returned his attention to the desk, though he was still aware of Zavanna behind him. As a kid, he'd desperately wanted Dune to speak, but he never did, no matter how much Jack wished for it. His first proper conversation with a kettu wasn't at all what he'd expected.

More than anything, he was surprised that there was more to Zavanna than barbed words and a mean right hook. He liked hearing her speak about her world, even if he couldn't fully understand what was going on. If nothing else, he sensed that he and Zavanna were beginning to understand each other.

He tried to focus. He picked up books at random, then scrutinised the film cells. What had Amelia hoped she would find in here? Something to take down Cutter. It was a vain hope. Jack couldn't imagine his father keeping anything to do with Cutter in his study.

Maybe he could reason with him. Make him understand. Maybe if he spoke to Cutter, fan to fan, he'd return Dune. Start to put things right. When he dialled Alden Smithee's number, though, a robotic voice answered.

'I'm sorry, the number you have dialled has not been recognised. Please hang up and try again.'

He tried again, and then hung up in frustration. Wesley Cutter had already changed his number. The only reason he'd do that was if he knew he'd be found out.

Renewed contempt flooded Jack's veins and he pocketed his phone, returning to his father's desk.

He cleared more notebooks and pamphlets, and then froze.

A VHS box stared up at him. The slipcase cover had been removed, replaced with a Post-it note that contained two words in his father's scrawl:

For Jack

THE SHADOW GLASS

1. The First Fragment
2. Dune's Theme
3. Ambush
4. Meet Rill
5. Domain of Nightmares
6. Lub & Wugs
7. Never Trust a Kettu
8. Nebfet
9. Dune's Story
10. Like Father Like Daughter
11. In Chains
12. Quartz Fortress
13. The Battle of Kettu
14. Friends & Guardians
15. The Shadow Glass

His ears rang. His knees felt like jelly.

Jack stared at the video box as if it might spontaneously combust. He considered leaving it where it rested, couldn't face what it contained if it was from his father, but then he picked it up and cracked it open. No tape rested inside, though. The box was empty apart from a small rectangle of plastic. A card.

Jack took it out and turned it over in his hand, staring at a jazzy eighties logo that was faded but still legible on the front.

'Mikes Video's,' he breathed. The misplaced apostrophe had always driven his dad crazy but Mike had refused to fix it, teasing Bob for being such a stickler.

'*It's perfectly imperfect,*' he'd drawl, winking through a cloud of cigarette smoke.

Jack hadn't thought of the video shop in decades. When he was little, he and his father had used this membership card almost every week to rent videos, even though they didn't need it. Bob co-owned the shop with Mike, his childhood friend.

Jack had no idea if the shop was still open. It would be a miracle if it was, but then Mike had always been a survivor, uncompromising as time. What if he knew where the Shadow Glass was?

'A curious object,' Zavanna said somewhere behind him.

Jack turned to see she was standing by a bookshelf, examining a spherical object. It was constructed from dozens of interlocking pieces of wood and was big in her hand, but would probably fit snugly in Jack's palm.

'The puzzle box,' he said, wandering over. 'I used to play with it as a kid. You move the pieces to unlock the treasure inside.'

He'd spent hours trying to solve it, clicking and sliding the pieces, but he had never succeeded in opening it.

He watched Zavanna slide one section around, then another, reconfiguring the object's shape.

'What is inside?' she asked.

'I never found out.'

He was still clutching the membership card. He turned it over and over but there was nothing else on it. He checked the video box and noticed a tiny scrawl in the corner of the Post-it note:

$$1/2$$

Jack frowned. At first, he thought it meant 'half', but then he realised what it was telling him.

This box was one of two.

There was a second somewhere.

Breathlessly, he went back to the desk and searched its contents, but it was no good. The second video box wasn't there.

'Dammit,' he said, straightening and massaging his lower back. It throbbed with tension but he knew he wouldn't be able to rest until this was over. Wasn't that always the way with quests?

Zavanna stood at the window, staring out at the evening sky. The clock on the wall said it was just after seven p.m.

'We have only one *cylar* remaining,' she said. 'By this time tomorrow, if the skalions discover the Shadow Glass before we do, Iri will be theirs for ever.'

'That will never happen,' Brol said.

He stood in the study door with Toby, who looked on edge, the lub balanced on his shoulder. The past hour flooded back in a queasy rush and Jack felt terrible.

'I'm glad you came back,' he told Toby, and he meant it. Throughout all of this, Toby had been unwavering in his enthusiasm. He'd helped the kettu without question and had been nothing but supportive of Jack. He'd even stuck around when Jack treated him like dirt.

Now, though, Toby said nothing. Jack wished he'd smile or crack a joke, make everything okay, and he knew it wasn't up to Toby to fix this. This was on him.

Jack pushed his good hand into his hair. 'Look, I wouldn't blame you if you never wanted to see me again,' he said. 'I've acted like an idiot ever since we met. I suppose I've been acting like one for a while. I'm still trying to get my head around a lot of things. I'm sorry.'

The teenager's forehead crinkled in surprise.

'I shouldn't have said those things about Dad,' Jack said. 'Those are my issues, not yours. What I'm trying to say is, I want to help. For real. Save Iri and get Dune back and find the Glass and, well, I'm sorry, and I thought— Can we start again?' He extended his uninjured hand, tugging his mouth into a smile. 'Hi, I'm Jack. Jack Corman.'

Toby's cheeks dimpled and Jack felt a tingle of relief as their hands met.

'Hi, Jack. It's good to meet you.'

They shook and, for the first time in as long as he could remember, Jack felt like he had done something right.

'What do you mean, "get Dune back"?' Zavanna asked.

'Right,' Toby said, looking uneasy. The kettu clearly had no idea about the Cutter deal. 'The statue from the attic—'

'I sold it,' Jack broke in. At Zavanna's stunned glare, he added, 'I'm sorry, I was desperate. I regret it. And we're going to get him back. I promise.'

Her look of disappointment made his chest thud. He'd ruined whatever understanding they had come to.

'We shall aid you in this, if it helps us to reclaim the Glass,' she said, but he could tell the damage was done.

'Here, I got you this,' Toby said, handing Jack a sandwich.

'Thanks.' He had no appetite.

Zavanna slipped the puzzle box into her bag.

'We have no option but to embark on a sight voyage,' she said.

Brol stepped forward, taking her hand. 'No, Zavanna. It is too dangerous.'

She tugged her hand free. 'We cannot allow fear to stop us, not when Iri hangs in the balance.'

Brol gave her a forlorn look and Jack couldn't believe they were still arguing about that. If sight voyages were so perilous, he had to agree with Brol. It wasn't worth the risk. He wondered how often Zavanna threw caution to the wind, and how often Brol had feared for her life.

'I have an idea,' Jack said, and the kettu looked wary. He realised he hadn't been that helpful since they appeared. 'I can have ideas sometimes.'

'We visiting another old friend?' Toby asked. 'Wait, is this

Bob's study?' He took in the room, his mouth forming a perfect
'O'. A familiar ache stirred in Jack and he couldn't bear being in
there any longer, didn't want to share this place with anybody.
Not yet.

'Let's go,' he said.

'Where?' Toby asked.

Jack smirked. 'How would you feel about renting a movie?'

★

Mikes Video's—the misplaced apostrophe was still there in the
weather-beaten sign—rested on the corner of a roundabout.
It was a relic from another time, the walls pebble-dashed, the
windows browning with sun-faded posters. It hadn't changed a
bit since the last time Jack visited, nearly twenty years ago, and the
sight of it made him feel both old and young as he remembered
how excited he always was when Bob took him there as a kid.

'I didn't even know this place existed,' Toby breathed.

'I think you're in the majority.' Jack had finally changed out
of the suit, finding an old pair of jeans and a faded Foo Fighters
T-shirt in his bedroom. The relief was enormous. On the way he
told Toby about Cutter's disconnected phone, and Toby texted
Huw asking him to search online for Cutter's address.

'You can do that?' Jack asked.

'Welcome to the millennium.'

Standing outside the shop now, the kettu delighted in the way the
flashing light bulbs around the window illuminated the pavement.

'What's *Lady Pain II*?' Toby asked, scrutinising a faded poster
in the window.

'The best one,' Jack said.

'Better than *Troll Mage 3?*' Another poster.

'I mean, if you want to compare unicorn horns…' Jack noticed the kettu sniffing the shop.

'You're coming in?' he asked, checking the street for passers-by. So far, there was nobody else around.

Zavanna thrust a defiant chin at him. 'You have proved you require a chaperone, your judgement cannot be trusted.'

He deserved that. He held up his hands. 'Actually, I have a feeling Mike won't have a problem with you.'

Zavanna's ears flicked and she seemed unsure if she should be irritated or relieved.

'This old friend Mike can help us?' Brol asked.

'He's our best shot right now. Come on.'

Jack pushed the shop door, which opened with a jingle, and he stepped into the 1980s. Video boxes lined the walls, row upon row of them, chunky and enticing, while Limahl's 'NeverEnding Story' fizzed from the sound system. A single stand of DVDs were the only hint they were anywhere but 1985.

It wasn't the sight of the shop that caused a shiver to travel down Jack's spine, though. It was the smell. Plastic and the aroma of warm videotape. It transported him back to a time when the world seemed surer, full of opportunity. In that smell he found a sparkling grain of something that he hadn't known in years: a sense that everything was going to be all right. Cynicism had no place at Mike's.

'What are these boxes?' Brol asked, prodding a *Terminator: Judgment Day* VHS.

'Films,' Toby said, grinning.

'The stories wrought in pictures,' Brol marvelled. 'The Scribes of Film must have worked to the grave. There are so many.' He turned in circles, taking in the rows of videos from one cover to the next, mouth agape.

'Holler if you need anything,' a voice said from the back of the shop.

Jack saw a man propped up behind the counter. It was as if he hadn't moved in the two decades since Jack last saw him. As he approached, though, Jack saw the cardigan and shirt were limp and greying, Mike's salt-n-pepper moustache thinner, his glasses thicker. He was crouched over a magazine, an unlit pipe in his hand, looking every bit like the man who had told Jack campfire stories as a kid, revelling in the grisly ones.

'How about a copy of *The Shadow Glass*?' Jack said.

'Shadow...?'

Mike looked up and fumbled with his pipe.

'Hi Mike.'

'Well stuff me and call me a puppet.' Mike peered at Jack without blinking and then broke into a hacking laugh, coming around the counter into the shop. 'Look at you! My word, you're a sore for very sight eyes. I mean, sight for very sore eyes. Ha!'

He threw an arm around him, drawing Jack into a hug that smelled of tobacco and something slightly less legal.

'You're still here,' Jack said, squeezing his arm.

'Only thing that changes are the number of holes in my socks.' Mike's grip slackened and Jack realised he had spotted Zavanna, Brol, Toby and the lub, who stood a little back, eyeballing the shop owner.

'What the...' Mike trailed off. He removed his glasses, blinked a few times, and then replaced them. 'Tell me I'm not dreaming. Are these—?'

'Kettu,' Jack said.

'And that's—'

'Lub,' Toby said. 'And I'm Toby.'

The lub barked and Zavanna offered a regal nod. 'Well met, Mike of the Video Shop.'

'Your treasury of film is as majestic as anything in Iri,' Brol added.

'Haha!' Mike laughed again. 'Man, this is the most interesting thing that's happened to me since Y2K.'

Going by the state of the video shop, Jack believed him.

'That reminds me.' Mike went back behind the counter. They heard him digging around for something, muttering and wheezing, before he finally set a VHS box on the counter. Jack leaned in to look at the cover, half anticipating another Post-it note from Bob. Instead, the cover showed a woman wielding a couple of flaming katana while a volcano erupted behind her.

'*Lady Pain III*,' he said.

'Finally got it in a few years ago,' Mike said. 'Kept it back here just for you.'

'For me?'

'Well, you reserved it, didn't you?'

Jack stared at him in astonishment. 'Yeah, in 1993.'

'Reserved means reserved, in my book. Go on.'

Jack took the video, enjoying the chunkiness of the box, the weight of it. They didn't make them like they used to.

'Thanks. I have to admit, I'm surprised you're still here.'

'Course I am!' Mike barked. 'Now don't get me wrong, there were a couple of slow years there when it seemed the old man was a fool to keep the place open, but then the kids got sick of hi-def and started craving analogue again, and who was there for them? Mike! Except now I'm a little older it's more difficult to keep up with demand.'

He eased himself onto the stool and put the pipe in his mouth.

'My-my-my, just look at you,' he breathed, admiring the kettu. 'Loyal sort, kettu. Always got your back.'

'Mike of the Video Shop,' Brol said, dipping his head in a bow. 'If you are indeed a Scribe of Film, it would be my great honour for you to filmify my finest battle. I was at Crooked Rock—'

'Not *now*,' Zavanna hissed, jabbing her elbow into Brol's ribs.

'He thinks you're a filmmaker,' Toby explained.

'Not me, alas,' Mike said. His gaze went to Jack. 'A shame about your old man. Lovely send off, though, the funeral. I looked out for you but my eyes aren't what they used to be.'

Jack winced. He'd avoided everybody at the funeral, allowed Amelia to take charge.

Mike took a tobacco packet from his cardigan pocket and began tapping it into the pipe. 'Say, did you ever do anything with that story of yours?'

Jack frowned. 'Story?'

'Yeah! You and your dad acted it out with your cousin, laid on a play upstairs for old Mike. Now that was a hoot.'

Jack blinked at him. He had a vague memory of visiting Mike's flat above the shop, but he couldn't remember ever putting on a play, especially not with his dad.

'I guess not,' Mike said. 'How is that cousin of yours, anyway?'

'Amelia? She's okay.'

'She runs Bob Co. now,' Toby added.

Mike's eyebrows hovered. 'That so? What are they doing over there these days?'

'A sequel, actually,' Jack said.

'*Shadow Glass 2*? Well I never.'

'That's the new movie you mentioned before? In the attic?' Toby had gone very still.

'Yes,' Jack said.

'They're making *Shadow Glass 2?*'

'They're trying to.'

'HOLY SHIT!' Toby bounced on the spot, drawing a startled glare from Zavanna. 'HOLY SHIT HOLY SHIT *HOLY SHIT!*'

Mike whooped with him and the lub puffed up to twice its size, beeping in tandem with Toby.

'*Holy shit,*' Toby stage-whispered, still slightly bouncing. 'A sequel. I never thought... I know your dad had concepts. He had notebooks full of ideas, right? You can see them in the *Through the Shadow Glass* documentary. But I never thought they'd actually make one. Holy crappola, Huw's going to lose his mind.'

Jack wished he hadn't mentioned it.

'Mike of the Video Shop,' Zavanna said, fixing him with a clear-eyed stare. 'We are in dire need of your help. The Shadow Glass is missing, and if we do not find it by the lunium, Iri shall be doomed to perish under skalion rule.'

Mike considered her. 'Been a while since anybody asked for *my* help,' he said.

'We're on kind of a quest,' Jack said. He nodded to the kettu. 'That's why they're here. Did Dad ever mention what happened to the Shadow Glass? I mean, the prop. It's sort of important that we find it.'

Mike chewed on his pipe.

'Glass... glass... glass... no. I don't think he ever mentioned what happened to it.'

'Are you sure?'

'Never!' He hacked a laugh, prodding his temple. 'Can't rely on this holey sponge anymore!' He sat wreathed in smoke and his eyes glimmered at the kettu. 'What a sight you are. Always thought it'd happen one day. Bob seemed so sure. And now here you are, living and blinking.' He sighed and shook his head. 'If only he could see it.'

'Sorry,' Toby said, 'what did you always think would happen?'

Mike jabbed his pipe at the kettu. 'Them! Iri! It had to find a way into our world sometime.'

'Find a way?' Jack said, not following.

The other man's gaze twinkled at him.

'Do you remember when you were a kid and you believed everything? You believed it so hard, you thought anything was possible.'

Honestly, Jack couldn't remember that at all.

Mike drew an exasperated breath and leaned against the counter. 'Imagine if a person never stopped believing that. Imagine if they truly believed anything was possible, that there was a place called Iri and there was a battle between two forces, one for good, another for evil. Imagine if they channelled that belief into creating something magical, not because they wanted to make art or a product or a franchise, but because they were trying to capture what they could already see, what they already believed existed. They could bring that thing to life simply by wishing it.'

'You're saying Dad created Iri.'

'*For real*,' Mike stressed. 'He poured so much into that film, him and Rick and Jenny, their crew, too. Their creativity—*pure* creative energy, man—made Iri real, somewhere in a parallel realm beyond our reach.'

As if on cue, the *Shadow Glass* soundtrack swelled into the shop, humming from the sound system.

'I knew it,' Toby whispered, gawking at Mike.

Jack wanted to scoff at him the way he always had at his father, tell Mike that was old-fashioned hippy nonsense. But for the first time in his life, he couldn't. Zavanna had talked about Bob creating Iri, too, and Jack had seen the images come alive in the study. It was getting difficult to deny it.

The more time Jack spent with the kettu, the more he felt he could almost sense Iri, as if it was just there, slightly beyond his grasp, lingering behind a gossamer veil. Waiting for him.

He was aware they were running out of time.

'We should get out of your way,' he told Mike.

'Not in my way!' Mike yelled good-naturedly. 'But I know what kids are like. Always moving, always shaking. Wish I had some of that energy. But you're always welcome.'

'Thanks.'

'Shame about the plays, though.' Mike chewed on his pipe, puffing smoke rings as he looked at Jack. 'You and your old man were thick as thieves back then. Sad to see that come apart. Now, I know what he was like. When we were growing up, he had a funny habit of taking people for granted. But my god he loved you, boy.'

Jack smiled weakly.

'You enjoy the movie,' Mike said.

Jack had forgotten he was holding the *Lady Pain III* video. He raised it in thanks. 'I will.'

'And Jack, a piece of advice from an old man whose adventures are over? Embrace it. Whatever's happening, jump on the back of it. Because if those adorable critters are anything to go by, Iri is right here, and it's not going away.'

Back at the van, Jack couldn't help feeling disappointed. As good as it had been to see Mike, all he had given them was a video Jack had forgotten he once wanted to watch.

'I'm starting to get the feeling those fragments don't want to be found,' he said as he climbed into the driver's seat.

'Any prize worth possessing is worth the effort to find it,' Brol said, strapping into his seat belt.

'Then the Shadow Glass must be one hell of a prize.'

'Of course,' Zavanna said. 'It is the Shadow Glass.'

'Hey, want some good news?' Toby asked. He flashed them a triumphant grin, waving his phone like a glow stick. 'We have Cutter's address.'

Lady Pain III

This article is about the 1989 fantasy film. For other uses, see *Lady Pain (disambiguation)*.

Lady Pain III is a 1989 sword and sorcery film and is the third instalment in the Lady Pain franchise, directed by Van Bruckmeier, starring Vivienne Hauer and Gaku Akaza as Lady Pain and Goro.

The film tells the story of Lady Pain's origins, as she returns to the village that spurned her years earlier, where she discovers an evil curse has transformed all men into onyx statues.

It was considered a box-office flop at the time of release, grossing $5.3 million during its US theatrical run[1]. The film's use of visual effects was considered groundbreaking, while Hauer's depiction of a strong female warrior earned considerable praise, and she won the 1990 Jupiter Award for Best Sci-Fi & Fantasy Female Performance.

The film received a mixed critical response, although *Bustblocking* magazine reappraised it in 2008 as a "stirring tale with a fascinating socio-political subtext"[2]. A sequel novel, *Lady Pain: Firebird*[3], written by Cam Jameson, was published in 1995.

11

Jack knocked on the grey front door, attempting to settle his nerves. Cutter wouldn't be happy about him showing up on his doorstep, especially as it was almost ten p.m., and Jack fully expected him to slam the door in his face. That was okay, though. He just needed to buy enough time for the kettu to search the house.

At his side, Toby peered up at the three-storey townhouse, and Jack spotted Zavanna and Brol scaling the brickwork as if they had been doing it for years. They were plan A. Kettu were skilled infiltrators, so they should have no trouble breaking into Cutter's home, locating Dune, looking for any sign of the Shadow Glass, and getting out of there before Cutter suspected a thing. All Jack had to do was keep him occupied until they had.

'Chin up,' he told Toby. The kid looked lost without the lub, which had remained in the VW. Jack was glad, though. Of all the Iri creatures, the lub made him the most uneasy.

'I—' Toby began, but then the door opened partway, the chain fastened, and a black-haired woman squinted through the gap.

'Yes?'

'Oh, hi, I'm sorry to bother you so late,' Jack said. 'Is Wesley in? I'm a friend.'

'He's not here.' She began to shut the door.

'Please,' Jack said. 'Do you know where he is?'

Green eyes glimmered at him, the skin around them deeply lined. 'Out. Never tells me where he's going. Never tells me anything.'

Despite the disappointment, Jack tried to keep his expression friendly. If Cutter was out, the kettu should have no problem taking Dune, assuming the puppet was here. He found himself staring at Cutter's mother with interest—they had the same cut-glass cheekbones—and he was surprised to find her staring back.

She was smiling now, as if he had said something charming.

'Said you'd come back,' she said. 'Took your time.'

She shut the door. As Jack shared a bewildered frown with Toby, he heard the jingle of the chain being removed, and then the door opened again, revealing a spindly woman in a black dress and blue bunny slippers.

'Living room's through here,' she said, disappearing through a doorway.

Jack hesitated. As much as he wanted to get Dune back, this suddenly felt wrong. Mrs Cutter had done nothing to him. His curiosity overpowered him, though, and he stepped into a dim, airless hall. The walls held no colour and the furnishings were sparse.

He and Toby followed Mrs Cutter into a lamp-lit lounge that smelled of candle wax and air freshener. The TV played a late-night game show and Cutter's mother perched in an armchair, her eyes fixed on the screen.

'Nice place,' Jack said, lowering himself onto the sofa with Toby, who looked like he was about to be sick.

'Old place,' the woman said. 'Everything around here's old now. Except you. You look as young as ever. Maybe shaving off the beard helped.'

She talked like she knew him. Like they'd been friends for years. But Jack had never had a beard and—

'You think I'm him,' he said, realising. 'Bob Corman.'

'That's right,' she said, scooping nuts out of a bowl and popping them into her mouth one at a time. The TV held her attention and Jack wondered how aware she really was of her guests. She seemed too at ease about having strangers in her home, as if they were part of a memory she was reliving in her mind. Alzheimer's, maybe, or a certain level of dementia.

'I'm afraid Bob passed away,' he said. 'A month ago. I'm his son, Jack. And this is Toby.'

'Oh.' The woman's hand paused on the way to her mouth. 'Oh, yes, of course. It was on the news.' She blinked, and then her frown smoothed as she smiled at him. 'You were so kind, though. I'll never forget how kind you were.'

Kind wasn't a word Jack immediately associated with Bob. Cutter's mother seemed so certain, though.

'When did you meet Bob?' he asked. 'I mean, *me*.'

Better not to confuse her.

The woman thought for a second, then got up and went to a dresser, tugging open drawers. 'In here somewhere. I keep everything. Can't help it. I had to hide it from him after what happened. Makes him angry. Oh, here it is.'

She took out a framed picture and went still, her head bent towards it. She sniffed and then passed the frame to Jack, along with something else. A dog-eared envelope with BOB scrawled on the front in childish letters.

'He wrote it before he passed,' Mrs Cutter said as she went back to her armchair. 'Never did send it. I suppose I couldn't let it go, that piece of him.'

Jack turned over the envelope, trying to figure out what she meant. It was still sealed.

'Wesley wrote it?' he asked.

'No, my other boy. Him in the picture.'

Jack looked down at a photo of a bald boy in a hospital bed. He could only be nine or ten, his skin pale and smooth where his eyebrows should be. Although he looked unwell, his smile dominated the picture. And beside him, smiling just as widely, was Bob.

'So much drama that day, I'll never forget it,' Mrs Cutter said. 'You were supposed to be there at midday. I remember because that's the time he usually had his second lot of meds. The boys were so excited, they couldn't wait to meet you.'

Jack clasped the frame tighter, realising he was looking at Alden Cutter, Wesley's younger brother, who died from leukaemia. He had never seen him before and he found it difficult to swallow. Alden seemed to be smiling right at him.

'I guess you got his letters, and you said you'd come visit him in hospital,' Mrs Cutter continued, and Jack reminded himself she must be talking about Bob. 'Then, of course, you didn't show up. We waited but you never arrived. Not all afternoon. The boys were upset but Alden kept smiling, that's the kind of boy he was. Wesley, though… he didn't take it as well. Made a bit of a scene, I'm afraid. My sister took him home and I stayed with Alden.'

She foraged for more nuts but then seemed to forget about them. 'I fell asleep in the chair, like I always did. Then I woke up to the sound of voices, and there you were, talking to him. It was past midnight, but you'd come after all. That visit gave him such a boost. He talked about it up to the end.'

She fell silent, a pained half-smile on her mouth. Jack looked at the photo. He'd had no idea. Bob had never mentioned visiting Alden, and Jack had never seen any articles about it. His father had visited Alden in secret. Not for the cameras. Not to combat the growing tide of bad press. But because it was the right thing to do.

He examined his father closer. Bob wore his usual tweed jacket, but his face was hollow-cheeked, sunken smudges beneath his eyes. The smile didn't quite reach them.

'I'm so sorry about your son,' he murmured. 'When did he pass away?'

'Nineteen-ninety. That picture was taken May sixth, a week before he passed.' The light from the TV flashed in Mrs Cutter's eyes but she didn't blink. 'Seems so long ago now.'

May sixth. Jack had only been seven years old. Still, he remembered that day because it was the day Bob failed to turn up to the summer festival at school. When Bob finally came to pick him up, he had smelled funny—a smell Jack now knew to be whisky. That's why he missed the fair and, apparently, the hospital visit.

'The book burning,' Toby murmured beside him. 'Wesley's protest was on May sixteenth.'

Jack realised he was right. Wesley staged his protest a week after Bob failed to show up at the hospital. The same week Alden died. Was that part of the reason he hated Bob so much?

'He looked up to him,' Mrs Cutter said. 'My boys never had a father. You should've seen Wesley's bedroom. Puppets and posters everywhere. He had such an imagination as a child. He wrote and wrote and wrote. I was sure he'd be an author. After his brother, though, he stopped all of that. Lost interest in everything. Except you. He talks about you all the time.'

Jack stiffened. The way Mrs Cutter looked at him now made the welt on his forehead pulse like a heartbeat, and hearing about Wesley's obsession with his father made him uncomfortable.

'He thinks I don't know, but I do.' She was staring at the game show, her eyelids pinned back. 'He won't stop until he's made you pay. That's why he came to see you.'

Jack's stomach squeezed.

'Came to see me?'

She didn't seem to hear him.

'Mrs Cutter, did you say your son came to see me?'

She laughed at the TV and Jack flinched, the sound harsh in his ears.

'Jack,' Toby murmured, and Jack sensed movement in the hall. The kettu had appeared. Even in the dark, he discerned their grim expressions. Brol shook his head dismally, then he and Zavanna disappeared through the front door.

No Dune or the Glass.

This whole excursion had been a waste of time.

Except for what Mrs Cutter had said. Wesley had visited Bob. Jack couldn't tell if she meant recently or back when Alden died. He had to know.

'Mrs Cutter,' he said, trying to keep his voice level. 'You said Wesley visited me. When was that?'

The woman looked at him. 'Did I say that?' A hint of fear flashed in her eyes, and he worried that she had realised he wasn't Bob. He was a stranger.

'We should go,' he said, his body trembling. He tried to keep up the facade on the way to the front door. 'It was so lovely to see you again.'

Mrs Cutter trailed after them, and Jack realised he was still holding the frame and Alden's letter. He tried to hand them back but the woman only took the picture, hugging it to her.

'Keep the letter,' she said. 'I'm glad I finally got it to you. He was such a sweet boy, my boy.'

'Uh, thank you,' Jack said, pushing the envelope into his pocket.

Her hand met his elbow. 'You look after that son of yours. Things don't always turn out the way you hoped. And you let me know if Wesley bothers you again.'

Jack swallowed and nodded.

★

In the van, he slumped into the driver's seat, feeling drained.

The atmosphere of Cutter's house clung to him like smoke. Grief had been in every fibre of Mrs Cutter's being, every gesture, as plain as day. He wondered what that did to people, if grief changed them; if it had changed Wesley.

Had Alden's death changed Bob, too?

Was that part of the reason for his breakdown?

Jack had always thought Bob was hung up on *The Shadow Glass* flopping in cinemas, but the photo of Bob with Alden had shown a man weathered by more furious storms. Although the book burning had yet to take place, he'd met a young fan who was terminally ill. A boy similar in age to his own son. A boy who couldn't be saved.

For the first time, Jack saw his father a little clearer; as a complicated human being rather than a deficient parental figure.

His injured finger throbbed again. They were no closer to finding the Shadow Glass and Wesley Cutter's whereabouts remained unknown. Worse, Jack had a horrible feeling the man's crusade had only just begun. His badgering of Bob Co. and the fan community was schoolyard stuff. Buying Dune had been a step up, and the way his mother talked, Cutter wouldn't stop until he was dancing on the ashes of Bob Co.

He sensed Zavanna shifting about in the back of the van and understood her agitation. They'd chased their tails for almost twelve hours with nothing to show for it.

He was failing her.

'What do you think is in Alden's letter?' Toby asked.

Jack shook his head. 'I don't know.' He couldn't bear to open it. It felt too invasive. Too private.

'I guess we know why Cutter had it in for Bob, though,' Toby said. 'He let him down, failed to show up that day at the hospital, and then to add insult to injury, he went to see Alden on his own. Wesley was left out completely.'

'Seems sort of a petty reason to keep hating somebody for so long.'

'I don't know.' Toby looked down at the lub. 'If I was fourteen and Bob said he was going to come see me, then he didn't, and then he ignored me, basically pretended I didn't exist, I'd be pretty upset. I can see why he'd hold a grudge. Especially as an obsessive.'

'And then the book burning earned him a following,' Jack said. 'A new family. Jesus, it's so messed up.'

He rubbed his face with his good hand. He got the feeling that Cutter had started something he couldn't stop even if he wanted to. He'd long since passed the point of no return, a slave to his own obsession.

'We must have faith,' Brol said, though he sounded weary. 'That's what Dune would say. Funny, I believed it more when he said it.'

'We have yet to find even one fragment,' Zavanna said. 'There must—'

'I knew it! Guys, look!'

They all jumped at Toby's cry.

He had opened the *Lady Pain III* video box and was grinning triumphantly. His eyes sparkled as he handed it to Jack. Something off-white was tucked beneath the tape. Hurriedly, Jack removed the tape and found a slip of paper staring up at him:

For Jack
2/2

Another clue from his father. The last one, if the numbers were to be believed.

'I knew Mike was helping us,' Toby said. 'I just knew it!'

Trembling, Jack flicked on the overhead light and drew out an A3 sheet of paper as Toby crowded him, the kettu peering over the seat. Jack unfolded the paper and stared at the bold lines that filled the page.

It was a map.

Not just any map, but a map of Bob Co.

It showed the main studio building, plus the twelve sound stages behind it. Other squares were labelled PROPS, ARMOURY and COSTUMES, while one was marked FUZZ TV ARCHIVES.

'It's Bob Co.,' Toby breathed.

'Bob Co.?' Zavanna asked.

'It's where the movie was made,' Toby explained. 'The one telling Dune's story.'

'The domain of the Scribes of Film,' Brol murmured reverently. 'Bouncing blunderblib, it worked! Dune always told us to have faith and now, look, another sign!'

Jack scoured the map for any special marks, something that might tell them where in Bob Co. the Glass was hidden, but there was no giant red X. It was just a map. Of course, it wouldn't be that easy. But it was their only clue.

'It looks like we're going to Bob Co.,' Jack said, but he wavered when he saw the manic light in Toby's eyes. 'But we're only going if you're cool about it.'

'Um, have we met?! There's no way I can be cool about Bob Co., so don't even ask.'

Jack softened. 'Well, at least try to use your indoor voice.'

Toby thought about it and nodded.

In the dark of the VW, Jack looked at Zavanna and Brol. They were definitely changing. Already the fine fur covering their bodies looked thicker, more real, and their eyes no longer resembled glass orbs. Whatever they were, whatever the truth was about Iri, if it really existed, if the skalions would destroy Earth the way they had the kettu plains, he knew he couldn't let them down.

'Bob Co.,' he said, 'here we come.'

Letter typed on paper with Bob Co. masthead.

BOB CO

To: The Staff
From: Bob
Date: 10 May 1985
FILMING UPDATE

Hi All,
Happy to report that week 10 has gone off without a hitch,
apart from Nebfet's malfunctioning eye. The footage is
pretty hilarious. We have just completed the scenes in the
nightmare swamp, where Dune happily emerged in one piece
(thanks to Jenny Bobbin for some quick thinking).

The lub and wugs are in a death match for the crew's
affection. They've proved so popular that we even found
Jack asleep among them at the end of a time-consuming
sequence. They must have sung him a lullaby. Meanwhile,
Kunin Yillda is proving to be every bit as grisly as expected
(eat your heart out, H.R. Giger). A lot of the crew can't stand
to be near her between takes. She has a way of staring that
is quite unnerving.

Otherwise, we're right on schedule and expecting to
complete on time. The studio will be happy, ho ho. Think
we're coming up with some fun stuff. Either that, or we'll
be scratching our heads in the edit suite wondering what
monstrosity we've brought into the world.

Until then,

12

Jack checked the time—11.17 p.m.—and then peered through the chain-link fence. In the distance rested the white collection of buildings that formed his father's studio, which glowed under the floodlights like some sort of retro space station. Beyond it loomed the sound stages, with their corrugated roofs and warehouse doors. To Jack it was as unremarkable as an industrial estate, but at his side Toby clung to the fence, his eyes bulging at the sight, as if he were trying to cram it all into his eye sockets.

'Woooooooow,' he breathed, the wind brushing through the lub's fur as it perched on his shoulder. 'This is where Bob worked. This is where he created the most important movie in modern history.'

Next to him, the kettu observed the compound with curious expressions. Zavanna's hand curled around her sword. The tension in her stance was unmistakable and Jack felt sure she was counting the hours, aware that Iri's fate rested almost entirely on her shoulders. He couldn't let her down any more than he already had.

All around them, the Essex countryside was dark, the van parked on the edge of a field a mile outside Bob Co.'s perimeter, and Jack couldn't help imagining the skalions emerging from the darkness in silent ambush.

'How are we going to sneak in?' Toby asked, the breeze pulling at his raincoat.

'There's a back way through the sound stages,' Jack said. 'Or there used to be. I'm pretty sure security only check it every hour or so.' Given his relation to Bob, he would probably be waved through the front gate without resistance, but he couldn't face Amelia finding out. Besides, he felt sure the kettu wouldn't play dead again. Breaking in was their only option.

Brol gazed up at Jack. 'This is your father's realm?'

He nodded.

'It is remarkable.'

'Just wait 'til you see inside.' Toby wiggled his eyebrows. 'I've only seen pictures but it's *insane*.'

'It is a madhouse?' Brol asked.

'Not that kind of insane.'

'Come on,' Jack said, leading them along the fence, away from the studio. They walked in the dark, the distant Bob Co. lights acting as a guide, and Jack hoped he was right. Somewhere in the depths of his father's labyrinth, the Shadow Glass was hidden. It was their last and only hope.

They reached the other side of the studio. The sound stages loomed above them, quiet and shadowy behind the fence.

'How do we—' Toby began.

Zavanna slashed her sword through the chain links as if they were made of string. She stepped back and raised an eyebrow at him.

'Were you planning on knocking?' she asked.

'Man, I love kettu,' Toby murmured, scooting through as Jack drew the fence back. He went in last, the kettu sniffing the air, their ears twitching as they scanned their surroundings.

'There is an ill wind,' Brol said. 'The nostrils never lie.'

'Just don't sneeze,' Toby said. 'Security might hear you.'

'The prop house is near Stage 9,' Jack said, surprised that information was still in his brain. He didn't even need the map. 'I figure we cross that off the list first. It's the most obvious place, but you never know with Dad.'

He led them to the first sound stage, where they stuck close to the wall, edging along it. Jack peered around the corner of the building and then jumped back.

'What—' Toby said.

'*Quiet!*'

Jack held his breath. The guard had only been fifty yards away, patrolling the avenue between the buildings, sweeping a flashlight ahead of him. Jack was sure he had been spotted, but the guard hadn't shouted or started running. Maybe he was a guard with poor eyesight.

A torch beam arced across the ground and Jack braced himself for action, but then the beam vanished and he heard footsteps retreating.

'That was close,' Toby breathed.

'You have much to learn about stealth.' Brol frowned at him.

Jack smirked. 'You just got owned by a kettu.'

'Shut up.'

Jack patted Toby's shoulder and led the way past Stages 7 and 8, before stopping outside a smaller building. A simple sign read: PROP STORE—AUTHORISED PERSONNEL ONLY. A keypad rested beside the door.

'Shit,' he muttered.

'We need a key,' Toby said.

Zavanna sniffed the device.

'We'll have to take down a guard,' Jack murmured. 'Steal his card.'

Zavanna reached into a pouch at her waist, then blew on her palm, directing a fine, glittering dust at the keypad. It stuck to four of the numbers, each button glowing with a different intensity.

'Dune taught me a few tricks he learned from Rill,' Zavanna said.

'Rill, the mystic,' Toby breathed. 'Have you met him?'

'Few ever have.'

'That means no.' Brol winked at him.

Zavanna ignored them. She punched the keys, starting with the one that glowed the brightest, and finally hitting the one that emitted only a faint luminescence. A green light flashed and the door disarmed with a *THUNK*.

Jack stared at her in disbelief. 'I thought only skalions had technology in your world.'

'A kettu must—' she began, but Jack interrupted her.

'—adapt to every climate and culture. Right.' He noticed Toby giving him a curious look. 'What?'

Toby smiled. 'Nothing.' He tried the handle and the door swung inwards. They hurried through into darkness.

'I can't see a thing.'

'Try to the left of the door. No, the right! The right!'

Light exploded around them. Jack turned to see Zavanna at the switch.

'I wonder how you accomplish anything in this world,' she said.

'With great difficulty, I imagine,' Brol commented, and they shared a knowing look before scanning their surroundings in awe.

It resembled a warehouse, but a warehouse so cavernous that it seemed to go on for ever, like something out of *Indiana Jones*. Rows of shelves ran into the distance, some towering at over twenty feet so that they reached the strip-lighting, and each was filled with exotic artefacts. The shelves nearest to them held silver goblets. Hundreds of them. Beyond them were plates and bowls, some of them silver, others fashioned from wood or clay. They sat in tottering piles as if somebody was preparing to load the dishwasher.

The whole building was categorised, Jack recalled.

'I think furnishings are further in,' he said. 'At least, they were. Wait!'

Toby had been about to amble down one of the aisles. Jack pointed to a CCTV camera above the door. If he'd stepped one foot further, he'd have been caught. Jack reached up and tipped the camera so it pointed at the ceiling.

'Watch out for others,' he told them.

Toby nodded and wandered in a daze down the aisle before them. The lub squeaked and cooed, bounding ahead of them with its tail waving like a pipe-cleaner.

Zavanna leapt at one of the shelves, scaling it to the top without so much as disturbing a ceramic mug. Jack admired her dexterity and watched as she shielded her eyes to scan the prop store.

'I do not see the Glass,' she called.

'If it's here, it'll be under wraps somewhere,' Jack said. 'Come on.'

She hopped down and they made their way along the aisle, scrutinising the shelves as they went, searching for anything that looked remotely mirror-shaped.

In the centre of the building rested the armoury, which was so huge it had been given its own sign, swinging from the ceiling. Toby turned on the spot, attempting to look at everything at once, his head tipped back.

'Kettu blades,' Zavanna murmured, running a finger down a stack of swords.

'And arrows,' Brol said. 'This bow is of the Fennek tribe. See how it curves.'

The lub nestled between the bows, rubbing its head against one of them. Jack had no idea how it had got in there.

'Where did you acquire these?' Zavanna asked.

'We made them.'

'This is all for your father's movings?' Brol asked.

'Movies. And a lot of it, not all.'

'It is its own empire,' Brol marvelled.

Jack had never thought of it that way, but he supposed he was right. The place was impressive. He stopped by a rack of swords, seeing that they were variations of the same model. Only a couple were marked *hero*. The hero swords were forged from real steel, the ones used in close-ups and for when the actor wasn't fighting. The lighter, Perspex doubles were used in action scenes or when the actor was climbing or running.

He was surprised by how much he remembered. The information was just there, sitting in a subterranean part of his brain.

As Toby and Brol went on, Jack noticed Zavanna had stopped. She stood examining a short blade, unblinking.

'Zavanna?' he said.

'My friend Gwyl has one just like this. She fought with us in Wugtown, just before the Glass cracked and we found ourselves here. I do not know what happened to her.'

'If I know anything about kettu, she's still fighting.'

'Perhaps.' Zavanna's grip on the dagger tightened. 'I only hope this does not spark another kettu war. That is what allowed the skalions to spread as they did. We were so busy fighting amongst ourselves, by the time we realised what the skalions had done, it was too late.'

Jack swallowed. The kettu seemed so unfazed by even the most incredible occurrences but the look on Zavanna's face hinted at pain she kept hidden. For the first time, he wondered how this was affecting her. She gave away so little. He felt the sudden need to reassure her.

'Bad things happen all the time,' he said. 'You can't blame yourself. You can only deal with them, one problem at a time.'

'Wise words, manchild.' Zavanna's mouth curved into a half-smile. 'You may yet be Bob's son.'

She replaced the blade on the shelf and continued down the aisle. Her words lingered, though, and Jack didn't know what to do with them. He'd tried for so long to be different to Bob, had run from place to place trying to avoid it, never settling, always moving… It never crossed his mind that he might possess some of Bob's less hideous qualities.

He picked up the dagger Zavanna had been examining. After judging its weight, he bent and slipped it into his boot. Better to be prepared, especially with one hand out of action.

'Comrades!' Brol called, appearing from another aisle. 'Hasten!'

Jack hurried after the kettu, finding Brol standing in a forest of mirrors. They were stacked like cards, fanning around an enclosed space in the corner of the store. Their frames were secured with foam padding and Jack found a dozen lubs blinking back at him. The creature rested at the centre of the mirrors, admiring its many reflections.

'Merciful Rithmar,' Zavanna breathed.

'Let's be quick,' Jack said. The more time they spent in here, the more likely their chances of being caught.

As one, they searched. Jack heaved mirrors up and away to reveal more behind. Oval, rectangular, some cracked, others worn with age, or at least aged to look worn.

'It has to be here,' Toby said. 'It just has to be.'

They examined each one carefully. Some looked a little like the Shadow Glass but none were an exact match. None were the real thing. And they were all complete mirrors. No fragments.

Jack sat back on his heels, kneeling before one of the frames, his heart thrumming with frustration.

'It's no good,' he said. 'Amelia will have already searched here.'

'Dammit,' Toby cursed. On the floor beside him, the lub trilled a grumble of annoyance.

'I'm sorry,' Jack said, turning to the kettu. 'We'll move on to the main building and—'

'Who's there?' a male voice interrupted. 'Don't move! How the hell did you get in here?'

A guard had appeared by one of the towering shelving units. Muscular and wearing a white shirt and black trousers, he had his hand at his hip, where a baton was holstered.

Jack's gaze darted to the kettu. They had frozen where they stood, blank expressions on their faces. Even though they were standing unaided, the guard didn't appear to notice. He must see puppets every day, he probably assumed they were being supported by an apparatus.

'It's okay,' Jack said, rising from the floor. 'I'm not an intruder. I'm Jack. Jack Corman.'

'Good for you,' the guard said. 'Don't move.'

'Jack *Corman*,' Jack repeated, in case he hadn't heard him.

'Son of Bob?' Toby added, holding up his hands. The lub peeked out from behind his leg, tail twined around his ankle.

'The guy who built this place?'

'Never heard of him. You're trespassing on private property. I'm going to have to detain you and report you to—'

'You're kidding, right?' Jack said. At the guard's granite expression, he muttered, 'You're not kidding.'

'I'm not the bad guy here,' the guard said, stepping forward. 'I just— Hey!'

He cried out as he lost his footing and stumbled into a shelf, only just remaining upright. Jack's gaze went down to a fluffy bundle of fur stink-eyeing the guard. The lub had zipped out from behind Toby's leg and tripped him.

'What the—' the guard began, but even as he regained his balance, a wooden club struck him on the back of the head. He crashed into a stack of picture frames, landing face down.

Toby shot Jack a breathless look of elation, still clutching the club. He must have slipped back and grabbed it from a nearby shelf. The lub gave a satisfied beep as it scuttled up his leg and into his rucksack.

'I thought you didn't hit people,' Jack said.

'Special circumstances. Also, RUN!'

'But—' Jack began, then he saw the guard wasn't unconscious, just dazed. The club must be a foam prop. The man groaned and wrestled with the frames, which had collapsed around him. It wouldn't be long before he recovered.

Shaking off the shock, Jack gabbed Zavanna and Brol, hissing, 'Don't move,' as he threw them over his shoulders. He was sure there were more security cameras around here, it was better if they played safe. He ran after Toby, hurrying down one of the aisles and spotting the exit at the far end.

'This is humiliating,' Zavanna spat.

'Are you sure we cannot be of aid?' Brol asked, his voice jumping as Jack ran.

'Just don't let him see you move.'

Jack realised he was worried for them. If the kettu were captured, who knew what would happen to them. The thought of them being strapped into mechanical equipment, prodded and poked and experimented on, make him feel sick.

Behind him, he heard the guard shouting into his radio.

'Intruders confirmed in the prop store. They're stealing puppets. Send backup, *NOW!*'

Jack didn't slow down, even as Brol's and Zavanna's claws dug into his shoulder blades, sending pain shooting into his neck. He felt their warmth, the lushness of their fur, and knew they were so much more than mere foam and fake fur now. They were real people. Real warriors.

At the door, Toby dashed outside and Jack went after him, skidding to a standstill just in time to avoid crashing into Toby's back.

'Why'd you stop?' Jack huffed.

Then he spotted the figure standing a few feet away, lit up by one of the security lights. Her arms were crossed over her chest, radio in one hand, her mouth pressed into a grim line.

'Hi, Amelia,' Jack panted.

His cousin said nothing. She took in the sight of Toby clutching his rucksack straps and Jack holding the kettu, and a series of expressions wrestled across her face. Irritation, then confusion, then anger. Before Jack could say anything, somebody seized his collar and the guard shouted in his ear.

'There's no need to be alarmed, Ms Twine, I've got him.'

Jack struggled to free himself but the guard held him in place.

'I found them in the prop store,' he said. 'I'll take them to—'

'That's all right, Larry. I can deal with this.' Amelia's voice was surprisingly level.

'Are you… are you sure?'

Amelia gave him a tense smile and nodded. After a pause, the guard roughly released Jack, shooting him a warning look before going back into the warehouse.

'Nice guy,' Jack said.

'What are you doing here?' Amelia didn't appear to be in the mood for games.

'Taking a walk down memory lane.'

She looked like she was chewing her tongue, speechless with anger. Jack knew he should back off, play nice, but then he heard himself say, 'I thought I'd give Toby a tour of the studio. He's never been.'

'Strange time to give a tour.'

'Strange time to be at work. Burning the midnight snake-oil?'

'If you wanted a tour, you could have asked.'

'I didn't want to trouble you. I know how busy and important you are.'

Amelia bristled. 'I don't know who you are anymore, Jack.'

'You have my sympathy.'

'Jack!' The look on her face withered his smirk. 'What is going on with you? You're acting like a fucking teenager! When are you going to grow up?!'

That stung. He opened his mouth to retaliate, but he couldn't think of a witty comeback.

Amelia shook her head. 'I don't have time for this. Just get out of here, however the hell you got in. I don't want to know.'

She turned stiffly and walked off towards the main studio building, which resembled a white box of light at the end of the avenue.

Jack released a breath. He'd half expected her to hand him over to the police. It would have been warranted. He *had* broken into private property.

'We should try the other side of the studio,' he said. No way were they leaving without the Glass.

'What if Amelia can help?' Toby asked.

'That is the Melia you spoke of?' Brol said, raising his head from Jack's shoulder. 'Now I understand your misgivings.'

Jack watched his cousin speed-walk away. He didn't want her help, couldn't stop thinking about the fact that Bob had chosen her to succeed him at the studio, how she apparently got all the good Bob had to offer, while Jack got all the bad. But he knew Toby was right. Amelia had intel he couldn't hope to gain access to. They needed her.

'Come on,' he muttered, chasing after his cousin. She had almost reached the lobby doors when he caught up.

'Look, I'm sorry,' he panted.

She ignored him, going inside. Jack butted the glass door and followed her into a pristine white lobby. A desk fashioned out of driftwood rested to the right, an artful selection of framed movie posters on the wall behind it. *Man-Hero*, *Riddlemaster* and *Twister Sister*. To the left, an impressive battle scene had been staged using creatures from movie properties Bob Co. had worked on. They fought against a backdrop of an electric-blue storm.

'I...' Jack began, but the words dried up as he felt eyes glimmering at him. A painting loomed at the rear of the lobby, a portrait of Bob that reached from the floor to the high ceiling, showing him sitting on the black stone throne.

It wasn't a glossy reprint like the ones in Huw's basement and Bob's study. It was the original painting, vast and inescapable. Jack couldn't look away from his father's face. The crooked smile and the otherworldly blue eyes that twinkled with amusement; eyes with a secret.

Finally, Jack blinked and looked at Amelia, who had stopped in front of the portrait.

'You broke into the prop store,' she said, 'you set off the sound stage alarm—what next, Jack? Are you going to trick—'

'Look, do you want to find the Shadow Glass or not?' he interrupted.

Amelia's expression froze. Jack set Zavanna and Brol on the reception desk and faced his cousin.

'That's why we're here. We're trying to find the Glass.' He nudged Toby, who grinned nervously.

'Uh, yeah. And is it really true you're making a *Shadow Glass 2?*'

Amelia thawed slightly but her anger was replaced with disbelief. 'Is this because of Cutter?'

'Sort of,' Jack said. 'Look, it's missing, right? Well, we're trying to find it. And you're welcome.'

She squinted at him. 'So I'm not a monster dancing on your father's grave?'

His back seized. 'I haven't decided yet.'

'And who are these? They're not ours.' She went to bend over the kettu, who were awkwardly splayed on the desk, limbs entangled, faces fixed. Jack wondered how they were managing to remain so still; if they were doing it purely because he'd asked them to. He felt a swell of affection for them.

'New characters,' Toby blurted. 'You know, a sequel has to expand the world and stuff. At least the best ones do, like *Man-Hero vs She-God.*'

Amelia drew Jack to one side. 'What are you really doing, Jack?'

He tried to think of an explanation that didn't sound insane.

'Look, this morning you told me to try, right?' He shrugged. 'Well, this is me trying.'

She considered him and, for the first time, the scorn bled from her expression, replaced with something brighter. Hope, perhaps.

He frowned, remembering what Amelia had accused them of. 'We haven't broken into any sound stages—'

'Uh, Jack?'

Jack turned to see Toby pointing at the portrait of Bob.

'*Look*,' he said, bobbing in his trainers. 'On his hand. The ring.'

Jack frowned. His father was wearing a ring on his left pinky, his hand resting casually on the arm of the throne. It was a thick band with a face bearing a swirling design. How had he never noticed it before?

'Did you ever see your dad wearing that ring?' Toby asked.

'No,' Jack murmured. 'Never.'

'That design, it's the kettu for—'

'—truth,' Jack finished for him. 'You think it's a clue?'

'It'd be like Bob to hide in plain sight.'

Jack agreed. 'Here. Help me with this.' He gripped the lower edge of the frame, careful not to knock his wounded right hand, and with Toby's assistance eased it away from the wall. It was heavy, but it hinged up a little so Jack could peer at the wall behind.

'What are you doing?' Amelia demanded. 'Stop it!'

'There!' Jack said. 'Look!'

The same symbol as the ring was painted in pink on the white wall.

'There's something behind there. There has to be.' He strained to keep the frame where it was, slipping a hand up and rapping on the wall. It resounded as hollowly as a cupboard door.

'Can you take it?' he asked Toby, easing back.

'Hurry,' Toby grunted.

Breathing hard, Jack scanned the lobby for something he could use to bust open the wall. His gaze settled on the display opposite the doors; the dynamic arrangement of puppets and props.

'You might want to look the other way,' he told Amelia as he wrenched a metal club from the display, ignoring the twinge in his destroyed finger.

'Jack!' she cried, but it was too late. Toby puffed and strained to draw the painting further back and Jack bludgeoned the wall where the symbol was painted. He was surprised at how easily the plasterboard gave. As Amelia emitted a shocked cry, Jack swung the club again, until a black hole gaped back at them.

'You're unbelievable,' Amelia hissed.

But Jack wasn't listening. He reached into the wall, his elbow scraping the ragged hole. His fingers scuffed the cavity, feeling wooden uprights and dry plaster and cobwebs. Then they scraped a smooth object that shifted at his touch. He thrust his arm in as far as it would go, his shoulder aching, sweat beading his forehead as he worked the object loose and, finally, dragged it free.

A wooden box.

He heaved it to the floor and Toby groaned with relief as he released the frame. Together, they crouched over their cargo.

It was the size of a toolbox, simple and with a modest clasp. Jack didn't allow himself to consider what it contained, wouldn't allow the wave of anticipation to grow, because he couldn't handle the possibility that it was another dead end.

Holding his breath, he flicked the clasp and opened the box.

The hairs bristled on his neck and Toby choked.

Inside rested a single piece of black wood, curved and gleaming. An intricate swirl of vines and animals and mountains dipped and coiled across the wood. All the creatures of Iri captured in a single exquisite motif. Jack hadn't seen it in years but he knew that polished sheen, the loving detail, and he shivered, a combination of relief and awe wrestling through him.

'We found it!' Toby gasped. 'It's a piece of the Glass!'

Before Jack could respond, he heard a shout—'Show me!'—followed by the sound of movement as Zavanna launched up from her position on the desk. She dashed past Amelia, whose mouth dropped open. As the kettu warrior fell to the floor beside Jack, staring down into the box, Amelia staggered backwards, the colour bleeding from her face as she butted against the desk.

'What—?' she croaked.

'Zavanna!' Brol hissed behind her. Amelia screamed and whipped around, staring at the male kettu, who was now sitting upright.

Jack ignored his cousin, grazing the carved timber with his fingers. 'Yes, it's a piece of the frame. See.'

He lifted it out and realised it was humming faintly, as if charged with ancient energy. It was heavier than it looked. His fingertips prickled as the fragment vibrated, and his arm hair stood on end.

'It's not a prop anymore,' he said. 'It's like you said, Toby. It's taken on the properties of the real Shadow Glass, just like the kettu.'

'Jack?' Amelia stared at the kettu in horror, her face pale with shock. 'They're moving.'

'Right,' he said.

'They're looking at me.'

'They do that.'

'No, Jack, they're *really looking at me!*'

'Where is the rest of it?' Zavanna scrutinised the wall containing the portrait. 'There must be more.' She no longer seemed to care that Amelia was staring at her as if she were the gilled monster in some classic creature feature.

'Jenny was right,' Toby said, sitting back on his heels. 'Bob broke the Glass into pieces. We have the first fragment!'

'I'm going to need somebody to explain what the hell is going on here,' Amelia snapped. '*Now.*'

All eyes turned to her, but before anybody could speak, the radio on the desk squealed. White noise hissed through the speaker, followed by a panic-stricken voice.

'*Miss Twine? There's been another break-in.*'

Amelia turned. Her hand shook as she grabbed the radio.

'Larry? Where? What's going on?'

'*There's something in the closed set.*'

'What do you mean, some*thing*?'

'*It look… uppet… I don…*'

'You're breaking up,' Amelia said, raising the radio to her ear. 'Larry? Can you hear me? Hello?'

A voice shrill with terror tore from the speaker.

'*OH MY GOD THEY'RE ALIVE!*'

One kettu is worth a thousand armies if she has
courage deep and blade sharp.

— *From the Kettu Saga of Agafripp*

13

'Stay here,' Amelia ordered, running for a door to the side of the reception. Her gaze skipped over the kettu as she fumbled with her key card, swiping it three times before the lock blinked green. 'All of you.'

She gave Jack a final, frazzled glare and then vanished.

'Amelia, stop!' He went after her, reaching the door just in time and elbowing his way into a long white corridor. There was no way he could let her run off on her own. Not after what he'd just heard over the radio. Already she was halfway down the corridor, marching for the door at the far end, the tails of her trench coat flapping.

'Wait! Amelia!' He stumbled on, giddy with the knowledge that they had found the first fragment, and that something awful could be happening further into Bob Co.

'Seriously, Jack, you've done enough already.' Amelia wasn't slowing down.

'If they're the intruders I think they are, you're going to need help.'

She swung around to jab a finger at him. 'See, it's things like *that* that make me worried you're—'

She broke off.

'Worried I'm what?' he asked.

'What really happened to your hand, Jack?'

He pressed his lips together and she screwed up her fists, growled, and continued down the corridor. Jack chased after her. 'Worried I'm *what?*'

'You don't want to know.'

'Wait!' Zavanna called behind them. She raced to catch up, Brol at her heels.

'Comrades!' Brol added. 'Permit us to aid you!'

They reached Jack with surprising speed, their swords unsheathed. Amelia ignored them.

She scanned another door and they went into another corridor that looked identical to the last, except the posters were for older movies and the carpet was even more threadbare. Bob Co. had always been a maze. The ex-Post Office depot was derelict when Bob bought it, and over the years he had added to it piece by piece, a wing here and a connecting stairwell there, until it became the sprawling warren that existed today.

Being back after so long made Jack feel off-balance, as if he really had slipped back in time. The world had changed around Bob Co. but these twisting corridors remained untouched. Jack recalled bouncing around them as a kid, opening doors to rooms that held strange treasures and eccentric workers. It even smelled the same, like acrylic paint and wood shavings.

'Where are we going?' he panted.

'The closed set. Iri.' Amelia tossed the last word back at him like a grenade.

He stumbled but managed to keep going. 'You've built sets?'

Amelia stopped by a door marked *ABSOLUTELY NO ADMITTANCE* and raised her radio.

'Hello? Come in? Anybody?'

Nobody answered. She tapped her keycard and pushed the door. It stuck. Jack joined her and together they forced it in, creating a gap big enough for Jack to squeeze through. He found himself in a dim, cavernous space and realised that he was inside one of the warehouse-like sound stages, the corrugated ceiling far above his head. He'd forgotten how big they were.

His toe caught on something and he landed beside what had been blocking the door. He bit down a cry as pain shot through his injured finger, but the complaint died in his throat as he saw the shapes beside him.

Bodies.

Three guards lay on the floor. At least, he assumed they were guards. It was difficult to tell through the layer of slime and blood coating their misshapen forms. Their limbs were bent at odd angles, like traumatised marionettes, and their fingers had been stripped of flesh, bare bone glinting. Jack shuddered at the sight of their empty eye sockets, which had been scooped clean.

'Oh god,' Amelia breathed as she squeezed through to join him.

A clanging sound came from a couple of wooden towers that rose so high they almost butted the corrugated ceiling. They resembled mini football stadiums, and Jack knew they must contain the enclosed Iri sets. Cables ran from each tower, more than he could count, snaking across the floor like black vines, and bits of machinery crowded the space around them; ladders and disused light stands and coffee cups.

Amelia was already running for one of the sets, but Jack hissed at her to stop. He pointed to a set of wooden stairs that ran around the outside of the nearest tower. They began to climb, the steps shuddering beneath their feet, the kettu at their heels.

At the top, they eased open a door onto a rocky ledge.

A sound like tribal music filtered through. Clanging drums and tinkling metal, maybe even a sand-shaker.

'We must see,' Zavanna hissed.

As one they crept across the ledge, and Jack saw that the platform they crouched on was at the summit of a spiral staircase. It ran all the way to the ground. He peered down at a dank, rocky chamber of black stone. Water trickled down the walls and a couple of barred windows filtered in green light.

Far below them, the floor had been painted with white symbols, and at the centre of the swirling motif rested Kunin Yillda. The skalion queen was starfished on the stone floor, lifeless, eyes closed, grey hair splayed like seaweed.

'What's going on?' Amelia whispered, transfixed by the sight of a figure hopping around Kunin Yillda. Nebfet was in her element, lumbering in drunken circles around the skalion queen, her rag dress flapping around her skeletal frame while she chanted. Her insectoid eyes flashed black and blue.

A dozen skalion soldiers stood guard against the walls, their swords drawn, nose-slits snorting steam.

'Seriously, who's making them do that?' Amelia demanded. 'And what are they doing?'

'They're performing a ritual,' Jack said.

'Thanks, Mr Obvious.' She got to her feet but Jack dragged her back down.

'They'll see us!'

'That's the point. Those puppets are worth more than both of us combined. I can't let anybody throw them around like that, especially not intruders who—'

'We must observe and then strategise,' Zavanna said, and Amelia gave the kettu a fearful glance before looking back at Jack.

'She's right,' Jack said.

'Tell me what the hell is going on right now or—'

'They're alive.' He held her gaze. 'I don't know how, or even really why, but they're here and they're alive and they think they're the characters from *The Shadow Glass*. They *are* the characters from *The Shadow Glass*. Maybe that's why they broke into the studio. This is Iri to them, this set.'

Amelia blanched. She looked as if she was about to spit, but she remained silent. Perhaps the sound of the truth, paired with the sight of the puppets, was more unnerving than the thought that Jack had lost his mind, and her along with him.

'They want the Glass, all of them,' Jack continued. 'And if we don't help the kettu return it to Iri by tomorrow's full moon, Iri will die.'

Amelia looked like she had been told Santa Claus had struck an exclusivity deal with Bob Co.

'Jack—' she said, but Nebfet's chanting became a shriek that shook the chamber. Lightning crashed above them. Jack saw that, in the cavernous roof space beyond the lighting rig, real lightning danced in a churning cloud vortex. The chamber flashed pink and green and a low rumble agitated the air.

'Arise, queen of Iri!' Nebfet crowed. 'Awaken and bless us with your divine presence!'

'Shit.' Jack's fingers dug into the edge of the platform. 'They really are trying to bring her here. Kunin Yillda.'

'Bring her *here*?' Amelia straightened, eyes narrowed at the scene below. 'This is ridiculous.'

'Tell that to my severed finger,' Jack said, raising his bandage. 'A skalion ate it.'

Amelia's mouth twisted in disbelief as Jack sensed movement below.

A new shape emerged from the shadows at the back of the set. A man in a white suit, his ash-coloured hair swept into messy peaks, his jaw thrusting arrogantly.

'Oh my god,' Jack said.

Of all the places he had expected to find Wesley Cutter, this was nowhere on the list. Jack craned forward to see if Dune's cabinet was with him, but there was just Cutter, who stood observing Nebfet, his face tight with anticipation. He didn't seem fazed by the fact that the puppets were moving. It was as if he were watching a scene from a movie, his gaze riveted by the unfolding drama.

'What's he doing here?' Amelia said. 'How did he get in?'

'I'm guessing the same way the puppets did.'

'This is really fucking unacceptable,' Amelia said, and before Jack could stop her she was running down the stairs, the radio still in one hand, her boots thumping loudly as she descended.

'Amelia!' Jack hissed. '*Amelia!*'

Swearing, he went after her.

'Bobson,' Zavanna called, but he ignored her.

The steps were slippery and he almost toppled over the edge. He clung on to the wall, hugging his injured hand to his chest as he hurried after his cousin.

'Halt!'

They skidded to a stop at the foot of the faux-stone stairs, confronted by a handful of skalion soldiers. One of them thrust a three-pronged spear at Amelia's throat. She batted it away and two more soldiers bounded forward, the three of them brandishing their weapons and forcing her back against the wall. The radio clattered to the floor.

'Stop this!' Amelia shouted.

'Get away from her!' Jack grabbed one of the spears and attempted to wrestle it from the skalion, but the soldier held fast, swinging the weapon and butting the side of Jack's head.

He cried out in pain. The world split in two and he tasted bile, staggering back, his ankles catching the lowest step and knocking him onto his backside.

He was only half aware of two more shapes leaping to Amelia's aid, the kettu descending on the soldiers like silent phantoms. He silently thanked them, relieved they were there, and squeezed his eyes shut, hearing strangled cries and grunts, forcing air into his lungs and dry-heaving at the pounding in his head.

'Jack.'

Cutter's voice broke through the nausea, nasal but strong. Jack opened his eyes.

Cutter remained to one side of the chamber, his mismatched gaze resting on Jack. His brows arched in surprise and then his lips spread in a blissful smile.

'I'm so glad you're here,' he said.

It took Jack a moment to find his voice. Finally, he said, 'What are you doing here, *Mr Smithee?*'

The man's smile shrank, then widened once more.

'You wouldn't hold a little subterfuge against a person, would you, Jack? After all, it was in service to a greater good. Dune belongs with those who care. Who understand. He belongs with me.'

'You stole him!'

Cutter shook his head. 'I can't imagine ever parting with something so precious. I was surprised you were willing to sell him. I suppose that's what makes us different.'

Jack struggled to respond as Nebfet's chanting grew louder.

Cutter called over her. 'I thought she was a vision, a prophet or an angel. She was there when I bought Dune, waiting in my car.' He laughed. 'I feared I had lost my mind, but she showed me everything. Iri. I saw it for the first time, Jack, really saw it, and it's magnificent.'

The wild light in his eyes spread a cold chill across Jack's neck. He didn't understand. Nebfet had found Cutter, but how? And why? Because he was an enemy of Bob?

With a shiver, Jack recalled Cutter's Mercedes speeding away from the house after the sale. Jack had seen a shape in the back seat, but he'd convinced himself he'd imagined it. Now, though, he realised he had been right. Nebfet had seen Cutter taking Dune, and now he was part of this.

She had been watching Kettu House this whole time. Waiting for her moment.

But why recruit Cutter?

Jack jumped as thunder boomed above their heads, and then more lightning cracked between the rigging, spitting in pink-green blasts before forking down into the chamber.

It bolted into the sternum of the Kunin Yillda puppet, which hopped where it lay, the limbs jerking as electricity twitched through them.

'It's real, Jack,' Cutter sang. 'All of it! It's beautiful and savage and everything we've ever dreamed of! And it's *right here*! The Glass is almost within our grasp!'

A thunderclap shook the set and then a bone-splitting shriek filled the chamber. It struck the black stones that formed the walls and penetrated Jack's chest, drilling into him like a physical thing. He watched in horror as Kunin Yillda jerked upright, her webbed claws in her hair, her mouth open and emitting a scream that made Jack's eardrums vibrate painfully.

Tensed over two slain skalions, Zavanna and Brol flattened their ears against their skulls, shrinking back. Other soldiers seized their chance, wrenching the kettu's wrists behind their backs and kicking out their knees. They sagged to the floor, cringing against the scream.

Jack saw that Amelia was still against the wall by the steps, her hands over her ears as she stared in disbelief at Kunin Yillda.

Cutter beamed.

Finally, the skalion queen fell silent, her breast heaving as she squinted at her surroundings, taking in the soldiers, the dripping walls, the soothsayer bowing before her, the blue light in her eyes dimming until they became sinister black orbs.

They all watched, waiting for what the skalion queen would do.

'Kunin Yillda, welcome.' Nebfet gripped the queen's shoulder with a skeletal hand. 'Far you have travelled but very welcome you are.'

The queen shoved her off and spoke in a proud voice thick with phlegm.

'Where are they?! Where are my jewelettes? My precious babies!'

'They remain in Iri, my queen, awaiting your return.'

The skalion queen clambered to her feet, which seemed to take considerable effort. Her movements were the rigid movements of a puppet. Her webbed claws kneaded her gut as she sneered up at the hangar-like ceiling, scrutinising the chamber with ribald interest.

'Another world, we have discovered,' Nebfet hissed. 'A place of wealth and wickedness far greater than that of our home world.'

Kunin Yillda's rattling breath eased. Finally, her gaze rested on Jack and Amelia, and her pock-marked face crinkled with disgust.

'What are they?!'

'Earthlings, my liege.'

'Erplings! So pink and spindling! *ACK!* Remove them! Now!'

Skalion soldiers surrounded Jack and Amelia, motioning with their blades.

'Majesty,' Cutter said, his tone dripping with subservience. He fell to one knee before her, his head bowed to the queen. Jack stared. Had Cutter completely lost it? Only a few hours ago he had been worshipping Dune. What was he doing bowing to the skalion queen?

'Who is this?!' Kunin Yillda shrieked, glowering at Cutter as if he were a tick she had found in the folds of her latex skin.

'Your humble servant,' Cutter said. 'Please, ask anything of me and it shall be yours.'

The skalion queen considered him and then licked her lips, her claws twitching. Nebfet swept before her.

'Herrrre,' the soothsayer hissed, sweeping a hand towards the back of the chamber. 'Replenish, my queen. You must regain your strength.'

Jack stared at Cutter, trying to figure out if he had totally lost his mind, but then the skalion soldiers attempted to herd him and Amelia towards the chamber doors. Jack pushed back against them and grabbed Amelia's wrist as shuffling shapes appeared at the rear of the set.

A couple of soldiers bore something heavy between them, grunting with the effort of dragging it across the floor towards Kunin Yillda. Jack glimpsed a white shirt and a thick head of dark hair.

He only recognised the guard as he was dumped at Kunin Yillda's gnarled feet.

Amelia gasped. 'Larry.'

The guard lay in a heap, unconscious, and the skalion queen bent to sniff him. She grimaced but a ravenous light glittered in her glass eyes.

'Please, regent, replenish,' Nebfet insisted, ushering Cutter back. The man stepped away but watched with interest as a warty tongue emerged from the swamp queen's mouth, jerking clumsily around her lipless maw.

Horror spasmed through Jack. The same horror he'd felt as a child when he cowered before the darkest scenes in *The Shadow Glass*, in which Kunin Yillda devoured her prey. He watched now as her mouth opened, her jaw distending and her tongue dancing, and his finger stump burned with the memory of razor teeth.

'No!' He went to run to help the guard but his foot caught on something—a skalion spear—and he crashed onto all fours. He screamed as agony blazed in his bandaged hand and, at his side, Amelia went down on her hands and knees with a cry. Half a dozen soldiers descended on them, pinning them while slippery hands wrenched at their heads, forcing them to watch.

'Yessssss,' a stinking voice rasped in Jack's ear. '*Seeee.*'

On the ground, the guard's eyes opened sluggishly and he appeared confused. Then he saw the thing looming over him and he emitted a blood-curdling scream.

Kunin Yillda laughed as she bore down on him. The guard kicked and thrashed but it was no good. The skalion queen held him fast, stronger than Jack imagined possible, even though she had yet to evolve beyond her puppet state like her subjects. She lowered her mouth over his head.

'Stop!' Jack cried.

'This isn't real, this isn't real, this isn't real…' Amelia said.

'Stop her!' Jack yelled at Cutter, but Cutter wasn't blinking, let alone listening, bewitched by Kunin Yillda's contorted form. 'Do something! What's wrong with you!'

On the other side of the chamber, Zavanna and Brol fought to free themselves from the skalion soldiers, but they remained pinned down, their jaws snapping with frustration.

Jack could only watch as the guard's head and shoulders disappeared into the skalion queen's throat, then an arm, and another. His screams became muffled and the brittle snapping of bones made Jack want to scream himself.

Finally, Kunin Yillda stood alone, grasping her belly and sighing as she slurped blood from her fingers.

Jack felt numb with terror. Cutter's face was pinched, his lips parted with a rapt smile.

Beside Jack, Amelia had fallen silent, staring at the floor, while Brol bucked against his captors and received a blow to the back of the head.

At the centre of the chamber, Kunin Yillda coughed and retched, her whole body convulsing. Just when Jack hoped she was going to choke to death on her food, she doubled over and dumped a slimy deposit on the ground. White and brown fabric. The guard's uniform.

He couldn't bear it anymore. He summoned every scrap of strength he had left and, bellowing, threw the soldiers off him. As he charged for the queen, though, Cutter's voice echoed through the chamber.

'Regent, this human has the Glass,' he said, gesturing at Jack.

Jack came to a stunned standstill.

'He took it, spirited away that which is rightfully yours,' Cutter continued. 'He is a thief in the night.'

Kunin Yillda squinted at Cutter, her jaw working, then she jabbed a barbed finger at Jack. 'You! Tell me! Where is my Glass?'

'Stolen,' Nebfet rasped. 'Snatched from us.'

'Silence!' the queen snapped. Straining with effort, she heaved forwards a step and screwed up her face. 'Where is it, erpling? Speak!'

Jack felt pinned in place by her stare. He tried to muster a response, but more than ever it seemed the world had gone mad. The fanboy who had made Bob's life hell had allied himself with the villain from his movie, and she was scowling at Jack, daring him to defy her, prolonging the moments before she devoured him in the same agonising way she had devoured the guard.

'Perhaps the erpling needs time to search its memory,' the swamp queen said. Her gaze moved past him and she ordered, 'Bring me the female.'

'No!' Amelia cried as she was wrenched to her feet by two skalion soldiers, and then shoved towards Kunin Yillda.

'Leave her—' Jack began, but claws clutched and held him back.

'So pretty,' the skalion queen cooed as Amelia was presented to her. Amelia cringed away from the queen's roving fingers. 'Such lovely skin. Let me touch you, *yesssss*.'

'Get the hell away from me,' Amelia said.

'STOP!' Jack shouted, but the queen ignored him. He blanched as her hungry gaze swept over his cousin, and he saw again the security guard being consumed, his uniform coughed back up in a glutinous deposit. He couldn't let that happen to Amelia. He raised his voice and shouted, 'I HAVE THE SHADOW GLASS!'

Cutter's head snapped in his direction just as the queen emerged from her trance.

She squinted at him. 'He lies.'

Jack felt Cutter's gaze on him, but he ignored it. 'I speak the truth,' he said, though his voice pitched awkwardly like a teenager's. He cleared his throat. 'I have the Glass. Let her go and I'll take you to it.'

Kunin Yillda's gibbous eyes shone with a savage light. She released Amelia, who staggered back, clutching her throat, her face registering shock as she went to the steps.

'Jack—' she began.

'Come,' Kunin Yillda grunted. 'Speak. Now.'

'I knew it,' Cutter whispered. Jack sensed his desperation. It must be the reason Cutter had bowed to Kunin Yillda. He knew that her ruthless drive to find the Glass was the most likely to yield results. All he had to do was stand by and let her find it for him. The fact that he was so ready to accept living puppets told Jack everything he needed to know about his mental state.

He ignored Cutter as the weight at his wrists snapped away. Trying to remain calm, he hobbled towards the queen, nearly choking on her rancid odour. He could taste it even from where he stood a few feet away.

'Kneel.'

He fell to one knee before her, forcing himself to look up into her countenance.

'Wellllll?' she brayed.

Jack fumbled with his pocket. 'I have it written down here. This is embarrassing. I'm sure—' As his right hand worked, he slipped the other hand into his boot. His fingers grazed metal—the dagger he had taken from the prop store—and in one swift motion, he wrenched free the concealed blade and drove it towards Kunin Yillda's neck.

He frowned.

The blade had stopped inches from her throat.

Pain cramped his hand. The queen had caught the blade and was squeezing his fingers tight. She eyed them hungrily.

'Where is my Glass?' she purred.

'Tell her, Jack,' Cutter said. 'Give it to her and this will be over.'

Jack trembled at the thought of Kunin Yillda's teeth, choking on the oily stench that was already collecting around her newly animated body. He prayed that Toby was okay, that the skalions hadn't found him in the lobby. Just thinking about Toby sparked new resolve and Jack knew he couldn't give in. He met Kunin Yillda's veiny eyeballs.

'It'll never be yours,' he spat. 'Never.'

Kunin Yillda shrieked with rage and Jack felt her tense as she prepared to drag him towards her waiting mouth. But then he heard a new cry behind him, followed by the clash of blades, and Zavanna shouting, 'Unhand him, wench!'

The kettu had fought free. The skalion queen was looking over Jack's shoulder, her attention diverted, and that was all the opening he needed. Jack jerked his hand free and stumbled backwards across the chamber floor. He collided with the wall beside Amelia, who watched as the kettu flipped through the air towards the queen. Jack had never felt more grateful for them.

Before they could reach her, though, Kunin Yillda's soldiers leapt forward, throwing up protective blades and blocking Zavanna's and Brol's attacks. The kettu came to a halt, hunched and panting as they faced the cluster of skalions.

'Come out and fight us, regent of all that is rancid!' Brol yelled.

Jack couldn't help smiling. If they got out of this alive, he'd teach Brol how to insult people Earth-style.

'Kettu!' cried the swamp queen. 'Fasc-i-na-ting!' Her bulbous eyes looked fit to burst. 'The great prize at the heart of your realm is mine by right, kettu scum. And why? For I am Iri's true queen. I am Kunin Yillda!'

'You are no queen!' Brol bellowed. 'You are lower than the parasite that burrows in the bowels of the fizzverm!'

'AGH!' Kunin Yillda's face crumpled as if she had been struck. 'Kunin—'

'You are more rancid than the sleesheet,' Zavanna cried, 'and twice as repugnant in appearance!'

A shocked gasp erupted from the queen's gullet. Her jowls shook and she mewled as she fussed with her limp hair.

'Lies, mistress,' Nebfet purred, hovering at her back. 'They mean only to distract you with callous words.'

Kunin Yillda's mouth pressed into a line and she pointed a clawed finger at Brol.

'You will kneel, kettu!' she shrieked. 'You will kneel before your true queen, as will all of Iri and Erp.'

'NEVER!'

Brol burst forward, launching himself at the queen as he drew his sword from his back. Before he could reach her, though, a skalion soldier charged him, and the kettu growled, swinging his legs around the creature's neck and flipping it through the air. The skalion landed with a crash that shook the set, and the sight snapped Jack from his stupor.

'Amelia, we have to get out of here!'

She nodded. There was no room for scepticism now. She had walked into the middle of an Iridian crisis, and there wasn't a puppeteer in sight to blame for what the kettu and skalions were doing to each other.

'This way.' Amelia tugged him towards the back of the chamber, to the cavity beneath the stairs, where she prodded the rocky surface, searching for something.

'There's a crew access door back here somewhere,' she said.

'Enjoying the show, Jack?' Cutter called. He prowled the other side of the chamber. 'You can't fight Iri! It will always win!'

'What do you want, Cutter?' Jack demanded. 'What are you doing here?'

The man smiled and went so still he might have turned to ice, but his eyes burned with fire.

'They follow me because I care, Jack. The fans who really believe in Iri and *The Shadow Glass*. That original vision meant so much to us, and Bob did nothing but pick it apart like carrion. Everything that came after only served to dilute it or develop a *franchise*.'

He spat the last word as if removing venom from a wound. 'But I always knew there was something special about the original film. Something primal. Your father tapped into a force he didn't understand. Somebody has to care, Jack. Bob would want *me* to have the Glass.'

He paused, stopped pacing. 'I made it right in the end. I was there, Jack. I was there when he died.'

Jack's lungs shrivelled to nothing. He didn't understand what Cutter was saying.

'Don't listen to him,' Amelia grunted, still working at the wall.

'I visited him a lot in that final year,' Cutter said. 'We became friends. Alden Smithee and Bob Corman. He was so desperate for company. I suspect he liked me because of my name. *Alden*. When he had the fit, I knew it was over. He begged to call you but you didn't answer. Why would you? His last communication was with your voicemail.'

Tears streaked his face. 'But I was there to hold his hand as he died, Jack. I watched the light leave his eyes. The mind that created all of this. Gone forever. And I forgave him for what he did, all the mistakes he made. In the end, I forgave him.'

Jack's ribcage seized and he felt as if the ground had fallen away around him. He was falling. All strength left his body.

'You see, they loved painting me as the villain,' Cutter continued, 'especially after the burning. But you're the one who abandoned an old man when he needed you. You're the one who turned your back on what he created. Don't you see, Jack? You're the villain, not me.'

Jack's insides calcified. Cutter was twisting the truth just like he had when he took Dune. He prepared to launch himself at Cutter, wanted nothing more than to crush his throat until he stopped talking.

'Give me the Glass,' Cutter said calmly.

He made it sound like he was doing Jack a favour, and for the briefest moment Jack was tempted. But then he thought about Toby, the way he talked about Bob and *The Shadow Glass*, and he remembered Zavanna's pain at losing Dune, her resolve to fight no matter what, and Jack knew he couldn't do it. For once, he wasn't going to run.

'No,' he said.

Irritation crossed Cutter's face. 'You have no place here, Jack. You're not him.'

His words triggered something in Jack's brain and every muscle in his body knotted together. He prepared to charge across the chamber, but then he heard a *click* and a section of wall swung open beside him.

'Crew access,' Amelia grinned, but then she frowned, turning towards the miniature door just as Jack felt the set judder.

Too late, he heard the symphony of trills, yelps and barks from beyond the set walls. Then came the sound of wings and the thunderous patter of padded feet as a mass of bodies surged through the crew door. Jack covered his face, falling back and yelling as airborne objects ricocheted off him and scampering creatures tangled in his feet.

What now?

Finally, the stream of bodies ended and he stared dumbfounded at the wildlife that flocked around the chamber. Witterbirds filled the air and six-legged viperhounds bounded about yelping. Yet more shell creatures scuttled and nipped at skalion feet, while a creature that appeared to be nothing but eyes rolled in a delirious blinking circle.

Understanding dawned in Jack's mind.

Nebfet's summoning ritual hadn't only awakened Kunin Yillda. It had awakened every puppet in the sound stage.

'GET THEM! KILL THEM! *STOP THEM!*' Kunin Yillda's voice thundered amid the chittering shriek of wildlife.

The main chamber doors crashed open and a herd of lopers cantered inside. Ghost-white with small, pointed heads, they towered on legs as long and knobbly as low-hanging branches.

'Zavanna!' Jack shouted. 'We have to go! Now!'

Across the chamber, the kettu's jaw tightened and, with Brol, she vaulted past skalions to join him. Together, Jack and the kettu ducked through the crew door, joining Amelia in the sound stage.

As the skalion queen bellowed at her army to apprehend them, Jack chased after Amelia, reaching a door that must lead back into the main Bob Co. building.

'Believe me now?' he panted as she flashed her card at the keypad.

'Let's just get the hell out of here,' his cousin said.

Jack paused to look back at the Iri wildlife streaming through the roof of the chamber set, tangling in the light rigging.

'What about them?' Zavanna asked.

'We'll figure it out later.'

[00:23:12] Ahh, here he is! You know, Gurchin wasn't in the script. As written, we were supposed to wend our way through the city of Rapell, following Dune as he slowly discovers it, but on the day we shot the sequence it just wasn't working. I had a very sleepless night trying to figure out why.

Anyway, the next morning I was giving my son, Jack, his breakfast. He was barely two years old and so more food ended up on his face than in his mouth. He looked like something that had crawled out of a sewer and WHAMMO!

There it was, the solution. It's funny how inspiration strikes. They say necessity is the mother of invention, but I think happy accidents are just as important to the creative process. Seeing Jack wearing his breakfast made me realise we needed a new character to lead us into Rapell, to let us know just how down and dirty it was, and in that moment Gurchin was born.

Of course, we had no time to create a new puppet for the role, and after a lot of agonising, I realised the answer was right in front of me. It seemed only right that Jack should play Gurchin.

Listen, here comes the line. 'That's good eatin'!' [chuckles] We fed him a lot of chocolate cake that day. He didn't seem to mind.

14

It was almost one a.m. when they pulled up outside the house. The lights were off and the street was so dark the sky swirled with stars. The moon hung above them like a timepiece, counting down the few hours they had left to save Iri.

Jack tried to ignore it. He had never been to this part of south London before and he eyed the house as he got out of the Land Rover, his legs aching, his finger numb.

They had escaped from Bob Co. in Amelia's car, piling into it as the studio came alive with the shrieks of Iri wildlife. They couldn't go back to Kettu House – it would be the first place Kunin Yillda would look for them – and Amelia had driven like a demon as she followed Toby's directions, white-faced and rigid with tension. In the back, the kettu had clawed the upholstery as the vehicle bumped over potholes, and while Jack was relieved they'd made it out of the studio in one piece, his thoughts were consumed with Cutter.

As the others got out of the vehicle, Jack noticed a sign hanging from the front of the house. Silver letters winked in the moonlight.

'Funeral home?' he said. He'd spent weeks organising his father's service, and he'd be happy not to see another undertaker for a very long time.

'Nell's parents have their own business,' Toby said, cradling the lub as he cricked his neck.

'Are they home?'

'Probably, but we're not going in there.'

Jack noticed Zavanna and Brol were still in the car. They sat with the fragment box between them, their attention directed through the windows. They must be exhausted, too.

'Are you…?' Jack asked.

'We shall remain here and guard the Glass,' Zavanna said.

'Okay.' He hesitated, checking them over for injuries. 'Are you all right?'

'Kunin Yillda must quadruple her efforts if she wishes to do us harm.'

Jack smiled. 'Right. Thanks for keeping us alive back there.'

Zavanna said nothing but nodded, a glint of warmth in her gaze. Jack sensed that things had changed between them again. Something modest and fragile had budded. Even if Zavanna hadn't forgiven him for selling Dune and failing to live up to her vision of Bob's son, he sensed he could earn her compassion. It was better than her pretending he didn't exist.

'At least Iri is safe for now,' he said, 'if Kunin Yillda is in our world.'

Zavanna's gaze darkened. 'Kunin Yillda is not the only threat to Iri. She has a sister.'

'Koruni Sleema is said to have been driven mad by the parasites of the southern swamps,' Brol whispered, as if speaking her name might summon her. 'She devoured their mother and delights in destruction. Her home is fashioned from the bones of skalions who crossed her.'

'*She's* the crazy one?' Jack shuddered at the thought of a creature even more repulsive than Kunin Yillda.

'If she is now in charge of the skalion army,' Brol said, 'there is no telling what fresh calamity Iri faces.'

No silver linings around here.

'Here.' Toby tried to pass the lub to Zavanna but the creature squealed and clung to his arm. 'It's okay, we won't be gone for long. I think.'

'I shall take him.' Brol carefully pried the lub free and petted it, cooing as he drew back into the car. 'There, there, small creature.'

The lub stared at him with undisguised contempt.

'Should I lock them in?' Amelia asked. She observed the kettu with a mixture of fear and awe. It was funny how their presence no longer unnerved Jack. He was getting used to having them around and he no longer flinched when Zavanna looked at him.

'No, they can look after themselves,' he said.

'I don't doubt it.'

Together, they walked up the shadowy drive running alongside the house. Toby led the way as Jack explained to Amelia how the kettu turned up in the attic on a quest to save Iri, which was real, apparently. He left out the part where he'd somehow brought them into the world himself.

'Do you believe them?' Amelia asked.

Jack merely raised his eyebrows in response. The front of his T-shirt was soaked through with sweat and skalion slime, and he felt filthy, bone-tired as they passed through a garden that resembled a solid block of darkness fringed by tall trees. They approached an arm of the house that seemed to have been added at some point in the recent past, and Toby rang the doorbell.

'Nell's gran used to live here,' he explained, 'before she died. Then Nell lost her job and took it over. It's so cool. One day I want to live in a granny annex.'

The door opened and Nell, the forty-something Guild member with multicoloured hair, blinked out at them. A familiar tingle of unease crept under Jack's skin.

'What's up?' Nell said, as if it wasn't past the witching hour and they had dropped by for a cup of tea. She still wore dungarees, although she had added unicorn slippers to the ensemble since Jack saw her at Huw's.

'Nelly!' Toby hugged her. 'You remember Jack, and this is his cousin, Amelia.'

'A pleasure,' Amelia said, extending her hand while Jack gave Nell a small wave with his good hand. Amelia stiffened in surprise as Nell hugged her. She went to draw Jack into a similar squeeze before she saw his slime-soaked T-shirt.

'Don't tell me, another dog? Come on in. We're halfway through *Man-Hero*.'

'We?' Amelia asked Jack through the side of her mouth, and he grinned. She had no idea what she was walking into.

Nell led them to a lounge dominated by a fifty-inch TV screen that was paused on a topless hunk standing atop a cliff, his sword raised.

'What time do you call this?' asked Anya, her blonde hair fixed in a high ponytail. She was on the sofa, sharing a duvet with Sumi, while Huw lounged in an armchair. They were all in their pyjamas.

'Don't tell me you need another finger sewing up,' Sumi said.

Jack smiled. 'Not tonight.'

She looked relieved.

'Why the location change?' Toby asked, remaining by Jack's side.

'My parents told us we were being too loud,' Huw said. 'But there's no way of playing Dune's Quest quietly, and *they're* the ones who failed to insulate the basement properly. Plus, you know, the night before All T'Orc is like Christmas Eve. No way we can be expected to be chill. So we came to Nell's. Where have you been? Why did you need Cutter's address?'

'Well…' Toby gave the Guild a secretive smile.

Jack realised it was still Saturday. The Shadow Glass Guild meeting was still in full swing, albeit in a new location. He couldn't believe that, just a few hours ago, he had met these people for the first time. It felt like weeks had passed since then.

'Oh!' Huw seized his laptop from the floor and flipped it open. 'I was just taking a break from researching the location of the Shadow Glass. I really feel like I'm about to make a breakthrough.'

Anya rolled her eyes. 'Yeah, you definitely haven't been snoring through the past twenty minutes of *Man-Hero*.'

He shot her a venomous glare through his black-framed glasses.

'M&Ms, anyone?' Nell offered them a bowl, and even though Jack's stomach felt as hard as stone, he grabbed a few and devoured them. They should probably get some food to the kettu, too. He was just hoping Nell didn't take that as a sign he liked her when a boxer dog probed his groin.

'Don't mind Fin, she never learned to respect boundaries,' Nell said.

'No kidding,' Jack grunted.

'She's never bitten off a finger, though, don't worry.'

The dog moved on from Jack, snuffling around the group, licking hands and shoes, its stumpy tail wagging.

'Wow, I haven't seen this film since I was a kid.' Amelia was staring at the man on-screen. Axel Backlund was a Swedish martial artist turned model turned actor, who made his indelible mark on the big screen playing Man-Hero in 1988. His English was so limited that half his lines were cut, which actually benefitted the film, affording Man-Hero a square-jawed mystique as he battled the evil Skullatrix.

'Oh, it's my favourite—' Nell began.

'Here she goes,' murmured Anya, though she was smiling.

'It was one of Bob's favourites, too,' Amelia said. 'What?'

Everybody in the room was staring at her. Sumi pushed her black fringe out of her eyes.

'What did you say your name was?'

'Amelia.'

Jack stepped back, knowing what was coming.

On cue, Huw jerked up from the chair.

'Oh, wow! Amelia Twine? *The* Amelia Twine? Of Bob Co.?' He hurried over to shake her hand and Jack choked down a laugh as Amelia stood speechless.

'Wow, hi. Oh my god. Wow.'

'It's lovely to meet you,' Amelia said. 'You're a fan.' She somehow extricated her hand from Huw's while he nodded. Jack wished he knew her trick. He supposed she'd had a lot of practice with fans.

'We all are,' Anya said, sitting up on the sofa. 'Unofficially.'

'Right, unofficially,' Huw said, looking cowed.

'You lost me,' Amelia said.

'Oh, we don't want to be accused of copyright infringement,' Anya said.

Sumi shook her head. 'Not again.'

Amelia straightened. 'Right. It's only just come to my attention that sites have been taking Bob Co.'s legal fire.'

'It was Cutter,' Toby said, going to stand in front of the TV.

'*Wesley* Cutter?' Nell asked, stroking Fin, who sat panting between her feet.

'The very one. It was never Bob Co. who tried to kill the sites, it was him.'

Jack's jaw creaked at the thought of Cutter in the chamber set, his crooked grin, the things he'd said. His hand hurt again.

'Forget about that, though,' Toby said. 'We still have to figure out where the rest of the Shadow Glass is.'

'It's in pieces,' Jack added, attempting to focus. 'We're trying to find out where each piece is hidden.'

'Just like the movie,' Nell said. 'We could watch the film for clues?' She was already moving to the bookcase, taking down a *Shadow Glass* Blu-ray and going to the TV. Jack shivered at the sight of it. He hadn't watched the movie in over two decades and he wasn't exactly in the mood now, having just lived through a real-life confrontation with the swamp queen of Iri.

'I need to make some calls,' Amelia said, and Jack realised that couldn't be more true. At least four of her security guards had been killed and, for all they knew, Bob Co. was now overrun with puppets. She had a lot to sort out.

'Oh, you can use the kitchen,' Nell said. 'Down the hall on the left.' She turned off *Man-Hero* and slotted in the *Shadow Glass* disc.

Jack found himself forced onto one end of the sofa next to Sumi. Beside her, Anya played a cat game on her phone.

'Is that your costume?' Toby asked Nell as he wriggled into the armchair by Huw. He pointed at a white and gold jumpsuit hanging from the door frame.

'Like you have to ask!' Nell said, settling into a beanbag chair, a bowl of crisps in her lap, the dog stretched out beside her. 'Bring on All T'Orc.'

'Right.' Toby groaned. 'I can't believe I forgot the mini-Con is tomorrow.'

'How could you forget the most important date in the *Shadow Glass* calendar?' Huw asked.

Toby yawned. 'I don't know myself anymore.'

Jack perched stiffly beside Sumi and Anya, watching as the disc menu loaded, showing a montage of film stills, and he crushed his good hand between his knees. There was Dune in the nightmare swamp, and the Shadow Glass beaming light through a dank cell, and Dune and Dorr on the rope walkway in Wugtown.

Jack's shoulders knotted painfully.

'Let's do this,' Nell said, pointing the remote at the TV.

The Bob Co. logo appeared, a cheerful wug winking at them as it peeked out from the second 'O', and then blackness settled over the screen.

Thunder drummed from the speakers.

An old male voice said, '*In a forgotten time, in a forgotten world, deep within a forgotten chamber few have ever seen, the Shadow Glass sees all.*'

Heat surged across Jack's back.

'*Jack? Boy-o?*'

He heard his father rasping down the line. His final phone call.

He couldn't do this. He had to get out.

'I, uh,' he began, trying to think of an excuse but failing. He staggered to his feet and ran for the door, bursting out into the night.

The air was cool on his skin, but he still felt hot and he couldn't stop, stumbling through the dark, not knowing where he was going, only that he had to put as much space as possible between him and that movie.

He was barely halfway across the garden when a voice hissed at his back.

'Jack, where are you going?'

He flinched and turned to face Amelia. In the moonlight she looked ghostly as she emerged from Nell's annex, tugging her torn coat around her, her pupils large and burrowing into him.

'I can't...' His shoulder blades squeezed, making his spine ache. 'I can't be in there right now.'

'Why not?'

He cast about for an answer. Their breath misted between them in the midnight chill. It was still pitch dark, the stars studding the sky and the moon disappearing behind a cloud. They could be the only two people in the world.

'I don't know if I can be the person they want me to be.'

He wished she would stop staring at him, and he kept hearing Cutter's words. *'You're the villain, not me.'* The more he thought about it, the more proof Jack found for that theory.

'What happened?' Amelia asked. 'When did you get like this?'

There was no answer for that, either.

'I'm really trying here, Jack. I want to help but you're freezing me out at every turn. That thing outside Uncle Bob's study, you were really angry. What's going on?'

He felt the handle in his palm, slamming the door, spitting at her to leave.

'It's where I found him,' he said, finally surrendering to the memory. He couldn't fight it anymore.

Amelia's tone softened. 'In the study? I didn't know.'

The back of Jack's throat burned and he tried to speak. Failed. Tried again.

'He tried to call me.' The words grew thick in his mouth. 'I saw the phone ringing, saw his name, and I ignored it. I *ignored* it. What kind of a son does that? He left a voicemail and he sounded so lost. I knew something was wrong. I came to the house as soon as I heard it, but I was too late. He was already gone.'

It felt good to say it. To prick that bubble of pain. It had been getting bigger in his chest for weeks, making it impossible to breathe or eat. He had felt it bubbling up while he talked to Jenny in her kitchen, and forcing it down had been painful. Just saying the words now eased the pressure. But the shame was overwhelming. It crashed over him in a black wave.

'The TV was on,' he said, recalling the way his reflection hit the curved screen. 'He was watching the movie on his own.'

'Jack, it's not your fault.'

He moved his head slowly. 'Of course it was.'

'Whatever happened between you, he was your father. He was everything you had, after your mum. And now he's gone, too. That must be a horrendous thing to deal with.'

The words shrank. He could barely say them. 'It's not just that. I hated him.'

'You didn't.'

'I did. He loved this stuff more than anything else. How do you think that felt? Knowing that?'

Amelia stared at him. Somewhere, an owl made a desolate sound that echoed in the night.

'Jack...' She shook her head. 'God, you're such an idiot sometimes! You can't see what's right in front of you. You're too busy creating this epic fiction in your head. This huge, imagined battle between you and your father. Don't you get it? There's a reason *The Shadow Glass* meant so much to him. Dune wasn't just a character to him. Dune is *you*.'

He stood stiffly, trying to understand what she was saying.

'How can you not see it?' She threw up her arms. 'It's all over the film. It wasn't about box office or critical acclaim. It was about Dune. It was about you.'

'What do you mean?'

Amelia looked like she was trying not to scream. 'Did you know there's an early draft of *The Shadow Glass* from before you were born? It's a pile of shit. It's awful. Hackneyed and empty, all about the spectacle. Bob wrote it before he knew what he wanted to write, before he had anything to say. It's locked in the vault at Bob Co. so nobody can ever read it. Then your mum got pregnant, and then she died and it was just you and him.'

'What's this got—'

'Suddenly he had something to write about, Jack. Some*body*. He poured all his love for you into that film, dammit. Into *Dune*. Every hope and wish. He created a hero who was vulnerable but determined, who wanted more, to learn how to be a hero despite the terrible things that had happened to him. He was writing about *you*, J.' Her gaze darkened. 'And you sold him to the highest bidder.'

He couldn't think.

'How do you know this?' he asked.

'It's so obvious! He talked about you constantly. When your mum died, all he had was you. And, for a while I guess, me. Why do you think I spent so much time at your house as a kid? My parents couldn't give a shit. They moved me to Florida a month after my eighth birthday then promptly stopped noticing I existed.'

Jack's whole body was shivering. He tried to take a breath but it didn't help. What she had said couldn't be true. *The Shadow Glass* wasn't for him. He wasn't Dune. How could he have missed that? How could he have got it all so wrong?

He felt the garden shadows growing around him.

'I'm sorry,' he said. 'I didn't realise. I should have realised things weren't great for you, either.'

'Yes, you should have.'

'Was it really that bad?'

She sighed and uncrossed her arms. 'Look, I'm not after a pity party. I mean, you just have to look at those kids in there to see they think I've got it made. And maybe I do. Professionally. But when I started working for Bob, I didn't imagine it would take over my life like this.'

'You don't have a life?'

'My wardrobe is all power suits.' Amelia rolled her eyes. 'Don't get me wrong, I love what I'm doing, but there has to be something else. It'd be nice to have friends, maybe even watch a freaking film every once in a while. I'm not exactly living my perfect life here, either, Jack.'

God, he was an idiot. He had been so lost in his own regret he couldn't see anything else. Anybody else. No wonder Amelia kept snapping at him, glaring and snorting. He was a mess.

And he was still thinking about himself.

'I'm sorry,' he said again. 'Let me help. I want to help.'

'You want to come work for me?'

He couldn't help smiling. 'I'm not sure I'd go that far.'

'You could be my assistant. Emphasis on *ass*.'

'I suppose I deserve that.'

Amelia raised an eyebrow at him and then smiled. She went to the patio and sat in a chair swing.

'What did he do?' she asked. 'Uncle Bob? The thing that was so unforgivable?'

Jack felt the familiar razor edge of pain that came with thinking about what Bob had said when he was fifteen, the thing that broke everything, and he was too tired to go near it. He couldn't face it.

'It was more all the things he didn't do,' he said. 'A big pile of them that grew every year. The birthdays he forgot, the lack of interest in how I was getting on at school, who my friends were, where I was going to university. He just didn't care. And then there was the drinking.'

He wasn't sure he could ever forgive him for that. It was the reason Jack rarely touched alcohol. Even the smell made him anxious and angry and a hundred other emotions he couldn't find names for.

Amelia released a breath. 'That must have been tough. Which I appreciate is an epic understatement. I think he drank to dull it all. He wanted people to love Iri so badly, he felt like the real world turned its back, so, eventually, he turned his. And deep down, I think he knew he was messing up with you.'

'Did you know he was dying?' Jack asked.

'Yes. I thought you did, too.'

His cheeks burned. 'I ignored a lot of calls in those final years. I still haven't listened to half the voicemails.'

He wasn't sure it would have made a difference anyway. The last time he saw his father alive, the meal had ended in raised voices and Jack storming out. Would knowing Bob was dying have changed that? Could they ever have worked through their issues?

'That's understandable,' Amelia said. 'But you want to know something insane? No matter what happened between you two, Uncle Bob's still here. He does care. All of this—the quest, the puppets, us—he's trying to connect with you. Maybe he realised too late what he'd missed out on. He's trying to fix it, even though he's not around anymore.'

Jack joined her at the chair swing.

'The key,' he murmured. 'Dad sent me the key to the attic. It turned up last week. It's where the puppets were. It's why I was at the house when you ambushed me.' He paused, thinking. 'Dad left me the puppets and he left you in charge of Bob Co.'

'Are we back into stating the obvious?'

'He knew you'd need the puppets to make the movie. You'd have to talk to me at some point to get them. And we haven't exactly been best friends for a while. It's like he set this whole thing up, all of it, not just the puppets coming to life, but all the things that would bring us back together.'

'You're saying Uncle Bob gave me a bitching job because he wanted to prove a point? Thanks.'

'No,' Jack said. 'Clearly you were overqualified. But I wasn't talking to him. So maybe he used the things he had at his disposal to do what he thought he should. Maybe this is his fucked-up way of helping me.'

Amelia tilted her head. 'Seems to me, once you throw talking puppets into the equation, anything is possible. So the question is: what do you want?'

Jack opened his mouth to answer but nothing came out. He couldn't begin to think about what his life might look like after this.

'Later,' he said. 'What are we going to do about Bob Co.?'

'That's what I'm trying to figure out. It's not like there's a box on your life insurance policy for "puppet massacre". Poor Larry.'

Jack nodded sombrely. He'd lost a finger. Larry had lost his life.

'She ate him,' Amelia said. 'How the hell did she *eat* him?'

'I don't know, but if the others are anything to go by, she's only going to get worse.'

'Worse?'

Jack shrugged. 'The skalions didn't bleed before. Now they do.'

'But it doesn't make any sense!'

Jack smiled. 'What did Dad always say? "After a sense of humour, nonsense is the best sort of sense."'

'I can't believe you're quoting your father at me.'

His smile dropped. She was right. When had that started?

'Look, that place has everything the skalions need,' he said. 'Armour, weapons, sets that feel like home. They'd be mad to leave. So we have to figure out a way to force them. And I think finding the Shadow Glass is key to helping us do that.'

Amelia looked at him. 'And Cutter?'

He scowled. 'I get the feeling he's going to be more difficult to deal with than the skalions. Plus… Cutter claims he was there when Dad died. He knew about the voicemail.'

'Shit.'

'I think Cutter's been trying to get his hands on Dune and the Glass for a while,' Jack said. 'It must be part of his plan to consolidate his following and bury Bob Co.'

Jack took some satisfaction in the knowledge that, so far, Cutter had failed, but a deeper sense of disquiet tunnelled through him. Because it was Jack's very absence that had given Cutter access to his father. How desperate must Bob have been to strike up a friendship with a stranger who pitched up on his doorstep?

With a sick feeling, Jack wondered if Bob had enjoyed their time together. If Cutter had made a prime replacement.

Maybe Jack *had* been acting like a villain. All the things Cutter accused him of were true, and Jack couldn't change them, even if he wanted to.

But he could change everything else.

'There's also this,' he said, digging a hand into his pocket for Alden's letter. He frowned and stood up, searching his other pockets, but he found only his phone, old chewing gum wrappers and the map of Bob Co.

The letter must have fallen out somewhere between Cutter's house and Nell's.

'Shit.'

'What is it?' Amelia asked.

Jack shook his head. Now he'd never know what Alden had written. How could he have been so careless?

He refocussed on Amelia. 'Just promise me one thing.'

She looked suspicious. 'What?'

'Promise me that no matter what, we're going to get Dune back, find the Glass, and make Cutter pay.' He held her gaze, making sure she understood how serious he was. 'We fix this, even if we have to tear the world apart to do it.'

'Finally!' Amelia grinned. 'There's the Jack I know.'

Posted by u/Witter19 1 hour ago

'It's sh*t,' says son of *The Shadow Glass* director Bob Corman in an exclusive interview with Wesley Cutter, aka the Keeper of Iri, about the film. During an intimate chat in which they discussed the franchise as a whole, Jack Corman revealed he hates the extended franchise and wishes his father had never written controversial and fanboy-slated comic series *Beyond the Shadow Glass*. keeperofiri.com/20190...

9 Comments

Witter19: Did you guys see this story?
Think it's legit?

Dun3: No way Bob's son said that stuff just Cutter stirring shit like always

Queen_Yillda: What if he did tho? All those rumours about them not getting on.

Witter19: Cutter can't just post lies.

Dun3: Never stopped him before.

Dun3: He's the one who tried to stop the Blu-ray release. He's anti-digital. Thinks it should only be watched on film.

Nellda: No chance Jack said that. I know him. He wouldn't say that.

Witter19: Hey Nellda, been a while. what's new?

Nellda: Loads. Guys, I need a favour.

15

Jack awoke to screaming. He jolted up from his makeshift bed on Nell's living room floor, instantly alert, and ran towards the sound, his limbs clumsy with sleep as he crashed down the hall. He rocked to a standstill, staring into a sea-green kitchen that had been turned upside-down. Scattered cereal, half-eaten chunks of bread and smashed mugs littered the floor, while the table had been flipped, chairs upended around it like prone turtles.

Amid it all, Huw stood shrieking. He pointed at the toaster, which was surrounded by coffee grains and torn teabags. Sumi and Anya hung back by the window, still in their pyjamas as they shot nervous glances at the toaster.

'What's going on?' Jack asked. Were the skalions attacking? Had Nebfet located them? He saw no armoured soldiers, though, only Nell dressed in a fluffy bathrobe and brandishing a broom as she approached the toaster.

'There's a rat or something,' Huw said. 'It's *huge!*'

Jack almost cried with relief, but a rat couldn't have caused this much destruction. The kitchen had been top-to-bottom trashed.

'Nell!' Anya shouted as something shot out from behind the toaster. A furry black-and-white shape darted forward and sank its teeth into the broom bristles, tugging as it growled, its tail whipping behind it like a live wire. Jack recognised it immediately.

'That's not a rat!' Sumi said.

'What is that thing?' Anya cried.

'Stop!' Jack shouted, preparing to go to the lub's aid, but it was too late. Nell swung the broom and the creature went with it, flapping wildly in the air before it finally released its grip on the bristles and sailed across the kitchen, smashing into an open cupboard.

'Wait,' Jack said, starting forwards, but then the window imploded.

As Anya and Sumi hit the floor to escape the shrapnel, Zavanna bowled inside, taking the table and counter in two confident leaps before she landed in a crouch by the cupboard.

'Is she here?' she demanded. 'Has Kunin Yillda descended?'

She crouched panting, positioned between the lub and the Guild. Her ears twitched and her gaze darted around the kitchen, taking in everything, braced for battle.

A stunned silence settled over the room. Jack had reached Huw's side and he sensed his shock. A whistling sound escaped his throat.

Nobody answered Zavanna's question.

'What… the…' Nell was propped against the counter, still clutching the broom.

Huw emitted a low hiss like air escaping a tyre. 'I'm-dreaming-I'm-dreaming-I'm-dreaming.'

'The lub,' Jack told Zavanna. 'It must have been hungry. Weren't you keeping an eye on it?'

Zavanna glanced behind her at the cupboard. 'I was guarding the fragment, not that impossible furball.'

'Who's screaming? What's happening?' Amelia appeared at Jack's side, her hair dripping, a towel in her hand. She took in the scene. 'Oh.'

'Is that what I think it is?' Anya murmured, steadying herself on a table leg as she stared at Zavanna.

'It's got to be animatronic,' Sumi said.

Jack considered agreeing with that, shielding both them and Zavanna from the truth, but the truth was right there in Nell's kitchen, unmistakably alive. She looked nothing like a puppet anymore, but a real-life kettu.

'She's real,' he said. 'So's the lub.'

'Lub,' Huw whispered. He hadn't moved from where he stood.

'Guys?' Toby staggered into the kitchen rubbing his eyes, his T-shirt and jeans rumpled. 'What's—' He stopped short at the sight of the mess, the stunned expressions, Zavanna tensed on the far side of the room, hackles raised.

Before Jack could try to explain, the cupboard emitted a happy yelp and the lub bounded out from its hiding place, hopping from the counter into Toby's arms. It buried its face in Toby's, a pink tongue scraping his cheeks, and he laughed.

'Hey, that tickles— Oh!'

The Guild gawped at him.

Huw looked like his jaw was about to fall off.

'Are the skalions here?' Brol asked as he materialised at Toby's side, struggling to hold on to the fragment box while brandishing his sword.

'There's two of them,' Huw whispered. He managed a short, stunned look at Brol before his eyes rolled back and he collapsed.

'Huw!' Toby yelled.

Jack grabbed him just in time and lowered him safely to the

kitchen floor, his damaged finger throbbing as he knocked it. He looked up at Amelia, who took a breath and turned to address the Guild.

'I suppose it's time we explained what's really going on.'

★

Ten minutes later, Nell handed Huw a coffee and squeezed his blanket-clad shoulder.

'I made it extra strong. It should help.'

Huw nodded and sipped, trembling as he sat at the kitchen table with Toby. The lub dozed in Toby's lap, its mouth open, while the kettu were seated on the other side of the table, their chins barely clearing the surface as they stuffed toast, bananas and chocolate croissants into their mouths.

Perched on a stool at the counter beside Anya and Sumi, Jack rubbed his neck and winced. The welt on his forehead still pounded, but it paled in comparison to the constant throbbing of his finger.

'So you're on a quest,' Nell said, buttering toast. 'A real quest.'

'Pretty much,' Jack said.

'That's awesome. And explains your T-shirt. Remind me to dig out some fresh clothes for you.'

'Thanks.'

There was an effortlessness about Nell that both put Jack at ease and made him nervous. He told himself to stop being an idiot. She wasn't anything like the SFF nerds he'd dated in the past. She was just being kind. Normal.

'We need to find the other fragments before tonight's lunium, uh, full moon,' Jack said, 'or Iri will become Kunin Yillda's for ever.'

'Kunin Yillda's real, too?' Huw looked a queasy shade of grey.

Toby pulled him into a hug. 'Don't worry, we'll protect you. Me and the lub. Man, it's so weird that I never heard of the lunium before this week. You'd think something as huge as an Iri Ragnarök would be common knowledge.'

'All we have now is this map of Bob Co.,' Jack said, tugging it out of his pocket and placing it in the middle of the table, 'which is pretty much useless—and Zavanna, where's the puzzle box?'

Zavanna set down her mug of coffee and retrieved the puzzle from her satchel.

'The dread sphere from Bob's study,' she said, placing it on top of the map. 'I feel certain it has broken greater minds than mine.'

Anya leaned closer to get a better look at it. 'What do you think is inside?'

Zavanna shrugged. 'You might ask the same of Bobson's skull.'

Toby snorted. Jack couldn't tell if he should be insulted or touched that she'd made him the butt of a kettu joke.

'May I?' At Zavanna's nod, Anya picked it up and gently shook it by her ear, frowning when no sound came.

'Anya once solved a Rubik's cube in seven seconds,' Nell said, patting Fin's side as the dog sat between her feet. 'That's only a few seconds shy of the world record.'

Jack smiled. She was talking to him like a friend. Like he was part of the Guild. It felt good.

'What are these numbers?' Sumi had picked up the map and was scrutinising a series of numbers in the upper right corner. Jack hadn't paid them much attention before. He had been too focussed on finding the Shadow Glass.

'I don't know,' he said.

'This long one, it looks like an ISBN.'

'So it's a reference to a book?' Toby asked.

Sumi nodded. 'Looks like it. Please talk among yourselves for a moment.'

She went into the living room, returning a few seconds later with an armful of books.

'Those were ordered alphabetically,' Nell said, her voice tight. Then she waved her hand. 'Ah, knock yourself out. I like alphabetising.'

While Anya worked the puzzle box, Sumi went back to the counter and started checking through the books.

'Do you go to the toilet?' Huw asked Brol meekly. At the kettu's blank look, he blushed. 'Sorry. I just wondered. You're eating and you look real, like not puppets, so I wondered... Never mind.'

Brol chewed slowly and said, 'I relieved myself in the wilderness before sunrise.'

Huw smiled.

'AHA!'

Sumi jumped up from her stool, a hardback book open in her hands. 'I knew it. The ISBN on the map matches the *Compendium of Iri Creatures and Creations.*' She lay the book on the kitchen table for them to see. 'And the second number, ninety-seven, I'm guessing that's a page reference.'

She flipped to page ninety-seven. It showed one of Rick Agnor's designs, an interconnecting motif of triangles and circles that filled two pages. They mapped out the stars, detailing Iri constellations, which were all named after figures from Iridian mythology.

'Bob wanted us to look at this page,' Sumi murmured. 'But why?'

'Something to do with Rick Agnor?' Jack asked. 'He helped Dad create Iri. Maybe he knows something.'

'I really hope not,' Amelia said. 'He's impossible to get hold of.

No email, no fax even. You have to call and there's no guarantee he'll answer.'

The Guild blinked at her.

Jack understood their interest: he had never met Agnor, either. At least, he had no memories of him. As far as he knew, Agnor hadn't been seen since he worked on *The Shadow Glass*, and there were no photos of him in any of the books. In fact, Jack wasn't sure he'd ever seen a photo of him. He made Bob look positively sociable.

'Do you think he'll be at the mini-Con?' Sumi asked.

Jack had forgotten the Con was happening today.

'I mean, it's at his old studio,' Sumi reasoned. 'What if he actually shows up this year?'

'What makes this year any different from last year?' Nell asked.

Sumi gestured at the kettu. 'I'd say they make things a little different.'

'Kudos,' Nell said. 'But we should stick to Bob's clues. They're the most likely to lead us to the fragments.'

Jack nodded in agreement and stared at the diagram in the book until he was sure his eyes were bleeding. It had to be relevant somehow.

Beside him, Zavanna stood on her chair to get a better view of the book.

'I do not see...' she began, but then she stopped. 'Wait.' She took the map of Bob Co. and laid it over the book page, pressing it flat against the diagram.

'Rithmar above,' she said.

'Holy shit,' Jack breathed.

Four squares on the map lined up with four of the constellations. Each constellation was annotated with a couple of letters, and the boxes on the map directly correlated with four of them.

'BC, JB, AT and RA,' Jack said. 'They look like initials.'

'Is this telling us where the fragments are hidden at Bob Co.?' Toby asked.

'I don't think so. I think it's telling us who has each one.'

'By Jove, I think he's right,' Anya said.

'BC must be Bob Co.,' Amelia said. 'That's where we found the first fragment. AT, those are my initials.'

Jack's heart raced. This felt so much like the breakthrough they had been waiting for, he could almost feel the fragments in his hands. 'Did Dad ever give you a box?'

She shook her head. 'No. I'm pretty sure I'd remember something as weird as that. AT has to be somebody or somewhere else.'

Anya jumped up, still clutching the puzzle box. 'All T'Orc! That's Rick Agnor's old studio. If BC means Bob Co., AT could mean Agnor's studio!'

'But RA has to be Rick Agnor,' Jack said.

'Maybe Agnor has two pieces?' Toby suggested. 'One at his studio and one at his home?'

Jack considered it. 'Seems like a stretch. Sort of dangerous, actually. It'd make it twice as easy for somebody to find half the Glass.'

'What about JB?' Anya asked.

'Jenny Bobbin,' Toby said.

Jack frowned. 'It can't be. She'd have told us she had it.'

'She told us the Glass had been broken up,' Toby said, stroking the lub. 'What if she knew that because she had one of the pieces?'

'But why wouldn't she tell us?'

Toby shrugged. 'Maybe we didn't earn it.'

He could be right. When they had showed up at Jenny's house yesterday afternoon, Jack hadn't exactly been on his best behaviour. What if Jenny had the piece but she had purposefully not told him?

'Shit,' he said. 'We have to go back there.'

'Agreed.' Toby nodded.

'Um, guys? Look.' Sumi was clutching her tablet. She propped it up on the counter so everybody could see. The screen showed the Bob Co. gates and, beyond them, the studio, which was half-concealed behind a sallow green fog. The sight caused Jack's stomach to hop into his throat.

At the gate, wearing a white suit that squeezed his neck, his hair slicked back, stood Wesley Cutter.

'Is that live?' Anya asked.

'It's on his website.'

'What's he doing?' Amelia asked, joining the others as they huddled around the screen. Jack hung back, frozen by the image of Cutter staring right at him. He stood at a podium and was clearly about to deliver some kind of speech. Jack wished he could reach into the screen and wrap his hands around Cutter's throat.

'*Thank you for coming*,' Cutter said. '*This is an auspicious day for Bob Co. and for film fans around the world.*'

'What is he doing?' Amelia demanded again. Everybody shushed her.

'*Bob Co. long ago proved it had lost its way*,' Cutter said, '*and it is my sad duty to report that Amelia Twine has chosen to step down as creative director of the studio. However, I am honoured and humbled that it has chosen me, a true film fan, to oversee the next phase of its productivity.*'

Jack felt paralysed.

All the colour drained from Amelia's face. She wasn't breathing. She stared at the tablet screen as if it were a gravestone. Jack noticed a suited man and a woman standing just behind Cutter. They smiled blithely but their smiles looked forced. They barely blinked.

'That's Frankie, the head of our legal team,' Amelia whispered. 'And Trent Smith-Williams, one of the stakeholders. What are they doing?'

'*From today,*' Cutter continued, '*I will oversee all operations at Bob Co. This is an exciting time for film and I believe Bob Co. should be at the forefront of cinematic endeavour. That is why, as new creative director, I am freezing all current productions in favour of a new slate that I am sure will excite fans of fantasy filmmaking. I want to thank you for your support during this transitionary period, and I guess all that's left to say is, well... action!*'

Cutter smirked down the camera lens as if his final word was a call to battle. One directed solely at Jack.

The livestream ended and Amelia paced the floor, then turned and yelled, 'What the *hell* is going on?'

'He's taken over Bob Co.,' Jack said, not believing it himself. He went to the screen and tried to rewind the broadcast.

'He can't!' Amelia cried.

'It seems nobody told him that.'

'But...' Amelia raked the air with her hands, didn't appear to know what to do with herself. Then she dug in her pocket and took out her phone. 'I'm calling Frankie.'

She tore from the room and he soon heard her shouting down the phone. The Guild exchanged bewildered looks. Toby had his arm around Huw, and Nell's knuckles shone white around her coffee mug.

'This is the man who allied himself with Kunin Yillda,' Zavanna said, joining Jack at the tablet. He had managed to pause the recording on Cutter's face. 'Who is he?'

'Dad's nemesis.'

Zavanna's eyes narrowed and she sniffed the screen with interest. 'I have seen this expression before. It is the look of one under Nebfet's thrall.'

'Cutter's been brainwashed?' Jack asked.

'The two behind.' Zavanna pointed. 'See the unnatural tint to their eyes. They are Nebfet's puppets now.'

She was right. The lawyer and the stakeholder looked unnaturally calm and there was a faint blue sheen to their eyes.

Cutter still looked like himself, though. He had finally achieved what he'd always dreamed of: Bob Co. was under his control. He could burn the place to the ground if he liked. But while he was smiling, there was no warmth in his expression. Cutter could claim to be the victor all he liked, but he didn't look triumphant. The victory was somehow hollow.

'He's older than I thought he'd be,' Anya said, still twisting the puzzle box.

'He looks like a ghost,' Sumi added.

'Does this mean there's not going to be a *Shadow Glass 2*?' Toby asked.

'CHRIST!'

Amelia stormed back into the kitchen, her cheeks flushed with fury. She looked like she was about to put her fist through a wall.

'Frankie says it's legitimate, it's really happening. But it can't be! She wouldn't just let Cutter take over Bob Co. She *couldn't* without my approval. And even then they'd need stakeholder approval and it would take *months*.'

'Nebfet's brainwashed her,' Jack said, 'and the stakeholder. Made the studio fall in line beneath Cutter and Kunin Yillda.'

'Nebfet's here, too?' Huw looked like he was about to vomit.

'Fuck,' Amelia breathed, her fury dissolving into despair.

'Why is Cutter doing this?' Sumi asked.

'He's the Keeper of Iri, right?' Jack said. 'He wants to control Iri as much as Kunin Yillda. And the best way to do that in *this* world is through Bob Co. The question is: why did Nebfet defend him in the chamber set? Why does she want him?'

Anya flicked her blonde hair as she stood. 'Because if a sovereign wants to invade new territory, claim it for herself, she needs somebody on the inside, somebody who knows that territory, its strengths and weaknesses. It's all over history. Cutter is her inside man. She's giving him what he wants so he'll serve her.'

'So she doesn't just want Iri—she wants *us* too,' Nell said. She cracked her knuckles. 'We really need to take this bitch down.'

'Hear, hear,' Anya and Sumi said.

'Cutter's posting all sorts of crap online, too,' Nell added. 'Last night he uploaded a story about you, Jack, that is clearly defamatory.'

A nerve twanged in Jack's temple. He almost daren't ask, wasn't sure he could take any more. 'Story?'

'Here.' Sumi sheepishly handed over her tablet and Jack looked at the screen, which showed an article with the headline: *'IT'S SH*T' — SON OF SHADOW GLASS DIRECTOR TRASHES FRANCHISE.* Anxiously, Jack scanned the story, seeing quotes attributed to him, his wounded forehead and finger thumping an anxious duet.

'What is this? Where's it posted?'

'Everywhere,' Sumi said, 'but it first went up on Cutter's site, Keeperofiri.com.'

'Shit. This is bad.'

Nell stood cradling her mug on the other side of the counter. 'You should report it. He can't make up stuff like that.'

A lump had formed in Jack's throat. He wanted to deny it all but he remembered Amelia asking him what he wanted, and he realised he wanted the Guild to like him. Which meant he couldn't lie to them.

'He didn't entirely make it up,' he said, so quietly he hoped nobody would hear him. When he saw that they were looking at him in question, he added, 'I was angry. I don't remember what I said.'

'You didn't say the franchise stuff was rubbish?' Sumi asked.

They weren't angry, he realised. They were hopeful he would deny it. But he had said those things during the Dune sale. Maybe not in as many words, but Cutter had teased out the sentiment behind his words. He had made Jack sound as vitriolic as possible.

'Jack?' Nell asked.

Even the kettu were looking at him now and Jack couldn't bear it. He felt the tug of doubt like somebody pinching his ear. The sense of unbelonging. He wasn't one of them. He wasn't part of the Guild. He jumped off the stool and paced from the fridge to the back door before circling back again, resisting the urge to run.

'Look,' he said, releasing a breath. 'I'm sorry, but yes, I said those things.'

'Why?' Nell asked. 'You didn't mean any of it.'

He almost laughed with relief. 'No, I didn't. Well, maybe at the time I thought I did. But not now.'

Toby crossed the kitchen and hugged him. Squashed between them, the lub squeaked in irritation and Jack felt four warm spots on his chest where the creature's feet pushed against him.

'It's okay, Jack.'

Jack nearly wept. He had thought they were about to turn on him. Instead, they had sided with him. They got it. He caught Zavanna looking at him in a curiously open way, her gaze uncharacteristically scorn-free. Was that approval in her expression?

'Cutter's going down,' Nell said, shaking her multicoloured hair. 'I've got the online community searching for anything that'll stop him on this ridiculous crusade. Don't worry, we're going to get him, Jack, even if we have to bust through a hundred firewalls to expose him as the snivelling cretin we all know he is.'

Jack almost couldn't speak. 'Thanks,' he said when he found his voice. 'Tell them to look into "Alden Smithee", too. It's a pseudonym he uses.'

'Affirmative.'

Jack rubbed his eyes with the heel of his hand and checked the clock on the microwave. It was already eight a.m. and light was beginning to glow through the smashed window.

'We should hit the road,' he said. 'If we split up we can cover more ground.'

'What's the plan, admiral?' Toby asked. One of Dorr's lines from the movie.

Jack smiled. 'I'll go to Jenny's with you. Amelia and the Guild, you head to All T'Orc, scout the place for anywhere Dad might have hidden a fragment. And the kettu should split up between us—they're the only ones with any battle training.'

'I don't have a pass to get into All T'Orc,' Amelia said.

Nell chuckled. 'I have a feeling they'll let you in.'

'You can have mine,' Toby said.

Amelia winked at him. 'Thank you.'

'We still get to go to the Con?' Huw asked. At their nods, he smiled and a little colour returned to his cheeks. 'What about Rick Agnor?'

'Assuming Jenny has the fragment,' Jack said, 'we'll go to Agnor's house after hers. Amelia, text me the address? Then we'll meet back up at Dad's house, by which point we should have the whole Glass. We can end this.'

'It is a sound plan, Bobson,' Zavanna said, gripping her satchel strap as she stood.

'Thank you,' Brol added, giving each of the Guild members an earnest look as he wiped crumbs from his chin. 'We are most humbled by your assistance, gilded comrades of new friend Toby.'

Huw burst into tears.

'Okay, let's—' Jack began, but Toby interrupted him.

'Wait wait wait.' He gave Jack a no-nonsense stare, gently rocking the lub in his arms. 'First, you have to say it.'

'Say what?'

'"I love *The Shadow Glass*."'

'Pffft.' Jack suppressed a laugh. 'I'm not saying that.'

'You are, or we can't help you.'

Jack found half a dozen sets of eyes riveted on him, and realised Toby wasn't joking.

'I…' he began. Behind the Guild, Amelia's mouth quirked into a smile. She was enjoying this.

'I…' Everybody leaned in, nodding encouragement. Jack swallowed. 'I don't hate *The Shadow Glass*.'

They all groaned and rolled their eyes. Toby patted him on the back. 'It's a start. We'll work on it.'

Leviathan

As rare as it is dangerous, the leviathan is a creature about which very little is known. Hulking at over fifteen feet tall, it is a fearsome carnivore with thick black fur, razor-sharp claws and enormous teeth evolved for shredding meat. It is best known for its violent temper and insatiable thirst for blood. In fact, its temper is so renowned throughout Iri that the leviathan remains one of the few Iridian creatures that skalions will actively avoid.

Fact file: *Baby leviathans have never been observed by another living creature, leading to the popular theory that leviathans emerge fully grown from enormous egg sacks buried in Iri caves.*

Mesaku

Birthed in the most violent of Iridian storms, the mesaku is one of the most formidable beasts in Iri. With a wingspan of over fifty feet, its grace is matched only by the wildness of its nature. Its rarity—they are glimpsed only in the most tempestuous lightning storms—means the mesaku has become a popular feature of Iridian myth. The Legend of Prip tells of a girl's quest to steal a mesaku egg, only for her to befriend the mesaku queen and join her ranks in battle against the ripozar (see p.59).

Fact file: The name 'mesaku' derives from the Japanese mesu kujaku, *meaning 'female peacock'.*

Jack changed into a faded bowling shirt Nell found in her wardrobe and dumped his ruined T-shirt into the kitchen bin.

'Frankie,' Jack said, reading the embroidered name on the pocket.

'My ex was a big fan. Here, take the hearse.' Nell dangled a pair of keys in front of him. 'It's not being used today.'

'Hearse?'

She shrugged. 'Amelia's Land Rover fits more people.'

He gulped and nodded, taking the keys and wishing they hadn't abandoned Bob's van on the outskirts of the studio. Then he, Toby and Brol left the Guild to change into their Con costumes. They went out the door just as Sumi started shouting about her missing bottle of fake blood, while Fin the dog ran past looking like roadkill.

On the road, Jack reassured himself that the hearse was just a car, nothing to get freaked out about, even if the air freshener swinging from the rear-view mirror seemed to be concealing all kinds of sinister scents. In the passenger seat beside him, Toby patted the lub, which perched on the dashboard like a living hood ornament, beeping with interest as it looked through the windscreen.

In the seatless back, Brol clung to the fragment box, blissfully unaware that the flat bed he sat on usually held a coffin. He wore a grey dog sweater over his armour, the hood pulled up over his ears. Nell had said it would help him blend in, but the effect was even more alarming than the sight of a living kettu.

It was odd seeing Brol without Zavanna. They came as a pair and Brol seemed somehow diminished without her. With a start, Jack realised he missed Zavanna. She was strangely calming. Her worldview straightforward. Her temperament unforgiving. Her consistency was reassuring and he hoped she was okay, then he scoffed. When had Zavanna ever *not* been okay?

'Do you really think Jenny has it?' he asked Toby. Driving with one less finger was still tricky and he avoided moving his hand as much as possible. Every time the bandaged stump knocked the wheel, he wanted to scream.

'I really hope so,' Toby said.

'I just hope she's in a good mood.'

Brol spoke up from the back. 'A fresh kill always improves Zavanna's temper. I ask her to take me on a hunt when I know I must broach a sensitive topic.'

Toby laughed. 'Yeah, maybe we should try that.'

It took them over an hour to reach Jenny's bungalow. As he parked, Jack saw that the clouds crowding the sky held a greenish tint, and he wondered if the sickly mist hanging over Bob Co. was spreading. Would it eventually engulf London and beyond?

In the driveway, a pair of legs stuck out from beneath an old Volvo, tools scattered around them. Jack told the others to wait in the car and hurried to the drive. The sparkly laces in Jenny's white sneakers were the only clue he needed that the pair of legs beneath the vehicle belonged to her.

'Uh, hi Jen,' he said.

She wheeled herself out from under the car and blinked up at him through a pair of safety goggles.

'Jackie? I didn't expect to see you for another ten years.'

'Touché.'

She got up from the ground, dusting herself off and pushing the goggles up into her silver hair. He tried to avoid looking at the damaged garage door, the site of his disfigurement, which she had covered with tarpaulin.

Jenny noticed the waiting hearse. 'Is everything all right?' Her California accent was as robust as ever.

'It's complicated.' His new favourite catchphrase.

'Okay.' She drew out the letters so that they formed a much longer word, one that contained roughly five different meanings, and he could tell she was worried his mere presence might result in yet more property damage. He offered her the best smile he could muster on five hours' sleep.

'Can we talk?'

'Christ on a croissant,' she huffed. 'Anybody else showed up here after what you did to my studio, I'd send 'em packing. But that smile, kid.'

She shook her head as she cleaned her hands on a cloth and beckoned him to follow her.

'Shoes,' she said at the door, and he wiped his scuffed soles before following her into the kitchen. Jenny repeated her tea-brewing routine as he leaned against the counter. Just twenty-four hours ago, he had struggled to be in here, found memories lurking in every corner. Today, though, he felt somehow safe. Jenny's bungalow folded around him like a hug.

'How's the hand?' she asked.

'Right, fine,' he said. 'Minor flesh wound.'

'Hmm.' Her pale eyes glimmered at him as she studied his face.

'I wanted to talk to you,' he said.

'Yes, you mentioned that.'

She was being deliberately cagey. Although he didn't blame her, he found it unnerving. She had wanted to talk yesterday and he had shut her down. Now, she was doing the same in return. He wished he could find a way to break down the barrier between them, not just because she might have a fragment, but because he really had missed her.

'I'm, uh, going through something,' he said. 'But I'm trying to do better. I'm trying to fix things.'

'Oh yes? You could start with the garage door.'

He definitely deserved that. Instead of shrinking away, though, he reached for the thorny bramble of emotions branching through his chest.

'Things were difficult,' he said. 'Dad was difficult. And I didn't make it easy for him. But he's gone now and I have to live with that.' He wiped his face with his non-bandaged hand. 'Look, I'm still looking for the Shadow Glass, and I think maybe Dad left a piece of it with you.'

She considered him for a moment, as if weighing something in her mind, and then sighed. She flicked off the kettle. 'Come.'

They went into the living room. It was every bit the artist's utopia, bustling with exotic art and so many patterns he thought he was having a bad trip. Maybe he was.

'It was the darnedest thing,' Jenny said as she opened the doors of an enormous dresser. 'Only way I got to see him in the past was by pitching up on his doorstep and forcing him to let me in. But then two months ago, boom, there he was on *my* front step, looking older'n Zeus and wanting to take a stroll down memory lane. I should've sent him packing right there and then.'

She huffed as she brought out a large brown object. The sight of it caused Jack's fingertips to hum. It was a box identical to the one they had found at Bob Co. He balled his good hand into a fist, stilling his excitement, watching as Jenny set it on the coffee table and stepped back.

'Course,' Jenny said, 'I never could say no to Bob, or his son.'

They stared at the box as if Bob himself was about to pop out of it brandishing flags and streamers.

'Do you mind if I…?' Jack asked.

'Knock yourself out.'

He trembled as he approached it. What if the box contained nothing more than a keepsake from his father and Jenny's time together? It could be old crockery or a puppet or the banjo they had sometimes played.

Please god, don't let it be the banjo.

His fingers found the clasp and he tugged, lifting the lid.

Black wood gleamed up at him, smooth and intricately carved, and there it was, nestled in purple fabric, almost identical to the one they had found in Bob Co.

The second fragment.

Like the first, it looked like more than a mere movie prop, and if he listened closely, he could hear it humming a series of notes. They trembled not in his eardrums but in the atoms of his being. Otherworldly but oddly calming.

There was no mistaking it.

Here was another piece of the real Shadow Glass, imbued with the spirit and hopes of Iri.

Jack crouched closer to make sure he wasn't seeing things, because this felt too easy. They had fought tooth and claw for the first fragment, but the second was just sitting there in Jenny's lounge. Where was the catch?

'I gotta admit, when I first saw what it was, I didn't understand,' Jenny said. 'But then I realised what it meant: the Glass belonged to all of us. Those of us who loved it first, before it became this cult thing the kids go crazy for. So he gave us a piece to keep forever. A month later, he was dead.'

He hadn't realised his father was so sentimental.

'Do you know who else has one?' Jack asked, still staring, as if the fragment might vanish at any moment.

Jenny's gaze became pointed. 'He said you'd come knocking one day. That you'd ask about the Glass. I thought it was his usual talk, but then who turned up on my doorstep, completely out of the blue?'

She considered the fragment. 'He said something I didn't understand until just now. That I shouldn't give this to you unless you were ready. That I'd know if you were.' She tutted, her eyes misting over. 'But it's the last thing he ever gave me. The only thing I have to remember him by.'

Jack bit down the tremor surging through him. He felt for her, but he needed the fragment. There was more than just her feelings at stake. He sensed what he had to do. Digging deep, he found the words he should have said when he first knocked on her door.

'I'm sorry,' he said. 'About everything.'

Her eyes crinkled in question.

'I know I owe you an explanation and a missing puppet and a cheque for the damage to your garage, but… and I know this sounds ridiculous, but I really need this fragment.'

'You want it, or you need it?'

'Both. And I can't explain why.' He took a breath. 'I felt like he was pushing me away. The whole time, ever since the book-burning in the nineties. Dad pushed me away, so I pushed him back. Made it impossible for him to hurt me. And it worked. Too well.'

He examined his bandaged hand.

'If I think about it, it probably started with Mum's death. I know Dad and I were inseparable when I was little. I've seen the pictures. He was amazing. Nobody told stories like him, but then the film came out and he started on this obsessive crusade that crashed and burned. For the longest time, I had nobody.'

'She died so young, your mother,' Jenny murmured. 'Labour isn't as straightforward as it is in the movies. I think you're right. Your mother's death left its mark on you both, how could it not? But it wasn't your fault, Jackie.'

'It's what he said,' Jack said, feeling pressure behind his eyes.

'What who said?'

'Dad. When I was fifteen, I found him in the kitchen. It wasn't even lunchtime, and he'd been drinking and looking at a picture of her. I tried to help him up to his room but he pushed me away, got angry, and he knocked over the picture. It smashed on the floor. He lost it. He said he wanted her, not me. He yelled at me to go away, to leave him alone. He only wanted her.'

He shivered, a chill creeping over his skin. He hadn't spoken to anybody about this. Not a single person for over twenty years. The worst thing Bob had ever said. The worst things

Jack thought about himself. That he had killed his own mother. That he was responsible for his father's misery. That he didn't deserve to live.

Jenny stepped towards him. 'He should never have said that. Christ, that man. The booze… He didn't mean it, Jackie. It wasn't your fault.'

He nodded. 'I know.'

'Jack, you have to believe it.'

The fragment blurred as his vision moistened with tears.

'He got me,' he said, his voice hoarse, 'but he lost her. How is that fair?'

'It's not. None of this is.'

His father's outburst changed things forever. From then on, Jack saw Bob as a thing that dwelled in darkness.

Only now was he beginning to see the man behind the monstrous behaviour. His impression of Bob was changing, the way a turn of a kaleidoscope refocuses its colours. He saw both the obsessive drunk and the old man broken by circumstance.

'I loved him,' Jack said. 'Even after everything, I loved him and I never told him. Not once in the past twenty years.'

Jenny's arms went around him and he shuddered against her.

'You didn't do anything wrong, kid,' she said. 'Not a thing.' She eased him back, her voice as soft as the stuffing in her many puppets. 'Your father always said to me he had two great loves of his life: you and that movie. Neither of you ever disappointed him.'

He stood absorbing her words, wanting to believe them, hoping they held at least a little truth. He wiped his face and smiled.

'You always had this effect on me.'

Jenny laughed and then shook her head at him, sighing.

'Take the damn fragment,' she said. 'But if you don't bring it back, I'll hunt you down and use your skin for a canvas.'

He wrapped his arms around her. 'Thank you. Thanks so much. You won't regret this.'

'I already am. You're going to be okay, Jackie. I wasn't so sure yesterday, but today something's different.'

He closed the box and lifted it from the table.

'Do you know who else has a piece of the Glass?' he asked.

'Now you're pushing it.' She smiled. 'Bob never said, but my guess would be Rick Agnor has one.'

Jack nodded. 'I'll be back. For some reason I have a hankering for a game of Hero Quest, and I know just the barbarian to play with.'

'I'll keep the fire alive.' One of Dune's lines. Her eyes twinkled at him.

Excerpt from A Compendium of Iri Creatures and Creations *by A.J. Lucas.*

Loper

With their long legs and slight build, lopers are made for long-distance excursions, so they are the perfect companions for explorers. Despite their impressive height they are incredibly swift, and are known to cover huge distances with greater speed than any other Iri creature. Although timid, they will attack if their habitats are threatened—a single kick can crack a skalion's skull.

Fact file: Lopers have a distinct cry that is said to be heard for miles. The claim that they are the only Iri animal that never sleeps remains unconfirmed.

17

'How'd Jenny's go?' Amelia asked as she led Jack, Toby and Brol away from the cobbled side street and into the warehouse.

Jack was still getting used to the fact that she was wearing a bright red wig. Amelia's lips were slicked the same black as her dress, and a red cape was fastened around her neck. She looked nothing like the studio exec who had ambushed him at Kettu House just yesterday.

'Oh, I'm Power Gal apparently,' she said, waving a hand as they approached a bank of security tables in the lobby. 'Nell insisted I costume up.'

Jack nodded, distracted by the hum of activity beyond security. He glimpsed the bustling warehouse space, seeing elf ears and purple wigs and leather bodices. A banner over the door read *ALL T'ORC MINI-CON*, a dragon curling through the letters.

If they had been anywhere other than the convention, Amelia would have stuck out like a troll at a tea party. Here, though, she fitted in completely. It was Jack and Toby who were conspicuous in their civilian clothes, although at least Toby had the lub on his shoulder.

Jack just hoped they had made the right decision coming to the Con rather than heading to Rick Agnor's house. The clues still didn't add up, and they couldn't afford to waste any time. The drive to Shoreditch alone had taken an hour and he felt tetchy with nerves, aware of every minute that slipped silently by. He had hidden the fragment boxes in the back of the hearse and triple-checked the car was locked before meeting Amelia.

Although she and the Guild hadn't found the third fragment, Amelia had secured three press passes from the event organiser. Apparently they knew each other.

Now, Jack, Toby and Brol flashed the badges at security, who let them through without so much as a second look.

They stepped through a set of doors into the main warehouse and the explosion of colourful stalls rendered Jack speechless.

All T'Orc clamoured with witches, monsters and elves. Everywhere he looked they gathered around stalls, checking out memorabilia, leafing through comics, and taking selfies with guests who sat signing their merchandise. There were banners and posters (*The New Adventures of Ellen Dritch!*) and stall after stall of geeky knick-knacks, tottering book towers, T-shirts (*'LUB YOURSELF!'*) and more props and figurines than he could count.

'It is a festival,' Brol marvelled. 'Is this neutral territory? Such intermingling of tribes should surely result in conflict.'

'Just don't get into a *Game of Thrones* versus Middle-earth debate,' Toby said.

Jack spotted a large cardboard cut-out of the Shadow Glass, which belonged to a stall selling kettu and skalion plushies, a whole fluffy table piled high with them. He noticed the novelisation of the film, plus Gurchin tea towels, badges, mugs and bookmarks. So much *Shadow Glass* merch he had no idea was out there.

None of this would exist without Bob. The laughing, smiling cosplayers living out their movie fantasies, becoming their favourite characters, living as heroes for a day. Bob had provided an escape for them, Jack realised. A safe place. This wasn't about using nostalgia as a shield, it was about celebrating the things that defined them, the characters that spoke to their heart's truth, the things that made them different and unique and powerful in their own special way. It united them.

Bob would have loved it.

'Jack,' Amelia said, snapping him back to attention. 'Do you have the second piece or not?'

'Right,' he said. 'Second fragment secured.'

'Shit, that's amazing! So there are only two left to find.'

'I wouldn't celebrate just yet,' Jack deadpanned, raising his bandaged hand.

'In Iri, we celebrate by drinking ranken blood,' Brol said.

Toby screwed up his face. 'That sounds disgusting.'

'It is, and magnificent.'

Somebody bumped Jack, and he moved out of the way of a tall man wrapped in a thick winter coat. Fur puffed up around the man's throat and fell to his knees, while his sweat-spackled bald head shone pasty white in the strip lighting. He glared at Jack as he lumbered past, then continued on into the convention, wading between the other guests like a giant in a forest.

'What's he supposed to be?' Jack said.

'Maybe one of the coats from Narnia?' Toby suggested.

Jack wrinkled his nose. A tangy metallic smell lingered in his nostrils. He shuddered, certain it had come from the fur-coat man.

'Where are the others?' he asked, refocussing on Amelia but fighting a sense of surrealism in the presence of her red wig and cape.

'They fanned out to search,' she said. 'There's just this room, plus a couple of gallery areas, and an off-limits staircase that must lead to the offices. Zavanna's with them, just in case. I think Sumi has a nerd-crush on her. I think I do, too.'

Jack smiled, but he was beginning to worry they wouldn't find the fragment here. He still didn't understand why his father would give half of the Shadow Glass to Rick Agnor. It seemed too risky. If the initials RA and AT referred to Agnor and his gallery, why not just group them together as one clue?

Meanwhile, he thought, as he scanned the sea of cosplayers, if the third fragment was here, how were they supposed to locate it amid all these people?

'There'll be a marker,' he said, 'like the one at Bob Co. Let's look.'

'Oh my god, you're adorable!'

A woman dressed as Winnie from *Hocus Pocus* had spotted Brol. She crouched down to get a better look at him, her buck teeth nearly popping out of her mouth as she smiled up at Jack.

'Is he yours? He's a kettu, isn't he? I love *Shadow Glass*! What's your name, little one?'

'I am Brol of the Vex tribe. Well met, new friend.'

The woman shrieked with laughter and dug in her purse. 'Oh god, he's killing me! Can you take our picture?'

'Actually—' Jack began.

'Here.' Amelia took the phone and the woman put her arm around Brol, smiling as their picture was taken. Brol looked dazed by the flash, his top lip creeping up in a show of pleasure.

As the woman took back her phone and got to her feet, her ginger wig rocked precariously on her head.

'This is going on Instagram *immediately*,' she said. 'You're so lucky you have a son who loves cosplay. Mine lives on his Xbox. Bill! Come look at this!'

A man wearing an eyepatch and leather trousers joined them. 'A kettu! Well met, bruv!'

Within seconds, a crowd had closed around them. Frodos, Madmartigans, Riddlemasters and Buffys goggled at Brol, cooing and attempting to push back his hood. Brol clung on to it, shrinking back from their delighted laughs.

'He looks so real!' one cried.

'That *fur*! It must have cost a fortune.'

'Can we get a picture?'

'Come on,' Jack said, ushering Brol ahead of him past a green-skinned witch. Disappointed sighs sounded behind him but he kept going, Amelia and Toby hurrying in his wake.

'Hey, is that a lub?' a unicorn asked.

'Just keep moving,' Jack said, pushing past him, 'and keep your eyes peeled.'

'This tribe is friendly if strange,' Brol said.

'You can say that again.'

'This tribe is friendly if strange.'

'Yeah, yeah.'

They passed a stall selling crystals, some of them carved into dancing kettu, others threaded onto slender chains. A collection of rings bore kettu symbols.

'Is that official merchandise?' Toby asked.

Amelia slowed as she studied the wares. 'I'll pretend I wasn't here.'

They kept going. Jack scanned the upper rafters of the building, looking for symbols that might help them uncover the fragment. And, he realised, he was keeping an eye out for Zavanna, too. Not because he worried about her but because, somewhere along the way, he'd started feeling better when she was close by. If Zavanna thought this was a waste of time, she'd waste no time telling him.

He spotted a coffee stand called Ye Olde Brewe serving fantasy drinks: Falkor Frappuccinos, Lub-ly Lattes and, he noticed with a grimace, Kunin Roast Koffee.

The bald man in the fur coat stood against the wall, watching him. His skin was marble-white, his eyes sunken into dark pits, and Jack couldn't tell if it was make-up or his real complexion that gave him the sickly appearance.

Something dripped from the hem of the man's coat. A speck of red stood out against the grey floor. Was he bleeding?

'Guys, you made it!'

A woman slapped Jack on the back. It took him a second to recognise Nell; she wore a winged gold headdress and a white-and-gold onesie. Of course she had come as She-God, Man-Hero's long-lost sister.

At her feet, Fin panted with excitement, dressed in a *Ghostbusters* jacket with a proton pack on her back. Sumi had transformed into an ice-skinned vampire, while Anya looked like something out of *Flash Gordon*, wearing a spiky gold headband and a metallic dress with pointed shoulders. Huw's camel-coloured tunic and curling snake necklace meant he could only be Atreyu.

'Where's Zavanna?' Jack asked.

'She's scouting the rest of the building,' Sumi said. 'She's like a ninja.'

'I wish I had my costume,' Toby said, eyeing his friends.

'Save it for MCM,' Huw told him.

'Jack, we can't get into the gallery,' Nell said. 'But I think they're letting press through. I figure if the fragment's anywhere, it's in there, away from the crowds. This way.'

Jack nodded and noticed that Anya was still working the puzzle box. She was so focussed on it that she kept bumping into other guests as Nell led them to the back of the warehouse, where a couple of guards stood either side of a stone arch.

'You guys keep looking out here,' Jack told them. 'Toby, Brol and I will search the gallery.'

There was still no sign of Zavanna, and Jack wondered if he'd done something wrong. If she was avoiding him.

He went to the gallery door and raised his pass at one of the guards, who nodded and stepped aside. Jack winked at Amelia, going through with Toby and Brol.

The sudden quiet rang in his ears.

They ambled into a softly lit space filled with paintings. Rick Agnor originals hung around the white walls, some of them small studies, others huge canvases swirling with watercolour. At the centre of the floor, a knotted tree spread branches up to the ceiling, fairy lights entwined around each limb to cast a warm aura over the gallery.

'The Yggram tree,' Brol breathed.

Jack wavered before it, awestruck by the detailing, the names etched into the bark, but he knew they were running out of time. They could sightsee another day.

'Look for symbols,' he said, moving around the walls, searching the paintings. He noted crouched goblins and frolicking fairies, waterfalls frothing with life, forests that looked dead until he moved closer and saw creatures poking out from every mushroom and plant.

But there were no symbols. Nothing that might lead them to the fragment.

'Iri,' Brol said.

Jack turned and saw him gazing up at a tiny frame. He went to stand behind the kettu, seeing that the picture was a rough ink study of the nightmare swamp. He scanned the frame and the wall around it for kettu symbols, but there was nothing.

He reached for the picture, preparing to check the wall, when a voice croaked behind him.

'Not my best work, I'll admit. Nevertheless, it's what I saw in my mind.'

Jack found a short man half-smiling up at him. He could be no more than three feet tall, but it wasn't his diminutive stature that surprised Jack, it was his attire.

The man wore a fluoro Hawaiian shirt under a black bomber jacket, his white hair slicked back from a face so creased with age the chestnut skin resembled soft leather. A gnarled hand rested on an equally gnarled cane, and the man took off his neon green sunglasses to squint up at Jack with mischievous eyes that flashed green-blue.

'You're Rick Agnor?' Jack murmured.

'Hello, Jack, I'm so glad you made it this far.'

Rick Agnor foreword taken from the book The Power of the Shadow Glass *(Goliath Publishing).*

My earliest memory of *The Shadow Glass* is of sitting in Bob Corman's study while he regaled me with stories of Iri. He was a natural storyteller and I would sit entranced as he talked of Dune and Dorr, their bravery as they set out to wrest the world of Iri back from the claws of the skalion queen. Even now, decades later, I recall the way his eyes lit up and his hands moved, casting shadows on the wall that seemed to dance with life. He was his own kind of magician.

It was raining the first day of shooting. I remember squelching through puddles to Bob's office, which I had visited many times before. When I got there, though, he was nowhere to be seen, and it was with irritation that I squelched back out into the rain, making my way to Sound Stage 9. By the time I reached it, I was soaked through and cursing, but when I stepped inside, I was transported.

Iri was everything I had ever imagined. I can say that with absolute certainty, as it was my drawings that partly inspired the images that ended up on-screen. But the wonderful production designers had worked wonders with my sketches. When I stepped into Rill's cosy dwelling for the first time, it was truly like coming home. The level of detail was quite staggering. I had no trouble imagining that Rill the mystic had lived there for centuries, helping Dune and giving him the lub before packing him off to fight another day.

The great challenge at the heart of *The Shadow Glass* was to create a brand new world that felt not only realistic, but also packed with history and meaning. I worked tirelessly with Bob to flesh out every part of Iri, from the smallest ceremonial spoon to the biggest leviathan and everything in-between, so that when you watched the film, you sensed there was more to this world than the small piece you were being shown on-screen.

In the end, I believe that is the power of *The Shadow Glass*. It is bigger, richer, and more complete than any fantasy film has any right to be. And therein lies its own kind of magic.

— *Rick Agnor, 2006*

18

'I believe you're looking for something?' Rick Agnor said.

Jack couldn't speak. Or blink. Or move. He stared at the man leaning on his cane, so different to how he had always pictured him in his mind, and yet in no way a disappointment. Deep wrinkles spidered from the corners of his eyes and he looked like he had stepped through a portal from 1986. Either that, or nobody had told him that fashion had moved on since the days of mullets and high-top sneakers.

Jack sensed the atmosphere ossifying about him. It was as if Agnor had his own centre of gravity, and Jack felt himself drawn towards him, leaning in, blood thumping in his ears while a strange sense of calm settled his mind.

Behind Agnor, at the gallery door, two men in black suits stood staring into space, earpieces spiralling into their shirt collars. Agnor, it seemed, had guards.

'It's a pleasure to meet you, Jack,' Agnor said, his voice scratchy with age and yet somehow still spritely, sparkling with affection.

'I… you too.' Jack swallowed, trying to scrape his thoughts back together. They had scattered across the floor the second he laid eyes on Agnor.

'How did you know we're looking for something?' he asked.

Agnor tapped the cane to his temple. 'It's possible to see with more than your eyes, young man. Come. All of you.'

He hobbled across the gallery, his sneakers squeaking as he disappeared through a small doorway Jack hadn't noticed before. In fact, he was sure it hadn't been there when they entered the gallery. He looked at Toby, who had clamped his mouth shut, perhaps to prevent another nerd-purge, the lub oddly silent on his shoulder. Then Toby mouthed, '*Come on!*'

In a daze, Jack ducked through the door after Agnor, Toby and Brol following behind him.

He found himself in a snug lounge festooned in eighties memorabilia. Movie and band posters plastered the walls, Gizmo and Marty McFly sharing space with Cyndi Lauper and Wham! A boom box crackled the deep-space melodies of Brian Eno, while the carpet zigzagged with a busy retro print.

Jack sensed something watching him and saw a cat. Then another. And another. They were everywhere, dozing on bookcases, legs dangling over the edges of tables, curled up by the heater that bathed everything in an ochre glow. The lub cooed from Toby's shoulder.

'I'm so happy you came,' Agnor said as he settled into a petite leather armchair that must have been custom made. 'Please, sit. Tea?'

Jack watched him tip a teapot shaped like ET's head, filling four teacups. He lowered himself into a larger armchair opposite Agnor as, beside him, Toby and Brol stood watching the man with interest. By the door, the guards stood with their hands clasped, staring ahead, as if this wasn't the strangest room they had ever seen.

'You really love the eighties,' Jack said.

'What's not to love?' Agnor chuckled. 'Pick any letter of the alphabet and the eighties had it covered. Look at "P". Polaroid cameras, Picard, Pound Puppies, Pacino, Push Pops, Pac-Man! Or "M"… mobile phones, Maverick, Madonna, Molly Ringwald, MTV! It was the pinnacle of popular culture. A veritable utopia! Now tell me, are you enjoying the convention?'

Toby nodded and Jack tried to wrestle free from the shock. He was having tea with Rick Agnor in a shrine to eighties pop culture. Reality seemed to have completely untethered itself from the universe.

'I've never been good with crowds,' Agnor said, 'but I love the energy the convention generates. This building hums with it months after the event itself. It's invigorating. I always paint best in those months.'

'I can't believe you're here,' Toby murmured.

'Had to be,' Agnor said, setting down the teapot. 'I couldn't miss out on a chance to meet you, Toby.'

'Me?'

Agnor nodded, passing him a teacup and saucer. 'Your love for Iri is a pure, white light. So pure I could sense it even if you were on the other side of the world. That kind of love transcends earthly restraints. It is special and should be treasured.'

Toby's hand shook, the tea spilling into the saucer.

'You must learn boldness,' Agnor said. 'Self-belief. It is there in you already. You just have to trust it.'

Toby nodded, quietly absorbing his words.

'And Brol.' Agnor shifted his attention to the kettu as he passed him another tea. 'How remarkable. A real-life kettu! I'm afraid I have no ranken blood to celebrate with, but I hope tea will suffice.'

Brol bowed. 'I shall pretend it tastes of ranken blood, wise one.'

'Most kind. I always wanted to see you in action,' Agnor said. 'Your reputation precedes you. I hear you are kind but fierce, a most potent combination.'

He passed the final teacup. 'Jack. Your journey has been the most unsettled. You have searched the longest, fought the hardest, and yet your quest is far from over. It is only just beginning.'

'How do you know these things?' Toby asked, his voice scratching.

Agnor smiled, his face wrinkling even more. 'Why, because of Iri.' His blue-green eyes sparkled. 'I am a creature of Iri, but you probably know me under another name. My first name. Back in the eighties, I was called Rill.'

Jack's thoughts scattered again, marbles skittering into the corners of the room. He stared at Agnor, trying to understand, to figure out the punchline to what was a very strange joke. But the more he looked at him, the more he saw the likeness between Agnor and the Rill puppet, the one that had appeared in *The Shadow Glass*. They had the same face shape and slight build, and beneath his bushy eyebrows, Agnor's eyes twinkled with an otherworldly wisdom, just as Rill's had.

'Rill?' Jack breathed. 'You can't be.'

'Here,' Agnor said. He set down his teacup and tugged up his sleeve, flashing his white forearm. Jack couldn't tell what he was trying to show him, but then he blinked and moved closer, seeing a faint, glimmering line running from Agnor's wrist to his elbow.

'Stitch line,' Agnor said, stroking it with short fingers. 'Almost gone but still there. We need reminders like this. Things that tell us where we've come from, where we've been, what has changed and what hasn't.'

'I don't understand,' Jack said.

Agnor winked. 'Funny how things come full circle, isn't it? It's the way of the universe. But, yes, before I was Rick Agnor, I was Rill. I've been Agnor the artist for so long I sometimes forget, but then I look at these stitch lines and I remember. I'm Iridian, always will be.'

'But I thought you helped Dad create *The Shadow Glass*? You drew Iri.'

'Oh yes.' Agnor pushed his sleeve back down. 'I suppose an occasion like this calls for a little exposition.' He squinted at Jack. 'Did you know your father based Rill on one of his childhood toys? It was made by his grandmother. When he was working on his first drafts of *The Shadow Glass*, that toy sat on his desk. Rill was the first character Bob imagined, a wise old mystic inspired by the toy his grandmother had made.'

He leaned closer. 'And do you know what happened? Bob imagined so hard that I came into being, animated the toy. I leapt from nothing to something.' He clicked his fingers. 'It was in your father's study that the first Iridian creature came to life.'

Jack couldn't believe what he was hearing. As much as he had been forced to set aside his scepticism, this was beyond all comprehension.

If that were true, Rill had been here since the eighties. Jack's gaze roved from the man's wizened face to his mittened hands. Then he peered at Brol. The kettu had become more lifelike in little more than a day, his black-and-brown fur thickening, his muscles hardening. Had the same thing happened to Rill? Was the man sitting opposite him the result of two decades spent in this world?

'I helped Bob,' Agnor continued. 'We were the original architects of Iri. He was words, I was pictures. We built it together, one creature at a time, until we had the makings of a universe. And, of course, there was Jenny Bobbin and the set designers, the lighting crew and the best boys. In their own way, they made Iri, too. A film is more than just one person, as is a world.'

He winked. 'Naturally, I played a small part in the movie, too. Bob himself puppeteered me, or so it seemed to the crew. In reality, it was my greatest performance. My *only* performance.'

'If you're Rill,' Jack said, 'why did you call yourself Rick Agnor? Why the charade?'

Agnor's eyebrows danced. 'I couldn't very well remain Rill in this world, now, could I? No, I had to create my own life, away from Bob. After *The Shadow Glass* was completed, I became Rick Agnor. I *am* Rick Agnor. Rick and Rill, both and neither.'

Jack puffed a breath. It was too much to take in. The idea that Rick Agnor was himself an Iridian seemed outrageous.

He realised he had found the answer to what would happen if they abandoned their search. If they failed to reassemble the Glass and Iri perished, Zavanna and Brol would be marooned on Earth for ever. Forced into hiding. Fugitives in an alien world. And it would only be a matter of time before the skalions poisoned everything they touched, creeping across the planet as a scaly, ravenous contagion, dooming Earth to the same fate as Iri.

'I can't believe it,' he murmured.

'Belief!' Agnor cried. He slapped his thigh. 'Belief is precisely what powers Iri! It has grown immeasurably since the eighties, fuelled by the singular love of the fans, those who experienced Iri on screens and in books. We forget how to accept the fantastical. Children accept everything, embrace every strange or mundane thing they encounter. We think we get older and wiser but we should be more like them. We *can* be. All we have to do is believe.'

'That's easy for you to say,' Jack said.

Brol stepped forward, his teacup tottering on its saucer. 'Rill, wise lord of Iri, we must call on your aid. Time runs thin and we must find the Shadow Glass before the lunium, or the balance shall for ever tip in the skalions' favour, and Iri shall be doomed. Will you help us?'

The smile on Agnor's face made the hairs on Jack's forearms bristle, because he was looking at Jack, not the kettu.

'The lunium, yes. A most interesting development.'

'You've heard of it?' Toby asked.

'Oh yes. It wasn't always a part of the fabric of Iri, but it is now. You see, Toby, Bob created Iri, but others have contributed to his world. That is the power of belief. If it is pure and true, it enables an idea to manifest. That is how the lunium came to be.'

'You're saying fan fiction created the lunium?' Toby asked.

Agnor nodded. 'It is possible.'

'Shiiiiiit.' Toby grinned. 'That's *sick*.'

Jack was still processing Agnor's words. The implications of what he'd said were huge. He thought about the All T'Orc attendees; the cosplayers and the fanatics. Their love for fantasy was clear. Was it possible they were unwittingly powering an alternate world, simply by loving it?

'If all it took to create Iri was belief,' Jack said, 'can't you just unbelieve in the skalions? Remove them from existence?'

'If only it were that simple. Ever heard the phrase, *You can't put the genie back in the bottle?*' Agnor smiled benevolently. 'You see, Jack, believing something into existence is one thing. But the second a creature draws breath, the second it has its first thought, it ceases to be an idea and becomes a reality. Its own entity, free from the shackles of its creation.'

Of course, Jack thought dismally.

Agnor's attention shifted to Brol. 'Life hangs in a delicate balance. Your world is under threat. Dying. The skalions have corrupted the natural order of things, destroyed it with their insatiable appetite for power. But who can blame them? After all, that is the way they were created.'

That was true, Jack thought. Nobody blamed Earth carnivores for killing, they did it to survive.

'If the skalions win,' Agnor whispered, 'if Kunin Yillda claims the Glass, it may be the end for not just Iri, but for our world, too.' His wrinkles bunched into grave lines. 'My question is: are you ready?'

'Ready for what?' Jack asked.

Agnor set down his teacup. 'The Shadow Glass requires a champion, one strong enough to step through its hallowed pane into the mirror realm. One strong enough to face their true self and overcome the darkest splinters of their own mind. A champion for Iri. Yes, the Shadow Glass requires a champion, now more than ever. I wonder who fits the bill?'

Brol placed a hand to his breastplate. 'I would be honoured to surrender to the will of the Shadow Glass.'

Agnor's gaze glittered at him. 'Yes, Brol of the Vex tribe. You are pure of heart and mind. Perhaps the Glass will choose you.'

His gaze slid to Jack, who felt a stab of pain in his wounded finger. He couldn't imagine reaching a point where they had pieced the Glass back together, let alone stood before it as it selected a champion. And the way Agnor stared at him made his throat itch.

'Do you have a fragment?' Toby asked. 'We're almost out of time.'

'Oh yes,' the mystic said, releasing Jack's gaze. 'Time is everything. Always too little, or too much. Always out of balance, like so much in this world. But yes. The box is in this very room. All you have to do is find it.'

Jack's chest clenched and he set down his teacup. He stared at the bookcases, the cats dozing lazily, the ET-shaped teapot.

'Are you really going to make us ransack your living room?' he asked.

The man's eyes twinkled as he put on his neon green sunglasses. 'It is easy enough to uncover. All you have to do is answer this simple question: when a kettu digs deep, what does she find?'

Jack searched his weathered face for the answer, but Agnor gave nothing away. Jack's gaze darted about him, looking from Toby to Brol to the guards, circling around the eighties shrine, scouring it for kettu symbols.

When a kettu digs deep, what does she find?

'It's from the comic,' Toby blurted. 'The riddle Zavanna solves.'

'Their soul,' Jack murmured. Somehow, he'd known the answer. 'But what does that—'

He stopped and looked down at the floor. At his feet, a floorboard stuck up fractionally around the others.

'You don't mean S-O-U-L, do you?' he said. 'You mean S-O-L-E.'

'Soul purpose. *Sole* purpose,' Agnor chuckled. 'Same thing, no?'

Jack fell upon the floorboard, scraping the wood with his fingernails and teasing it up to reveal a dark hollow. Light spilled across a carved box. Breath hitched in Jack's throat as he took it out, his neck creaking with tension. He rested it on the arm of the chair, examining it.

'You can't blame me for having a little fun,' Agnor said. 'It's been so long since I got to flex my old mystic muscles.'

Jack frowned. The box was the same size as the others. 'Are there two pieces in there?'

'One box, one fragment,' Agnor said simply.

'What about the fourth? AT?' Toby asked.

'I am afraid Bob gifted me only one.' Agnor looked concerned. 'Have you not uncovered all four?'

Jack stood. 'No. Shit. Sorry. I knew it was too good to be true. Do you know who has the final piece?'

'Alas no, even mystics have their limits. It seems that is something you must discover for yourself.'

Jack sensed he was deliberately withholding information, but he didn't have time to waste arguing.

'We should find the others,' he said. Brol exchanged his teacup for the box, holding it tight as he bowed to Agnor, his snout almost brushing the carpet.

'Our thanks, wise and colourful one.'

'What about Cutter?' Toby asked. 'How do we stop him?'

'Ah, yes, the keeper of Iri.' The mystic's mouth tugged into a troubled smirk. 'The answer to that question is already known to you.'

Jack shook his head. 'We might need a little more than that.'

Agnor squinted at him through his neon sunglasses. 'A man driven by envy is easily undone. Simply confront him with his own irrefutable truth.'

That seemed to be as much as he would say.

'Go,' he urged, hopping off the armchair. 'Save Iri. It must endure.'

Jack nodded and prepared to head back into the gallery when a hulking figure crashed through the door, taking half the wall with him. He saw a bald skull and thick fur as it backhanded one guard, then the other, rendering them unconscious, then lumbered towards Jack. Jack recognised the man who had glowered at him on the Con floor.

'Hey—' he began, but the man knocked him to one side, his bloodshot eyes seeking out the box in Brol's hands.

'*Yesssss,*' he hissed. Liquid dripped from him to the floor. Red. He seemed to be bleeding but Jack couldn't discern an injury.

With a strangled cry, the man lurched for the box, big hands roving, a metallic reek swirling around the room.

Before he could seize the fragment, though, Brol dropped to the floor, ducking between the man's legs. Scooting the box across the carpet, he burst towards the part-demolished door, vanishing through it.

The man bellowed with rage, causing a number of the dozing cats to awaken and hiss, and he whirled around to give chase. Something about the way he moved made Jack queasy. The stranger's head bobbed as if he were having trouble keeping it upright, and his elbows and knees stuck out at odd angles.

As the man staggered for the door, Jack seized his arm. He gasped in disgust. The coat was sopping wet, the fur squelching like a soaked sponge. The man swung in a circle, butting Jack away, and Jack's back struck the wall. He stared down at his palm. It was coated in red.

The man's coat was soaked in blood.

'What the—' Jack began, but the man had gone, loping back into the gallery.

'Go,' Agnor urged. 'Stop her!'

'Her?' Jack asked, but the sound of the man crashing through the gallery spurred him into motion. Together, he and Toby ran from the room, the lub scuttling into Toby's backpack.

'Giiiiive,' the man bellowed as he pounded through the gallery, smashing the Yggram tree with a huge fist as he chased Brol. The kettu didn't slow down, dancing through the gallery and disappearing into the main warehouse just as the Yggram tree groaned and collapsed.

'Oh no,' Jack moaned, hurrying to the archway. He scanned the Con, but Brol had vanished. The man in the fur coat staggered between the stalls, knocking people out of the way as he tried to keep up with the kettu. The guests cried out as they were shoved aside, finding themselves smeared with blood.

'Jack,' Amelia called, tugging at her cape as she ran to his side. 'What happened?'

'Brol has the fragment, but that fur-coated freak is after it.'

Amelia stared after the retreating figure. 'Who is it?'

'I have no idea.' He was already running, charging into the throng. He skidded to a stop when he saw the bald man had halted in the centre of the avenue between stalls. At first, Jack couldn't tell why, but then he saw the lithe shape poised before him.

Zavanna stood blocking the man's path, her sword held out to one side as she spat, 'Get back!'

Jack's heart slammed his ribs with relief. Zavanna was here. Their blood-soaked attacker didn't stand a chance.

'Fragment,' the man gurgled. 'Give ussss.'

His head wobbled, turning as he scanned the warehouse for Brol.

Amelia gasped. 'It's Harry. One of the Bob Co. guards. I didn't recognise him before, but it's definitely him. He looks awful.'

'What's he doing here?' Jack hissed.

'Final piece!' the man demanded, the words choking from his throat as he tottered before Zavanna. He waved a hand, almost losing his balance but managing to stay upright. 'Tell now!'

'I said get back, fool!' Zavanna snarled.

The man whirled to faced Jack. His mouth foamed with white globules that thickened over his chin. His complexion was as pale as boiled meat.

Jack tried to take the man's arm but he jerked it out of the way. Jack tried to grab his other arm and the man growled, his body flailing.

As the man twitched and attempted to free himself, his coat fell open and Jack froze. Before he could fully comprehend what he was looking at, he heard himself cry out in horror.

He stared at what lay inside the coat, not understanding, his heart thumping.

Where the man's torso should have been, a hunched creature squatted, nestled in his guts. Its blue eyes beamed out at Jack and it cackled, glistening with blood and bile, the stench of death rising to clog his nostrils.

'Nebfet,' Jack choked, staggering backwards, his mouth gaping in shock.

'*Jack*,' the soothsayer said, and the man's mouth moved at the same time, spitting the word in a bubbling hiss. '*Tell us, Jack, where is the final piece?*'

Excerpt from The Shadow Glass *screenplay, dated 1 Dec. 1984,*
written by Bob Corman.

INT. CELL – NIGHT

Dune SITS UP as the cell door creaks open. A shadowy
figure slips inside and Dune JERKS FORWARD to seize
it, but the CHAINS attached to the wall prevent him. On
the floor before him, the lub YAPS and GROWLS at the
newcomer, who raises her hooded head to reveal it is –

                    DUNE
        Dorr.

She moves towards him.

                    DORR
        Here.

                    DUNE
        Get away from me.

She pauses. The lub continues to BARK.

                    DORR
        Shh! I'm here to free you.

                    DUNE
        More mind games! You showed

your true allegiance when you gave
the fragment to your father.

                    DORR
              (dips her head)
I was wrong. Foolish. He wants peace
no more than Kunin Yillda herself.

The lub falls silent.

                    DORR
I want to make it right. Please, Dune.

She moves forward again and unlocks his wrists.
Dune sighs and rubs them, then LEAPS AT HER. He
grips her shoulders.

                    DUNE
If this is another trick–

She KISSES HIM.

Dune blinks in surprise.

                    DORR
I love you, you idiot.

                    DUNE
Oh.

Jack stared in horror. Nebfet was controlling the guard from the inside, making him move and talk. She had used his dead legs to chase Brol and his dead hands to grope for the fragment box. Now, the seer leered up at Jack, coiled in the cavity where the man's abdomen should be, her shell-like exoskeleton bathed in blood and her honeycomb eyes lasering into him.

Around them, bystanders gawked. The whole Con had ground to a halt as costumed guests crowded around the scene at the centre of the warehouse.

'That's messed up,' a man said, wrinkling his nose at Nebfet.

'I didn't know they were doing a show,' another said.

'There's so much blood!'

'It looks totally fake.'

Jack barely heard them. All he saw was the soothsayer.

'I think I'm going to throw up,' Toby said.

Before Jack could respond, Nebfet leapt from the corpse, shrieking as she fell upon Jack. The dead guard's body crumpled to the floor amid a chorus of surprised shouts from the bystanders. Nebfet seized hold of Jack's shoulders, sinking her talons into his flesh. He cried out in pain and found himself trapped by her eyes. They were all he could see.

'Let us in, yes, Jack. Let Nebfet see. You must know.'

He was vaguely aware of more yelling and then Nebfet tumbled off him, her claws carving away ribbons of flesh as they released his shoulders, her presence withdrawing from his mind.

'Jack, snap out of it!' Amelia yelled. She brandished a Man-Hero sword she must have seized from one of the stalls, and he realised she had knocked the soothsayer off him. He spotted a pair of feet disappearing behind one of the stalls as Nebfet withdrew, but when Amelia circled around, ready to strike again, she stopped short and gave Jack an apprehensive look.

'Gone,' she said.

Jack shook off a chill, trying to ignore the hollowed-out body on the floor as a man dressed in a hat and coattails nudged it with his boot.

'Where's Brol?' Jack asked, searching the rafters and the stalls but only seeing bewildered guests.

'He ran that way,' Anya said, appearing at his side with the rest of the Guild. She pointed at the exit, which seemed so far beyond their reach—only just visible past the crowd of cosplayers—that Jack despaired. Before he could suggest making a break for it, the doors burst open as if kicked from the outside, and a projectile sailed into the warehouse.

With a cry, the clustered cosplayers parted, only just getting out of the way in time for a metal ball to *thunk* down the aisle, trundle across the floor, and roll to a stop at the centre of the room. It sprouted claws that clamped onto the tiles, and then a shaft of green light beamed up from it, filling the air.

Kunin Yillda's engorged face appeared, fuzzy with transmission interference, lines scrolling up and down her warty countenance. She surveyed the crowd with no attempt to hide her revulsion.

'People of Erp,' she shouted. 'Among you stands a traitor to Iri. One who does not belong. This man must be stopped at all costs. Find him! Find Jack Corman, and you will be generously rewarded.'

A delighted murmur rippled through the warehouse. Everybody thought it was part of the show. Jack wished it was.

'Who the frell is Jack Corman?' somebody asked.

Jack found Amelia scowling at him, the Guild mesmerised by the skalion queen. Nell put her arm around Huw, while Anya and Sumi held hands. At their feet, Fin growled. Over Toby's shoulder, the lub trembled inside the rucksack, only its eyes visible.

'Now you will bow, all of you, to your new queen!' shouted the flickering transmission.

Glass exploded around the warehouse as armoured shapes crashed through the windows. Skalions swung from the walls, ziplining into the gallery and spreading out, swords drawn, visors engaged as they rallied around the cosplayers. Jack counted twenty, but he was sure only a dozen had been animated in his father's attic. He couldn't account for how many there were now.

'Holy shit,' Huw uttered. 'They're even uglier than in the film.'

'They look different,' Nell murmured. 'What happened to them?'

'They've evolved,' Jack said.

A diminutive shape darted past him. It bounded between the attendees, heading for the spherical transmitter at the centre of the floor and then leaping into the green light it emitted. Nebfet hung suspended in the light, which turned blue the moment her eyes ignited with their wild energy, and Jack shuddered at the sight of the soothsayer spinning slowly in the air.

'*Earthlings, look at me, see me!*' she cried.

'Cover your eyes!' Jack shouted, throwing one arm over his face, his other in front of the Guild.

'What's she doing?' Anya grunted, her head down so that her seventies headdress poked Toby's elbow.

'*Be in me,*' Nebfet hissed. '*Yessssss. Be in meeeeee.*'

The atmosphere in the warehouse changed. Jack sensed it even before a hand seized his arm and he found himself staring into the face of a middle-aged, improbably ripped Man-Hero whose eyes burned with unnatural blue light.

Behind him, the cosplayers turned as one to glower at Jack, their faces slack, their eyes glowing.

'She's hacked them,' Jack said, shaking off the Man-Hero, who remained where he was, glowering at him but not moving. The Guild pressed together, facing the drooling crowd, and as Jack moved closer to Amelia he saw the attendees had formed a ring around them, penning them in. There was no escape.

'Zavanna,' Jack said. 'Where's Zavanna?' She had to be somewhere beyond the crowd.

A bang rang out at the entrance, and Jack craned to look at the gallery doors. Long-legged creatures galloped inside, whinnying and jerking their heads as they wrestled with the restraints jammed into their mouths. The lopers that had been animated at Bob Co. bore skalion soldiers on their backs, and the riders sneered as they stabbed their heels into the creatures' ribs, forcing them to do their bidding.

'This can't be happening,' Jack said, gripping his head in his hands as he turned around in a circle, seeing skalions and brainwashed cosplayers everywhere, tightening around them, their knuckles twisted, jaws set, all of them resembling Halloween ghouls, their sheer number leaving no room for them to break free.

'*Seize them!*' Nebfet cried, jabbing a finger at Jack and the others.

Everything happened at once. The crowd surged forward as a single, many-armed entity, hands outstretched as it lunged for Jack and the Guild. Fin started barking while the Man-Hero went for Jack, his hands closing around his neck and squeezing. Jack gagged and gritted his teeth, knowing a real man was in there, not some movie monster. He was just a man being puppet-mastered by an Iri seer.

But he couldn't *not* fight back.

'I'm sorry,' he gulped, punching Man-Hero. The hands released his throat but Man-Hero didn't look like he was backing off, his blue eyes searing the air between them. 'I'm really sorry,' Jack said, punching him again.

The man toppled backwards, crashing against one of the stalls, but more cosplayers rushed to replace him, zombie-like fingers tearing the air, a sea of eerie blue eyes blazing.

'Hey, get off him!' Huw cried, striking a Lion-O that had seized Toby's arm and was attempting to drag him away from the Guild. The Lion-O released him and melted back into the throng, and Toby smiled, dragging Huw into a kiss.

'Thanks.'

Jack kicked his leg free of a hand clasping from the floor. He glimpsed Zavanna beyond the scrum, flipping around skalion soldiers. Her blade grew bloodier as she ducked and wove, but there were too many of them. She was struggling to keep up with the onslaught. The thought of them gaining the upper hand sent fear spasming through Jack's gut but he couldn't reach her to help.

The Guild remained with their backs together, armed with whatever they had to hand. Fin nipped nearby ankles while Huw swung his necklace like a slingshot, beating cosplayers on the side of the head. On Toby's shoulder, the lub yapped and bit anything that got too close.

'The doors!' Jack cried, grappling with a woman dressed as a cyclops. 'We have to get to the doors!'

He shoved off the cyclops, ducking beneath a pair of vicelike arms to seize a fake sword from a stall. He swept the sword before him in an arc, hacking again and again, the plastic weapon bluntly striking anything that came near him. It was enough of a deterrent to force the possessed cosplayers back and, somehow, Jack managed to clear a path through them.

'Get them out of here,' he told Toby, and Toby nodded, pushing his friends through the closing gap, avoiding snatching hands as they went. They made it through but skidded to a stop at the warehouse doors, where the skalions atop their lopers had moved to block them.

'Bacccck!' the skalions spat, jabbing their spears at the Guild. 'Bacccck now!'

Fin and the lub barked, and the lopers squealed. They reared up, throwing off their skalion captors. As the riders crashed to the floor, the lopers wheeled about and charged for the exit, bursting out into the street.

'Go!' Amelia yelled at Jack's side, just as he butted the handle of his sword into the nose of a wizard. 'Help Brol!'

He saw the Guild making for the door, but his relief atrophied at the sight of movement just behind them. One of the skalion riders jerked its head forward to reveal the deadly quills protruding from its spine.

'Toby—' Jack began, but it was too late. The skalion's back spasmed and its needle-tipped spears shot through the air. The Guild ducked and, for a brief moment, it seemed they were all right—but then Anya fell.

Her legs went out from under her and she slumped to the ground, her hand wrapped around a cluster of black barbs at her neck. She'd taken a direct hit.

'Anya!' Nell cried. The Guild surrounded her as the skalion cackled and wiped saliva from its mouth. Toby screwed up his fists and charged, barrelling into it.

Jack didn't see what happened next because something seized his hair, yanking so hard that his eyes streamed. He could only make out a blurred shape as knuckles pummelled his abdomen and he retched, sure he was about to purge half his insides. A smear of red entered his vision and the hand snapped free from his hair.

'Jack, are you okay?' Amelia panted, helping him upright.

'Yep,' he wheezed. 'Please keep rescuing me.'

He wiped his eyes, clutching his bruised abdomen, and spotted Zavanna wrenching her blade free from a skalion soldier. She was only a few metres away from Nebfet, who remained suspended in the air above the transmitter, blue energy crackling around her as she puppeteered the assault.

'Stop her!' Jack shouted at Zavanna, pointing at the soothsayer. If they took down Nebfet, it might sever her connection to the cosplayers. Return them to normal.

Zavanna nodded and dipped a hand into her satchel.

'What happened to Anya?' Amelia panted.

'She got hit.'

He saw Sumi using the hem of her dress to tug the darts free from Anya's throat, before tossing them to the floor. She pressed a piece of torn fabric to the wound and placed Anya's hand over it to keep it in place. Then she, Nell and Toby heaved her up.

Anya looked half-conscious, her eyes rolling and her legs barely taking her weight, and Jack could already see the poison discolouring her throat, making the skin glisten and pull tight. Together they stumbled for the exit, the lub jumping onto Fin's back as she dashed after them.

'We have to help her,' Jack said, but found he was talking to himself. Amelia had vanished. 'Amelia?'

He searched the crowd for her, but a cosplay ogre seized his shirt collar and stale coffee breath blasted Jack's face.

'*You're ourrrrrs,*' the ogre hissed, his off-green make-up running into his mouth.

'You wish,' Jack grunted, ripping his shirt as he freed himself and twisted, sprinting for the doors, where he spotted Amelia waiting. He had to make sure Brol and the fragment were safe, that Anya was okay. He batted away grasping hands, crashing into blue-eyed cosplayers and sending them flying as he ran.

An explosion rocked the floor and Jack only just retained his balance, feeling a rush of heat behind him. He slowed at the edge of the gallery, just as the blue light bathing the walls extinguished. A sudden hush fell over the cosplayers.

Jack watched as they lowered their hands, then pushed them into their hair, shaking their heads, their eyes no longer glowing. They blinked around them in confusion, and Jack shared their bewilderment until Zavanna leapt into view, bounding away from the centre of the hall.

She had destroyed Kunin Yillda's transmitter. Nebfet's power was spent.

'Nice!' Jack shouted.

'Move!' Zavanna cried back, dodging between the cosplayers, and Jack joined her to bowl outside into the alley. His relief at escaping the warehouse was short-lived as he stopped to search for Brol, Amelia and the Guild. Zavanna swiped her blade at yet more skalions, who instantly charged them. How many were they now? How had their numbers grown?

Jack spotted Amelia and the Guild further down the alley. They gathered around Anya, who was propped against the warehouse wall, unconscious, unresponsive. Huw stood with his hands covering his mouth, observing as Sumi soothed Anya's forehead with wet fabric. She had her phone to her ear and Jack wondered who she was calling, who could possibly help them.

'You took your time, Bobson,' Brol said.

Jack turned and saw him standing by the hearse, bloodied and panting, surrounded by skalion corpses. He had defended the fragments alone, and Jack saw he had stowed the third fragment box in the back of the car.

'If this doesn't earn you a place in the Kettu Sagas,' Jack said, 'nothing will.'

'It would be a most welcome if tardy honour, friend.'

'We need to help the others—' Jack began, but then Zavanna soared over his head, crashing into the All T'Orc sign and tearing it down with her as she landed at Brol's side. She bounded quickly to her feet as a dozen skalions surrounded them, sniggering as they closed in, trapping Jack and the kettu with the hearse. They looked madder than Jack had ever seen them, a ravenous light boiling their eyes.

'Kettu and erpling, tasty treats,' one gurgled.

'Give us pieces, yesssss,' hissed another, eyeing Jack hungrily.

Jack managed to seize a skalion sword from the ground just

as the battalion charged. Brol and Zavanna clashed with four of them, while Jack tackled a fifth, ducking its lunge and stabbing it from behind. As it thrashed and wailed, Jack saw the hearse rocking as a couple of skalions piled into the front seats.

'There's no way—' he began, but then the engine sputtered to life. The car revved and began to trundle over the cobbles, away from the warehouse.

'STOP THEM!' Jack bellowed, then winced as a skalion leapt up to loop a cable around his throat. It yanked hard and Jack found himself on the ground, his throat burning. Through the pain, he saw Brol and Zavanna fighting a scrum of skalions while the hearse bobbed down the street away from him. If they picked up speed, they would make off with all three fragments.

He couldn't let that happen.

With a burst of energy, he swept the skalion off its feet and tore the cord from his throat. The creature rose quickly, but Jack seized its sword and twisted it into the skalion's gullet. Black blood foamed from its throat, and Jack found himself facing Zavanna, who stood clutching her own slick blade.

'A clean kill, Bobson,' she panted. 'Well done.'

'Thanks.' Jack smiled, feeling for the first time what it must be like to be a kettu warrior; comrades together against the world. Then he remembered the hearse. 'Just keep them away from the Guild.'

With a cry, he launched himself at the vehicle, catching hold of the back door handle. His legs fought for purchase on the cobbles as he was dragged along, and the vehicle picked up speed, the engine roaring. Pain erupted in his injured hand as he clung on, his palms sweaty, and the knowledge that he wouldn't be able to hold on for long sent waves of despair through him. He glanced over his shoulder and saw Zavanna watching him with that same look she'd given him in Nell's kitchen. Something verging on pride. Then she whirled to confront a fresh skalion horde.

The car bumped over a pothole and Jack lost his grip, collapsing onto the cobbles as the hearse rattled on.

Growling, he struggled to his feet and seized the handle again, attempting to inch it upwards. If he got it open, he could climb inside and drag out the fragments.

He opened his mouth to call for help, then saw Brol raising his sword to lop off the head of a fallen skalion. The kettu shot Jack a triumphant smile, then Brol's face froze. He looked down at the serrated blade that had appeared in his chest.

Behind him, a skalion loomed, victory in its eyes as it gripped the sword it had thrust through Brol's back.

Cold shock flushed through Jack. 'No,' he whispered.

The car lurched up a gear and knocked him loose. Jack collapsed onto the cobbles, panting, seeing Brol, the blade, the kettu's eyebrows arching in shock. It couldn't be true. It *couldn't*.

'Brol!' Zavanna's cry rang against the brick walls.

Brol's gaze found her and he smiled, reaching for her with bloody fingers. He said something Jack couldn't hear, pain and love etched into his face, and then he slumped forward. Went still.

The skalion tore the blade from his back, dumping Brol's body on the ground, and Zavanna flew at him, spitting and shrieking, sinking her teeth into the soldier's throat and tearing away its flesh. Black blood erupted in a torrent and the skalion laughed and screamed at the same time, finally collapsing to gurgle into the cobbles, its limbs thrashing as it bled out.

Zavanna dropped to the ground beside Brol.

Lying on the road, Jack twisted to see the hearse bump around a corner and vanish.

They were too late.

It was gone.

He struggled to his feet and stood watching Zavanna.

She tore at her armour and released a tortured howl that caused the hairs on Jack's arms to stand on end. She pulled Brol's body into an embrace and sat rocking him, making noises Jack had never heard a kettu make. He hobbled towards her, numb with shock at the sight of Brol so still. Not moving, not laughing, eyes closed.

More noises came from within the warehouse. The sound of crying, confused shouting and skalions gibbering. By the wall, Amelia broke away from the Guild, tugging off her red wig as she observed the kettu with a pained expression. She must have seen it happen, too.

All Jack knew was that they had to get away from here. But the hearse was gone and he had no idea where Amelia had left the Land Rover.

'The lopers,' he murmured, seeing the creatures milling around the other end of the alley. Five of them. It was their safest bet right now. Although he wanted to stay with Zavanna, he hurried over to the Guild and stopped still as Toby turned a tear-streaked face to him. The lub mewled in his arms, and Jack saw Anya still slumped against the wall, her skin yellow. Her friends looked shell-shocked, especially Sumi.

'She's gone,' Toby said.

At first Jack didn't understand, but then he saw how still Anya was, her chest not moving, the black veins splintering across her face.

Before Jack could say anything, a siren filled the alley and he saw an ambulance at the end of it. Sumi must have called it. In a daze, he watched a couple of paramedics hurry towards them, talking to Sumi, bending over Anya, then looking at each other, the urgency leaving their stances.

No. She couldn't be dead. She couldn't.

Jack felt numb with horror. His eyes wouldn't leave Anya, seeing the skalion poison blackening her veins, knowing it was his fault.

'You should go,' Sumi was saying to him, her voice an echo. She squeezed his arms. 'Jack!'

He looked at her, blinked. The paramedics were on the radio. They must be calling for backup.

'I'm staying with Anya,' Sumi said. 'You have to help the others get out of here.'

He felt himself nodding.

'The lopers,' he said, pointing. 'We can use the lopers to get away.'

The Guild hugged Sumi and then went to the lopers at the end of the alley. Nell manoeuvred onto one of the creature's backs, her shoulders shaking with sobs, while Amelia climbed onto another. Huw and Toby shared a third, holding each other tight, their faces frozen with shock. Jack approached Zavanna, who was still cradling Brol's body on the ground.

'Zavanna, we have to go,' he said.

She didn't move for a few seconds, and then she took Brol's arm and draped it around her neck, tugging him to her. Standing, she carried him to a loper and lay him over the creature's back, before pulling herself up next to him.

Shaking, Jack struggled up onto the remaining loper, clinging on to its hide as he awkwardly seated himself over its back. Then, as one, the herd jerked into motion, racing away from the chaos of the convention and into the busy London streets.

Cry happy
Cry sad
Dam never breaks

— *Old wug proverb*

They had nothing. That was all Jack could think as the lopers barrelled through East London, their long legs carrying them with alarming speed as they lumbered past pedestrians and dodged through traffic, leaving double-takes and startled shrieks in their wake.

Jack clung on to the creature's soft hide, dizzy and exhausted, vaguely aware of Fin running alongside them, keeping pace with the herd. He saw the blade bursting through Brol's chest over and over again, the black veins branching from Anya's throat, spreading up to her temple. He wished he had been quicker, that he could have saved them.

Just a few hours ago, they'd had two of the fragments and were on their way to claim the third. They'd had Brol. Now, Kunin Yillda had most of the Shadow Glass, and Brol and Anya were dead.

They were dead.

And it was already past midday. Only a few hours of daylight remained. Soon the moon would rise and Iri would be beyond saving.

Jack slumped into the loper's warm pelt, smelling straw and sweat. The herd moved with purpose and he resigned himself to wherever he was being taken, trying to make his mind go blank but failing, seeing the Bob Co. guard's ruined corpse, Nebfet's eyes, and Brol's surprise as the skalion skewered him.

His hand hurt again, radiating pain up to his shoulder, and he wished he could escape into the dark void that kept opening up before him—but even that was denied him.

Eventually, the loper trotted to a standstill. Jack pushed himself upright and saw they were outside his father's house, the sky oozing black and green as the sun lowered itself behind the rooftops. A handful more lopers surrounded his, and he saw Amelia clambering down from one, Toby and Huw from another.

The creatures had brought them home. Home to his father.

Jack slid clumsily off his snorting steed and landed on legs that almost crumpled on impact. He saw Nell, Toby and Huw hugging each other, their faces tear-streaked, and their costumes only added to the sense of surreality that threatened to overpower him. Nell was still dressed in her She-God jumpsuit, while Huw's Atreyu outfit was torn and bloodied.

Jack saw Zavanna dropping down from her loper, ignoring everybody as she tugged Brol's body off the creature, cradling him in her arms. Without a word, she carried him into the front garden, disappearing down the passage that ran along the side of the house.

'Here,' Jack said, handing Amelia his keys. 'Let yourselves in. I'll be there in a second.'

She looked at him in question, but Jack didn't have time to explain. Zavanna had already disappeared. He herded the lopers the way she had gone, urging them down the passage and into the back garden. It wasn't big, London gardens never were, but it was green, filled with fir trees and overgrown bushes that kept out the rest of the world. The lopers went to graze in the far corner.

To one side, Zavanna stood by an old picnic bench. Brol was laid out on its surface, his eyes closed, his armour blood-smeared.

If she heard Jack approach, Zavanna showed no sign of it. Her ears remained flat as she bent over Brol's prone form and Jack could only imagine what she felt. Kettu believed in the twin soul. One spirit, two beings. They mated for life. She would feel Brol's death in her bones, as if it were she who had been speared by the skalion's blade.

He shivered with cold. 'Zavanna, I'm so sorry—'

A growl rumbled in her throat and she whirled to glower at him. The pain in her face cut him to the marrow.

'What do you know? You are nothing! Your words mean nothing to me.'

He straightened, shocked by the ferocity of her words. 'Zavanna, please—'

'Fool! You cannot see yourself. You cannot see anything. Leave us be.'

He staggered back a few paces as if she had dealt him a blow. 'I'm trying to help you.'

'Now?' She stepped forward, shoulders tensed, hands twisted into claws, and he saw the power in her. For the first time since she attacked him in the attic, he felt afraid of her.

'Now you want to help?' she demanded. 'What of before? When you sought to rid yourself of us, moments after we stumbled into this terrible world?'

Her expression challenged him, half sneering, half broken.

'We have to find the Glass,' he said. 'There's still time—'

She shook her head, dismissing him. 'Go back to your life, such as it is. We do not need you.'

Her snarl faded and she turned back to Brol. Jack knew this wasn't the time.

Shivering, he went into the house via the back door.

From the hall, he saw Amelia and the Guild in the lounge, but he couldn't face them. Their grief was intense and he was responsible for it. Their friend had died trying to help him. There was nothing he could say to change that.

He slipped upstairs and went into his father's study. There had to be something here that would tell them where the final fragment was, put everything right. Maybe remaking the Glass would reset everything that had happened, bring back Anya and Brol. Maybe even Dune, too.

Still feeling disoriented, fighting the sense of defeat, he began going through the same piles of notebooks and script pages he had searched yesterday, willing for some solution to present itself.

One of the desk drawers contained a box full of USBs and a second-hand laptop. The latter didn't have a password lock, and he quickly went through the files on the USBs, finding more notes. More stories about Iri. A whole treasure trove of them written by his father. This was what Bob had been doing all these years. Crafting his own encyclopedia containing every myth, character and story in Iri. It was endless. Document upon document of Bob's singular vision.

No wonder he'd had trouble whittling it down to a single script for *Shadow Glass 2*. There was enough material here for fifty movies. For an entire world.

He spotted a childish drawing poking from beneath a notepad.

Tugging it free, he found it wasn't just a drawing; it was a comic.

The Revenge of Kunin Yillda, written by Jack Corman.

The title was drawn in thick letters and Jack immediately recognised it. It was one of the stories he wrote as a kid. He'd not seen it in years. He flipped the pages, smiling at the clumsy dialogue bubbles and colouring in, the green circles that must be skalions and the kettu wielding enormous swords.

He stopped as a capitalised word jumped out at him.

LUNIUM.

'Can I help?'

Toby stood in the doorway, his face weary but determined.

Jack turned and forced himself to meet his gaze.

'How are you doing?' he asked.

'Okay.'

'I'm... Anya seemed so...' Everything Jack tried to say died on his tongue. Felt inadequate. Finally, he said, 'I'm so sorry.'

Toby nodded. He blinked hard and Jack could tell he was fighting fresh tears. Instead, Toby focussed on the study. Yesterday Jack had ushered him out, couldn't bear to have anybody in there with him. Now, though, he wanted Toby to see Bob's inner sanctum. It was the least he could do, and he found he wanted to share it with him. It didn't feel as much of an invasion.

'Take a look if you want,' he said.

'Can I?'

Jack nodded and watched Toby tread carefully inside. He went to the bookcase and leaned in to read the spines and ponder the curios on the shelves.

'This is where he wrote,' Jack said, wishing he could find a way to help Toby feel better. 'He loved it in here. Called it his snug. He'd spend hours writing and drawing, researching. Sometimes he didn't come out for days. Everything he needed was in here.'

Toby looked down at his hands, his head bowed. 'I'm sorry, Jack.'

Jack frowned. 'What could you possibly be sorry for?'

'When we first met, I said a lot of stupid things. How lucky you were having Bob as a dad, how amazing he was. I didn't know how complicated things were.'

He looked so awkward, nothing like the grinning teenager who had bounced into the front garden a day ago. Jack hated to think of Toby beating himself up over anything he'd said. And especially not after Anya.

'You don't have anything to be sorry for,' Jack said firmly. 'Listen, things weren't great with Dad. I spent so long angry at him, it sort of took over. I could only see the monstrous parts of him, the things that made life so impossible. I've been trying to escape it for years but, well, then you came along and you reminded me how great Dad could be. You helped me remember the good, Toby.'

Toby turned his head, his eyes glistening.

'If anybody should be apologising, it's me,' Jack said. 'I brought you and your friends into this, and now Anya…' He couldn't finish the sentence.

'She loved *The Shadow Glass*,' Toby said. 'I mean, obviously. She wanted to help. You're not responsible for what happened to her.'

Jack wanted to believe him.

'Christ, how did you get so level-headed?' he asked. 'I wish I could've been like you back then. Things might have been different.'

'Hardly,' Toby said. 'My parents want me to be the best at everything. I just know I'm going to disappoint them—'

'Impossible.'

'But—'

'Impossible,' Jack repeated. 'You're brilliant and nobody should ever tell you otherwise.'

He smiled, feeling twitchy with emotion, and Toby smiled back. His entire face lifted and Jack wanted to hug him, tell him he was the coolest, most put-together person he'd ever met, and he'd never disappoint anybody, even if he tried.

But then he remembered the comic in his hands.

'Remember what Agnor said about fans helping to build Iri?' He held up the comic. 'Check this out. I wrote it when I was eight.'

Toby came over and looked at the page. 'Wait, *lunium*? What's that doing in your comic?'

'I think *this* is why you'd never heard of the lunium. It's from my story. *I* made it up.'

'Shit! Jack! Agnor wasn't kidding. You wrote Iri lore that actually became part of the world!'

'I guess I really loved Iri back then.'

'You're already connected to it,' Toby said, 'the way Bob was.'

Jack nodded, searching his memory. 'I wrote tons of stories but this one was special because it was epic, the idea of an Iri apocalypse. I remember wanting to write something huge and dangerous. Something world-changing.'

'Based on what we've been through the past few days, I'd say you succeeded.'

'It also means I really am the reason Zavanna and Brol turned up in the attic,' Jack said. 'I created the lunium. Thirty years ago, I set the board for the skalions to have a chance of taking power in Iri. I just didn't know it at the time. This was always my fight, maybe even more than theirs.'

'I have a headache,' Toby said.

'Really? It makes total sense to me.'

Toby grinned. 'So humble.'

Jack set the comic back on Bob's desk. He surveyed his father's possessions, feeling connected to them in a way that he hadn't in decades. He didn't know how the magic of Iri worked, how certain ideas turned into a reality, but he remembered Zavanna's words. *Sometimes it is better if there are no answers.*

All he knew was that he was directly responsible for the trouble in Iri, and he had to find a way to make everything all right again.

'We should talk to the others,' he said.

★

In the lounge, Amelia perched on the sofa, twisting something in her hands. The puzzle box, Jack saw from the door. Anya must have given it to her before she died.

At the other end of the sofa, Nell sat with a blotchy face, scrolling through her phone with Fin at her feet. Toby went and squashed himself into an armchair beside Huw, putting his arm around him.

'Hey,' Jack said.

They all looked up.

'Hey,' Amelia said.

'I'm, uh, I'm so—' Jack began, but Toby cut him off.

'Found anything, Nell?' he asked, giving Jack a meaningful look. Jack understood. No more apologies.

'Everybody on the fan forums saw Cutter's press conference,' Nell said, sniffing. 'They're going crazy. Some of them have dug up a load of stuff about him that's, well, not exactly flattering.'

'Like what?' Jack asked.

'He wrote a load of Iri fan fiction under that pseudonym you mentioned, Alden Smithee. It's pretty bad. There are a couple on Wattpad. They're at the top of the fantasy chart right now. The comments are sort of tearing him apart.'

Jack remembered Cutter's mother saying he had written stories when he was younger. Had he never stopped?

He thought about the lunium and how fan love had added to Bob's world, and hoped desperately that Cutter's stories hadn't changed anything in Iri. Jack got the feeling that only those who truly loved Bob's world had any influence over it. Cutter's contributions to Iri would have been dead on arrival, just like his prose.

'He used the same pseudonym to troll other writers,' Nell said. 'It's pretty horrible. He told one writer they were so untalented they should hang themselves.'

Jack ignored the prick of anger and tried to focus on something else. Thinking about Cutter made him think about stabbing and ripping and tearing, and he hated that one person, one man, could make him feel that way.

'Have you heard from Sumi?' he asked.

'She's at the hospital,' Huw said.

Amelia emitted a cry that made everybody jump. Jack found her giving him a stunned look as she held up the puzzle box.

'I did it,' she whispered. 'I actually did it.'

Jack saw that a portion of the puzzle had slid to one side, revealing the dark interior. Amelia had solved it. He glimpsed something glinting inside.

'It was easy, actually,' Amelia said. 'Once I remembered Anya talking about Sikake-Bako boxes. Turns out this is a variation of that.'

'What's in it?' Huw asked, the question on everybody's mind.

They craned forward as she tipped out a gold object and held it up.

A necklace winked in the lamplight. It was shaped like a sideways teardrop, almost the size of her palm, curling with intricate flourishes. With a start, Jack realised what they were looking at.

'It's an Iri Eye,' he breathed.

They were sacred in kettu clans, the symbol of good fortune.

'But it's just a necklace,' Huw said, looking dejected.

Jack couldn't help feeling the same way. Of all the things he had hoped the puzzle box might contain—a cure for skalion poison, or some clue about the final fragment—a necklace hadn't factored in. The trinket didn't hum the way the Shadow Glass fragments had. The Iri Eye may be an optimistic symbol but, at this point, it was next to useless.

Jack saw Huw's disappointment mirrored in everybody else's face. Nell's cheeks glistened with tears and Amelia looked like she wanted to spit. He sensed the air curdling, the hopelessness suffocating them. He felt it, too, but he couldn't let them give up. There was still time. They could still fix this.

'Here,' he said, 'let me show you something.'

He produced the laptop from his father's study and plugged in a USB. He set the laptop on the coffee table.

'What are you doing?' Toby asked.

'Just watch.'

They crowded around the screen, Amelia and Nell on one side, Huw and Toby on the other, giving Jack a bemused look.

He hit 'play' on the video.

As violin music eked from the speakers, swelling mournfully, the screen showed a crumbling town that had succumbed to wildlife. A figure darted between rock piles and twisted trees, breathing heavily.

Dune.

'*What now?*' asked Dune's voice. '*What now?! Run. Get away. Quick!*'

It was the scene from towards the beginning of *The Shadow Glass*, when Dune was alone after the kettu fellowship had been slaughtered by the skalions.

The next bit was new, though. Instead of cutting to Dune wading into the nightmare swamp, where he would face his worst fears in the rotting flesh, he dashed across a town square dappled in blue and pink twilight.

'*Come play with us!*'

A cheerful voice broke the sound of Dune's panicked gasps.

'*We'll help you suss—*'

'*—out how to be a Gloomy Gus!*'

Dune skidded to a halt and turned on the spot, searching the ruins for who had called out.

A head emerged from behind a broken window, a hairless black face bordered with snow-white fur and small nub-like ears. Electric pink eyes glowed above a modest snout with large nostrils. Another appeared at an empty doorway; a third from a low wall.

'*You don't need to be alone!*' one sang.

'*Come with us into the unknown!*'

Dune's voice rang out, heavy with fear. '*Who are you?*'

The creatures sprang out into the open, revealing themselves as lemur-like beings with purple hands and feet. They were muscular and lean, prowling around Dune in a circle. A percussive beat stirred and the violins surged, this time sharp and teasing.

Toby stared at Jack.

'It's the musical number,' he said. 'Jack, it's the cut musical number!'

'Holy shit,' Huw breathed.

The creatures hopped and cavorted around Dune, singing in tune with the beat.

'When life's run you dry my friend
And you're out of turns, don't bend
There's magic in the air to mend
Your spirit and that's sure to send
You right to us!
Come dance with us!
Shake it high and hurl your guts!'

As they frolicked, the ruins faded and were replaced with a whirling pink and gold vortex, through which the characters danced. Dune stood at their centre, bewildered but with a growing look of amazement on his face.

The creatures produced bright fabric out of thin air, threading it around Dune's torso and arms, binding him tight.

'Stop!' he cried. 'I don't like it!'

The creatures cackled and jerked the fabric so that Dune's arms and legs spread like a starfish. He stared around in horror, struggling to get free.

'Play with us!'

'You know you must!'

'We're the ones who you can trust!'

Dune cried, 'Please!' and thrashed harder. 'LET ME GO!'

He jerked and fought, finally snatching a dagger from his belt and severing one of the threads. He slashed another and another until the fabric unspooled, spinning him on the spot.

Panting, he collapsed on all fours, back in the town square. The creatures were gone. The music was replaced with the sigh of a breeze.

Dune checked himself over quickly and then ran.

The screen faded to black.

Jack closed the laptop and looked at Toby, while Nell sank back against the sofa.

'That was un-fricking-believable!' Toby said. 'Oh my god! Why'd they cut it?'

'I've never heard of Gloomy Gusses,' Nell said. 'How did they keep all of that under wraps?'

Jack shrugged. 'Pre-internet, that was pretty simple.'

'Wow,' Toby breathed.

They sat in various states of astonishment.

Jack stood to address them all.

'I have an idea for how we can find the final fragment,' he said.

'But the lunium—' Toby began, gesturing at the window, where the light was fading behind the curtains.

'Isn't here yet,' Jack said. 'We have time. Not much, but some. We have to do this. For Brol. For Anya. But we're going to need Zavanna's help.' He turned to Amelia and said, 'Mind if I borrow this?'

She shook her head and he took the Iri Eye.

'Meet me in the attic in a few minutes.'

★

Out in the garden, a breeze tousled his hair. Light flickered in the trees at the end of the lawn, and Jack found Zavanna standing over a modest bonfire, her back to the house. Brol's weapons lay by the fireside. Jack approached, feeling wary but knowing what he had to do.

'His name deserves a place on the Yggram tree,' he said.

Zavanna bowed her head and then turned to look at him, her eyes bright.

'The moon is almost at its zenith,' she said, and he saw the silver disc peeking above the trees. It shone ghostly and full. They were almost out of time.

'Look, I wanted to… give you this.' He chewed his lip as he thrust the necklace between them. It twirled, catching both the moonlight and the fire, glinting green and gold.

Zavanna stopped still and stared, transfixed.

'An Iri Eye,' she murmured.

'For protection.' He hoped she couldn't hear his heartbeat.

'I thought they were lost,' Zavanna said, her ears trembling. 'When the skalions raided Irindell.'

'They failed to raid my dad's office.' He smirked. 'It was inside the puzzle box.'

She raised a hand to cup the pendant and its light sparkled in her eyes, which shifted and dilated, glittering with life. Her evolution was complete. She was no longer the puppet he had first encountered in the attic but a full-blooded creature in her own right. A fierce warrior.

'I cannot,' she said, withdrawing her hand.

'Please.' He pushed it towards her. 'What is it the kettu say? *"The act of gift-giving is more important than the gift being given."*'

Her brow knitted into a frown. Then she blinked and avoided his gaze as she murmured, 'I should not have said the things I said.'

It took him a moment to realise she was apologising, and he was so stunned he struggled to reply.

'Uh, thanks?'

'I was angry and… upset.' This was difficult for her. 'I regret my words. I wish I had not spoken them.'

'I'm sorry I've been so useless,' he said.

She didn't correct him. Finally, she gave a curt nod and took the necklace, fastening it around her neck. The eye gleamed against her breast. Jack thought it completed her. She looked more formidable than ever.

'Thank you,' she said.

'You're welcome.' He fiddled with the bandage on his hand and thought of their talk in the study the previous day, her measured, earnest words about his father. Quietly, he added, 'The bad memories are easier to remember than the good.'

Her eyebrows lifted and he scratched the back of his neck, searching the trees.

'Even before Dad died, all I could remember was the bad stuff. None of the good. It was like anything good that had existed between us, no matter how small, died when I moved away. And then he really did die. I think that's what grief does to you. It becomes its own entity, like a haunting, and it thrives on unhappiness.' He drew a breath, pushed it back out through dry lips. 'So I'm not going to let it anymore. I'm going to remember the good things. I can't forgive everything my father did, but I can try to make peace with it.'

Zavanna nodded.

He thought she might remain silent, but then she said, 'Brol was brave. Even when I treated him unfairly, he remained by my side. Always loyal. He will be missed more than I can say.'

Jack recalled what she had said about her brother.

'He's just on the other side of the glass,' he said. 'Just waiting, like Dune.'

'Thank you, Bobson.'

Jack smiled sadly and looked up at the moon, his mind returning to what he had gone out there for. 'Will you come inside? We need your help.'

★

In the attic, he found Amelia pacing and typing on her phone while Nell, Toby and Huw sat on the edge of the sofa. Wugs circled the attic, humming a soulful tune. They must sense time was almost up.

Everybody watched Zavanna enter but the kettu ignored them, moving silently to stand beside a creaking wardrobe, the necklace flashing at her breast. Jack felt he understood her a little more each day. She hid her vulnerabilities, showed only strength and courage, but, for the briefest moment, she had permitted him to see her pain. The real Zavanna. He felt honoured.

'What's the plan?' Amelia asked, pocketing her phone.

Jack felt awkward with everybody staring at him but he pressed on.

'Zavanna, it's time we did your sight voyage.'

Her ears pricked, then lowered. It was one of the first things she had suggested in their search for the Shadow Glass, but Brol had convinced her it was a last resort.

'Yes,' she said. 'It is time.'

'Hold up,' Amelia said. 'Sight voyage? That's your plan for finding the final fragment?'

Jack glanced at a dusty grandfather clock. 'It's three p.m., so we have roughly two and a half hours until the moon reaches its apex. At this point, it's our only option.'

'Don't you need special herbs and stuff for that sort of thing?' Toby asked.

Jack nodded at Zavanna. 'You have herbs, don't you?' He eyed the pouches fastened at her belt. He was sure he could smell the contents from where he stood, a bitter combination of flowers and earth.

'It is how kettu mystics commune with the ether,' she said. 'Although using them comes with no certainty that you will ever return.'

'Which is why I'll do it,' Jack said. The kettu scowled at him but he shrugged. 'You're too important to risk. Besides, I could do with a little vision right now.'

Zavanna looked like she might argue but then she nodded. 'We need space.'

Nell and the boys helped clear the centre of the room, pushing the coffee table against the wall while Amelia straightened the rug. The lub sat on the sofa with Fin and the wugs, its head rotating to observe everybody in action.

When the rug was cleared, Zavanna ordered Jack to sit cross-legged at its centre. He did so, winking at Amelia as she watched, her arms crossed and her mouth pinched. The others gathered on the sofa. Toby patted the lub, which yawned.

'Here.' Zavanna held out the pouch, and the aroma was so strong Jack thought he might pass out.

'Aren't we supposed to pound it into a paste or drink it or something?'

She shook her head. 'The herbs are more potent in their raw state.'

The word *raw* caused Jack's stomach to flip, but he took the pouch and tipped its contents into the palm of his hand. His skin itched. He peered down at the herbs. Maybe this was a bad idea, but it was their only idea. He thought of Anya and Iri and the kettu's plight and knew he had no choice.

'Bottoms up.' He gave the Guild a nervous smile and tipped the herbs into his mouth, forcing himself to chew, little bits sticking between his teeth and scraping his tongue. They formed a prickly ball in his mouth and it took all of his willpower to resist spitting them back out.

He swallowed.

Nothing happened.

'How do you feel?' Zavanna asked.

'I don't—' he began but then he saw her eyes were winking different colours. Red and green, like otherworldly traffic lights. More eyes winked into existence on her face, ten, twenty, thirty of them, all blinking at him, and her limbs became string-like, lengthening as he looked, stretching her body until she resembled a looping nightmare version of herself.

He looked down at his hands and his fingers had become snakes, writhing and spitting at each other. The severed one spurted green liquid.

He started to scream but Zavanna's voice cut through the panic.

'Breathe, Bobson, breathe. Slow and deep. Focus on what you wish to know.'

He forced himself to inhale. The taste of the herbs caused saliva to flood his mouth while his stomach spasmed, desperate to purge its contents. He forced an exhale and another inhale and his fingers—including the bandaged stump—returned to normal.

'Zavanna?' he asked, because she no longer stood before him. The whole room had vanished. Instead, he was staring at a canvas of stars that pulsed with multicoloured lights.

He had no body. He tried to look down at himself but there was nothing, only more stars, moving faster now, zipping past like bullets, and he was rushing with them, so fast he could feel his joints separating.

'Jack!'

Zavanna's voice was deafening and it anchored him, bringing him to a standstill.

The stars ran like paint on a black wall and he realised it *was* a wall, but there was no ceiling or door. A black whirlpool sucked at the middle of the floor. He felt its force, a gravitational pull that tugged at him, desperate to consume him. He resisted.

'*Focus, Bobson.*'

He clenched his hands into fists, or at least where he thought his hands should be, and there was no pain from his severed finger, which was both worrying and a relief. He tried to think about the Shadow Glass. He pictured it in his mind, each separate piece, and as he thought of them they appeared before him, spinning in the air above the vortex in the floor.

Zavanna's voice became a distant echo.

'*What do you see?*'

Only three pieces of the Shadow Glass twirled before him. Where the fourth fragment should hang, the air remained empty.

He pondered the sucking vortex and knew what he had to do.

Taking a breath, he plunged into it.

Black water flooded his mouth and ears, roaring so loudly it sounded like screaming.

He felt crushed, the water pounding him on all sides, the pressure so intense he thought he might be smashed out of existence.

He gasped and found himself whizzing through enormous rooms. He glimpsed Kunin Yillda atop her old throne, but the Iri landscape around her was nothing more than a watercolour painting. He surged into another cavernous space, this time glimpsing an enormous mechanical wheel that spat blue electricity. Before it, Nebfet chanted and stared at him with pulsing eyes that burned into his soul.

Jack screamed and threw up his arms. When he lowered them, he was somewhere dark, silence hissing in his ears.

He had come to a standstill and the world felt solid again.

He was in a cramped space, wooden panels close on either side of him, while a sheet of glass rested between him and the light beyond. He stared through the glass at an office. It was small and messy, a desk piled with papers, a bookcase spanning a wall and a rubber plant by the door.

Where am I?

'Zavanna?' he asked, and his mouth felt strange.

She didn't reply.

He looked down at his hands and he had three fingers and a thumb. His hands weren't made of flesh but a kind of plastic, and he wasn't wearing his clothes, he was wearing a leather bodice adorned with a kettu pattern.

Dune's armour.

Oh god oh god oh god!

He moved forward and stared at his reflection in the glass pane.

Dune stared back.

Jack opened his mouth and watched as Dune's did the same. He blinked and watched Dune's eyelids flicker closed and open.

With a shriek of horror, he realised where he was. What had happened. He was inside Dune's cabinet, the one Cutter had taken—and he was no longer inside his own body.

He was inside Dune's.

Excerpt from The Shadow Glass *screenplay, dated 1 Dec. 1984, written by Bob Corman.*

INT. QUARTZ CASTLE – NIGHT

Dune peers from the window. The lub sits on the ledge.
POV: The land beyond the castle gates teems with
skalion SOLDIERS.

> DORR
>
> There are so many.

> DUNE
>
> What are they doing?

A LARGE SHAPE is trundled towards the gates.

> DUNE
>
> What is that?

A sheet is tugged from the object, revealing a
mechanical device shaped like a wheel. It begins to spit
GREEN ENERGY, the wheel spinning.

> DORR
>
> There are tales of skalion devices.
> They call it teck-noll-gee.

> DUNE
>
> I don't like it.

The green energy crackles and shakes the ground.

It BLASTS the gates, destroying them in a torrent of
flying debris.

                    DUNE
        They're coming.

Jack couldn't breathe. The cabinet held no air. He hammered the glass with fists that weren't his own. He twisted in the cramped space, his shoulders hitting one side and then the other, the back of his head striking the back of the cabinet.

'OH GOD! OH FUCKING GOD!'

His voice sounded strange. Muffled. And his tongue felt heavy, fuzzy.

'I'm not Dune,' he cried. 'I'm not Dune!'

He had to wake up. He had to end the sight voyage *now*. But as he banged his latex fists against the glass, he felt the cold pane and saw his juddering reflection. He felt Dune's body, lighter than his own, smaller, and he smelled the interior of the box, its aroma of stale wood and preserved leather.

This wasn't part of the sight voyage.

This was real.

He was Dune.

A fresh howl tore from his throat as he threw himself against the glass. The box teetered for a second and then rocked forwards. He was thrown off balance, the carpet rushing up to meet him as the cabinet toppled from its perch. Glass smashed and darkness snapped around him.

'Zavanna,' Jack grunted, lying in the cradling dark. 'What have you done to me?'

He heaved a few breaths. He couldn't move. At least without any light he didn't have to look at himself, and that felt good. He could think. What if this really was still part of the sight voyage? What if it was a test?

He shifted against the carpet and winced as glass sliced his palms.

There was only one way to find out if this was real.

He panted a few quick breaths, psyching himself up, and then threw the cabinet off him. It crashed back against a filing cabinet and lay motionless.

Jack stood in the middle of the office, surrounded by glass shards. He was sure he recognised the place, with its Overlook-style carpet and art deco windows. He peered up at the desk, which in itself was surreal. He felt as if he were kneeling but he knew he was standing as tall as Dune's body would allow.

At the front of the desk, with its piles of paperwork, notebooks and collection of Iri-styled paperweights, rested a name plaque.

BOB CORMAN.

It was his father's office at Bob Co.

He was at the studio.

The office had been trashed. The floor was covered in paper and the filing cabinet was open, spewing yet more documents into the room. It looked as if a gremlin had been let loose. Jack remembered how ordered his father had kept the office and felt annoyed for him.

He became aware he was moving only because it felt so strange. His legs were strong but light, stiff from lack of use, and the armour was tight around his abdomen. Muttering, he moved around the desk and clambered up onto the chair, scanning the surface before he found what he needed.

He grabbed the old rotary phone, fumbling with it in his newly small hands, and raised it to one of the ears atop his kettu head, hearing the dialling tone.

'Shit.' He had no idea what Amelia's mobile number was. Who knew anybody's number nowadays? The only number he knew was his own and… his phone was in the real Jack's pocket! And the real Jack was, hopefully, still in the attic with the Guild. He dialled and waited.

Finally, the line clicked.

'Hello?' Amelia said.

'Amelia! Thank god you're there. I wasn't sure you'd hear my phone but—'

'Jack?'

Her tone stopped him short.

'You're calling from Bob Co.?' Amelia asked. She must recognise the number. '*How* are you calling from Bob Co.?'

One thing at a time.

'Am I still there?' Jack asked. 'I mean, my body. Am I okay?'

She didn't say anything for a second. When she spoke, her voice was quiet. 'Jack, you're here with us at the house. Unconscious. Something happened. We've been trying to wake you up but—'

A wave of vertigo almost sent him toppling off the chair. So this was real. He wasn't still in the sight voyage. He was at Bob Co., inside Dune… He swallowed and hiked the phone back up to his ear, which was higher than his regular ear.

'I'm fine,' he said. 'Well, not fine, I'm completely screwed, but I'm alive. You're not going to believe this—'

Amelia cut short a laugh. 'The list of things I'm not going to believe is getting pretty short these days.'

'I'm Dune.'

'You're...'

'Dune. I'm in the puppet.'

More silence. He imagined her face, mouth half-open, blue eyes unblinking. Classic 'understated freaking out' Amelia.

'You're Dune.'

He heard a voice in the background but he couldn't tell who had spoken. Maybe everybody. But he didn't have time to go through all the confusion and wacky theories. The sight voyage had done this for a reason.

'You're a puppet,' Amelia breathed.

'Seems that way.' He shook his head. 'Look, if we know anything from the movies, it's that I won't be able to get out of here until I've completed some kind of karmic journey. Probably finding the final fragment. So we need to figure this out. Amelia?'

'I'm putting you on speakerphone.'

The Guild chorused 'Shit', and 'You okay?' and 'Fucking hell'. He shouted over all of them.

'Why would the sight voyage bring me here? To Dune? This doesn't exactly help us.'

Nell's voice came through. 'What did the voyage show you, Jack? Before the body-swapping hijinks?'

He tried to think through the gnawing sense of unreality that had its teeth around his brain.

Brain. The puppets aren't built with physical brains. How am I thinking?

'The Glass,' Jack said, suppressing the thought. 'It showed me the three pieces we had before Kunin Yillda took them, and then it showed me Kunin Yillda and Nebfet in front of some kind of wheel thing, and then I was inside Dune's cabinet. I was Dune.'

'This is messed up!' Huw said.

Toby said something that Jack didn't catch.

'The vision took you to the box,' Toby said, coming through clearer now. He must have moved closer to the phone.

'Yes,' Jack said, eyeing the cabinet on the floor.

'Jack, what if that's where the final piece is?'

Jack shook his head. 'But the initials are wrong. Dune was at Dad's house and he isn't AT.'

'But I am,' Amelia said. 'Think about it. We assumed BC meant Bob Co. because that's where we found the first fragment, but that's also where I work, or used to anyway, before Cutter. For all intents and purposes, I *was* Bob Co., so AT could mean me, the first fragment at Bob Co., and BC could mean Bob Corman—Uncle Bob's house. Dune.'

'That actually makes sense,' he said excitedly. 'Let me look.'

He hopped off the chair, dragging the phone with him. Paper cascaded off the desk, a couple of paperweights thumping to the carpet, but he ignored them, hurrying to the cabinet. Avoiding the broken glass, he heaved the box over and peered inside. There was nothing else in there, though.

'Jack?'

His ears swivelled towards the phone and he almost lost his balance. He wasn't used to having such active appendages and he realised he could still hear Amelia, even though the receiver was resting on the carpet. Kettu hearing really was good.

'There's nothing,' he called.

'Are you sure?' Toby asked.

'Let me look again.' He got into the cabinet and ran his hands over the wood panels. He stopped as his fingers brushed a ridge in the wood. Squinting, he ran his fingers over it again, attempting to make it out. He stared at a segment of the panel that formed the back of the cabinet.

It was carved with a symbol.

An Iri Eye.

'Holy shit,' he whispered.

He reached over the edge of the cabinet to grab the phone.

'We need Zavanna,' he breathed. 'Now.'

A sound came at the door. Footsteps.

'Somebody's coming,' he said. 'Guys, we need the Eye. It's a key to the final fragment, I think. I could try smashing the box but that might damage the Glass. We need the key.'

'We're on our wa—' Amelia said, but Jack dropped the receiver and leapt behind the desk just as the office door opened.

He tried not to breathe, curling up in the shadows beneath the desk. He heard a hitched inhale and the faint patter of a heartbeat. Whoever had entered must have spotted the broken cabinet. Jack had no time to wonder at his newfound super-hearing, though, because then a voice croaked, 'Dune?'

It was Cutter.

Jack remained hidden.

'Dune? Are you in here?'

Glass crunched and Jack heard the cabinet being lifted from the floor, Cutter's breath rattling with the effort. He was sure he even heard the air popping in the man's joints.

Nothing happened for a moment, then the office door closed.

Silence.

Jack counted to twenty and then crept out from under the desk. Cutter was gone, and so was the cabinet.

'Shit,' he whispered. Where had Cutter taken it? Had he noticed the Iri Eye, too? If he had figured out the fragment was in the cabinet and taken it to Kunin Yillda, it was game over. Jack had to leave the office, head into Bob Co., even though it had become enemy territory and he was outnumbered.

He stepped towards the door and glass cracked beneath his boot. He bent and picked up a framed photo that must have been knocked off the desk in his haste to get to the cabinet. The photo showed the *Shadow Glass* castle set that had once been here at Bob Co. A pink-cheeked toddler snuggled in a onesie as a jumble of skalions, wugs and kettu crowded around him. And there, standing over him protectively, was Dune.

His father had taken the picture during a break in filming, and the look on toddler Jack's face was one of pure joy. That was before it all went wrong. Back then, there was only a baby sitting in a fantasy menagerie, grinning from ear to ear.

And now the skalions had taken over Bob Co.

One kettu is worth a thousand armies if she has courage deep and blade sharp.

He heard Dune's voice but he couldn't tell where it was coming from, if he had imagined it entirely. It was oddly comforting. Regardless, he clenched his fist and knew he didn't have a choice. He had to find that cabinet. Save his father's worlds; both of them.

Jack checked his weapons, finding a dagger attached to his belt, Dune's sword swinging between his shoulder blades. He scoured the office for supplies, seizing a heavy glass paperweight and a handful of drawing pins, which he stuffed into a pouch. His fingers hovered over a pair of Ray-Bans, then he pocketed those as well.

Creeping to the door, he listened, then stuck his head into the corridor. It was wreathed with a fine green mist that made him think of the skalion swamps.

It was quiet. When he was a kid, Bob Co. had been a bustling hive. Now, though, it seemed drab and grizzled. It had suffered in Bob's absence and Jack thought again about Iri—how it, too, was falling apart—and he felt more certain than ever that Bob's declining health, his impending death, had been the cause of Iri's own decline.

'Iri needs you!' Bob had said, and Jack hadn't listened. He could make up for that now.

Somewhere beyond this corridor, he heard sounds. His ears twisted as he crept down the hall, unable to decipher the random chorus of footsteps and clanging and shouting.

He marvelled at how light he felt, how noiseless his movements were. The kettu had always been his favourite Iri creatures, but now that he was one, he was newly awed. He felt he could do anything.

The only limits are those we place on ourselves.

Dune's voice again, a comforting whisper somewhere in his mind. It strengthened Jack's resolve, made him feel less alone.

He carried on down the hall, taking the stairs to a fire escape and listening before he pushed open the door.

Wind tousled Dune's hair, and as Jack scanned the village of warehouses a thousand scents thrilled his nostrils. Tarmac and grass, rain and petrol, and something else, a putrid stench that made him want to retch.

'Skalions,' he whispered, sniffing the toxic fog that hung over the studio. The knowledge that Kunin Yillda was fouling Bob's empire, his legacy, caused a jag of anger to shoot through him. It quickly soured into regret.

Jack had no time to consider why, because at that moment footsteps rang in his ears and he shrank back. The sound clanged in his head and he peered through a crack in the door.

A troop of men and women carted props and bits of furniture across the studio lot, skalion soldiers poking them with spears and jostling them along. The humans' mouths hung slack, their sunken eyes tinged with blue, and their movements seemed robotic. They looked exactly how the cosplayers had at All T'Orc, and Jack realised they were all under Nebfet's thrall. One by one, they vanished into Stage 9.

'What are they doing?' Jack whispered. He frowned, spotting a couple of the workers in uniforms. They looked like police, but they must be security guards.

After waiting for the last worker to disappear inside, he leapt out from his hiding place. Dune's body seemed to know what to do and he found himself tucking and rolling across the tarmac, keeping to the shadows until he was outside the Stage 9 door.

Clanging and hammering sounds came from within.

Just what were they doing in there?

He eased the door open to peer inside, and the work sounds doubled in volume, almost deafening him. He tried to make out what was going on, but a wooden panel a few feet away shielded his view of the sound stage. Green and yellow light flickered across the space and Jack felt sure they were building something. If only he could see what.

A sudden wave of despair clutched at him.

How could he possibly stop them?

Bob's creations were running wild, taking over the studio. Had Bob set all of this in motion knowing it would end in chaos? Was that his final trick? The sick punchline to a joke that Jack was still struggling to understand?

Fight this. Fight until there is no fight left.

The kettu voice echoed in the back of his head and this time he felt it as more than just a voice. It was a presence. Some lingering aspect of Dune urging him on, speaking the words Jack needed to hear. But they only magnified the sense of failure.

He had done everything Bob wanted; helped the kettu, followed the breadcrumbs that led to the Shadow Glass. He had even started to remember the good things, the Bob that existed before the booze, public humiliation and ranting voicemails. But it still wasn't enough. Bob's world was spiralling out of control and nothing Jack did seemed to make a difference.

He heard movement a fraction of a second before the skalion lunged for him.

It burst out of the darkness of the sound stage, butting through the stage door and knocking Jack backwards as it emerged. Panting, Jack staggered back, keeping his eyes trained on the creature as it leered at him, then slurped the air with delight.

'Kettuuuuu,' the creature gurgled.

It charged.

Before Jack knew what he was doing, he'd seized the soldier's arm and used it to propel himself up and over the skalion's domed head. He wrenched the arm back as he landed behind the skalion, hearing the satisfying crunch of breaking bone and kicking out its legs. As the soldier gurgled in pain, Jack dealt a blow to its skull.

In that moment, he saw his father. Not the man who had filled his childhood with laughter, but the crouched, nocturnal monster he had become in Jack's teen years. As he struck the skalion, he saw Bob's sallow complexion, the dead look in his eyes, and Jack gritted his teeth, anger surging into his fists.

He heard the schoolyard echoes that had followed him through adolescence.

'Hey, Crackers Jack, what's your dad taken today?'

'Did you hear the one about the film director and the puppet?'

He saw Bob drooling, cradling an empty bottle, stinking of whisky.

'I want her! Not you.'

Everything his father said in those drunken stupors was twisted. Poisoned words from a poisoned mind. But the pain remained, sharp and icicle white, stabbing Jack's heart as painfully now as it ever had.

The skalion went down face first and rolled over just as Jack pounced. He snarled, spitting as he pummelled the creature's face, his heart racing.

He saw his father's vacant stares, the days where the study door remained closed, the fevered monologues about Iri, about Hollywood, about how nobody understood him. He kept hitting the thing beneath him and with each punch he saw a new face.

Dune.

Anya.

Brol.

Zavanna.

Zavanna in pain. Zavanna howling. The skalion laughing as it bled into the cobbles. He'd do anything to stop Zavanna making that sound ever again. The sound of something inside her splitting down the middle like lava rock, forever scarred.

'Die!' he shouted. 'Die! Die! DIE!'

He kept hitting long after the creature had stopped thrashing. With a gasp, he drew back, staring at the puddle of goo that had once been the skalion's head, his fist coated in slime and brain matter.

He staggered back, shocked at what he had done, but it had felt good. He wanted more of them. More things to kill.

Calm, the voice said. *Find the calm. There is no joy in killing.*

Jack ignored it. More skalions emerged from the sound stage, hunching around him, and Jack grinned, drawing Dune's sword from his back.

'Come on, then,' he snarled, and the skalions plunged as one. Dune's body flipped and kicked, the sword snaking with deadly precision, hacking flesh, separating limbs from bodies. He felt more alive than he had in years. He felt free, surrendering to the anger that for so long had been bubbling beneath the surface, only just kept in check.

He had no idea how long he fought for. Finally, though, he sat panting, leaning on his bloodied sword, a ring of corpses around him. The sight of them caused his stomach to squeeze and he trembled uncontrollably, no matter how hard he tried to stop.

Peace, Bobson. Peace.

Before he knew it, he was crying. Not for the slain monsters or for Bob but for himself. For the anger he hadn't realised was in him. It had been there for so long it was a part of him, a festering second heart made up of every bad memory, every regret, and it had pumped hatred through his every waking moment.

For the first time in his life, he wished he could have helped Bob, but he had been a kid. Just a kid. He couldn't have done anything different. It was only now, looking back, that he saw his father for who he truly was. An arrogant dreamer whose fantasies were his gift and his undoing.

He couldn't hate him anymore.

Hating him was killing Jack.

It was time to let it go.

Finally, he wiped the downy fur covering Dune's cheeks and raised his head.

He had to move. He had to find a way to stop Cutter and Kunin Yillda, salvage what remained of Bob's legacy.

He wiped Dune's sword on one of the skalions and holstered it between his shoulder blades. As he prepared to slip into Stage 9, though, he heard the soft patter of heartbeats, and a mechanical roar filled his ears. It wasn't coming from the stage, but somewhere near the main studio building.

Jack ran towards it, shredding the circling mist as he went. He paused by the car park, reaching it just in time to spot a vehicle as it smashed through the security booth. It sped across the tarmac, headlights on full, and with a start Jack realised it was his father's camper van. The one they had abandoned in the wake of Kunin Yillda's resurrection. Amelia and the Guild must have gone back for it.

He whooped as the van tore across the tarmac, but the cheer died on his lips as he saw that it wasn't slowing down. The Volkswagen was barrelling with alarming speed straight for the studio.

'Wait!' he shouted, running to block its path. 'STOP!'

But it didn't slow down. He leapt out of the way and watched the van slam into the lub statue at the front of the building. With a *BOOM*, it hammered into the building itself, shattering the glass door and disappearing inside amid a chorus of destructive sounds.

Silence fell.

Excerpt from The Shadow Glass *shooting script, dated 1 Dec. 1984,*
written by Bob Corman.

INT. CELL – NIGHT

CLOSE-UP: Nebfet's blue eyes GLOW amid the sound of
SCREAMING.

We PULL BACK to reveal the soothsayer is in a DANK,
DRIPPING CELL.

A wug is strapped to a chair, its eyes PINNED OPEN by
a BARBARIC DEVICE. It WAILS in horror.

> KUNIN YILLDA
> What does the snivelling gnat know?
> Speak!

> NEBFET
> Alas, regent, nothing, it seems.

Kunin Yillda shrieks and SEIZES Nebfet, pinning her to
the wall.

> KUNIN YILLDA
> I MUST KNOW WHERE IT IS! I MUST KNOW ALL!

> NEBFET
> (choking)
> Please, regent, I am close, I sense it.

Do not fear. The Glass shall be yours.

The skalion queen TOSSES her to the cell floor.

She eyes the panting wug. LICKS her THIN LIPS.

> KUNIN YILLDA
> Everything is Kunin Yillda's.
> Yeeeesss. Ev-er-y-thing.

She approaches the wug, her bulk FILLING the FRAME.

OS: The WUG SCREAMS as a GURGLING, CHOMPING
SOUND fills the darkness.

Jack stood panting, horror shuddering through him.

Had Amelia lost control of the vehicle?

Before he could chase across the tarmac, a shrieking stampede kicked into life. He watched as skalions poured out of Stage 9, charging for the main building. A screaming war cry filled the air as they fought their way inside, weapons raised, and Jack heard a screech of metal as they tore at the Volkswagen.

He gritted his kettu teeth and prepared to launch after them, but then a new shape bounded out from behind a parked car. It pinned him against the vehicle, and Jack grimaced as an enormous tongue swiped his face.

'Fin,' a voice hissed. 'Heel!'

The dog fell off him and turned circles by the car as Jack spotted five figures emerging from behind another vehicle. A clapped-out Beetle with rusted orange paint. His father's car. The last time he had seen it was when they took the camper van from the garage. What was it doing here?

As he attempted to figure out what was going on, he spotted Amelia, her eyes wide with shock as they focussed on him. Flanking her, Toby and Huw's mouths fell open, while Nell went to Fin, drawing the dog back.

'Jack?' Zavanna asked, stepping out from behind the others, her gaze skipping over him. He knew what she saw. Not him, but her brother, alive again, returning her stare. She hadn't seen Dune since the attack on Wugtown. The one that cost Dune his life.

'Yeah,' Jack said. 'It's me.'

She didn't look away and her unblinking stare was painful to endure. There was too much feeling in her eyes, too much conflict and yearning and anguish. He wished he could be Dune for her, but he wasn't, not even close. Still, he felt a flutter in Dune's chest cavity, as if the puppet recognised its kin. His arms twitched, instinctively reaching for her, and Jack resisted.

'I'm, uh, sorry,' he said, unable to think of anything else. The fact that he was inside the body of her dead brother was wrong in roughly ten thousand ways.

At the sound of his voice, Zavanna's expression softened and she took both his forearms, gripping them tightly as she smiled.

'I'm glad you're back,' she said, and he wasn't sure if she meant him or Dune. Maybe both.

'Thanks.' He cleared his throat. 'Speaking of, where's the real me?'

Toby jerked a thumb over his shoulder. 'In the Beetle. Your dad really loved Volkswagens. We brought you along just in case, I don't know, we needed you or something.'

'The decoy was Toby's idea,' Amelia said.

Even though the thought of his body lying unconscious in the Beetle made Jack feel sick, he smiled at Toby. 'Brilliant.'

'Thanks.'

'We need to find Dune's cabinet,' Jack said. 'Cutter took it.' The wind carried the sound of screeching and smashing as the skalion horde tore apart the camper van. The ground trembled as if something was shifting beneath the surface, and Jack saw that the others felt it, too. It was too intense to be made by the skalions. It felt like an engine groaning beneath their feet.

'What's doing that?' Huw asked.

'They're doing something in Stage 9,' Jack said. 'I think that's their base of operations.'

Amelia straightened. 'Then that's where we're going. It makes sense. The Iri sets are in Stage 7, which is connected to 9, don't ask me why. I think Bob purposefully designed this place to be confusing.'

'Iri sets?' Nell asked.

'For *Shadow Glass 2*,' Toby explained.

'Right!' Nell said. 'If only we could watch that *before* we're eaten by Kunin Yillda.'

'You still want a sequel?' Jack asked. 'After all this?'

'Do skalions lay deadly spawn sacs in the woods?'

They all looked at her. Nell offered an apologetic smile.

'Sorry, gross.'

Amelia laughed, shaking her head while Nell blushed.

'Stage 9 it is,' Jack said.

The ground continued to shudder as they skirted around the studio, forming what Jack realised was surely the most ragtag troupe in history. A studio executive, two kettu, a lub, a trio of excitable fankids and their dog. He just hoped that what they had in pop culture smarts made up for what they lacked in numbers.

He felt the others staring at him and gave them an irritated snarl.

'Quit it,' he said.

Toby chuckled. 'It's so weird, your voice coming from Dune's mouth.'

'Don't get used to it.'

'How does it feel?' Amelia asked.

'Furry.' He couldn't tell them about the voice he kept hearing. They'd only think he was crazier than the situation already suggested.

They stopped outside Stage 9. The ground shook even more violently there, causing the warehouse to rattle and groan.

'What the hell is doing that?' Amelia hissed.

'Whatever's in there,' Jack said. 'Plan?'

'We charge,' Zavanna said. 'Swift and savage.'

'What if we're outnumbered?' Toby asked.

'There are seven of us, lub not included.' Huw shrugged. 'So that's pretty much a given.'

'One kettu is worth a thousand armies,' Zavanna said.

'If she has courage deep and blade sharp,' Jack finished for her. He met her surprised stare and noted the way the corner of her mouth lifted.

Family, murmured the voice in his head. *Without family, we are nothing.*

'Let's do this.'

Jack tugged open the stage door and eased his eye to the crack. Just inside, a couple of skalions guarded the entrance. They smelled worse this close and Jack resisted putting a paw to his nose. Instead, he gave the others a warning glance and then tore the door open. He threw himself at the skalions and, taking advantage of their surprise, knocked their craniums together.

They collapsed with a wet *thwack*. Unconscious.

Skalion scum!

Jack beckoned for the others to follow him into the warehouse. The cement floor shook even more, a deafening, mechanical whirring sound throbbing in his ears, but Jack still couldn't tell what was causing it. Blue lightning danced beyond a wooden screen that shielded their view of the sound stage.

'Yes! It is done!' Nebfet's cry echoed coarsely around them.

The door slammed behind Jack and he turned to see a couple of skalions blocking their exit. They squatted with delight contorting their features as their eyes gleamed at the gathering of humans.

'Shit,' Jack said, giving the others a nervous look.

A final blast of blue light bathed the warehouse, and then abruptly fell away.

The floor stopped vibrating. The mechanical sound dulled until silence fell.

The screen moved sideways and the studio was revealed to them.

Tensed where he stood, Jack saw the floor was lined with puppets. Skalions and kettu and wugs, at least fifty in total, more than he had ever seen en masse. And they were moving.

Fifty of them cranked upright, gasping, blue light burning in their irises. Beyond them, standing before a huge mechanical wheel, Nebfet cackled, her arms spread wide as she surveyed them.

'Yes! Welcome! Welcome to the beginning of the end!'

The newly animated creatures stood, blue eyes agleam, creating an unblinking sea of light that turned the sound stage neon.

Jack panted with dread. He shared a look with Zavanna and her jaw firmed as she drew the sword from her back.

'The sequel prototypes,' Amelia murmured. 'They're the test puppets for *Shadow Glass 2*.'

Jack's gaze moved past the puppets to the mechanical wheel. It was a junkyard version of the weapon the skalions used in *The Shadow Glass*, at least fifteen feet in diameter, over which slack-jawed Bob Co. workers fawned. They had created it from bits of old set and what looked like parts from the crew's cars. The machine shook and steamed as it powered down.

'Christ,' Jack breathed. His fur bristled as he realised what was happening. Nebfet had repeated the ceremony she had performed on Kunin Yillda, but on a grander scale. That was why there were now so many skalions, how they had overrun both All T'Orc and Bob Co.

She had created an army.

'Welcome, also, Bobson,' Nebfet rasped, and Jack found her attention on him, her lips peeling into something resembling a smile. 'You have made it just in time.' She raised a skeletal finger and pointed. 'Take them!'

The puppet army turned. More skalions and blue-eyed wugs than Jack could count whirled to face them, teeth bared, snarls reverberating against the walls. The skalions' visors were engaged, their breath snorting against the glass, while the wugs growled, their adorable faces warped with uncharacteristic malice.

Jack raised a hand to shield his eyes from the burn of their eyes, and then he remembered the Ray-Bans. He slipped them on, dulling the light just in time for him to see them surge forward.

'Charge!' Zavanna cried, and together they broke into a run, hurtling towards the horde.

Within seconds, Jack was swallowed up by it. He battled against the tide of blows and jabs, wielding Dune's sword. A skalion spear lanced his arm but he ignored the pain, seeing that Amelia and the Guild had entered the fray. Fin bounded about, unable to resist the sight of the puppets, and the others had foraged weapons from somewhere.

Low, said the voice. *Strike from below.*

They danced between their attackers and Jack marvelled at how swiftly he moved, how easy it was to dodge around the skalions, and his blade flashed and dove, tearing out blood-smeared stuffing. These puppets were freshly animated; they hadn't evolved in the way Zavanna had, and their insides were a mixture of fluid and fluff.

He caught sight of Zavanna tearing off a wug's head. She bared her teeth in a grin and he felt himself smiling back, sensing something new between them. They were in this together.

'How does it really feel to be a kettu, Bobson?' Zavanna called.

'Pretty freaking—' Jack began, but he winced as teeth sank into his arm. He seized a wug by the throat, then dropped to his knees as a blade whirred over his head, nearly clipping his ears.

'Do you require aid?' Zavanna shouted, her tone mocking.

'Just focus on your own fight!'

At the sound of her laughter, he tossed the wug aside. He plunged his dagger into a soldier's groin, then yanked his weapon free and prepared to spear another.

'Jack!' Amelia shouted, and he spotted her by a door at the far side of the sound stage. He nodded and, alongside Zavanna, hurried to join the others, battling his way between wugs and snarling kettu. Finally, they leapt over the threshold, and Toby and Nell slammed the door, throwing their backs against it.

Clanging blows immediately followed as Nebfet's army fell upon the door, but it held firm for the moment.

Jack cast a look around them, seeing tombstones and gnarled trees. He realised they had made it to Stage 7. A graveyard set rested before them, graves jutting from the uneven earth as branches raked the air.

Somewhere, a skalion cackled, the sound reverberating through the warehouse.

If the Glass and Kunin Yillda were anywhere, it was here.

'*Dead Spaces* just wrapped, we hired out the sound stage to them,' Amelia whispered, motioning for them to follow her into the cemetery. Crouching low, they went after her, traipsing between the graves. Toby, Huw and Nell gazed around in awe while Fin stopped to sniff a tree and Nell whispered at her to keep up.

Amelia ducked into the shadows at the back of the set and Jack heard the creak of another door opening. They followed her into a fifties-style living room, the flowery wallpaper artfully aged, the chairs draped with doilies. In front of an electric heater, a coffee table held a bowl of Werther's Originals.

'Don't tell me you're making soap operas, too,' Jack said.

'I actually have no idea what this set is,' Amelia said.

Jack's kettu ears swivelled as they picked up a sound and he held up a warning hand to the others. They stilled, listening.

He heard a scuffling like something brushing against the inside of the walls, and then a long, hairy arm smashed through the lounge window. It grabbed Toby, dragging him back towards the window frame. Zavanna leapt to his aid, but then Huw cried out as his legs were yanked from beneath him. Something hauled him behind the sofa.

'Huw?' Jack said, just as Amelia shouted in surprise, wiping clear, gloopy liquid from her shoulder.

Jack looked up.

Hundreds of blue eyes blinked back.

Creatures were crammed into the catwalks running over the set, drooling with glee as they lay in wait. Somehow, Nebfet's army had made its way into Stage 7. They began to gibber and shriek, the sound reverberating around the set, and Jack saw them preparing to launch themselves inside, but then a voice hissed, 'Silence!'

A clicking sound shuddered around them, the sound of a swarm, and the hairs on Jack's forearms shivered. With Zavanna's help, Toby wrestled free from the thing at the window, and he held out a hand to tug Huw up from behind the sofa.

As they recovered, Nebfet dropped from the ceiling, landing a few feet from Jack. The soothsayer's eyes pulsed with light and her gnarled claws knotted together before her. That was all he saw before the lights went out.

Darkness dropped over Jack's eyes.

He blinked, straining to see, but it was no use. Even with his new kettu senses, he couldn't pick out anything in the pitch dark.

He heard something scurrying about, though, the scrabbling all around them, coming from the walls, then the ceiling, then the floor. Nebfet's blue eyes had vanished but Jack heard scuttling, buzzing insect noises. She was in here somewhere, and her army with her.

'Zavanna?' he hissed.

A claw snatched at Jack's ankle and he yelled, stomping his foot. The claw released him.

'Jack?' Toby's voice was distant.

The scuttling sound grew louder and Jack's head jerked from side to side, searching.

'There.'

Nebfet's breath was cold in his ear and he cried out as claws pincered his shoulders. A weight dropped onto him from above and he staggered back, crashing into something solid, maybe the wall, and then his legs gave way beneath him. He hit the floor with a grunt, his back against soft cushion. The sofa.

'*There you are.*'

Twin slivers of blue light blinked open, becoming full and round, and he found himself staring into Nebfet's segmented eyes.

'*Surrender to the dark,*' she cooed, the rustling insect noises vibrating in his ears, deafening him. '*This is not your fight, Bobson. Surrender to the dark. Iri is not yours, it never will be. Be mine. Be miiiiiine.*'

Jack struggled to free himself, revulsion bristling through him as he strained to lower his eyelids against the light. Even with the sunglasses, it was painful to endure. A growl rumbled up from his gut and he drew on every scrap of strength he could, both his and Dune's, feeling it in the sinew of his artificial muscles.

Be strong, urged the voice in his head, even as Nebfet's will clawed at his mind. *Together. Defeat her together.*

With a howl, Jack threw Nebfet off him.

She crashed against the coffee table and recovered quickly, spinning to face him. Just as Jack wondered how he was able to see her in the dark, he realised a new light had entered the room.

Zavanna's face was illuminated with a green luminescence.

At her breast, the Iri Eye gleamed.

It beamed a livid radiance around them, painting the lounge green and illuminating Toby, who stood panting beside the coffee table, his eyes wide, while Nell, Amelia and Huw were tensed by the fireplace. The light picked out the corrupted Iri creatures, who shrank into the back of the set, becoming shadowy outlines awaiting their moment.

Nebfet crouched on the table, and for the first time she looked afraid.

'The Eye!' Jack cried, and Zavanna seemed to understand. She tugged the pendant away from her breast, aiming it at Nebfet as she paced towards her.

'Iri sees you, witch,' Zavanna hissed. 'It is displeased.'

The soothsayer shrieked, shrinking back and shielding her honeycomb eyes.

'*No! No!*'

She flopped off the coffee table, scuttling for the lounge door. Jack leapt to stop her, but he was too slow. The door opened and she vanished.

'Get her!' Jack cried, lunging after the soothsayer, leaping through the door into darkness.

He stopped and turned around in a confined space. As his eyes adjusted to the sudden lack of light, he spotted cables looping above his head and the wooden joists that formed the backs of set walls. He was in the cramped space between sets.

It was only as the others pushed in behind him that he spotted the white-clad figure at the far end of the walkway.

He resembled a paper man, a pale piece of origami, his suit as white as his complexion. His high cheekbones whittled dark hollows into his face but his mismatching eyes shone bright. Despite his sickly appearance, Wesley Cutter managed a thin smile.

'Dune,' he whispered, looking at Jack.

'Near enough,' Jack said.

Cutter's brow creased. 'Jack?' His lips trembled. 'What have you done?'

Jack ignored the question. 'Where's the cabinet, Cutter?'

For a moment, Cutter remained motionless, his eyes glassy. Then he seemed to recover. He cast a look over Amelia and the Guild, drawing himself up to his full height as his expression sharpened.

'Amelia Twine, I'm so grateful to you for surrendering the studio to me. I think you'll find it will thrive under my care.'

'As delusional as ever,' Amelia spat.

His tone became conversational. 'You don't care, not really. You think you make movies, nothing more. I'm afraid you have been horribly misguided. Even now, you must see it. When Bob Corman made *The Shadow Glass*, he captured something remarkable. He captured what so few people manage. Pure, unbridled creativity. He captured a truth. That is why I have fought so long to preserve that vision. That *original* vision.'

A jag of loathing cut through Jack at the thought of the book-burning demonstration. A younger Cutter encouraging fans to throw their graphic novels into the pyre. The effect it had on his father, the way he withered like the pages eaten by the flames.

Agnor had said belief powered Iri. Jack wondered if Cutter had unwittingly contributed to Iri's erosion.

Cutter wasn't protecting Iri, he was killing it, one fan at a time, simply by turning people against it.

Jack's knuckles throbbed. He felt every sinew aching to pummel something, expel the emotional charge, preferably the man raking his claws through his father's legacy. He wished he hadn't lost Alden's letter. He might have been able to use it somehow.

Unhappiness is the source of all evil, whispered the voice.

'You're crazy if you think I'm going to let you take Bob Co.,' Jack said.

Cutter laughed, unhindered. 'Oh Jack, why else do you think they call us fanatics?'

Something trilled in Jack's ear and he saw the lub had poked its head out of Toby's backpack. It blinked around in fear. Toby whispered something reassuring and petted its head.

'You think you're a fan?' Jack demanded. 'You don't love anything, Cutter. You want to seal it behind glass. Keep it away from other people in case they contaminate it.'

'It must be somebody's duty to protect that which is sacred and vulnerable.'

'You have no idea what made that film special. None!'

Cutter's smile hardened.

'How disappointed your father must have been. The heir of Iri so casually dismissive of it. It's a wonder he lasted as long as he did with a cuckoo in his nest.'

Anger exploded in Jack's chest, but he felt a surge of confidence.

'Is this really what Alden would have wanted?' he asked. 'He's why you're doing this, right? It's his hatred of that book that gave you the idea to burn it in the nineties. The book that ruined Iri for Alden. Or is this more about what *you* wanted? What did you think would happen if Bob came to see you that time in the hospital? Did you think he'd take you under his wing? Give you the attention you deserved?'

Cutter's lips thinned into a reptilian leer. 'Don't—'

'It's not really about Alden, is it?' Jack continued. 'It's about you.'

Cutter's face had become hard with horror. Or fear. Or grief. Probably all three. His eyes were glassy with emotion. He looked as if he was about to say something, maybe confess he'd made a mistake, that his hate campaign was futile. Had ruined lives.

But then his face smoothed into something almost serene.

Zavanna's voice filled the space. 'Jack, look.'

The wall beside them was shifting. It slid sideways, drawn by invisible hands, reconfiguring the space, opening it up. He found himself staring into a vast chamber that guttered with candlelight. It resembled the interior of a Gothic castle, black cobbles running across the floor and up the walls, while onyx columns supported a vaulted ceiling carved with glittering, web-like structures.

The chamber was filled with snarling Iridians. Brainwashed lopers, witterbirds and wugs prowled and drooled, ready for battle.

And at the far end, beneath a stained-glass window that dappled the chamber in green light, rested the skalion queen's throne. In it sat Kunin Yillda.

'Welcome erplings!' she shouted. 'Let us finish this, hmmm?'

Final blog post by Bob Corman, posted on BobCorman.com *on 19 February.*

It's the old cliché, isn't it? It's not the destination, it's the journey. We don't watch *Willow* because we want to see Madmartigan and his bride. We don't watch *The NeverEnding Story* to see Bastian riding Falkor, even if that is a magnificent visual. It's the stops along the way. The subtle notes between the showstopping musical numbers. When I first wrote *The Shadow Glass*, the ending with Dune *[SPOILER REDACTED]* was intended to be emotional, but I believe it worked because the journey is so huge, so seemingly impossible, and yet it was accomplished by a so-called 'pup', the least likely hero imaginable.

Endings are, in my opinion, overrated.

But the journey? Now there's something to write home about.

The skalion queen studied them and Jack heard a clatter of metal as her soldiers emerged from the shadows, lining the walls, their spears drawn, eyes trained on Jack and his friends. Purple tongues stroked thin lips.

'Oh my god,' Toby breathed, and Jack saw what he had spotted.

The Shadow Glass rested to the right of Kunin Yillda's throne. It remained incomplete, still missing the top left of its frame. The final fragment. And the oval mirror was nowhere in sight. The queen had yet to complete it, yet Dune's cabinet sat beside the Glass. Did she know it held the final piece? What was she waiting for?

'Admiring my prize, erplings?' Kunin Yillda spat. 'Is it not impressive? Enjoy it while you still can. It shall never be whole again.'

Jack's chest pinched. The swamp queen really had no intention of putting the Glass back together. She wanted it solely for her collection. A status symbol. A shiny bauble, just as Brol had said. And as long as the Glass remained in Kunin's keeping, broken and scattered, Iri would continue to waste away.

'We have to get to that cabinet,' Jack hissed.

'How are we supposed to fight them all?' Toby asked, eyeing the army of Iridians. Cutter strolled between them, approaching the throne.

'My liege,' he called to Kunin Yillda, gesturing behind him. 'I have secured the traitors. They await your judgement.'

'Zavanna,' Jack whispered. 'Get to the cabinet, the final piece. Now.'

Before she could respond, he leapt forward, shouting as he strode down the aisle, ignoring the blue-eyed wugs and lopers that pawed the cobbles, desperate to attack.

'I've just realised something, Cutter,' Jack called, drawing the man's attention. 'All this time I've been trying to figure out how to stop you, what you're planning, but you're nothing. You'll never be the keeper of Iri. You'll always be a sad, lost little boy who wishes he had a speck of the talent my father possessed.'

Cutter's face pinched.

'Your father was lucky,' he said. 'He had one brilliant idea. One. And then he ruined it.'

'And yet you remain its prisoner,' Jack said. 'There's nothing special about you, Cutter. There will always be people like you.'

'Yeah!' Toby shouted, following in Jack's wake. 'You're not a fan, you're a fake.'

Cutter peered at Toby down his long nose. 'I place no value in the opinions of teenagers.'

'You wish you had half the passion and creativity he had,' Jack snarled. 'You claim to be a protector but all you want to do is destroy.'

'Bob didn't make *The Shadow Glass* for people like you,' Toby said.

'No,' Jack said. 'My father would hate what you've done.'

'And yet who remains standing while he festers in his grave?'

Jack lunged for Cutter. The man crumpled beneath him and Jack landed on top of him, preparing to bury his fists in his face. Then he froze.

Something sharp dug between his ribs. A triumphant light entered Cutter's eyes.

'Yes, I have a few tricks of my own,' he hissed.

It was a blade, small but deadly, pressed to Jack's side. It had already gone through Dune's armour and Jack felt it nick his skin, the pain sharp and bright. Would Cutter do it? Would he really kill Dune?

'You're nothing,' Jack snarled. 'You've wasted your life hating a man who created something you could never dream of. Why? Because of your brother? Alden—'

'Don't say that name!'

Cutter pressed the blade further, but a fresh shriek interrupted them.

'Kettu!' a skalion soldier cried, pointing.

Zavanna had been discovered. She froze behind a black column, just a few feet from Kunin Yillda's throne. Another few seconds and she would have reached the dais where the cabinet rested.

'AGH!' the swamp queen screamed. 'SEIZE HER!'

Jack felt Cutter's grip slacken and he grabbed his chance, batting the knife away and leaping off the man just as the chamber juddered and shook. Panting, Jack stared up at the warehouse ceiling, which was sliding open like the lid of an enormous eye. It peeled back to reveal the night sky, the moon stamped in silver-green against a star-studded backdrop, bathing the chamber in an eerie pall.

'The lunium!' Kunin Yillda gasped, her tone croaking with uncharacteristic reverence. 'Our fates are almost decided.'

The set erupted with movement.

As one, the brainwashed Iridians charged. Witterbirds flocked into the air and pelted Zavanna, their beaks tearing at her armour, while a pack of six-legged volks yapped as they surrounded Amelia, Nell, Huw and Fin.

'How do we stop them all?' Toby panted at Jack's side.

To the left of Kunin Yillda's throne, Nebfet's eyes pulsed as she observed the battle, and Jack knew what he had to do.

'Don't move,' he told Toby, then he vaulted into motion. Flipping through the air, he sprang over the snapping jaws of a volk and bounded towards the throne. As he ran, he rearranged his Ray-Bans, praying they would shield him against Nebfet's gaze.

In his other hand, he clutched Dune's dagger. He pounced, sailing over a brainwashed wug and crashing into the soothsayer.

She screamed as he crushed her against the back wall, her skeletal fingers lunging for his face, shredding the air as the blue of her eyes almost blinded him.

'Hey, Nebfet,' Jack grunted, squinting through the sunglasses, seeing only light. 'Take a look at this.'

He plunged the dagger into one of her eyes. As she yowled, he yanked the blade free and sank it into her other eye, extinguishing the nuclear-bright glow as the shriek abruptly died on her lips. He tugged the dagger from her and, as purple blood dripped from it, Kunin Yillda's soothsayer collapsed lifeless to the floor.

Flushed with exhilaration, Jack stepped back from the blood pooling at his feet. He turned to see that the brainwashed puppets had all frozen where they stood. The blue glow dimmed in their eyes. Amelia kept her spear raised while Fin continued to tear at a wug, spraying the ground with fluff.

'I did it,' Jack whispered in shock. 'I did it.'

Around the chamber, every puppet that had been under

Nebfet's thrall dropped to the cobbled floor. All that remained of Kunin Yillda's army were the skalions who had sprung to life in Bob's attic. And Wesley Cutter.

Jack was about to whoop in celebration, perhaps attempt one of those elated one-liners the good guys always dropped in the heat of battle, when he spotted Toby. He had taken advantage of the chaos and crept up behind Kunin Yillda, a knife clenched in his fist, jaw tensed with determination. His backpack rested against one of the pillars, the lub quivering as it peeked out the top, black eyes wet with fear.

'Toby—' Jack murmured, but it was too late.

With a cry, Toby leapt at the skalion queen and pressed the blade to her throat.

'Don't move!' he shouted.

A rattling gasp escaped Kunin Yillda's gullet and she tensed, her eyes narrowing into slits.

'This is for Dune!' Toby cried. He drew back the knife, preparing to drive it into the queen's flesh. Even as the blade descended, though, Kunin Yillda convulsed, her back arching, and Toby sucked in a shocked breath. His face registered pain.

At first Jack couldn't tell what had happened, but as he staggered around the dais he saw a monstrous black barb protruding from Kunin Yillda's back.

It had speared Toby's shoulder.

For a second they remained pinned together, Toby's mouth sagging, Kunin Yillda's violet lips spread wide with triumph. Then, with a grunt, the queen retracted the stinger and Toby toppled to the floor, his body twitching into the dais.

'None touch Kunin Yillda!' the queen shrieked, towering over Toby's stricken form.

'TOBY!' Huw howled, but he was held at bay by skalion soldiers on the other side of the chamber. Nell stood with three spears pointed at her, while Fin had been muzzled and restrained.

'Get away from him!' Jack sprang towards Kunin Yillda at the same time as Zavanna. A moment of understanding passed between them and Zavanna charged the skalion queen, battling her backwards while Jack fell to Toby's side, pulling him away from the dais. He was heavier than Jack had anticipated, but he summoned all his strength and finally got him to the onyx pillar, where the lub still trembled in the backpack. Jack eased Toby against the faux stone, eyeing the mashed-up flesh of his shoulder.

'Almost got her,' Toby gasped.

'I'm so sorry,' Jack said. He fought his ballooning panic as he clutched Toby's hand. He saw Anya, pale and bloated with venom, and knew he had failed. The one person who had seen the good in him, the one person he had to protect at all costs, was already shutting down from the inside.

'Her poison kills you dead in minutes,' Toby had said just yesterday.

Tears stung Jack's eyes and his mind whirred in search of a solution, anything that could save him.

'Do you think I'll go to Iri?' Toby asked. 'When it happens?'

Jack tried to speak but his throat had sealed shut. He saw skalion soldiers dragging Zavanna away from Kunin Yillda, forcing her to her knees as they attempted to muzzle her. The queen barely noticed. She stood bathed in silver-green light. Above her, the green disc of the moon hovered.

'The lunium arrives!' she crowed.

Jack felt a weak squeeze at his hand.

'You're the champion,' Toby said. 'It's you, Jack.'

'Save your strength,' Jack said, but Toby shook his head,

struggling to swallow.

'Listen, Jack. The Glass always chooses one. It's going to choose you, I know it. You can do this. You can be a champion. You can save Iri and our world.'

'I don't…' Jack began, but he found no more words. Toby was wrong, there was no way the Glass would choose him, but he was right about the fact that he had to finish this. He just had to figure out how.

To his right a mewling sound trilled, and his gaze moved to the rucksack.

'The lub,' he murmured. Big eyes blinked at him and an idea formed in Jack's mind, a new voice echoing in the recesses of his memory. They had to get to the final fragment, and Jack realised the lub was just what he needed to do that.

He reached in to take out the creature, which squeaked and struggled in his grip, straining for Toby.

'Quiet,' Jack hissed, and the lub puffed up but fell silent.

'Hold on,' he told Toby. 'Don't let go.'

Toby coughed but nodded. 'I believe in you.'

Jack fought the emotion surging through him, and saw that Wesley Cutter was bent on one knee before Kunin Yillda.

'In the dawning of a new age,' Cutter drawled, 'I pledge my undying servitude, regent. My home is yours and shall be forever. Just tell me what you require and it shall be done.'

'Yesssss,' Kunin Yillda gurgled as Cutter pressed his lips to her clammy hand.

The sight sent a cold shudder through Jack's abdomen and he saw his chance. He knew exactly how to make Cutter pay for everything he had done.

'He lies,' he shouted, getting to his feet. 'Cutter doesn't want to serve you. He wants to imprison you. Collect you.'

Kunin Yillda's brow knitted into a sallow expanse of wrinkles.

'Do not listen to him,' Cutter oozed. 'I live for you, my queen.'

'He'll poison you in your sleep,' Jack yelled, still holding the lub. 'Make you compliant. He wants to control you.'

The queen's liquid gaze fell from Jack to the man kneeling before her. Although she appeared ugly and stupid, Jack knew how her mind worked. He'd spent years watching her in *The Shadow Glass*. He knew every one of her weaknesses, he just hadn't figured out how to use them to his advantage. But now he saw the wheels turning as she studied Cutter.

'No, no,' Cutter whimpered, his hands raised. 'He doesn't understand. He never did. I am your most humble slave.'

'He wants to control you,' Jack repeated, sensing he was getting through to her. Push too much and she'd see through him.

The queen gave a wet snort. 'None control Kunin Yillda!'

'No, of course not.' Panic edged into Cutter's voice. 'I merely wish to serve you. Stay here with me and I will be yours forever.'

'Stay?' Her eyes narrowed, dark pupils like supernovas. She cackled and rested a hand on the crown of Cutter's head. 'Yesssss, erpling. We shall be together forever.'

He nodded and bowed.

Kunin Yillda seized his shoulders, her claws ribboning his white jacket as she dragged him towards her mouth, her teeth flashing.

'What are you doing?' Cutter shrieked. 'No! Please!'

As he struggled in her grasp, Jack felt a thrill of satisfaction. Cutter was the reason Bob changed. He was the reason Anya and Brol were dead. That Toby was hurt. This was what Cutter deserved. To be devoured by the monster he had allied himself with. To finally pay for all the pain he had caused.

Cutter managed to jerk himself free, his jacket shredded and bloody. He spun away from Kunin Yillda but tripped and landed on his front. The queen seized his foot and hauled him backwards with alarming strength.

Cutter's fingernails gouged the floor.

'Please! Help!'

The fear in his face sent a jolt through Jack. The exhilaration soured and he shook himself. What was he doing? As much as he hated Cutter, he didn't deserve to die, not like this. Jack couldn't stand by and let it happen, the way Cutter had when the guard was eaten alive. He'd find another way to make him pay.

'Shit,' he muttered. Leaping over dead-eyed puppets, he made for Cutter. He set down the lub and then seized Cutter's hands, bracing himself against the floor as he strained with all his strength.

'Dune, please,' Cutter gasped, his eyelids pinned back, his cheekbones hollowing skeletal shadows across his face. 'No!'

Cutter's fingers slipped and Jack adjusted his grip, clinging on tightly. Cutter thrashed and writhed and Jack feared he wasn't strong enough, but he heard Dune's voice in his head, urging him on, and he gave a final heave.

He fell back as Cutter came free. The man sprawled against the cobbles, panting as Jack sprang back to his feet.

'Thank you, thank you,' Cutter whimpered. 'Dune—'

Jack punched him and the man's head dropped to the floor. He lay motionless, rendered unconscious.

Shaking off the pain in his hand, Jack went to retrieve the lub. Before he had the chance, Kunin Yillda bounded to his side, seizing his head and dragging him to her so that he could count every one of the boils oozing in her repugnant face.

'Finally,' she hissed. 'You are mine, Bobson.'

Her padded fingers found his collar and hauled him forwards. He resisted, but her determination doubled her strength, made her unstoppable.

'Amelia,' Jack shouted, trapped in Kunin Yillda's ravenous yellow gaze, 'promise me you'll end this!'

'But—' Amelia said somewhere behind him.

'Promise! Open the cabinet, get the fragment, now!'

'I promise.'

Jack closed his eyes. 'Good.' As Kunin Yillda wrenched him towards her waiting maw, he took a breath and shouted, 'LUB! IT'S TIME!'

The swamp queen wavered. She glared at him in confusion.

'LUB! SHE HURT TOBY! HE'S GOING TO DIE UNLESS YOU HELP! NOW!' Jack shouted again, knowing it was now or never.

'*Why are lubs dangerous, Dad?*' he'd asked one night while his father tucked him into bed. The previous evening, Bob had told Jack never to trust anything as adorable as a lub, and Jack hadn't understood why. They were so loveable in the movie.

'*Promise not to tell anybody?*' his dad asked.

Jack had nodded, eyes wide.

'*Nobody knows this, boy-o, and it's not written anywhere, so this is just between you and me. Lubs are the offspring of one of the most feared creatures in Iri.*'

The floor rumbled beneath him, and Jack saw that Kunin Yillda had frozen where she stood. Her ferocious gaze wasn't on him any longer but peering past him, and he felt her quake in fear.

The rumbling grew louder, causing the floor to bounce beneath him. Seizing his chance, Jack wrestled free from the swamp queen, rolling on the floor and sitting up to face the commotion at his back.

The lub convulsed against the floorboards, its mouth open and shrieking, its feet pounding a frantic rhythm. Jack watched in awe as the creature began to grow.

As it writhed and screamed, its fur puffed up and its body changed shape. It doubled in size. Then it doubled again. Its scream morphed into a roar and its limbs stretched, its claws sharpening, its eyes blazing purple. Its shadow fell over the skalion queen as its wing-like ears rose up towards the ceiling.

'No,' Kunin Yillda groaned, her mouth gaping as she stared up at the lub.

No, not a lub any longer.

'Leviathan,' Jack whispered.

The lub had transformed.

It towered over them, its fangs leaking saliva strings. Its penetrating glare fell upon Kunin Yillda and the swamp queen released a strangled cry.

Her remaining soldiers abandoned their attempts to subdue Zavanna and leapt to their queen's aid, forming a barrier between her and the lubiathan. The monstrous beast swung a bristled arm that knocked them over like skittles. As they flailed, the lubiathan lunged for the queen.

Kunin Yillda dodged the monster's gnashing teeth by throwing herself at its feet and scrabbling between its legs.

'Thanks, Dad,' Jack murmured. His plan had worked. The queen and her army were distracted. Now was their chance. He checked that Toby was safe, seeing that a shaken-looking Huw was cradling him. Although Toby looked only half alive, he was staring up at the lubiathan in awe, an exhausted smile on his lips.

Jack turned to search for back-up.

'Zavanna!' he cried. 'Amelia! The cabinet!'

Everybody had stopped to watch the lub, but at Jack's cry they jerked into motion.

As Kunin Yillda attempted to flee, Amelia ran for the dais, reaching the cabinet.

'Zavanna,' she called. 'I need the Eye.'

On the other side of the chamber, the kettu raced towards them, tearing the necklace from her throat and tossing it as hard as she could.

Skalions leapt skywards, their webbed claws outstretched, but the necklace sailed over them, glittering in the moonlight. With a triumphant cry, Amelia snatched it from the air. As Jack clambered to her side, she thrust the Iri Eye into the back of the box. They looked at each other and then she twisted it.

The panel came away before them and he stared down at what was revealed.

The mottled surface of an ancient mirror.

His and Amelia's reflections blinked back, dark and exhausted. He ignored the tremble of shock at seeing Dune panting, moving, knowing he was the reason the puppet appeared alive. Instead, he eased free the glass and handed it to Nell.

A shriek reverberated through the chamber as Kunin Yillda fought the lubiathan.

The monster scooped her up in a huge claw.

'You will release me! I am Kunin Yillda and I—'

Whatever she was, they never found out as her shriek became lost in the gale of the lubiathan's breath.

Jack refocussed on the cabinet.

'Where is the final fragment?' Zavanna panted as she joined them.

For a moment, Jack feared he had been wrong. The final piece wasn't here after all. Then he examined the base of the box and spotted a modest bronze catch. He reached in and drew up the false bottom, revealing a shallow cavity.

There, nestled in purple velvet, was the final part of the Shadow Glass.

The lubiathan screeched and Jack saw it had been impaled by a skalion spear.

Kunin Yillda wrestled free from its grasp and thumped to the cobbles below, her crown slipping in her greasy crop of hair. As her soldiers surrounded the lubiathan, the queen's rheumy gaze found Jack.

'Get away from there!' she shrieked, clambering to her feet, her fatty folds swinging.

Fin leapt forward to block her path and Jack didn't waste his moment.

'Quickly,' he breathed, striding to the part-assembled glass. Nell handed him the mirror, and he slotted it into place. Then he took the final fragment from Zavanna.

'If this doesn't work,' he began.

'Don't say—' Amelia said.

'If it doesn't,' he interrupted. 'I wanted to say thank you. All of you.' They blinked back at him, smeared with black blood and dirt, their eyes bright with fatigue. He reached out a hand. Zavanna placed hers on top, followed by Nell and Amelia.

'Get away from there!' Kunin Yillda cried, batting Fin out of the way and stomping towards them.

'For Iri,' Jack said.

'For Iri,' the others repeated.

He turned and placed the final piece of the Glass in position.

A blast of energy punched him in the chest. He hurtled backwards, the back of his head striking one of the onyx columns, and he slumped against it, dazed. Every part of him ached and he wanted to stay there, his eyes closed, but the air felt different. It pulsed with heat and he forced his eyes open.

He blinked. At first all he saw was golden light shimmering over the chamber. It flickered in waves, as if reflected by water. And then he saw it.

The Shadow Glass stood complete.

Its surface glowed, beaming a soft radiance that he felt in his skin. A low hum vibrated in his ears and dust motes swirled before him like embers, pink and gold. Everything seemed to slow down to half-speed.

He got to his feet, finding Zavanna and Amelia either side of him. Nell and Fin hung back while Toby struggled to keep his eyes open, Huw helping him to sit up. They clung to each other, jaws dropping.

All Jack saw was the Glass.

'It's beautiful,' he breathed.

'It is the Shadow Glass,' Zavanna said.

They stood gazing at it.

The sound of shifting debris drew Jack's attention and he saw Kunin Yillda heaving herself up from the floor. The blast must have knocked her over, too, but she had recovered, and her expression was twisted with fury.

'It's mine!' she cried. 'The Glass is Kunin Yillda's! Get back!'

Jack's heart beat faster as he approached the Glass, ignoring the queen's shrieks.

'Jack?' Amelia said behind him.

'I'm going in.' He felt its pull, an alien gravity. It tugged at his chest as if it were a part of him. Even if Toby wasn't right, and he wasn't the champion, Jack had to try. He couldn't let anybody else. The legends said that those who entered the Glass were never seen again.

He couldn't allow that to happen to Zavanna or Amelia or anybody.

This was on him.

He was the champion, self-made or not.

'No, Jack,' Zavanna said, her ears flat against her skull. 'It should be me.'

'Get back!' Kunin Yillda bellowed, limping forwards.

'I finally understand,' Jack said, smiling at the kettu. 'I understand why Dad loved the kettu and all the creatures of Iri.'

He remembered that tingle of being a child. Hugging Dune while they watched *The Shadow Glass*. Wishing he would speak. As he looked at Zavanna, seeing her determination, he couldn't bear to think of her suffering, dying. He could do something about it. He had to.

'STOP!' Kunin Yillda cried.

A shape charged through the wreckage and Jack was shoved out of the way. He stumbled, correcting his balance just in time to see Cutter racing for the Glass. He had regained consciousness.

'No!' Jack cried, but Cutter didn't stop. He shot a look over his shoulder at Jack, his mouth warped in a grin, then he plunged into the Glass.

Nobody moved.

They all stared in shock as Cutter vanished.

'The Glass is MINE!' Kunin Yillda caterwauled, flopping forwards.

Jack stood braced before the Glass, expecting Cutter to emerge at any moment, but the golden radiance continued to spill from it, tugging at his chest. Cutter didn't return. Jack was vaguely aware of Kunin Yillda growling, tearing at her hair, but then she was being held back by Zavanna. The kettu put herself between the skalion queen and Jack, digging her blade into the queen's sternum.

'Move another inch and your blood shall be my wine.' She shot Jack a glittering stare. 'Well, if you're going, go! Now!'

Jack nodded and approached the Glass, Kunin Yillda shrieking and spitting, but held at bay by the kettu.

Standing bathed in the spectral luminescence, Jack took a breath, inflated his lungs, sensing Bob Co. around him, his father's realm, the place that had been his childhood. A sense of calm settled over him, folding him in an embrace. If this was the last thing he ever saw, he was okay with that.

He turned to look at Toby, who shuddered and twitched, dark shadows beneath his eyes, which were wet with tears.

'Hey, Toby,' Jack said.

Toby nodded a fraction to show he could hear him.

'I love *The Shadow Glass*,' Jack told him. 'I always did.' He winked and smiled at Amelia. 'Time for one last adventure.'

'Jack!' Amelia choked.

'NO!' Kunin Yillda bawled.

Before anybody could stop him, Jack turned and stepped into the Shadow Glass.

Transcript from an interview with Bob Corman, broadcast on BBC Radio 1 on 27 June 1986.

INTERVIEWER: Sorry, real? What do you mean, Iri is real?

BOB CORMAN: *[laughs]* I know it sounds crackers but I don't care. I've learnt not to. I think a person should believe whatever their heart tells them, so long as it isn't hurting anybody. If I learned anything making *The Shadow Glass*, it is that. True belief, no matter if it falters or fades, is the most powerful force in this universe. After love, of course.

24

Water rushed beneath him. A great river of silver flecked with foam. It sliced through the land and, in its glassy surface, he glimpsed the reflection of huge wings and a feathered underbelly as it soared through the air.

His own reflection stared back and he saw that he was himself again, not Dune, but Jack Corman. Jack Bobson. Borne aloft by a great beast, wind whipping through his hair.

He clung on to soft down, digging his knees into a muscular back, and he felt the power of the enormous creature carrying him. Its frost-tipped wings spread either side of him and its long neck tapered into a proud head crowned with feathers. The white peacock bore him with ease, its feathers crackling and spitting pale sparks while its tail feathers streamed behind them in a tangle of white fire.

'A mesaku,' Jack murmured. He was riding an Iridian dragon, a rare beast considered lucky by some, a portent of doom by others.

'Where am I?' he asked.

'You already know,' the mesaku said. White embers danced between its flight feathers and he remembered all mesaku were born in storms, forged from lightning.

To his right, a snow-capped mountain towered over a blackened forest.

He stared about him in awe.

'Iri,' he whispered.

His wonder was short-lived, though, for the further they travelled, the more troubled he became. Vast craters that had once been lakes now lay arid and hissing green steam, while entire forests had withered, the earth cracked and bleeding green lava.

Iri was dying.

They soared above great plains littered with half-rancid corpses and giant skeletons. Far below, he glimpsed shapes darting underground, perhaps kettu, perhaps some other hardy scavengers, doing their best to survive in a decaying world; a world on the brink of ruin.

'Where are we going?' Jack asked.

'You will see.'

A mountain loomed before them. It was a solid black triangle that seemed to have been cut out of the sky.

They flew to its peak and the mesaku landed on a dusty outcrop, her wings dragging soot and black soil into the atmosphere.

'This is where you will find answers,' she said.

Jack climbed off, trying not to tug at her feathers, and set his feet on the rocky ground. An updraught buffeted him as the mesaku beat the air and took off, soaring up and away from the mountain, higher into the crackling clouds, until she vanished amid the forking light.

'Jack.'

A male voice spoke behind him and a shiver electrified Jack's spine. He turned.

The kettu stood a few feet away, the wind tangling in his long hair, his expression set somewhere between pensive and curious. The lightning reflected in his eyes.

'Dune,' Jack uttered.

'It has been a while.'

Jack wasn't sure what he meant. The kettu looked wild and alive, his fur thick and gleaming, his feet set apart in a stance that spoke of quiet resilience.

'You're alive,' Jack said. 'I thought in the battle, you...' He shook his head. 'What am I doing here?'

'Is that the question you really wish to ask?'

Jack frowned and attempted to calm his racing thoughts. He had too many questions. Dune strolled to the edge of the outcrop to stare at the toxic landscape.

'Iri is dying,' he said. 'It has been eroding for years, falling apart, losing its lustre. Now it takes its final breaths.'

'Why?' Jack asked. 'Why is this happening?'

Dune didn't look at him. 'I do not pretend to understand the source of Iri's power, but I know it wouldn't exist without Bob. His belief in this world birthed us, and when he shared Iri with others, their own stories and love for it sustained us. Gave us history and adventure. As Bob aged and people forgot, so Iri began to crumble.'

Jack had been right. Iri and his father were connected, and in Bob's final years—as he grew ill, as his spirit tired and frayed—that pain echoed in Iri.

And Cutter had done his own damage. His condemnation of those who loved Iri the 'wrong way' had further eroded this world.

He stepped forward. 'We can save it. The Glass—'

Dune's gaze was heavy. 'It may be beyond saving.'

'That's not what Zavanna said. We found the Glass, that's what we had to do. Find the Glass—'

'So that you might come here.'

'—and save Iri.' He registered what Dune had said. 'What?'

Dune's ears twitched as if he'd heard something and he looked over his shoulder. Jack turned to peer at a dark gap in the rock that must lead to chambers within the mountain. He thought he saw movement in the shadows, but it was too dark for him to be sure.

'The Glass brought you here,' the kettu said. 'That was its purpose. But there is one last thing that might save Iri.'

'What? Tell me!'

Dune glanced down at his hands. 'Death comes to all, eventually. I was never afraid of it. To die in battle, to have your name etched upon the Yggram tree along with brave ancestral warriors, is a great honour. A gift. But now I see my world like this, torn apart by greed and hate, and I do not know what is worse.'

'The skalions,' Jack said, searching for an answer amid Dune's melancholy.

'Their will is strong. They are pure force, wild nature at its most unforgiving, driven and inevitable. It is their will that is destroying Iri.'

'So we stop them,' Jack said. 'Break their will and free Iri.'

'There is no time.'

Jack threw up his hands. This wasn't the Dune he had loved as a child. Where was the hero who faced every battle with a grin? Who lived for Iri and his people? Who wanted nothing more than to protect this world and every creature in it?

'There has to be something,' he said.

Thunder boomed in the distance as Dune's gaze settled on him. 'There is.'

'What?'

'You, Jack.'

He stated it so simply, it could be the most obvious thing in Iri. Something thumped hard in Jack's chest.

'This world meant so much to you once,' Dune said. 'Do you remember? Those images you watched as a child, so enraptured that you forgot your own world. The stories you conjured, adding to Iri piece by piece, imagining new adventures for its inhabitants. Do you remember?'

'Yes. I remember.'

'What changed, Jack? Why did you abandon us?'

Jack felt a lump in his throat. 'I didn't mean to.'

'We were cast out. Forgotten.'

He was right. Jack had turned from Iri, too.

'I never forgot!' he said. 'I just got older.'

'I was with you all that time,' Dune said. 'We visited Iri together. And then you turned your back on us. On me.'

Tears pricked Jack's eyes. 'I'm sorry. I didn't know. I didn't mean to.'

'You can make it right.'

'Just tell me how!'

Dune gave him an uncertain look. 'Iri needs people to believe in it, Jack, but it needs one person most of all. One person who knows it from the smallest blu-verm to the tallest tussu tree. Somebody who loves it, heart and soul, who feels it in the bones of their bones, in the heart of their heart, and whose belief sustains it in a hundred ways I will never understand. Somebody like you, Jack.'

Belief? That was really all it took? Somebody who believed in Iri?

He had believed in it once, long before irrefutable proof smashed its way into his father's attic.

'Your father meant to pass the mantle to you, before he died,' Dune said.

Jack heard his father begging him in the restaurant.

It's all falling apart, boy-o. It's crumbling around them.

Jack had walked away.

'What do I do?' he asked.

'He did not die, Jack,' Dune said. 'He is here with us.'

His gaze went past Jack again, and Jack glanced back at the rocky recess. He was sure somebody was in there watching him. He looked back at Dune.

'Dad died,' he said. 'I saw him. I found him.'

'His body, yes, but his spirit lives on.'

Jack turned back again, seeing that the figure was tall and thin but still shrouded in darkness.

'He's here?' he asked. A tremor ran through him.

Dune nodded. The ground shifted beneath Jack's feet. The mountain groaned. Rocky shrapnel spat around them as the mountain shook, and Jack watched as, far below them, torrents of green fire spewed up from great fissures in the earth.

It was all he could do to remain standing. He tore his eyes from the flaming horizon.

'Dune?' he yelled over the elemental cracking and groaning of a world coming apart.

'We are almost out of time,' the kettu said, hair whipping his face. 'You are the only one who can save Iri. You must decide.'

'*Jack?*' a voice croaked behind him. '*Jack? Boy-o? Are you there?*'

'Decide?'

The kettu's eyes were glassy with tears.

The ground lurched beneath them and Dune staggered back. He stopped just inches from the outcrop edge.

'Dune?' Jack asked.

'You have to decide what you prize most!' Dune said over the roaring wind.

'*I need you, Jack. Will you come? Please?*'

Jack turned to peer into the shadows of the rock face.

'Dad?'

Dune's voice rang against the hard mountainside. 'There's always a choice, and this is yours. Save Iri or see your father one last time.'

The mountain shook once more, as if attempting to hurl them off.

'That's…' Jack struggled to find the words. 'That's not fair!'

'That's the way it is!' Dune yelled. 'You have to choose!'

'I can't!'

A violent tremble shifted through the mountain and Dune pitched backwards. He lost his footing, tumbled, and vanished over the edge.

'DUNE!'

Jack threw himself forward. At the brink, he got down on his knees and peered over, dreading what he might see.

A small hand clung to a flinty perch.

Dune stared up at Jack, his eyes wide as he clutched at the mountainside.

'Jack!' he shouted. 'Do it!'

'Take my hand!' Jack cried, reaching down, tears hot on his cheeks.

'You have to choose!'

Dune was just out of reach. Jack shot a look over his shoulder, glimpsing the figure in the darkness, his chest aching.

A fiery explosion of lava rocked the base of the mountain and Jack watched in horror as Dune slipped. He skidded down a few feet before catching hold of the rock face. He threw up a panicked shout.

'Jack!'

Jack squeezed his eyes shut. He sensed the presence at his back, the scent of wood shavings and instant coffee, and he knew what he had to do.

'I'm sorry,' he whispered.

He leapt to his feet, screwing up his face.

He filled his lungs with air and bellowed over the storm.

'IRI! I CHOOSE IRI!'

White light blinded him as lightning struck the mountaintop just metres behind him. Silence rang in his ears as Jack was pitched forwards, his feet leaving the ground as he soared over the edge of the outcrop and into the air.

He fell.

Letter addressed to Bob, dated 7 May 1990.

Dear Bob,

Thank you so much for coming to see me last night, it was a dream come true—I've dreamed of meeting you ever since I first watched The Shadow Glass. Iri is so beautiful I just wish I could visit it for real. I love all the characters, even Kunin Yillda, because I just feel like she's misunderstood. Villains aren't all bad (even the ones who eat people). I think Kunin is just really unhappy.

I really loved the story you told me about what happens next, and how the story is never really finished. I love that Iri keeps going no matter what. Dune is my and my brother's favourite character and I'm glad he turns out okay in the end.

One day, I hope you make a Shadow Glass 2. I'm sad I won't get to see it but I'm happy I got to meet you, and don't worry, I promise not to tell anybody the secret you told me. I mean, who would I tell?

Sincerely,
Alden Cutter

PS. Thanks for signing my copy of Beyond the Shadow Glass. I loved reading about Iri's origins and Zavanna's story. Please write another one.

Jack bolted upright with a gasp. He winced as his bandaged hand dabbed at the welt on his crown, then he cast a look around him. He was on the back seat of a car. Through the window, he saw Bob Co., the green mist burning off, the car park littered with bodies.

He looked down at himself, seeing the torn bowling shirt, his missing finger still bandaged up, and a shiver of relief went through him. He was himself again. In the back of the Beetle, just as Toby had said.

'I'm back,' he panted.

The elation quickly faded. He remembered feeling the wind in his hair as he flew the mesaku, talking to Dune atop the mountain, turning his back on his father. Choosing Iri. But it would all be for nothing if Toby died.

He stopped, frowning, feeling an object in his bandaged hand. A small glass vial winked up at him. He raised it, peering at the clear liquid, instinctively knowing what it was.

'I'm coming, Toby.'

He fumbled with the car door, stumbling out before it had properly opened and cracking his head on the frame. Not caring, he limp-ran across the parking lot, weaving between the puppets, which had become lifeless once more. Fear pumped through him. What if he was too late? He urged his legs to move faster, tearing through the studio lot until he reached Stage 7.

His footsteps echoed around the throne room, which had fallen eerily silent.

On the dais, the Shadow Glass stood complete, no longer glowing, but observing with a cool reserve the inanimate puppets scattered throughout the room. Jack saw limp wugs and witterbirds and more skalion soldiers than he could count, the floor slick with black blood and stuffing.

'Jack?'

Across the set, Amelia released Nell from a hug as she spotted him. But Jack's relief at seeing his cousin was cut short by her expression. She looked like she had been crying, her face pale and wrung out. Nell's arm remained around her, her own cheeks tracked with tears.

'Toby,' Jack whispered, almost tripping over weapons and puppets in his haste to get to them. As he reached Amelia's side, he looked down at the teenager propped against the column. Toby's complexion was ashen, his eyelids rheumy slits, and Huw clutched his hand to his cheek, whispering words Jack couldn't quite hear.

As Jack fell to Toby's side, Toby managed a weak smile.

'What... did you see?' he wheezed.

With fingers that felt thick and unwieldy, Jack unstoppered the vial and raised it to Toby's mouth.

'Drink it,' he urged. Toby's parched lips trembled open and Jack helped him, wincing as a few precious drops were lost.

Finally, Toby lay back with a sigh. Tension ticked in Jack's temples and he clutched Toby's other hand, squeezing it hard.

'Come on,' he said. 'You have to live. You have to. Who else will scare me by popping out of random places shouting my name?'

Toby had stopped breathing.

Jack fought the panic surging through him. Why wasn't the elixir fixing him?

He remembered Toby had taken a direct hit from Kunin Yillda. Maybe he was beyond saving.

'I think he's—' Huw said, but then Toby sat up with a gasp. He coughed, clutching his injured shoulder, which no longer seemed to pain him. He looked from Jack to Huw, and then grinned, leaping forward to drag them both into a hug.

'Thank god,' Jack said, hugging him back.

'Thank *you*,' Toby said.

'Not so tight,' Huw grunted. 'Can't breathe.'

Toby laughed and let them go. His eyes shone at Jack.

'I knew you could do it. I knew it! You went into the Glass. And you came back.'

'Seems that way.'

'You— Oh no, the lub,' Toby murmured. He eased out of the hug, and Jack followed his gaze to a ball of fluff with a tail that rested on the floor. 'He's just a puppet again.'

'They all are,' Amelia said. She didn't sound happy about it. Jack saw she was crouched beside Zavanna, who sat with her back against a slain skalion. Beside her rested Dune. They were inanimate once more, their eyes polished glass, their mouths rigid. The only hint they had ever been alive was the blood and dirt smearing Zavanna's armour.

Jack couldn't bear her stillness. He couldn't lose them again.

He approached Dune and stared into his dark eyes. He looked into Zavanna's face, moving from side to side, watching for any micro-movements in the puppet's expression. When she first came to life, Jack had wished Zavanna would stop staring at him. The weight of her glare was too much to bear. Now, he'd give anything for her to look at him, just once. Just for a second.

He willed her to sneer at him. Call him an imbecile and a manchild. Tell him he was useless, a terrible fighter, a colossal disappointment.

But Zavanna remained motionless.

Lifeless.

The back of his throat stung.

Jack looked away, pressure building behind his eyes.

'They're gone,' Toby murmured, getting to his feet.

'Why doesn't this feel like a happy ending?' Huw said.

Jack turned and caught movement. He squinted at the Shadow Glass, sure the movement had come from there. Something like hope surged through him, but as he went to stand before it he found only his own startled reflection staring back.

'Jack,' Toby whispered, joining him. 'Look at it.'

The Shadow Glass winked, its black frame polished and smooth, its mirrored surface no longer mottled with age but as clear as a window.

'I never dreamed I'd get to see the real thing,' Toby breathed.

Jack was only half listening because he was looking closer at the mirror. Something felt off about the reflection. He stepped up to it, staring into the mirror image of the studio, finding the reflected versions of Zavanna and Dune.

With a shock, he watched the reflected Zavanna get to her feet.

He whirled to face the chamber set, staring across at the puppet. But she remained still beside her brother. She hadn't moved.

In the mirror, though, Zavanna ambled towards him, raising a hand in welcome.

'Bobson,' she said.

He blinked at her in shock. 'Tell me I'm not dreaming. Ow!'

Toby had pinched Jack's arm. 'Not dreaming.'

Jack returned to Zavanna, unable to contain the relieved grin that spread across his face. 'You're okay. You survived.'

'Thanks to you.' She dipped her head in gratitude, and Jack saw that she was no longer standing in the throne room set but beside a rippling lake. Two suns shone full above her, trees murmuring by the water, and a wug danced on the spot as colourful witterbirds buzzed through the air.

'You're home,' Jack murmured. Iri looked every bit as wild and colourful as Zavanna had described it to him that day in the study. The thought came tinged with sadness. He hadn't known at the time how special that moment was. The first time they talked plainly.

'It is good to be back,' Zavanna said.

'What about Brol?' Toby asked. 'And Dune?'

Melancholy seeped into Zavanna's expression. 'It appears some realms are more difficult to cross. They shall live on in songs and stories.'

Tears streaked Toby's cheeks and Jack put an arm around his shoulders, feeling the loss too. Not just of the kettu, but of his father. He took small comfort in the knowledge that he had chosen correctly. He had chosen Iri. He had finally done what his father had wanted all along.

Toby hiccupped. 'Are the skalions gone?'

Zavanna smiled. 'They have been exiled to the wastelands of western Iri, liberated of their terrible teck-noll-gee.'

'And Iri's okay?' Jack asked.

'It has never been better.'

Zavanna threw a look over her shoulder as if she had heard something. A call from Iri, maybe.

'It is time,' she said.

'No, not yet.' Jack couldn't bear to watch her leave. 'We need you. *I* need you.'

Her mouth creased at the corners. She raised a hand and pressed it to the pane between them, her gaze resting on his.

'I'm just on the other side of the glass, Jack,' she said softly. 'Waiting.'

Jack swallowed, his eyes burning. He pressed his palm to the same spot. He could almost imagine he felt their hands meet.

Zavanna's gaze didn't leave him. 'Know that I shall carry you with me across every plane and stream, Bobson. You will be with me always, and I with you. Believe me when I say that your father would be proud. And mine, also, I think.'

'He would be,' Jack said, the pane warming his palm. 'I know it.'

'Goodbye, Jack. Be well.'

The kettu bowed and turned, walking towards the lake as the other Iridians followed in a jumbled stream, wugs tottering across the shore and lubs bouncing and mewling, while witterbirds flashed bright colours above their heads.

Zavanna passed a tree and vanished.

A tremor travelled through Jack and he tasted tears. Lowering his hand, he sent up a silent thank-you that he'd been given the gift of meeting her.

Zavanna of the Vex tribe.

His friend.

When the Glass had faded to reflect only Jack and Toby, Jack wiped his cheeks and saw that Toby was blowing snot bubbles as

he silently cried. Jack squeezed him in to his side, smiling back at
Amelia, Nell and Huw.

'I just realised something,' Toby said. 'The Glass was in the
attic the whole time, hidden in Dune's cabinet. That's why the
kettu appeared in the attic during the storm. They came through
the Glass.' He shook his head with a mixture of awe and dismay.
'If we'd just searched that cabinet first, we'd have saved ourselves
a lot of trouble.'

'Let's pretend you didn't just say that,' Jack said.

Toby frowned. 'Hey, what's this?'

He bent down to tug something from beneath the Shadow
Glass. It looked like a piece of paper. No, an envelope. Jack
couldn't believe it, but he recognised the shaky letters.

BOB.

Alden's letter.

Jack must have dropped it here at Bob Co. during their first
fight with Kunin Yillda, and now the studio was returning it.

He shared a look with Toby, who, understanding, carefully
opened the envelope and removed a slip of paper. Together they
read the handful of neat paragraphs, and Jack's heart skipped faster
as he absorbed Alden's words. By the time he reached the end, his
chest was vibrating and Toby's hands shook.

It was one of the most beautiful things Jack had ever read.

'He loved it,' Toby murmured. 'Alden loved the book. And Bob.'
He looked up at Jack. 'What did you see? When you went into
the Glass?'

'NOTHING!' cried a nasal voice. It came from behind them.
Jack turned to see Wesley Cutter leaning against a black column,
his white suit dirty and torn, his cheeks sunken. He emitted a
stinging laugh.

'There was nothing. Nothing!' He tore at his hair, his body wracked with sobs as he approached.

'You didn't see Iri?' Jack asked.

Cutter snarled and flew at him, his bony hands aiming for Jack's neck. Jack caught them easily and held Cutter at bay. The man appeared weakened. Broken.

'It's over, Cutter. Just stop.'

He pushed the man back and took Alden's letter from Toby. He contemplated it for a moment, and then held it out to Cutter.

'You know what this is, don't you?'

Cutter eyed the letter fearfully.

'This was never about Alden or my father,' Jack said. 'This was about you, your issues. I'm not sure even you understand them. But if *I* can move on, make peace with who my father was, my god, I'm sure you can.' He released a breath. 'It's over, Cutter. For good.'

Cutter held his gaze, a vein flickering in his temple.

'You can't—' he began.

A crash resounded through the set and Jack startled. He half expected Kunin Yillda to lurch up from the floor, claim her last hurrah the way villains always did in the movies, but then a blonde woman in a police uniform appeared on the other side of the chamber.

'Jack Corman?' she called.

'Uh, yes?' Jack said.

'I'm Special Officer Barrow. I have reason to believe you know the whereabouts of a Wesley Cutter.'

Jack stared at her in bewilderment. As she drew closer he felt sure he had seen her before, and, with a jolt, he realised he *had*. She had been among the brainwashed workers tending to Nebfet's generator.

'What—' he began, but then he heard footsteps. Cutter was running.

'That's him!' Huw yelled, pointing as Cutter made for a large, studded door to one side of the chamber. As he tugged it open, though, it revealed a brick wall. The door was a fake. There was no escape.

Two more officers joined Officer Barrow and Jack recognised them, too. They had all been under Nebfet's thrall. He watched as the officers wrestled Cutter up against the wall. As he resisted the cuffs being snapped around his wrists, they read him his rights.

'Wesley Cutter, you're under arrest for criminal theft, money laundering and internet fraud. You have the right to remain—'

'Get off me!' Cutter cried, his face pressed into a column as the officer continued to read out his rights. 'Dune! Kunin! Help me!'

'Do you understand these rights as they have been read to you?'

Cutter stopped thrashing and twisted to give the officers a brittle stare. 'They'll eat you alive! The skalions always repay their debts. Turn your backs and they'll tear out your spines!'

Special Officer Barrow joined Jack. She looked exhausted. 'He's talking about the puppets, isn't he?'

'Seems that way.'

'Have you been with him all day?' she asked.

'Uh, a lot of it. What's going on?'

'We've had an arrest warrant for Mr Cutter for over a month, but he's a tricky man to find. This morning, we received a tip-off about his video announcement here at the studio.'

'How interesting,' Nell said, looking so overtly intrigued that Jack was left with no doubt she was the one behind the call. Something told him she'd also found out about the arrest warrant. Perhaps the internet wasn't so bad after all.

'Strangest thing is,' Officer Barrow said, 'I have no memory of what happened when we got to the studio. My mind's a blank. I'd love to know where the past few hours went.'

Jack sensed she hoped he could tell her, but how could he explain that she and her colleagues had been brainwashed by a puppet?

'This place has that effect,' he said.

The sound of a scuffle drew their attention, and Jack found Cutter eyeballing him as he strained to free himself from the officers, his hands behind his back.

'Jack, tell them!' Cutter pleaded. 'Tell them about Iri and the others! Tell them the truth!'

Jack's gaze went from him to Officer Barrow. He shrugged.

'I have no idea what he's talking about.'

'No! Please! The skalions! They're alive! THEY'RE ALIVE!'

Cutter was dragged through the chamber door. It slammed behind him, and the sound echoed with a pleasing sense of finality.

He wasn't Jack's problem anymore.

'LOST' *SHADOW GLASS* NOVEL TO GET LAVISH RE-RELEASE

Goliath Publishing has announced it will release graphic novel *Beyond the Shadow Glass*, a spin-off of classic eighties fantasy movie *The Shadow Glass*.

The long out-of-print title was originally published in 1990, and became a rare collector's item following a small fan uprising opposing its release.

Next spring, Goliath will publish a glossy hardback edition of *Beyond the Shadow Glass* complete with a new foreword by Jack Corman, the son of visionary director Bob Corman.

'We're so excited to be dusting off this fantastic story for fans old and new,' says Goliath's Lydia Baylay. 'This story is as vital and epic as ever, and now is the perfect time for people to rediscover Iri.'

26

A week later, Jack stood in the downstairs foyer of the Prince Charles Cinema watching people filter into the cinema screen. Some had plaited their hair like kettu warriors, while others wore skalion make-up. Two dedicated fans had dressed their kids as wugs.

'It's unreal, isn't it?' Amelia said, checking her own braided hair. Dressed in a variation of Zavanna's armour, she handed out kettu badges to patrons as they went into the screen.

'I think we've found our people,' Jack said.

'Is it okay if we get a picture with the Shadow Glass?' asked a woman wearing Kunin Yillda's crown, her arm around what could only be her daughter. The likeness was uncanny.

'Of course,' Jack said. 'In fact, let me take it.'

He took their phone as they posed beside the Glass, grinning. It was the event's *pièce de résistance*, giving fans the chance to take selfies with the movie prop that was lost for decades and had only just, according to a Bob Co. press release, been found in a dusty forgotten part of the studio. Well, the real story was a bit far-fetched.

It no longer hummed. Whatever power it briefly possessed had returned to Iri when they beat Kunin Yillda.

Jack handed back the phone.

'You know, this is Gurchin,' Amelia told the woman.

'Seriously? Oh my god, you *are*! Can we get a picture with you, too?'

Jack felt the familiar ripple of annoyance, but then laughed and posed for a selfie.

'Gurchin got *old*,' the woman's daughter said as they went into the screen.

'Thanks for that.' Jack bumped Amelia, who failed to suppress a laugh as she resumed handing out badges.

'It's good for you.'

'Jack, Amelia, hi!'

Huw appeared from the other side of the foyer, laden with popcorn and drinks, his fellow Guild members in tow. They all wore *Shadow Glass* T-shirts (Nell's read *I Kettu Like Nobody Else*) and Sumi had an Eye of Iri necklace.

'Hey,' Jack said. 'You get good seats?'

'If you consider front row good,' Sumi said, rolling her eyes.

Huw gave her a withering look. 'You're free to move.'

'Thank you, master.'

Amelia smirked.

'Are you really making a *Shadow Glass* sequel?' Huw asked. 'You don't have to say anything, I know there are all kinds of NDAs about that stuff, but just give me a sign, like a nod or a wink or something.'

Jack looked at Amelia, who rolled her eyes and turned to Huw.

She winked.

'OH-MY-GOD OH-MY-GOD OH-MY-GOD!' After a second, his elation dimmed. 'Man, Anya would've loved to see it.'

'Yeah,' Nell said. 'She would've.'

They fell silent and Jack felt guilt spreading through his chest like winter frost. He still lay awake at night thinking about that moment in the alley. They'd lost their friend because of his quest.

'I'm so sorry—' he began.

'If you're going to say it was your fault again, stop,' Sumi said. 'We all knew what we were getting into. We love Anya, we always will, but she knew too.'

Jack couldn't help doubting Anya would have agreed to take part if she knew there was a chance she'd die, but he appreciated Sumi trying to make him feel better.

'Thanks.'

'Hey, did you hear?' Nell asked. 'About Cutter?'

'What about him?' Amelia pressed her lips together. At least the vein in her throat had stopped pulsing at the mention of his name. In the wake of the Bob Co. takeover, she'd been busier than ever cleaning up Kunin Yillda's mess, while fielding questions from two dozen exhausted employees who had lost a day of their lives but had no memory of what they'd done while brainwashed by Nebfet.

And, of course, there were the guards who had died. Their memorials were happening in a week and Amelia was cooperating with police in the investigation into their deaths. Meanwhile, Cutter was still in custody.

'Oh, he's facing life behind bars,' Nell said nonchalantly. 'With zero access to anything *Shadow Glass*-related. It's not good for his mental state, apparently.' Her satisfied expression told Jack all he needed to know.

'Thank you,' he said.

'No, really, thank you,' Amelia said, clasping her hand. 'Here, have all the kettu badges you want.'

'Oh don't thank me, thank the law.' Nell winked. 'But I'll definitely take a badge.'

Jack noticed a splash of colour rising in Amelia's cheeks and looked between her and Nell. Something was definitely going on there. He was glad, and not just because it meant he didn't have to worry that Nell had a celebrity crush on him.

While everybody took their seats, Jack found Toby at the front of the cinema. They stood to one side by the emergency exit. The *Shadow Glass* title card filled the screen with its reflective mirror lettering, and for the first time in forever, Jack felt warmed by the sight of it.

'I'm definitely going to be sick this time,' Toby said, squinting at the seats as they filled up.

'You'll be great,' Jack said. 'Just breathe.'

'I was born to be behind the scenes. Now I'm going to make a scene. A bad one.'

'Just imagine them all—'

'In their underwear?'

Jack pouted. 'I was going to say as wugs, but whatever floats your boat.'

'Oh god, my parents are here. Oh *god*.'

Jack spotted a couple deep in conversation with Huw. They waved at Toby, beaming with pride, and he raised a hand, smiling feebly.

'I wish Zavanna and Brol were here,' he said.

'Me too.'

'And the lub. I miss it so much.'

'Uh, Mr Corman?' A steward offered Jack a microphone.

'Thanks. Looks like it's about that time.'

Jack gave Toby a reassuring shoulder squeeze before he strolled over to stand beneath the screen. He surveyed the audience, over two hundred *Shadow Glass* fans, and wished Bob was here to see them. He wondered if somewhere, somehow, Bob could.

'Hi,' he said into the mic. 'I'm Jack Corman. You might recognise me as the fat toddler who loved eating garbage in *The Shadow Glass.*' Laughter filled the cinema and somebody hollered, 'THAT'S GOOD EATIN'!'

The audience settled down and Jack cleared his throat. 'I won't talk for long because there's somebody more important who'll introduce the film, but I just wanted to say... Look, we're all friends here. You all know my father was a complicated man. He could be difficult, infuriating sometimes. He wouldn't mind me telling you he was a mess a lot of the time. He had his demons and they impacted me in ways I wish they hadn't. That's something I've made peace with, mostly.

'What really mattered to him, though, was you. The people who loved his film. It wasn't just a film to him. It was a window into another world, a place that he filled with everything he loved, every fear, every hope. Which sounds incredibly pompous and highfalutin for a film starring a cast of puppets, but it's true. And I'm so glad he made it.'

He meant it, too.

'Anyway, that's enough from me.' Jack raised his voice. 'It is my great honour to introduce the biggest *Shadow Glass* fan I know, and somebody I consider a friend. Please give it up for Toby Taylor!'

The audience erupted with cheers and Toby stumbled over to join him. Jack hugged him and handed over the microphone, retreating to the side. He scanned the back row, seeing Amelia on the aisle seat. She was crying but gave him an 'OK' sign, and he saw Jenny Bobbin and Mike seated beside her. He blinked and looked again when he saw a diminutive figure in the seat beside the video shop clerk. Rick Agnor.

They were all here.

'Uh, thanks Jack,' Toby stammered into the mic. 'I'm pretty sure everybody here now hates me because *everybody* thinks they're the biggest *Shadow Glass* fan, right?'

'Hell yeah!' a woman shouted.

'Right.' Toby's smile twitched. 'But anyway, this isn't about me, or anybody else, really. It's about somebody I've admired my whole life, who took a risk on something he loved and created a film I think we all agree is pretty fucking—sorry, Mum—*freaking* amazing. And that person is Bob Corman.'

Deafening whoops and claps filled the cinema.

'Here's the thing,' Toby said when everybody had settled down. 'It's been thirty-plus years since *The Shadow Glass* came out, and we're still here, still talking about it and buying the merchandise and wishing we had been to Iri and stuff. And that means something. We all know *The Shadow Glass* was considered a failure at the time because it didn't make a crap-ton of money, but that's not the point. The point is, Bob gave us something, a part of himself, that we can enjoy over and over again. Something that's ours now as much as his. We'll always have him with us. And that's worth more than a billion dollars at the box office any day.'

He shifted the mic to his other hand. 'So, yeah, without further ado, it's a privilege and an honour to introduce this special celebratory screening of...' He bowed. '...*The Shadow Glass*.'

Amid more cheers and whistles, he passed the mic to a steward and then joined the Guild in the front row.

The lights dimmed and Jack stood to the side, grinning as the winking wug in the Bob Co. logo elicited more cheers. The screen faded to black.

Thunder rumbled from the sound system, reminding Jack of the storm that had brought Iri back into his life.

A cracked voice said, *'In a forgotten time, in a forgotten world, deep within a forgotten chamber few have ever seen, the Shadow Glass sees all.'*

The words THE SHADOW GLASS appeared, glimmering darkly like a mirror, and the audience went wild.

As the camera roved through a steamy, bubbling swamp, Jack walked towards the back of the cinema.

He crouched by Amelia and whispered, 'I'll see you tomorrow.'

'Aren't you staying for the movie?' she whispered back.

He pointed to his head. 'It's all up here. Besides, I'm on the clock now, right?'

She smiled, hugging him, and he waved at Jenny, Mike and Agnor before slipping out into the night.

Back at his father's house, Jack fixed himself a strong coffee and went up to the study. He sat at the desk and booted up his laptop, cracking his knuckles. He opened a blank document and stared at it for a while, sipping coffee and wondering if he'd been mad to agree to this, but trying not to overthink it. He already knew what he was going to write.

Amelia was right. It had been unreal seeing all those *Shadow Glass* fans up close. He had felt the same way when Toby introduced him to the Guild. An intermingled sense of pride and regret. He had missed out.

He had been trying to cram himself into the wrong-shaped hole for so many years, it was a relief to find the right one. It had been there the whole time, just waiting for him.

Finally, he started typing.

The Shadow Glass II: Zavanna Rising

screenplay by Jack Corman
based on characters created by Bob Corman

ACKNOWLEDGEMENTS

So MANY PEOPLE helped piece together *The Shadow Glass*. First and foremost, though, I'd like to thank Jim Henson. *The Dark Crystal* and *Labyrinth* made a life-long fantasy fan of this young muppet, and I've lost count of how many times I've escaped into their worlds, discovering new wonders with every watch. This book wouldn't exist without you and I hope that it stands as a fittingly grotesque/quirky/heartfelt tribute to everything you achieved. Thanks, Jim.

Thank you to my agent/champion Kristina Pérez at Zeno Agency for guiding me through the weird world of publishing with a neverending supply of good humour and grace.

Everybody at Titan deserves a triumphant ride on Falkor. Thank you to my excellent editor Craig Leyenaar for making this book roughly 3,000 times better than it was when you bought it. Thanks to Lydia Gittins, Polly Grice and Katharine Carroll for spreading the word as swiftly as any luck dragon, and to George Sandison and Fenton Coulthurst for getting Jack and co over the finish line. Particular thanks to Julia Lloyd for the best retro cover EVER.

The first people to read this book were my friends and fellow fantasy fans. Thank you Troy Gardner, Erin Callahan, Roberta, Carrie, and Kate Baylay. Your undying enthusiasm kept me writing when my brain was down in the underground.

Fellow writer pals who help me escape the Swamps of Sadness over and over again: William Hussey, Paul Cunliffe, Matt Glasby, Rosie Fletcher, Katharine and Elizabeth Corr, Fran Dorricott, Jack Jordan. You're all heroes.

People who haven't read the book (yet) but supported me in a thousand ways they'll never know: Chelley, Emma, Sue, Ben, Christina, Jess, Meggie and the Trehernes, Rob, Dibbers, Pixie, Rich, John, Isla, Becca, Sam, Hugh, Jez, Bobby, Rachel, Polly, Kirsty, Steve, Teddy, my gorgeous nephews Arthur, Alfie and Leo, the Guild (Eddie, Maz, Will, Lydia and Rory), Lisa and Charlie, and anybody else my addled brain has momentarily forgotten.

Readers, bloggers, book fans and Insta buddies, thanks for loving books and for sharing that love so tirelessly. And a big thank you to everybody who kindly blurbed *The Shadow Glass*— I'm thrilled I tricked you into enjoying it.

Thank you Dad for always letting me do what I dream, and Mum for always making this little boy feel important. Thank you Penny for the daily reminders that something cute can also be deadly. And thank you Thom for always believing. There's a fox on the cover because of you. With all my lub.

ABOUT THE AUTHOR

JOSH WINNING is a senior film writer at *Radio Times*. He is contributing editor at *Total Film* magazine, writer at *SFX* and *Den of Geek*, and the co-host of movie podcast *Torn Stubs*. He has been on set with Kermit the Frog (and Miss Piggy), devoured breakfast with zombies on *The Walking Dead*, and sat on the Iron Throne on the Dublin set of *Game of Thrones*. Josh lives in London and dreams of one day convincing Sigourney Weaver to yell "Goddammit!" at him.

For more fantastic fiction, author events,
exclusive excerpts, competitions, limited editions and more

VISIT OUR WEBSITE
titanbooks.com

LIKE US ON FACEBOOK
facebook.com/titanbooks

FOLLOW US ON TWITTER AND INSTAGRAM
@TitanBooks

EMAIL US
readerfeedback@titanemail.com